IT HAPPENED ONE SUMMER

Also by Tessa Bailey

HOT & HAMMERED
Fix Her Up • *Love Her or Lose Her* • *Tools of Engagement*

THE ACADEMY
Disorderly Conduct • *Indecent Exposure* • *Disturbing His Peace*

BROKE AND BEAUTIFUL
Chase Me • *Need Me* • *Make Me*

ROMANCING THE CLARKSONS
Too Hot to Handle • *Too Wild to Tame*
Too Hard to Forget • *Too Close to Call* (novella)
Too Beautiful to Break

MADE IN JERSEY
Crashed Out • *Rough Rhythm* (novella)
Thrown Down • *Worked Up* • *Wound Tight*

CROSSING THE LINE
Riskier Business (novella) • *Risking It All* • *Up in Smoke*
Boiling Point • *Raw Redemption*

LINE OF DUTY
Protecting What's His • *Protecting What's Theirs* (novella)
His Risk to Take • *Officer Off Limits*
Asking for Trouble • *Staking His Claim*

SERVE
Owned by Fate • *Exposed by Fate* • *Driven by Fate*

BEACH KINGDOM
Mouth to Mouth • *Heat Stroke* • *Sink or Swim*

STANDALONE BOOKS
Unfixable • *Baiting the Maid of Honor*
Off Base (with Sophie Jordan)
Captivated (with Eve Dangerfield)
Getaway Girl • *Runaway Girl*

IT HAPPENED ONE SUMMER

a novel

Tessa Bailey

AVON

An Imprint of HarperCollinsPublishers

IT HAPPENED ONE SUMMER. Copyright © 2021 by Tessa Bailey. All rights reserved. Printed in the United States of America. No part of this book may be used or reproduced in any manner whatsoever without written permission except in the case of brief quotations embodied in critical articles and reviews. For information, address HarperCollins Publishers, 195 Broadway, New York, NY 10007.

HarperCollins books may be purchased for educational, business, or sales promotional use. For information, please email the Special Markets Department at SPsales@harpercollins.com.

FIRST EDITION

Designed by Diahann Sturge

Library of Congress Cataloging-in-Publication Data has been applied for.

ISBN 978-0-06-304565-1 (paperback)
ISBN 978-0-06-308235-9 (hardcover library edition)

21 22 23 24 25 LSC 10 9 8 7 6 5 4 3 2 1

Acknowledgments

This book was my mental escape during the Great Quarantine of 2020 and will always have a special place in my heart. When everything got too overwhelming, I was able to close my office door and travel to Westport to help two people fall in love—and I'm very grateful for it. I couldn't have written this book without my husband, Patrick, who kept a confused nine-year-old occupied without the benefit of school or any sense of normalcy for months on end.

Thank you, as well, to my friends—Nisha, Bonnie, Patricia, Michelle, Jan, and Jill—who bolstered my spirits via text or socially distanced visits, from the curb, while I shouted from the porch in sketchy pajamas. Thank you to the character Alexis Rose from *Schitt's Creek*, whom I fell so madly in love with that I needed to give her a happily ever after via Piper. Thank you to the essential workers and medical personnel who worked tirelessly at the risk of their health throughout 2020 and beyond. You are heroes. As always, thank you to my fantastic editor, Nicole Fischer; my agent, Laura Bradford; and, of course, the readers who continue to read my stories. I treasure each and every one of you.

IT HAPPENED ONE SUMMER

Chapter One

The unthinkable was happening.

Her longest relationship on record . . . over in the blink of an eye.

Three weeks of her life *wasted*.

Piper Bellinger looked down at her lipstick-red, one-shoulder Valentino cocktail dress and tried to find the flaw but came up with nothing. Her tastefully tanned legs were polished to such a shine, she'd checked her teeth in them earlier. Nothing appeared amiss up top, either. She'd swiped the tape holding up her boobs while backstage at a runway show in Milan during fashion week—we're talking the holy grail of tit tape—and those puppies were on point. Big enough to draw a man's eye, small enough to achieve an athletic vibe in every fourth Instagram post. Versatility kept people interested.

Satisfied that nothing concerning her appearance was glaringly out of place, Piper trailed her gaze up the pleated leg of Adrian's classic Tom Ford suit made of the finest sharkskin wool, unable to quell a sigh over the luxurious peak lapels and monogrammed buttons. The way her boyfriend impatiently checked his Chopard watch and scanned the crowd over her shoulder only added to the bored-playboy effect.

Hadn't his cold unattainability attracted her to him in the first place?

God, the night of their first meeting seemed like a hundred years ago. She'd had at least two facials since then, right? What *was* time anymore? Piper could remember their introduction like it was yesterday. Adrian had saved her from stepping in vomit at Rumer Willis's birthday party. As she'd stared up at his chiseled chin from her place in his arms, she'd been transported to Old Hollywood. A time of smoking jackets and women traipsing around in long, feathered robes. It was the beginning of her own classic love story.

And now the credits were rolling.

"I can't believe you're throwing it all away like this," Piper whispered, pressing her champagne flute between her breasts. Maybe drawing his attention there would change his mind? "We've been through so much."

"Yeah, tons, right?"

Adrian waved at someone across the rooftop, his expression letting whoever it was know that he'd be right with them. They'd come to the black, white, and red party together. A minor soiree to raise money for an indie movie project called *Lifestyles of the Oppressed and Famous*. The writer-director was a friend of Adrian's, meaning most of the people at this gathering of Los Angeles elite were his acquaintances. Her girls weren't even there to console her or facilitate a graceful exit.

Adrian's attention settled back on her reluctantly. "Wait, what were you saying?"

Piper's smile felt brittle, so she turned it up another watt, careful to keep it one crucial notch below manic. *Chin up, woman.* This wasn't her first breakup, right? She'd done a lot of the dumping, often unexpectedly. This was a town of whims, after all.

She'd never really noticed the pace of how things changed. Not until lately.

At twenty-eight, Piper was not old. But she *was* one of the oldest women at this party. At every party she'd been to recently, come to think of it. Leaning on the glass railing that overlooked Melrose was an up-and-coming pop star who couldn't be a day older than nineteen. She didn't need tape from Milan to hold up her tits. They were light and springy with nipples that reminded Piper of the bottom of an ice cream cone.

The host himself was twenty-two and embarking on a film career.

This was Piper's career. Partying. Being seen. Holding up the occasional teeth-whitening product and getting a few dollars for it.

Not that she needed the money. At least, she didn't think so. Everything she owned came from the swipe of a credit card, and it was a mystery what happened after that. She assumed the bill went to her stepfather's email or something? Hopefully he wouldn't be weird about the crotchless panties she'd ordered from Paris.

"Piper? *Hello?*" Adrian swiped a hand in front of her face, and she realized how long she'd been staring at the pop star. Long enough that the songstress was glaring back.

Piper smiled and waved at the girl, pointing sheepishly to her glass of champagne, before tuning back in to the conversation with Adrian. "Is this because I casually brought you up to my therapist? We didn't go in depth or anything, I promise. Most of the time we just nap during my appointments."

He stared at her for several seconds. Honestly, it was kind of nice. It was the most attention she'd gotten from him since almost slipping in puke. "I've dated some airheads, Piper." He sighed. "But you put them all to shame."

She kept her smile in place, though it took more determination than usual. People were watching. At that very moment, she was in the background of at least five selfies being captured around the roof, including one of Ansel Elgort. It would be a disaster if she let her sinking heart show on her face, especially when news of the breakup got out. "I don't understand," she said with a laugh, sweeping rose-gold hair over her shoulder.

"Shocking," he returned drily. "Look, babe. It was a fun three weeks. You're a smoke show in a bikini." He shrugged an elegant Tom Ford–clad shoulder. "I'm just trying to end this before it gets boring, you know?"

Boring. Getting older. Not a director or a pop star.

Just a pretty girl with a millionaire stepfather.

Piper couldn't think about that now, though. She just wanted to exit the party as inconspicuously as possible and go have a good cry. After she popped a Xanax and posted an inspirational quote on her IG feed, of course. It would confirm the breakup, but also allow her to control the narrative. Something about growth and loving herself, maybe?

Her sister, Hannah, would have the perfect song lyric to include. She was always sitting around in a pile of vinyls, those giant, ugly headphones wrapped around her head. Damn, she wished she'd put more stock in Hannah's opinion of Adrian.

What had she said? Oh yeah.

He's like if someone drew eyes on a turnip.

Once again, Piper had zoned out, and Adrian checked his watch for the second time. "Are we done here? I have to mingle."

"Oh. *Yeah*," she rushed to say, her voice horrifyingly unnatural. "You couldn't be more right about breaking things off before the boring blues strike. I didn't think about it like that." She clinked her champagne glass against his. "We're consciously uncoupling. *Très* mature."

"Right. Call it whatever you want." Adrian forced a wan smile. "Thanks for everything."

"No, thank *you*." She pursed her lips, trying to appear as non-airhead-like as possible. "I've learned a lot about myself over the last three weeks."

"Come on, Piper." Adrian laughed, scrutinizing her head to toe. "You play dress-up and spend your daddy's money. You don't have a reason to learn anything."

"Do I need a reason?" she asked lightly, lips still tilted at the corners.

Annoyed at being waylaid, Adrian huffed a breath. "I guess not. But you definitely need a brain that functions beyond how many likes you can get on a picture of your rack. There's more to life than that, Piper."

"Yes, I know," she said, prodded by irritation—and more than a little bit of reluctant shame. "Life is what I'm documenting through photos. I—"

"God." He half groaned, half laughed. "Why are you *forcing* me to be an asshole?" Someone called his name from inside the penthouse, and he held up a finger, keeping his gaze locked on Piper. "There's just nothing to you, okay? There are thousands of Piper Bellingers in this city. You're just a way to pass the time." He shrugged. "And your time has passed."

It was a miracle Piper kept her winning smile intact as Adrian sailed away, already calling out to his friends. Everyone on the roof deck was staring at her, whispering behind their hands, feeling sorry for her—of all the horrors. She saluted them with her glass, then realized it was empty. Setting it down on the tray of a passing waiter, she collected her Bottega Veneta satin knot clutch with all the dignity she could muster and glided through the throng of onlookers, blinking back the moisture in her eyes to bring the elevator call button into focus.

When the doors finally hid her from view, she slumped back against the metal wall, taking deep breaths in through her nose, out through her mouth. Already the news that she'd been dumped by Adrian would be blasted across all the socials, maybe even with video included. Not even C-list celebrities would invite her to parties after this.

She had a reputation as a good time. Someone to covet. An "it girl."

If she didn't have her social status, what *did* she have?

Piper pulled her phone out of her clutch and absently requested a luxury Uber, connecting her with a driver who was only five minutes away. Then she closed the app and pulled up her favorites list. Her thumb hovered over the name "Hannah" momentarily, but landed on "Kirby," instead. Her friend answered on the first ring.

"Oh my God, is it true you begged Adrian not to break up with you in front of Ansel Elgort?"

It was worse than she thought. How many people had already tipped off TMZ? Tomorrow night at six thirty, they would be tossing her name around the newsroom while Harvey sipped from his reusable cup. "I didn't beg Adrian to keep me. Come on, Kirby, you know me better than that."

"Bitch, I do. But I'm not everyone else. You need to do damage control. Do you have a publicist on retainer?"

"Not anymore. Daniel said me going shopping doesn't need a press release."

Kirby snorted. "Okay, boomer."

"But you're right. I do need damage control." The elevator doors opened, and Piper stepped off, clicking through the lobby in her red-soled pumps, eventually stepping out onto Wilshire, the warm July air drying the dampness in her eyes. The tall buildings of downtown Los Angeles reached up into the smoggy summer night sky, and she craned her neck to find the tops. "How late is the rooftop pool open at the Mondrian?"

"You're asking about hours of operation at a time like this?" Kirby griped, followed by the sound of her vape crackling in the background. "I don't know, but it's past midnight. If it's not already closed, it will be soon."

A black Lincoln pulled up along the curb. After double-checking the license plate number, Piper climbed inside and shut the door. "Wouldn't breaking into the pool and having the time of our lives be, like, *the* best way to fight fire with fire? Adrian would be the guy who broke up with a legend."

"Oh shit," Kirby breathed. "You're resurrecting Piper twenty fourteen."

This was the answer, wasn't it? There was no better time in her life than the year she turned twenty-one and ran absolutely buck wild through Los Angeles, making herself famous for being famous in the process. She was just in a rut, that was all. Maybe it was time to reclaim her crown. Maybe then she wouldn't hear Adrian's words looping over and over again in the back of her head, forcing her to consider that he might be right.

Am I just one of thousands?

Or am I the girl who breaks into a pool for a swim at one o'clock in the morning?

Piper nodded resolutely and leaned forward. "Can you take me to the Mondrian, instead, please?"

Kirby hooted down the line. "I'll meet you there."

"I've got a better idea." Piper crossed her legs and fell back in the leather seat. "How about we have *everyone* meet us there?"

Chapter Two

$\mathcal{J}$ail was a cold, dark place.

Piper stood in the very center of the cell shivering and hugging her elbows so she wouldn't accidentally touch anything that might require a tetanus shot. Until this moment, the word "torture" had only been a vague description of something she'd never understand. But trying to *not pee* in the moldy toilet after roughly six mixed drinks was a torment no woman should ever know. The late-night Coachella bathroom situation had nothing on this grimy metal throne that mocked her from the corner of the cell.

"Excuse me?" Piper called, wobbling to the bars in her heels. There were no guards in sight, but she could hear the distinctive sounds of *Candy Crush* coming from nearby. "Hi, it's me, Piper. Is there another bathroom I could use?"

"No, princess," a woman's voice called back, sounding very bored. "There isn't."

She bounced side to side, her bladder demanding to be evacuated. "Where do *you* go to the bathroom?"

A snort. "Where the *other* non-criminals go."

Piper whined in her throat, although the lady guard went up a notch in her book for delivering such a savage response without hesitation. "I'm not a criminal," Piper tried again. "This is all a misunderstanding."

A trill of laughter echoed down the drab hallway of the police station. How many times had she passed the station on North Wilcox? Now she was an inmate.

But seriously, it had been one hell of a party.

The guard slowly appeared in front of Piper's cell, fingers tucked into her beige uniform pants. *Beige.* Whoever was at the helm of law enforcement fashion should be sentenced for cruel and unusual punishment. "You call two hundred people breaking into a hotel pool after hours a misunderstanding?"

Piper crossed her legs and sucked in a breath through her nose. If she peed herself in Valentino, she would voluntarily remain in jail. "Would you believe the pool hours weren't prominently posted?"

"Is that the argument your expensive lawyer is going to use?" The guard shook her head, visibly amused. "Someone had to shatter the glass door to get inside and let all the other rich kids in. Who did that? The invisible man?"

"I don't know, but I'm going to find out," Piper vowed solemnly.

The guard sighed through a smile. "It's too late for that, sweetheart. Your friend with the purple tips already named you as the ringleader."

Kirby.

Had to be.

No one else at the party had purple tips. At least, Piper didn't think so. Somewhere between the chicken fights in the pool and the illegal firecrackers being set off, she'd kind of lost track of the incoming guests. She should have known better than to trust Kirby, though. She and Piper were friends, but not good enough for her to lie to the police. The foundation of their relationship was commenting on each other's social media posts and enabling each other to make ridiculous purchases, like a four-thousand-dollar purse shaped like a tube of lipstick. Most times, those kinds of surface-level friendships were valuable, but not tonight.

That's why her one phone call had gone to Hannah.

Speaking of whom, where *was* her little sister? She'd made that call an hour ago.

Piper hopped side to side, dangerously close to using her hands to keep the urine contained. "Who is forcing you to wear beige pants?" she gasped. "Why aren't they in here with me?"

"Fine." The guard flashed a palm. "On this we can agree."

"Literally any other color would be better. *No* pants would be better." Trying to distract herself from the Chernobyl happening in her lower body, she rambled, as she was wont to do in uncomfortable situations. "You have a really cute figure, Officer, but it's, like, a commandment that no one shall pull off nude khaki."

The other woman's eyebrow arched. "You could."

"You're right," Piper sobbed. "I totally could."

The guard's laugh faded into a sigh. "What were you thinking, inciting that chaos tonight?"

Piper slumped a little. "My boyfriend dumped me. And he . . . didn't even look me in the eye the whole time. I guess I just wanted to be seen. Acknowledged. Celebrated instead of . . . disregarded. You know?"

"Scorned and acting like a fool. Can't say I haven't been there."

"Really?" Piper asked hopefully.

"Sure. Who hasn't put all their boyfriend's clothes in the bathtub and poured bleach on top?"

Piper thought of the Tom Ford suit turning splotchy, and shivered. "That's cold," she whispered. "Maybe I should have just slashed his tires. At least that's legal."

"That's . . . not legal."

"Oh." Piper sent the guard an exaggerated wink. "*Riiiight.*"

The woman shook her head, glancing up and down the hallway. "All right, look. It's a quiet night. If you don't give me any trouble, I'll let you use the slightly less shitty bathroom."

"Oh, thank you, thank you, thank you."

With her keys poised over the keyhole, the guard hit her with serious eyes. "I have a Taser."

Piper followed her savior down the hall to the bathroom, where she meticulously gathered the skirt of her Valentino and eased the unholy pressure in her bladder, moaning until the final drop fell. As she washed her hands in the small sink, her attention caught on the reflection in the mirror. Raccoon eyes looked back at her. Smeared lipstick, limp hair. Definitely a long way from where she'd begun the evening, but she couldn't help but feel like a soldier returning from battle. She'd set out to divert attention from her breakup, hadn't she?

An LAPD helicopter circling overhead while she led a conga line had definitely reaffirmed her status as the reigning party queen of Los Angeles. Probably. They'd confiscated her phone during the whole mug shot/fingerprint thing, so she didn't know what was happening on the internet. Her fingers were itching to tap some apps, and that's exactly what she would do as soon as Hannah arrived to bail her out.

She looked at her reflection, surprised to find the prospect of breaking the internet didn't set her heart into a thrilling pitter-patter the way it did before. Was she broken?

Piper snorted and pushed away from the sink, using an elbow to pull down the door handle upon leaving. Obviously the night had taken its toll—after all, it was nearly five o'clock in the morning. As soon as she got some sleep, she'd spend the day reveling in congratulatory texts and an inundation of new followers. All would be well.

The guard cuffed Piper again and started to walk her back to the cell, just as another guard called down to them from the opposite end. "Yo, Lina. Bellinger made bail. Bring her down to processing."

Her arms flew up in victory. *"Yes!"*

Lina laughed. "Come on, beauty queen."

Vigor restored, Piper skipped alongside the other woman. "Lina, huh? I owe you big-time." She clutched her hands beneath her chin and gave her a winning pout. "Thank you for being so nice to me."

"Don't read too much into it," drawled the guard, though her expression was pleased. "I just wasn't in the mood to clean up piss."

Piper laughed, allowing Lina to unlock the door at the end of the gray hallway. And there was Hannah in the processing area, wearing pajamas and a ball cap, filling out paperwork with her eyes half closed.

Warmth wiggled into Piper's chest at the sight of her younger sister. They were nothing alike, had even less in common, but there was no one else Piper would call in a pinch. Of the two sisters, Hannah was the dependable one, even though she had a lazy hippie side.

Where Piper was taller, Hannah had been called a shrimp growing up and never quite hit the middle school growth spurt. At the moment, she kept her petite figure buried under a UCLA sweatshirt, her sandy-blond hair poking out around the blank red hat.

"She clear?" Lina asked a thin-lipped man hunched behind the desk.

He waved a hand without looking up. "Money solves everything."

Lina unlocked her cuffs once again, and she shot forward. "*Hannnnns*," Piper whimpered, throwing her arms around her sister. "I'll pay you back for this. I'll do your chores for a week."

"We don't have chores, you radish." Hannah yawned, grinding a fist into her eye. "Why do you smell like incense?"

"Oh." Piper sniffed her shoulder. "I think the fortune-teller lit some." Straightening, she squinted her eyes. "Not sure how she found out about the party."

Hannah gaped, seeming to awaken at least marginally, her hazel eyes a total contrast to Piper's baby blues. "Did she happen to tell you there's an angry stepfather in your future?"

Piper winced. "Oof. I had a feeling I couldn't avoid the wrath of Daniel Q. Bellinger." She craned her neck to see if there was anyone retrieving her phone. "How did he find out?"

"The news, Pipes. The news."

"Right." She sighed, smoothing her hands down the rumpled skirt of her dress. "Nothing the lawyers can't handle, right? Hopefully he'll let me get in a shower and some sleep before one of his famous lectures. I'm a walking *after* photo."

"Shut up, you look great," Hannah said, her lips twitching as she completed the paperwork with a flourish of her signature. "You always look great."

Piper did a little shimmy.

"Bye, Lina!" Piper called on the way out of the station, her beloved phone cradled in her arms like a newborn, fingers vibrating with the need to swipe. She'd been directed to the back exit where Hannah could pull the car around. *Protocol*, they'd said.

She took one step out the door and was surrounded by photographers. "Piper! Over here!"

Her vanity screeched like a pterodactyl.

Nerves swerved right and left in her belly, but she flashed them a quick smile and put her head down, clicking as fast as she could toward Hannah's waiting Jeep.

"Piper Bellinger!" one of the paparazzi shouted. "How was your night in jail?"

"Do you regret wasting taxpayer money?"

The toe of her high heel caught in a crack, and she almost sprawled face-first onto the asphalt but caught the edge of the door Hannah had pushed open, throwing herself into the passenger side. Closing the door helped cut off the shouted questions, but the last one she'd heard continued to blare in her mind.

Wasting taxpayer money? She'd just thrown a party, right?

Fine, it had taken a considerable amount of police officers to break it up, but like, this was Los Angeles. Weren't the police just waiting around for stuff like this to happen?

Okay, that sounded privileged and bratty even to her own ears.

Suddenly she wasn't so eager to check her social media.

She wiped her sweating palms on her dress. "I wasn't trying to put anyone out or waste money. I wasn't thinking that far ahead," Piper said quietly, twisting to face her sister as much as she could in a seat belt. "Is this bad, Hanns?"

Hannah's teeth were sunk into her lower lip, her hands on the wheel slowly navigating her way through the people frantically snapping Piper's picture. "It's not good," she answered after a pause. "But hey, you used to pull stunts like this all the time, remember? The lawyers always find a way to spin it, and tomorrow they'll be onto something else." She reached out and tapped the touch screen, and a low melody flooded the car. "Check it out. I have the perfect song cued up for this moment."

The somber notes of "Prison Women" by REO Speedwagon floated out from the speakers.

Piper's skull thudded against the headrest. "Very funny." She tapped her phone against her knee for a few seconds, before snapping her spine straight and opening Instagram.

There it was. The picture she'd posted early this morning, at 2:42, accused the time stamp. Kirby, the traitorous wench, had snapped it using Piper's phone. In the shot, Piper was perched on the shoulders of a man whose name she couldn't recall—though she had a vague recollection of him claiming to play second string for the Lakers?—stripped down to panties and boob tape, but like, in an artistic way. Her Valentino dress was draped over a lounge chair in the background. Firecrackers went off around her like the Fourth of July, swathing Piper in sparkles and smoke. She looked like a goddess rising from an electric mist—and the picture was nearing a million likes.

Telling herself not to, Piper tapped the highlighted section that would show her exactly *who* had liked the picture. Adrian wasn't one of them.

Which was fine. A million other people had, right?

But they hadn't spent three weeks with her.

To them, she was just a two-dimensional image. If they spent more than three weeks with Piper, would they scroll past, too? Letting her sink into the blur of the thousand other girls just like her?

"Hey," Hannah said, pausing the song. "It's going to be all right."

Piper's laugh sounded forced, so she cut it short. "I know. It always turns out all right." She pressed her lips together. "Want to hear about the wet boxers competition?"

Chapter Three

$\mathcal{I}$t was *not* all right, as it turned out.

Nothing was.

Not according to their stepfather, Daniel Bellinger, revered Academy Award–winning movie producer, philanthropist, and competitive yachtsman.

Piper and Hannah had attempted to creep in through the catering entrance of their Bel-Air mansion. They'd moved in when Piper was four and Hannah two, after their mother married Daniel, and neither of them could remember living anywhere else. Every once in a while, when Piper caught a whiff of the ocean, her memory sent up a signal through the fog, reminding her of the Pacific Northwest town where she'd been born, but there was nothing substantial to cling to and it always drifted away before she could grasp on.

Now, her stepfather's wrath? She could fully grasp that.

It was etched into the tanned lines of his famous face, in the disappointed headshakes he gave the sisters as they sat, side by side, on a couch in his home office. Behind him, awards gleamed on shelves, framed movie posters hung on walls, and the phone on his L-shaped desk lit up every two seconds, although he'd silenced it for the upcoming lecture. Their mother was at Pilates, and out of everything? *That* made Piper the most nervous. Maureen tended to have a calming effect on her husband—and he was anything but calm right now.

"Um, Daniel?" Piper chanced brightly, tucking a piece of wilted hair behind her ear. "None of this is Hannah's fault. Is it okay if she heads to bed?"

"She stays." He pinned Hannah with a stern look. "You were forbidden to bail her out and did it anyway."

Piper turned her astonishment on her sister. "You did what?"

"What was I supposed to do?" Hannah whipped off her hat and wrung it between her knees. "Leave you there, Pipes?"

"Yeah," Piper said slowly, facing her stepfather with mounting horror. "What did you want her to do? *Leave* me there?"

Agitated, Daniel shoved his fingers through his hair. "I thought you learned your lesson a long time ago, Piper. Or *lessons*, plural, rather. You were still flitting around to every goddamn party between here and the Valley, but you weren't costing me money or making me look like a fucking idiot in the process."

"Ouch." Piper sunk back into the couch cushions. "You don't have to be mean."

"I don't have to be—" Daniel made an exasperated sound and pinched the bridge of his nose. "You are twenty-eight years old, Piper, and you have done nothing with your life. *Nothing*. You've been afforded every opportunity, given anything your little heart could ask for, and all you have to show for it is a . . . a digital existence. It means *nothing*."

If that's true, then I mean nothing, too.

Piper snagged a pillow and held it over her roiling stomach, giving Hannah a grateful look when she reached over to rub her knee. "Daniel, I'm sorry. I had a bad breakup last night and I acted out. I won't do anything like that ever again."

Daniel seemed to deflate a little, retreating to his desk to lean on the edge. "No one handed me anything in this business. I started as a page on the Paramount lot. Filling sandwich orders, fetching coffee. I was an errand boy while I worked my way through film school." Piper nodded, doing her best to appear deeply interested, even though Daniel told this story at every dinner party and charity event. "I stayed ready, armed with knowledge and drive, just waiting for my opportunity, so I could seize it"—he snapped his fist closed—"and never look back."

"That's when you were asked to run lines with Corbin Kidder," Piper recited from memory.

"Yes." Her stepfather inclined his head, momentarily pleased to find out she'd been paying attention. "As the director looked on, I not only delivered the lines with passion and zeal, but I *improved* the tired text. Added my own flair."

"And you were brought on as a writer's assistant." Hannah sighed, winding her finger for him to wrap up the oft-repeated story. "For Kubrick himself."

He exhaled through his nose. "That's right. And it brings me back to my original point." A finger was wagged. "Piper, you're too comfortable. At least Hannah earned a degree and is gainfully employed. Even if I called in favors to get her the location scout gig, at least she's productive." Hannah hunched her shoulders but said nothing. "Would you even care if opportunity came knocking on your door, Piper? You have no drive to go anywhere. Or do anything. Why would you when this life I've provided you is always here, rewarding your lack of ambition with comfort and an excuse to remain blissfully stagnant?"

Piper stared up at the man she thought of as a father, stunned to find out he'd been seeing her in such a negative light. She'd grown up in Bel-Air. Vacationing and throwing pool parties and rubbing elbows with famous actors. This was the only life she knew. None of her friends worked. Only a handful of them had bothered with college. What was the point of a degree? To make money? They already had tons of it.

If Daniel or her mother had ever encouraged her to do something else, she couldn't remember any such conversation. Was motivation a thing that other people were simply born with? And when the time came to make their way in the world, they simply acted? Should she have been looking for a purpose this whole time?

Weirdly, none of the inspirational quotes she'd posted in the past held the answer.

"I love your mother very much," Daniel continued, as if reading her mind. "Or I don't think I would have been this patient for so long. But, Piper . . . you went too far this time."

Her eyes shot to his, her knees beginning to tremble. Had he ever used that resigned tone with her before? If so, she didn't recall. "I did?" she whispered.

Beside her, Hannah shifted, a sign she was picking up on the gravity of the moment, too.

Daniel bobbed his head. "The owner of the Mondrian is financing my next film." That news landed like a grenade in the center of the office. "He's not happy about last night, to put it quite mildly. You made his hotel seem like it lacks security. You made it a laughingstock. And worse, you could have burned the goddamn place down." He stared at her with hard eyes, letting it all sink in. "He's threatened to pull the budget, Piper. It's a very considerable amount. The movie will not get made without his contribution. At least not until I find another backer—and it could take me years in this economy."

"I'm sorry," Piper breathed, the magnitude of what she'd done sinking her even farther into the couch cushions. Had she really blown a business deal for Daniel in the name of posting a revenge snap that would make her triumphant in a breakup? Was she that frivolous and stupid?

Had Adrian been right?

"I didn't know. I . . . I had no idea who owned the hotel."

"No, of course not. Who cares who your actions affect, right, Piper?"

"All right." Hannah sat forward with a frown. "You don't have to be so hard on her. She obviously realizes she made a mistake."

Daniel remained unfazed. "Well, it's a mistake she's going to answer for."

Piper and Hannah traded a glance. "What do you mean by"— Piper wiggled her fingers in the shape of air quotes—"'answer for'?"

Their stepfather took his time rounding his desk and opening the bottom filing drawer, hesitating only a moment before removing a manila folder. He tapped it steadily on his desk calendar, considering the nervous sisters through narrowed eyes. "We don't talk a lot about your past. The time before I married your mother. I'll admit that's mostly because I'm selfish and I didn't want reminders that she loved someone before me."

"Awww," Piper said automatically.

He ignored her. "As you know, your father was a fisherman. He lived in Westport, Washington, the same town where your mother was born. Quaint little place."

Piper started at the mention of her birth father. A king crab fisherman named Henry who'd died a young man, sucked down into the icy depths of the Bering Sea. Her eyes drifted to the window, to the world beyond, trying to remember what came *before* this swanky life to which she'd grown so accustomed. The landscape and color of the first four years of her life were elusive, but she could remember the outline of her father's head. Could remember his cracking laugh, the smell of salt water on his skin.

Could remember her mother's laughter echoing in kind, warm and sweet.

There was no way to wrap her head around that other time and place—how different it was from her current situation— and she'd tried many times. If Maureen hadn't moved to Los Angeles as a grieving widow, armed with nothing more than good looks and being a dab hand at sewing, she never would have landed a job working in wardrobe on Daniel's first film. He wouldn't have fallen in love with her, and this lavish lifestyle of theirs would be nothing more than a dream, while Maureen existed in some other, unimaginable timeline.

"Westport," Hannah repeated, as if testing the word on her tongue. "Mom never told us the name."

"Yes, well. I can imagine everything that happened was

painful for her." He sniffed, tapping the edge of the folder again. "Obviously she's fine now. Better than fine." A beat passed. "The men in Westport . . . they head to the Bering Sea during king crab season, in search of their annual payday. But it's not always reliable. Sometimes they catch very little and have to split a minor sum among a large crew. Because of this, your father also owned a small bar."

Piper's lips edged up into a smile. This was the most anyone had ever spoken to her about their birth father, and the details . . . they were like coins dropping into an empty jar inside of her, slowly filling it up. She wanted more. She wanted to know everything about this man whom she could only remember for his boisterous laugh.

Hannah cleared her throat, her thigh pressing against Piper's. "Why are you telling us all of this now?" She chewed her lip. "What's in the folder?"

"The deed to the bar. He left the building to you girls in his will." He set the folder down on his desk and flipped it open. "A long time ago, I put a custodian in place, to make sure it didn't fall into disrepair, but truthfully, I'd forgotten all about it until now."

"Oh my God . . ." Hannah said under her breath, obviously predicting some outcome to this conversation that Piper was not yet grasping. "A-are you . . . ?"

Daniel sighed in the wake of Hannah's trailed-off question. "My investor is demanding a show of contrition for what you did, Piper. He's a self-made man like me and would like nothing more than to stick it to me over my spoiled, rich-kid daughter." Piper flinched, but he didn't see it because he was scanning the contents of the file. "Normally I would tell any-one who demanded something from me to fuck off . . . but I can't ignore my gut feeling that you need to learn to fend for yourself for a while."

"What do you mean by"—Piper did air quotes again—"'fend'?"

"I *mean* you're getting out of your comfort zone. I *mean* you're going to Westport."

Hannah's mouth dropped open.

Piper shot forward. "Wait. What? For how long? What am I supposed to do there?" She turned her panicked gaze on Han-nah. "Does Mom know about this?"

"Yes," Maureen said from the office doorway. "She knows."

Piper whimpered into her wrist.

"Three months, Pipes. You can make it that long. And I hope you would do it without hesitation, considering I'll maintain my film budget by making these amends." Daniel came around the desk and dropped the manila folder into Piper's lap. She stared at it like one might a scuttling cockroach. "There is a small apartment above the bar. I've called ahead to make sure it's cleaned. I'm setting up a debit account to get you started, but after that . . ." Oh, he looked way too pleased. "You're on your own."

Mentally listing all of the galas and fashion shows that would happen over the course of three whole months, Piper got to her feet and sent her mother a pleading look. "Mom, you're really going to let him send me away?" She was reeling. "What am I supposed to do? Like, fish for a living? I don't even know how to make toast."

"I'm confident you'll figure it out," Maureen said softly, her expression sympathetic but firm. "This will be good for you. You'll see. You might even learn something about yourself."

"No." Piper shook her head. Didn't last night yield the revelation that she was good for nothing but partying and looking hot? She didn't have the survival skills for a life outside of these gates. But she could cope with that as long as everything stayed familiar. Out there, her ineptitude, her uselessness, would be *glaring*. "I—I'm not going."

"Then I'm not paying your legal fees," Daniel said reluctantly.

"I'm shaking," Piper whispered, holding up a flat, quaking hand. "Look at me."

Hannah threw an arm around her sister. "I'm going with her."

Daniel did a double take. "What about your job? I pulled strings with Sergei to get you a coveted spot with the production company."

At the mention of Sergei, Hannah's long-standing crush, Piper felt her sister's split second of indecision. For the last year, the youngest Bellinger had been pining for the broody Hollywood upstart whose debut film, *Nobody's Baby*, had taken the Palme d'Or at Cannes. Most of the ballads constantly blaring from Hannah's room could be attributed to her deep infatuation.

Her sister's solidarity made Piper's throat feel tight, but there was no way she'd allow her sins to banish her favorite person to Westport, too. Piper herself wasn't even resigned to going yet. "Daniel will change his mind," she whispered out of the side of her mouth to Hannah. "It'll be fine."

"I will not," Daniel boomed, looking offended. "You leave at the end of July."

Piper did a mental count. "That's, like, only a few weeks from now!"

"I'd tell you to use the time to tie up your affairs, but you don't have any."

Maureen made a sound. "I think that's enough, Daniel." With a face full of censure, she corralled the stunned sisters out of the room. "Come on. Let's take some time to process."

The three Bellinger women ascended the stairs together, climbing up to the third floor where Hannah's and Piper's bedrooms waited on opposite sides of the carpeted hall. They drifted into Piper's room, settling her on the edge of the bed, and then stepped back to observe her as if they were medical students being asked to make a diagnosis.

Hands on knees, Hannah analyzed her face. "How are you doing, Piper?"

"Can you really not get him to change his mind, Mom?" Piper croaked.

Maureen shook her head. "I'm sorry, sweetie." Her mother fell onto the bed beside her, taking her limp hand. For long moments, she was quiet, clearly gearing up for something. "I think part of the reason I didn't fight Daniel very hard on sending you to Westport is . . . well, I have a lot of guilt for keeping so much of your real father to myself. I was in so much pain for a long time. Bitter, too. And I bottled it all up, neglecting his memory in the process. That wasn't right of me." Her eyelids drifted down. "To go to Westport . . . is to meet your father, Piper. He *is* Westport. There's so much more history . . . still living in that town than you know. That's why I couldn't stay after he died. He was surrounding me . . . and I was just so angry over the unfairness of it all. Not even my parents could get through to me."

"How long did they stay in Westport after you left?" Hannah asked, referring to the grandparents who visited them on occasion, though the visits had grown few and far between as the sisters got older. When Daniel officially adopted Piper and Hannah, their grandparents hadn't seemed comfortable with the whole process, and the contact between them and Maureen had faded in degrees, even if they still spoke on holidays and birthdays.

"Not long. They bought the ranch in Utah shortly after. Far from the water." Maureen looked down at her hands. "The magic had gone out of the town for all of us, I think."

Piper could understand her mother's reasoning. Could sympathize with the guilt. But her entire life was being uprooted for a man she didn't know. Twenty-four years had gone by without a single word about Henry Cross. Her mother couldn't expect her to jump all over the opportunity now because she'd decided it was time to dump the guilt.

"This isn't fair," Piper groaned, falling backward on her bed, upsetting her ecru Millesimo bedsheets. Hannah sprawled out beside her, throwing an arm over Piper's stomach.

"It's only three months," Maureen said, rising and floating from the room. Just before she walked out, she turned back, hand poised on the doorframe. "Word to the wise, Piper. The men in Westport . . . they're not what you're used to. They're unpolished and direct. Capable in a way the men of your acquaintance . . . aren't." Her gaze grew distant. "Their job is dangerous and they don't care how much it scares you, they go back to the sea every time. They'll always choose it over a woman. And they'd rather die doing what they love than be safe at home."

The uncharacteristic gravity in Maureen's tone glued Piper to the bed. "Why are you telling me this?"

Her mother lifted a delicate shoulder. "That danger in a man can be exciting to a woman. Until it's not anymore. Then it's shattering. Just keep that in mind if you feel . . . drawn in."

Maureen seemed like she wanted to say more, but she tapped the doorframe twice and went, leaving the two sisters staring after her.

Piper reached back for a pillow and handed it to Hannah. "Smother me with this. Please. It's the humane thing to do."

"I'm coming with you to Westport."

"No. What about your job? And Sergei?" Piper exhaled. "You have good things happening here, Hanns. I'll find a way to cope." She gave Hannah a mock serious face. "They must have sugar daddies in Westport, right?"

"I'm definitely going with you."

Chapter Four

*B*rendan Taggart was the first Westport resident to spot the women.

He heard a car door slam out by the curb and slowly turned on the barrel that passed as a seat in No Name. His bottle of beer paused halfway to his mouth, the loud storytelling and music filling the bar fading away.

Through the grubby window, Brendan watched the pair exit on opposite sides of a taxi and immediately wrote them off as clueless tourists who obviously had the wrong address.

That is, until they started hauling suitcases out of the trunk. Seven, to be exact.

He grunted. Sipped his beer.

They were a ways off the beaten path. There wasn't an inn for several blocks. On top of misjudging their destination, they were dressed for the beach at night, during a late-summer rain, no umbrella to speak of—and visibly confounded by their surroundings.

It was the one in the floppy hat who caught his eye right away, purely because she looked the *most* ridiculous, a lipstick-shaped purse dangling from her forearm, wrists limp and drawn up to her shoulders, as if she was afraid to touch something. She tilted her head back and gazed up at the building and laughed. And that laugh turned into what looked like a sob, though he couldn't hear it through the music and pane of glass.

As soon as Brendan noticed the way the rain was molding the dress to Floppy Hat's tits, he glanced away quickly, going back to what he'd been doing before. Pretending to be interested in Randy's overboard story, even though he'd heard it eighty goddamn times.

"The sea was boiling that day," Randy said, in a voice equivalent to scrap metal being crushed. "We'd already hit our quota and then some, thanks to the captain over here." He saluted Brendan with his frothy pint. "And there I was, on a deck slipperier than a duck's ass, picturing the bathtub full of cash I'd be swimming in when we got home. We're hauling in the final pot, and there it was, the biggest crab in the damn sea, the motherfucking grandpappy of all crabs, and he tells me with his beady little eyes that he ain't going down without a fight. Noooo, sir."

Randy propped a leg up on the stool he'd been sitting on earlier, his craggy features arranged for maximum drama. He'd been working on Brendan's boat longer than Brendan had been captaining it. Had seen more seasons than most of the crew combined. At the end of each one, he threw himself a retirement party. And then he showed up for the next season like clockwork, having spent every last dime of last year's take.

"When I tell you that sucker wrapped a leg around the arm of my slicker, right through the pot, the mesh, all of it, I'm not lying. He was hell-bent for leather. Time froze, ladies and gen-tlemen. The captain is yelling at me to haul in the pot, but hear me now, I was *bamboozled*. That crab put a spell on me—I'm telling you. And that's when the wave hit, conjured by the crab himself. Nobody saw it coming, and just like that, I was tossed into the drink."

The man who was like a grandfather to Brendan took a pause to drain half his beer.

"When they pulled me in . . ." He exhaled. "That crab was nowhere to be found."

The two people in the crowded bar who hadn't already heard the legend laughed and applauded—and that was the moment Floppy Hat and the other one decided to make their entrance. Within seconds, it was quiet enough to hear a pin drop, and that didn't surprise Brendan one bit. Westport was a tourist stop to be sure, but they didn't get a lot of outsiders stumbling into No Name. It was an establishment that couldn't be found on Yelp.

Mainly because it was illegal.

But it wasn't only the shock of non-locals walking in and disrupting their Sunday-night bullshit session. No, it was the way they *looked*. Especially Floppy Hat, who walked in first, hitting the easy energy of the room with shock paddles. In her short, loose dress and sandals that wrapped around her calves, she could have stepped out of the pages of a fashion magazine for all those . . . tight lines and smooth curves.

Brendan could be objective about that.

His brain could point out an attractive woman without him caring one way or the other.

He set his beer down on the windowsill and crossed his

arms, feeling a flash of annoyance at everyone's stupefied expressions. Randy had rolled out the red carpet in the form of his tongue lolling out of his mouth, and the rest of the men were mentally preparing marriage proposals, by the look of it.

"Little help with the luggage, Pipes?" called the second girl from the entrance, where she'd propped open the door with a hip, struggling under the weight of a suitcase.

"Oh!" Floppy Hat whirled around, pink climbing the sides of her face—and hell, that was some face. No denying it, now that there wasn't a dirty windowpane distorting it. Those were the kind of baby blues that made men sign their life away, to say nothing of that wide, stubborn upper lip. The combination rendered her guileless and seductive at the same time, and that was trouble Brendan wanted *no* part of. "Sorry, Hanns." She winced. "I'll go get the rest—"

"I'll get them," at least nine men said at once, tripping over themselves to reach the door. One of them took the suitcase from Floppy Hat's companion, while several others lunged into the rain, getting stuck side by side in the doorway. Half of those jackasses were on Brendan's crew, and he almost disowned them right then and there.

Within seconds—although not without some familiar bickering—all seven suitcases were piled in the middle of the bar, everyone standing around them expectantly. "What gentlemen! So polite and welcoming," Floppy Hat crooned, hugging her bizarre handbag to her chest. "Thank you!"

"Yes, thanks," said the second girl quietly, drying the rain off her face with the sleeve of a UCLA sweatshirt. *Los Angeles. Of course.* "Uh, Pipes?" She turned in a circle, taking in their surroundings. "Are you sure this is the right place?"

In response to her friend's question, she seemed to notice where she was standing for the first time. Those eyes grew even bigger as she catalogued the interior of No Name and the people occupying it. Brendan knew what she was seeing, and already he resented the way she recoiled at the dust on the mismatched seats, the broken floorboards, the ancient fishing nets hanging from the rafters. The disappointment in the downturned corners of her mouth spoke volumes. *Not good enough for you, baby? There's the door.*

With prim movements, *Pipes*—keeper of ridiculous names and purses—snapped the handbag open and drew out a jewel-crusted phone, tapping the screen with a square red nail. "Is this . . . sixty-two North Forrest Street?"

A chorus of yeses greeted the strangled question.

"Then . . ." She turned to her friend, chest expanding on quick breaths. "Yes."

"Oh," responded UCLA, before she cleared her throat, pasting a tense smile on a face that was pretty in a much subtler way than Pipes's. "Um . . . sorry about the awkward entrance. We didn't know anyone was going to be here." She shifted her weight in boots that wouldn't be good for anything but sitting down. "I'm Hannah Bellinger. This is my sister, Piper."

Piper. Not Pipes.

Not that it was much of an improvement.

The floppy hat came off, and Piper shook out her hair, as if they were in the middle of a photo shoot. She gave everyone a sheepish smile. "We own this place. Isn't that crazy?"

If Brendan thought their entrance had produced silence, it was nothing compared to this.

Owned this place?

No one owned No Name. It had been vacant since he was in grade school.

Originally, the locals had pooled their money to stock the place with liquor and beer, so they'd have a place to come to escape the tourists during a particularly hellish summer. A decade had passed since then, but they'd kept coming, the regulars taking turns collecting dues once a week to keep the booze flowing. Brendan didn't make it over too often, but he considered No Name to be theirs. *All* of theirs. These two out-of-towners walking in and claiming ownership didn't sit right at all.

Brendan liked routine. Liked things in their place. These two didn't belong, especially Piper, who noticed him glowering and had the nerve to send him a pinky wave.

Randy drew her attention away from Brendan with a baffled laugh. "How's that now? You own No Name?"

Hannah stepped up beside her sister. "That's what you call it?"

"Been calling it that for years," Randy confirmed.

One of Brendan's deckhands, Sanders, disentangled himself from his wife and came forward. "Last owner of this place was a Cross."

Brendan noticed the slight tremor that passed through Piper at the name.

"Yes," Hannah said hesitantly. "We're aware of that."

"Ooh!" Piper started scrolling through her phone again at the speed of light. "There's a custodian named Tanner. Our stepdad has been paying him to keep this place clean." Though her smile remained in place, her gaze crawled over the distinctly *not* clean bar. "Has he . . . been on vacation?"

Irritation snuck up the back of Brendan's neck. This was a

proud town of long-standing traditions. Where the hell did this rich girl get off waltzing in and insulting his lifelong friends? His crew?

Randy and Sanders traded a snort. "Tanner is over there," Sanders said. The crowd parted to reveal their "custodian" slumped over the bar, passed out. "He's been on vacation since two thousand and eight."

Everyone in the bar hoisted their beers and laughed at the joke, Brendan's own lips twitching in amusement, even though his annoyance hadn't ebbed. Not even a little bit. He retrieved his bottle of beer from the windowsill and took a pull, keeping his eyes on Piper. She seemed to feel his attention on her profile, because she turned with another one of those flirtatious smiles that *definitely* shouldn't have caused a hot nudge in his lower body, especially considering he'd already decided he didn't care for her.

But then her gaze snagged on the wedding band he still wore around his ring finger—and she promptly looked away, her posture losing its playfulness.

That's right. Take it somewhere else.

"I think I can clear up the confusion," Hannah said, rubbing at the back of her neck. "Our father . . . was Henry Cross."

Shock drew Brendan's eyebrows together. These girls were Henry Cross's daughters? Brendan was too young to remember the man personally, but the story of Henry's death was a legend, not unlike Randy's evil crab story. It was uttered far less often lest it produce bad luck, whispered between the fishermen of Westport after too much liquor or a particularly rough day on the sea when the fear had taken hold.

Henry Cross was the last man of the Westport crew to die

while hunting the almighty king crab on the Bering Sea. There was a memorial dedicated to him on the harbor, a wreath placed on the pedestal every year on the anniversary of the sea taking him.

It was not unusual for men to die during the season. King crab fishing was, by definition, the most dangerous job in the United States. Every fall, men lost their lives. But they hadn't lost a Westport man in over two decades.

Randy had dropped onto his stool, dumbfounded. "No. Are you . . . You ain't Maureen's girls, are you?"

"Yes," Piper said, her smile too engaged for Brendan's peace of mind. "We are."

"Holy mackerel. I see the resemblance now. She used to bring you girls down to the docks, and you'd leave with pockets full of candy." Randy's attention swung to Brendan. "Your father-in-law is going to shit himself. Henry's girls. Standing right here in his bar."

"Our bar," Brendan corrected him quietly.

Two words out of his mouth were all it took to drop a chill into the atmosphere. A couple of the locals shrunk back into their seats, drinks forgotten on the crates that served as tables.

Brendan finished his beer calmly, giving Piper a challenging eyebrow raise over the glass neck. To her credit, she didn't blanch like most people on the receiving end of one of his looks. A stony stare through the wheelhouse window could make a greenhorn shit himself. This girl only seemed to be evaluating him, that limp wrist once again drawn up against her shoulder, that long mane of golden-rosy-honey hair tossed back.

"Aw. The deed says otherwise," Piper said sweetly. "But

don't worry. We'll only be killing your weirdly hostile vibe for three months. Then it's back to LA."

If possible, everyone retreated farther into their seats.

Except for Randy. He was finding the whole exchange hilarious, his smile so wide Brendan could count his teeth, three of which were gold.

"Where are you staying?" Brendan asked.

The sisters both pointed up at the ceiling.

Brendan bit off a laugh. "Really?"

Several patrons exchanged anxious glances. Someone even hopped up and tried to rouse Tanner at the bar, but it was nothing doing.

This whole situation was absurd. If they thought the bar was in shambles, they hadn't seen anything yet. They—especially *her*—wouldn't last the night in Westport. At least not without checking in to one of the inns.

Satisfied with that conclusion, Brendan set his beer aside and pushed himself to his feet, kind of enjoying the way Piper's eyes widened when he reached his full height. For some reason, he was wary of getting too close to her. He sure as hell didn't want to know what she smelled like. But he called himself an idiot for hesitating and strode forward, picking up a suitcase in each hand. "Well, then. Allow me to show you the accommodations."

Chapter Five

*W*ho the fuck. *Even. Was* this douche?

Piper forced her chin up and followed the beast to the back of the bar—the bar which was essentially the size of her closet back in Bel-Air—and up a narrow staircase, Hannah in tow. God, he was freakishly big. Just to make it up the stairs, he had to bend down slightly, so his beanie-covered head wouldn't hit the ceiling.

For a split second, she'd found the silver-green eyes under the band of that beanie kind of captivating. His black beard was decently groomed. Full and close cropped. Those shoulders would have been seriously valuable in the chicken-fight competition a couple of weeks ago, to say nothing of the rest of him. He was *large* all around, and not even his beat-up sweatshirt could conceal the beefy musculature of his chest, arms.

He'd been staring at her, so she'd done what she did best when a man seemed interested. She did a little stationary flossing.

It was as natural as breathing, the subtle hip shift. Finding the light with her cheekbones, drawing attention to her mouth and sucking his soul out with her eyes. It was a maneuver she normally performed with a high success rate. Instead, he'd only looked pissed off.

How was she supposed to know he was married? They'd walked into a crowd of two dozen people. Into her father's bar, which had apparently been commandeered by a group of townies. There'd been a lot to take in at once, or she might have noticed the gold band. He'd seemed to purposefully flash it at her, and as she was definitely not the type to go after someone who was taken, she'd shut down her come-hither glance immediately.

Piper rolled her shoulders back one by one and decided to try being friendly to the beast, at least one more time. It was kind of admirable of him, wasn't it? To be aggressively faithful to his wife? If she ever got married someday, she hoped her husband would do the same. Once he realized she wasn't trying to catch his eye, maybe he'd chill. She and Hannah would be living in Westport for ninety days. Making enemies right off the bat would suck.

"Don't we need to get an apartment key from Tanner?" Piper called up the stairs.

"Nope," he responded shortly. "No locks."

"Oh."

"The bar entrance has a lock," he said, kicking open the apartment door and disappearing inside. "But almost everyone downstairs has a copy."

Piper chewed her lip. "That doesn't seem very secure . . ."

His derision was palpable. "Are you worried someone is going to break in and steal your lipstick purse?"

Hannah sucked in a sharp breath. "He went there."

Tenaciously, Piper held on to her poise and joined him in the apartment. The light hadn't been turned on yet, so she stepped aside to let Hannah in and waited, more grateful than ever that her sister was stubborn and refused to let her be banished to Westport alone. "I think we might have gotten off on the wrong foot," Piper said to the man. Wherever he'd gone. "What did you say your name was?"

"I didn't," came that mocking baritone from the dark. "It's Brendan."

"Brendan—"

The light flipped on.

Piper gripped Hannah's arm to keep from collapsing.

Oh no.

No no no.

"Ohhhh fuuuuuck," Hannah whispered beside her.

There had to be some mistake.

She'd googled Westport and done some nosing around, if minimally. Everywhere else was simply *not* Los Angeles, so what did it matter? Her search told her Westport was quaint and eclectic, located right on the cusp of the Pacific Ocean. A surfing destination. A cute village. She'd imagined an ocean view in a rustic but livable apartment, with lots of photo ops of her roughing it, with the hashtag #PNWBarbie.

This was not that.

Everything was in *one room*. There was a paper-thin partition blocking off the bathroom, but if she went three steps to the left, she'd be in the miniature kitchen. Three to the right, and she'd ram into the bunk bed.

Bunk. Bed.

Had she ever even seen one of those in real life?

Brendan's boots scuffed to a stop in front of the sisters. He crossed his arms over his wide chest and surveyed the apartment, his disposition suddenly jovial. "Second thoughts?"

Piper's eyes tracked along the ceiling, and she lost count of the cobwebs. There had to be an inch of grime on every surface—and she hadn't even seen the bathroom yet. The one window looked directly at the brick wall of the building next door, so the musky odor couldn't even be aired out.

She started to tell Hannah they were leaving. They would take the pittance Daniel put in their debit accounts and use it to rent a car and drive back to Los Angeles. Depending on how much it cost to rent a car, that was. It could be a thousand dollars or fifty. She had no clue. Other people usually arranged these kinds of things for her.

Maybe if they called Daniel and told him his custodian had been cashing a check and doing none of the work, he would relent and allow her and Hannah to return home. How could he say no? This place was unlivable. At least until it was scoured clean—and who was going to do that for them?

Brendan's unwavering gaze remained on her, waiting for her to crack.

She *was* going to crack, right?

Multiple voices drifted back to her, tightening the nape of her neck.

You play dress-up and spend your daddy's money.

You don't have a reason to learn anything.

There's just nothing to you, okay?

You have no drive to go anywhere. Or do anything. Why would you when this life I've provided you is always here, rewarding your lack of ambition with comfort and an excuse to remain blissfully stagnant?

Brendan's smugness was suddenly cloying, like glue drying in her windpipe. How original. Another man who thought she was worthless? How positively breathtaking.

He didn't matter. His opinion was moot.

Everyone's low expectations of her were beginning to wear kind of thin, though.

One look at her and this prick had become as dismissive of her abilities as her stepfather and her ex-boyfriend. What was it about her that courted such harsh judgment?

Piper wasn't sure, but after being dumped and banished to this murder hostel, she didn't really feel like taking another lump, especially when it wasn't warranted.

One night. She could do one night. Couldn't she?

"We're good, aren't we, Hanns?" Piper said brightly. "We never got to do the whole summer-camp thing. It'll be fun."

Piper glanced over at Hannah, relieved when her face warmed into a smile. "We're good." She sashayed across the space like she was surveying a million-dollar penthouse. "Very versatile. Cozy. Just needs a splash of paint."

"Mmmm," Piper hummed in agreement, nodding and tapping a finger against her chin. "Form *and* function. That abandoned pallet in the corner will make a lovely display shelf for my shoe collection."

When she risked a look at Brendan, it stressed her out to find his superior smile hadn't slipped an iota. Which was when she heard the scratching. It reminded her of a newspaper being crumpled in a fist. "What is that?" she asked.

"Your other roommate." Brendan tucked his tongue into his cheek, sauntered toward the exit. "One of several, I'm guessing."

No sooner had the words left his mouth than a rodent scurried across the floor, darting one way, then the other, his itty-bitty nose twitching. What was it? A mouse? Weren't they supposed to be cute? Piper scrambled onto the top bunk with a yip, Hannah hot on her heels. They met in the middle and clung to each other, Piper trying not to gag.

"Enjoy your night, ladies." Brendan's arrogant chuckle followed him out the door, his boots making the stairs groan on his way back down to the bar. "See you around. Maybe."

"Wait!" Gingerly, Piper climbed down off the bunk and shuddered her way out onto the landing where Brendan had paused, keeping her voice low. "You wouldn't happen to know a good, um . . . exterminator slash housekeeper in the area, would you?"

His derision was palpable. "No. We clean our own houses and catch our own vermin here."

"Catchy." She checked around her ankles for hungry critters. "Put that on the town welcome sign and watch real estate prices soar."

"Real estate prices," he echoed. "That kind of talk belongs in LA. Not here."

Piper rolled her eyes. "What is it like having such an accurate sense of where things belong? And who belongs where?" Still scouting for critters, she said absently, "I can be in a room full of people that I *know* and still not feel like I belong."

As she played that statement back to herself, Piper's eyes snapped up to find Brendan frowning down at her. She started to smooth her blurted truth over with something light and diverting, but her exhaustion made it too much of an effort.

"Anyway, thanks for the warm welcome, Mayor Doom and Gloom." She retreated a step back into the apartment. "You've sure put me in my place."

He squinted an eye. "Hold on." Weirdly, Piper held her breath, because it seemed like he was going to say something important. In fact, she kind of got the feeling he didn't say much *unless* it was significant. But at the last second, he seemed to change his mind, dropping the thoughtful expression. "You're not here to film a reality show or some shit, are you?"

She slammed the door in his face.

Chapter Six

Brendan locked the door of his house and double-checked his watch. Eight fifteen, on the dot. As was a captain's habit, he took a moment to judge the sky, the temperature, and the fog density. Smelled like the sun would burn the mist off by ten o'clock, keeping the early August heat minimal until he could finish his errands. He pulled on his beanie and took a left on foot toward West Ocean Avenue, traveling the same route he always did. Timing could make all the difference to a fisherman, and he liked to stay in practice, even on his off days.

The shops were just opening, the squawking calls of hungry seagulls blending with bells tinkling as employees propped open doors. The drag of a chalkboard sign being hauled out to the curb advertising fresh catches, some of which Brendan's crew had caught themselves on their last outing. Shopkeepers called lazy good mornings to each other. A couple of young kids lit cigarettes in a huddle outside the brewery, already dressed for the beach.

Since they were nearing the end of tourist season, there were markdowns advertised everywhere. On fishing hats and postcards and lunch specials. He appreciated the cycle of things. Tradition. The reliability of weather changing, and the shifting seasons setting people about a routine. It was the consistency of this place. Enduring, just like the ocean he loved. He'd been born in Westport, and he never intended to leave.

A ripple of aggravation fanned out beneath his skin when he recalled the night before. The stone tossed into the calm waters of how things were done. Outsiders didn't simply show up and claim ownership of things here. In Westport, people worked for everything they had. Nothing was handed over without blood, sweat, and tears. The two girls didn't strike him as people who had an appreciation for the place, the people, the past it was built on. The hard work it took to sustain a community on the whims of a volatile ocean—and do it well.

Good thing they wouldn't be sticking around for long. He'd be shocked if Piper made it through the night without checking in to the closest five-star hotel.

I can be in a room full of people that I know and still not feel like I belong.

Why did his mind refuse to let that drop?

He'd gnawed it over for far too long last night, then again this morning. It didn't fit. And he didn't like things that didn't fit. A beautiful girl—with admittedly sharp humor—like Piper could belong anywhere she chose, couldn't she?

Just not here.

Brendan waited at a stoplight before crossing Montesano, breezing through the automatic door of the Shop'n Kart, the wrinkle of irritation smoothing itself out when he saw that everything was in its place. He waved at Carol, the usual register attendant. Paper gulls hung from the ceiling and blew around in the breeze he'd allowed inside. Not many people were in the store yet, which was why he liked to come early. No conversations or questions about the upcoming crab season. If he expected a big haul, the course he'd charted. If the crew of the *Della Ray* would beat out the Russians. Talking about his plans would only jinx them.

As a seaman, Brendan was all about luck. He knew he could only control so much. He could construct a tight schedule, guide the boat in a direction of his choosing. But it was up to the ocean how and when she gave up her treasures. With crab season quickly approaching, he could only hope fortune would favor them once again, as it had the last eight years since he'd taken over from his father-in-law as captain.

Brendan picked up a handcart and headed west, to the freezer aisle. He didn't have a list and didn't need one, since he got the same groceries every time. First things he'd grab were some frozen burger patties and then—

"Siri, what should I make for dinner?"

That voice, drifting over from the next aisle, made Brendan stop in his tracks.

"Here's what I found on the Web," came the electronic reply.

A whine followed. "Siri, what is an *easy* dinner?"

He ground a fist into his forehead, listening to Piper speak to her phone as if it were a living, breathing human being.

There was some frustrated muttering. "Siri, what is *tarragon*?"

Brendan dragged a hand down his face. Who had let this girl child out into the world on her own without supervision? Frankly, he was kind of shocked to find her in a supermarket at all. Not to mention this early in the morning. But he wasn't going to question her. He didn't *care* about her explanation. There was a schedule to adhere to.

He trudged on, ripping the burger patties out of the freezer and throwing them into the handcart. He turned to the other side of the lane and picked out his usual bread. No-frills wheat. He hesitated before turning down the next aisle, where Piper was still yacking at her phone . . . and couldn't help but draw up short, a frown gathering his brows together. Who the fuck wore a sequined jumpsuit to the grocery store?

At least, he thought it might be called a jumpsuit. It was one of those deals women wore in the summertime with the top attached to the bottom. Except this one had shorts that ended right below her tight ass and made her look like a goddamn disco ball.

"Siri . . ." Her shoulders sagged, her handcart dangling from limp fingers. "What is a meal with *two* ingredients?"

Brendan let out an inadvertent sigh, and with a toss of hair, she glanced up, blinking.

He ignored the stab of awe in his chest.

She'd gotten prettier overnight, damn her.

With a roll of his shoulders, he tried to ease the tension bracketed by his rib cage. This girl probably inspired the same reaction in every man she ever came across. Even in the harsh supermarket lighting, he couldn't pick out a single flaw. Didn't want to *look* that closely. But he'd have to be dead not to. Might as well admit it. Piper's body reminded him, for the first time in a long, long time, that he had needs that couldn't be satisfied forever by his own hand.

Add it to the list of reasons her stay in Westport couldn't be over fast enough.

"Still here?" Jaw bunched, Brendan tore his eyes away from her long, achingly smooth-looking legs and moved down the aisle, dropping pasta and a jar of sauce into his basket. "Thought you'd be long gone by now."

"Nope." He could sense how pleased she was with herself as she fell into step beside him. "Looks like you're stuck with me at least one more day."

He lobbed a box of rice into his basket. "Did you make peace with the mice horde?"

"Yes. They're making me a dress for the ball right now." She paused, seeming to study him to see if he got the *Cinderella* reference. But he gave away nothing. "Um . . ."

Did he just slow his step so she could keep up with him? Why? "Um, what?"

To her credit, she didn't bat an eyelash at his shitty tone. Her smile might have been a little brittle, but she kept it in place, chin up. "Look, I sense you're in a hurry, but . . ."

"I am."

That fire he'd seen in her eyes last night was back, flickering behind the baby blue. "Well, if you're late for an appointment to go roll around in fish . . ." She leaned forward and sniffed. "Might as well cancel. You're already nailing it."

"Welcome to Westport, honey. Everything smells like fish."

"Not me," she said, cocking a hip.

"Give it time." He reached for a can of peas. "Matter of fact, don't."

She threw the hand holding her phone, let it slap down against the outside of her thigh. "Wow. What is your problem with me?"

"Bet you're used to men falling all over themselves to make

you happy, huh?" He tossed the can up in the air, caught it. "Sorry, I'm not going to be one of them."

For some reason, his statement had Piper's head tipping back on a semi-hysterical laugh. "Yes. Men *salivate* to do my bidding." She used her phone to gesture between them. "Is that all this is? You're being rude to me because I'm spoiled?"

Brendan leaned close. Close enough to watch her incredible lips part, to catch the scent of something blatantly feminine— not flowers. Smoky and sensual, yet somehow light. The fact that he wanted to get closer and inhale more pissed him off further. "I saw your judgment of this place before anyone else last night. The way you looked up at the building and laughed, like it was some cruel joke being played on you." He paused. "It's like this. On my boat, I have a crew, and each member has a family. A history. Those roots run all through the town. They've lived a lot of it inside No Name. And on the deck of my boat. Remembering the importance of each member of my crew and the people waiting on shore for them is my job. That makes this town my job. You wouldn't understand the character it takes to make this place run. The persistence."

"No, I don't," she sputtered, losing some steam. "I've been here less than one day."

When sympathy—and a little regret over being so harsh— needled him in his middle, he knew it was time to move on. But when he turned the corner into the next aisle, she followed, trying to look like she knew what she was doing by putting apple cider vinegar and lima beans in her cart.

"Jesus Christ." He set his cart down and crossed his arms. "Just what the hell are you planning on making with that combination?"

"Something to poison you with would be nice." She gave him one last disgruntled look and stomped off, that work-of-art backside twitching all the way to the end of the aisle. "Thank you for being so neighborly. You know, you obviously love this place. Maybe you should try being a better representation of it."

All right. That got him.

Brendan had been raised by a community. A village. By the time he was ten years old, he'd seen the inside of every house in Westport. Each and every resident was a friend of his parents. They babysat him, his parents returned the favor, and so on. His mother always brought a dish to celebrations when the men came back from sea, did the same for acquaintances who were sick. Kindness and generosity could be counted on. It had been a damn long while since he'd wondered what his mother would think of his behavior, but he thought of it now and grimaced.

"Fuck," he muttered, snatching up his basket and following Piper. Spoiled rich girl or not, she'd been right. About this *one* thing. As a resident of Westport, he wasn't doing this place justice. But just like the rare times he got off course on the water, he could easily correct the path—and get the hell on with his day. "All right," he said, coming up behind Piper in the baking aisle and watching her shoulder blades stiffen. "Based on the conversation you were having with your phone, it sounds like you're looking for a quick meal. That right?"

"Yes," she mumbled without turning around.

He waited for Piper to look at him, but she didn't. And he definitely wasn't impatient to see her face. Or anything like that. This close, he judged that the top of her head just about reached his shoulder, and felt another minor pang of regret for being a dick. "Italian's easiest, if you don't need it to be fancy."

Finally, she faced him, mid–eye roll. "I don't need fancy. Anyway, it's mostly . . ." She shook her head. "Never mind."

"What?"

"It's mostly for Hannah." She fluttered her fingers to indicate the lined shelves. "The cooking. To thank her for coming with me. She didn't have to. You're not the only one with important people and roots. I have people who I want to look out for, too."

Brendan told himself he didn't want to know anything about Piper. Why exactly she'd come, what she planned to do here. None of it. But his mouth was already moving. "Why are you in Westport, anyway? To sell the building?"

She wrinkled her nose, considered his question. "I guess that's an option. We haven't really thought that far ahead."

"Think of all the giant hats you could buy."

"You know what, assho—" She turned on a heel and started to bail, but he caught her elbow to halt her progress. When she ripped out of his hold immediately and backed away with a censorious expression, it caught him off guard. At least until he noticed she was looking pointedly at his wedding ring.

The temptation to put her misconception to rest was sudden and . . . alarming.

"I'm not interested," she said flatly.

"I'm not, either." *Liar*, accused the tripping of his pulse. "What you said before, about your sister being your roots. I get that." He cleared his throat. "You've got other ones, too. Here in Westport. If you feel like bothering."

Her disapproval cleared slightly. "You mean my father."

"For a start, yes. I didn't know him, but he's part of this place. That means he's part of us all. We don't forget."

"There are barely any memories for me to forget," she said. "I was four when we left, and after that . . . it wasn't spoken about. Not because I wasn't curious, but because it hurt our mother." Her eyes flickered. "I remember his laugh, though. I . . . can hear it."

Brendan grunted, really beginning to wish he'd stepped back and considered her from more than one angle before going on the defensive. "There's a memorial for him. Across from the museum, up on the harbor."

She blinked. "There is?"

He nodded, surprised by the invitation to bring her there that nearly snuck out.

"I'm almost scared to go look at it," she said slowly to herself. "I've gotten so comfortable with what little memories I have. What if it triggers more?"

The more minutes ticked past in Piper's presence, the more he started to question his first impression of her. Was she actually an overindulged brat from the land of make-believe? He couldn't help but catalogue everything else he knew about her. Such as, she wouldn't pursue an unavailable man. Thought she couldn't belong in a room full of people she knew. And she was in the store at eight thirty in the morning to buy ingredients to make a meal for her sister. So. Maybe not as selfish as he'd originally thought.

Honestly, though. What the hell did his impression of her matter?

She'd be gone soon. He wasn't interested. End of.

"Then I guess you'll have to call your therapist. I'm sure you've got one."

"Two, if you count my backup," she responded, chin raised.

Brendan staved off his interest in inspecting the line of her throat by rooting around in his basket. "Look. Make your sister an easy Bolognese sauce." He transferred his jar of marinara into her basket, along with the flute of pasta. "Come on."

He turned to make sure she was following on the way to the meat aisle, where he picked up a pound of ground beef and wedged it in along with her other purchases, which still included the lima beans and apple cider vinegar. He was kind of curious if she'd buy those two items just to be stubborn.

Piper looked between him and the meat. "What do I do with that?"

"Put a little olive oil on the pan, brown it up. Add some onions, mushrooms if you want. When it's all cooked, add the sauce. Put it over pasta."

She stared at him like he'd just called a football play.

"So like . . . everything stays in layers?" Piper murmured slowly, as if envisioning the actions in her head and finding it mind-blowingly stressful. "Or do I mix it all up?"

Brendan took the sauce back out of her basket. "Here's a better idea. Walk up to West Ocean and grab some takeout menus."

"No, wait!" They started a tug-of-war with the sauce jar. "I can do it."

"Be honest, you've never used a stove, honey," he reminded her wryly. "And you can't sell the building if you burn it down."

"I won't." She gave a closed-mouth scream. "*God*, I feel sorry for your wife."

His grip loosened automatically on the jar, and he snatched his hand back like he'd been burned. He started to respond, but there was something caught in his throat. "You should," he said finally, his smile stiff. "She put up with a lot."

Piper paled, her eyes ticking to the center of his chest. "I didn't mean . . . Is she . . . ?"

"Yeah." His tone was flat. "Gone."

"I'm sorry." She closed her eyes, rocking back on her heels. "I want to curl up and die right now, if it makes you feel any better."

"Don't. It's fine." Brendan coughed into his fist and stepped around her, intending to grab a few more things and check out. But he stopped before he could get too far. For some stupid reason, he didn't want to leave her feeling guilty. There was no way she could have known. "Listen." He nodded at her basket. "Don't forget to have the fire department on speed dial."

After the briefest hesitation, Piper huffed at him. "Don't forget to buy soap," she said, waving a hand in front of her face. But he didn't miss the gratitude in those baby blues. "See you around. Maybe."

"Probably not."

She shrugged. "We'll see."

"Guess we will."

Fine.

Done.

Nothing more to say.

It took him another handful of seconds to get moving.

And hell if he didn't smile on his way back up West Ocean.

Chapter Seven

After the groceries had been purchased and organized in the mini-fridge, the Bellinger sisters decided to go exploring—and escape the grunge of the upstairs apartment. Now Piper sat perched on the wooden railing overlooking the harbor, head tilted to allow the early afternoon breeze to lift the hair from her neck, sunshine painting her cheek. She looked inspired and well rested, fashion-forward in a scoop-back bodysuit and skinny jeans. Chloe ankle booties that said, *I might go on one of these boats, but someone else will be doing the work.*

"Hanns," she said out of the side of her mouth. "Lift the phone and angle it down."

"My arms are getting tired."

"One more. Go stand on that bench."

"Piper, I've gotten no fewer than forty shots of you looking like a goddess. How many options do you need?"

She gave an exaggerated pout. "Please, Hannah. I'll buy you an ice cream."

"I'm not a seven-year-old," Hannah grumbled, climbing onto the stone bench. "I'm getting sprinkles."

"Ooh, that would be a cute picture of you!"

"Yes," her sister replied drily. "I'm sure all nineteen of my followers would love it."

"If you'd let me share just *once*—"

"No way. We talked about this. Tip your head back." Piper complied, and her sister snapped the pic. "I like being private. No sharing."

Piper swung herself off the rail, accepting her phone back from Hannah. "You're just so cute, and everyone should know it."

"Uh-uh. Too much pressure."

"How?"

"You're probably so used to it by now, you don't stop to think of how . . . all these strangers and their responses to your posts are determining your enjoyment. Like, are you even experiencing the harbor right now, or are you trying to come up with a caption?"

"Oof. Below the belt." She sniffed. "Is 'Feeling a little nauti' cute?"

"Yes." Hannah snorted. "But that doesn't mean you can tag me."

"Fine." Piper harrumphed and shoved her phone into her back pocket. "I'll wait to post it so I won't be checking for likes. I can't get any reception, anyway. What should I look at with my eyeballs? What does reality have to offer me? Guide me, O wise one."

With an indulgent grin, Hannah locked her arm through Piper's. They each got an ice cream from a small shop and headed toward the rows of moored fishing vessels. Seagulls circled ominously overhead, but after a while, the sight of them and their shrill calls became part of the scenery, and Piper stopped worrying about being shat on. It was a clammy August afternoon, and tourists in sandals and bucket hats shuffled past signs advertising whale watching and boarded boats that bobbed in the water. Others stood in circles on the edges of the docks dropping what looked like steel buckets into the blue.

Piper noticed up ahead the white building proclaiming itself the maritime museum and recalled what Brendan had said about Henry Cross's memorial. "Hey. Um . . . not to spring this on you, but apparently there's a memorial for our father up here. Do you want to go look?"

Hannah considered. "That's going to be weird."

"So weird," Piper agreed.

"It would be weirder for his daughters *not* to visit, though." She chewed her lip. "Let's do it. If we wait, we'll keep finding reasons to put it off."

"Would we?" Not for the first time today, it occurred to Piper how little they'd spoken about the weird elephant in the room. Also known as the blurry start of their lives. "Finding out about Henry is something you'd want to avoid?"

"Isn't it?" They traded a glance. "Maybe following Mom's lead on this is just natural."

"Yeah." Only it didn't feel natural. It kind of felt like a chunk was missing from her memory. Or like there was a loose string in a sweater that she couldn't ignore. Or like perhaps Brendan's judgment had gotten to her in the supermarket. Her mother and grandparents had kept important details about Henry from her, but she could have found out about him on her own, right? Maybe this was her chance. "I think I want to go."

"Okay." Her sister studied her. "Let's do it."

Piper and Hannah continued along the harbor, scanning for the memorial. They returned the wave of an elderly man who sat on the museum lawn reading the paper. Shortly after, they spotted a brass statue outlined by the sea. Their steps slowed a little, but they kept going until they stopped in front of it. Gulls screeched around them, boats hummed in the distance, and life continued as usual while they stood in front of an artist's rendering of their long-lost father.

There he was. Henry Cross. He'd been standing there, immortalized, the whole time. A larger-than-life brass version of him, anyway. Maybe that's why his frozen smile and the metal ripple of his fisherman's jacket seemed so impersonal, foreign. Piper searched for some kind of connection inside of her, but couldn't find it, and the guilt made her mouth dry.

A plaque positioned at his feet read: *Henry Cross. Deeply Missed, Forever Remembered.*

"He looks like a young Kevin Costner," Piper murmured.

Hannah huffed a sound. "Oh shit, he really does."

"You were right. This is weird."

Their hands met and clasped. "Let's go. I have that Zoom call with Sergei in ten minutes, anyway."

Hannah had agreed to do some remote administrative work while in Westport, and she needed time to brush her hair and find a good background.

Their pace brisk, the sisters turned down the street that would guide them back to No Name and their apartment, but neither spoke. Hannah seemed deep in thought, while Piper tried to contend with the guilt—and a mild sense of failure—

that she hadn't been . . . grabbed by her first encounter with Henry.

Was she too shallow to feel anything? Or was the beginning of her life so far removed from her reality, she couldn't reach it so many years later?

Piper took a deep breath, her lungs rejoicing from the lack of smog. They passed fishermen as they walked, most of the men on the older side, and every single one of them gave the sisters a tip of the cap. Piper and Hannah smiled back. Even if they stayed a year in Westport, she'd probably never get used to the friendly ease of the locals, as they went around acknowledging other humans for no reason. There was something kind of nice about it, though she definitely preferred the bored indifference of Los Angeles. Definitely.

There was also something to be said for not looking at her phone as she walked. If she'd been responding to comments on her post, she might have missed the woman putting fresh fish into the window of her shop, two seagulls fighting over a French fry, a toddler trundling out of a candy shop stuffing saltwater taffy into his mouth. Maybe she should try to put her phone down more often. Or at least take in the real moments when she could.

When they reached No Name, Piper was surprised to find a man leaning up against the door. He appeared to be in his sixties, slightly round at the middle, a newsboy cap resting on top of his head. He watched them approach through narrowed eyes, a slight curve to his mouth.

"Hi," Hannah called, getting out her keys. "Can we help you?"

The man pushed off the door, slapped a hand against his thigh. "Just came to see Henry and Maureen's girls for myself, and there you are. How about that?"

After living two decades without hearing her father's name at all, it was a jolt to hear it out loud, have it connected with them. And their mother. "I'm Piper," she said, smiling. "This is Hannah. And you're . . . ?"

"Mick Forrester," he said affably, putting out his hand for a shake, giving each sister a hearty one. "I remember when you were knee high."

"Oh! It's nice to meet you as adults." She glanced at Hannah. "My sister has a work thing. But if you'd like to come in, I think there's still some beer in one of the coolers."

"No, I couldn't. I'm on my way to lunch with the old-timers." He smoothed his thick-knuckled hands over his belly, as if pondering what he'd order to fill it. "Couldn't let a day pass before I stopped by to say hello, see if you girls ended up favoring Maureen or Henry." His eyes twinkled as he looked between them. "I'd have to say your mother, for sure. Lucky, that. No one wants to look like a weathered fisherman." He laughed. "Although, Henry might have had that ocean-worn look about him, but, boy, your dad had a great laugh. Sometimes I swear I still hear it shaking the rafters of this place."

"Yeah." Inwardly, Piper winced at this stranger having more substantial memories and feelings for her own father. "That's kind of the only thing I remember."

"Shoot." Hannah's smile was tight. "I'm going to be late to the meeting. Pipes, you'll fill me in?"

"Will do. Good luck." Piper waited until Hannah had disappeared, the sound of her running up the back stairs of No Name fading after a moment. "So, how did you know Henry?"

Mick settled into himself, arms crossing over his chest. A classic storytelling stance. "We fished together. Worked our way up the ranks, side by side, from greenhorns to deckhands to crew, until eventually I bought the *Della Ray* and became my own captain." Some of the luster dulled in his eyes. "Not to bring up a sad subject, Piper, but I was right there in the wheelhouse when we lost him. It was a dark day. I never had a better friend than Henry."

Piper laid a hand on his elbow. "I'm sorry."

"Hell, you're his daughter." He reared back. "I'm the one should be comforting you."

"I wish . . . Well, we don't remember much about him at all. And our mother . . ."

"She was hurting too much to fill in the blanks, I'm guessing. That's not unusual, you know. Wives of fishermen come from tough stock. They have nerves of steel. My wife has them, passed them on to my daughter, Desiree." He gave a nod. "You might have met her husband, Brendan, the other night when you arrived."

Desiree. That was Brendan's late wife's name? Just like that, she was real. Someone with a personality. Someone with a face, a voice, a presence.

Sadness had turned down the sides of his mouth at the mention of his daughter. "Wives of fishermen are taught to lock up their fears, get on with it. No crying or complaining. Your mother rebelled against the norm a little, I suppose. Couldn't find a way to cope with the loss, so she picked up and left. Started over in a place that wouldn't remind her of Westport.

Can't say I wasn't tempted a time or two to do the same after my daughter passed, but I found it was worth staying the course."

Piper's throat felt tight. "I'm sorry. About your daughter."

Mick nodded once, weariness walking across his face. "Listen, I've got a lot more to tell you. Since you're staying awhile, I figure we'll have chances. A lot of us locals remember your father, and we never miss a chance to reminisce." He took a piece of paper out of his back pocket, handed it over to Piper. An address was written on it, blunt but legible. "Speaking of locals, I figured there's one who'd be more eager to catch up than any of us. This here is the address for Opal. I wasn't sure if you'd had a chance to stop over and see her yet."

Was Opal a woman Piper was supposed to know?

No clue.

But after visiting Henry's memorial and not being moved the way she should have been, she wasn't up for admitting her cluelessness, on top of the lingering guilt. Plus, there was something else she'd been wondering about and didn't want to miss her chance to ask.

"Opal. Of course." Piper folded up the piece of paper, debating whether or not she should ask her next question. "Mick . . . how exactly did Henry . . . ?" She sighed and started over. "We know it happened at sea, but we don't know the details, really."

"Ah." He removed his hat, pressed it to the center of his chest. "Rogue wave is what did it. He was standing there one minute, gone the next. She just snatched him right off the deck. We always thought he must have hit his head before going into the drink, because no one was a stronger swimmer than Henry. He had to be out cold when he went overboard. And that Bering Sea water is so damn frigid, there's only a minute's window before it sucks the breath right out of a man's lungs."

A shudder caught her off guard, goose bumps lifting on every inch of her skin. "Oh my God," she whispered, imagining the robust man made of brass being pitched over the side of a boat, sinking to the bottom of the ocean all alone. Cold. Did he wake up or just drift off? She hoped it was the latter. Oddly, her thoughts strayed to Brendan. Was he safe when he ventured out on the water? Was all fishing this dangerous? Or just crab fishing? "That's terrible."

"Yeah." Mick sighed and replaced his hat, reaching out to pat her awkwardly on the shoulder. Until he touched her, Piper didn't realize her eyes were wet. "I promise I won't make you cry every time I see you," he said, obviously trying to lighten the mood.

"Just once in a while?" She laughed.

Amusement lit his eyes again. "Here now, listen. We're having a little party on Friday night. Just us locals having some drinks, a potluck. Sharing memories. Consider yourself and Hannah invited." He pointed toward the harbor. "Up that way, there's a bar called Blow the Man Down. We'll be in the party room downstairs, around eight in the evening. I hope we'll see you there."

"I do love a party." She winked at him, and he blushed.

"All right, then." He gave her the signature Westport hat tip. "Great meeting you, Piper. You have a good day now."

"You too, Mick."

"Henry Cross's daughter," he muttered, heading off. "Hell of a thing."

Piper stood and watched him walk for a little before going inside. She didn't want to interrupt Hannah's Zoom call, so she took a seat on one of the barrels, letting the quiet settle around her. And for the first time, No Name felt like a little more than four walls.

Chapter Eight

Later that night, Piper stared down at the package of ground beef and tried to gather the courage to touch it with her bare hands. "I can't believe meat looks like brains before it's been cooked. Does everyone know about this?"

Hannah came up behind her sister, propping her chin on Piper's shoulder. "You don't have to do this, you know."

She thought of Brendan's smug face. "Oh, yes I do." She sighed, prodding the red blob with her index finger. "Even if we could find a way to stretch our budget to cover takeout for every night, you should have home-cooked meals." Shifting side to side, she shook out her wrists, took in a bracing breath. "I'm the big sister, and I'm going to see that you're properly nourished. Plus, you cleaned the toilet from hell. You've earned dinner and sainthood, as far as I'm concerned."

She sensed her sister's shiver. "I can't argue with that. There were stains in there dating back to the Carter administration."

After her work call, Hannah had tripped over to the hardware store for cleaning supplies. They'd found a broom, dustpan, and a few rags in a supply closet downstairs in the bar, but that was it. Meaning they'd been forced to spend a chunk of their budget on bleach, a mop, a bucket, paper towels, sponges, cleaning fluids, and steel wool to block the mouse holes. All eight of them. When they'd dragged the bunk bed away from the wall, the panel running along the bottom had resembled Swiss cheese.

They'd been cleaning since midafternoon, and the studio, while still irreversibly grungy, looked a whole lot better. And Piper could admit to a certain satisfaction that came along with making her own progress. Being part of a before and after that didn't involve makeup or working with a personal trainer.

Not that she wanted to get used to cleaning. But still.

It smelled like lemons now instead of rotting garbage, and the Bellinger sisters of Bel-Air were responsible. Nobody back home would believe it. Not to mention, her manicurist would shit a brick if she could see the chipped polish on Piper's nails. As soon as they were settled, finding a full-service salon that did hair, nails, and waxing was top of the agenda.

But first. Bolognese.

Looking at the lined-up ingredients forced her to recall her impromptu morning shopping trip with Brendan. God, he'd been smug. Right up until she'd brought up his deceased wife. He hadn't been smug then. More like distraught. How long had the woman been gone?

If Brendan was still wearing his wedding ring, the death had to be recent.

If so, he had a thundercloud attitude for a good reason.

Despite her dislike of the burly, bearded fisherman, she couldn't stave off a rush of sympathy for him. Maybe they could learn to wave and smile at each other on the street for the next three months. If growing up in Los Angeles had taught her anything, it was how to make a frenemy. Next time they crossed paths, she also wouldn't mind telling him she'd mastered Bolognese and had moved on to soufflés and coq au vin.

Who knew? Maybe cooking was her undiscovered calling.

Piper turned the stove burner on, holding her breath as it clicked. Clicked some more.

Flames shot out of the black wrought iron, and she yelped, stumbling backward into her sister, who thankfully steadied her.

"Maybe you should tie your hair back?" Hannah suggested. "Fingers might be sacrificed tonight, but let's not lose those effortless beach waves."

"Oh my God, you're so right." Piper exhaled, whipping the black band off her wrist and securing a neat ponytail. "Good looking out, Hanns."

"No problem."

"Okay, I'm just going to do it," Piper said, holding her spread fingers above the beef. "He said to cook it on the pan until it turned brown. That doesn't sound too hard."

"Who said?"

"Oh." She made a dismissive sound. "Brendan was in the supermarket this morning being a one-man asshole parade." Closing her eyes, she picked up the meat and dropped the whole thing into the pan, a little alarmed by the loud sizzle that followed. "He's a widower."

Hannah came around the side of the stove, propping an elbow on the wall that was much cleaner than it had been this morning. "How did you find that out?"

"We were arguing. I said I felt sorry for his wife."

"D'oh."

Piper groaned while poking the meat with a rusty spatula. Was she, like, supposed to turn it over at some point? "I know. He kind of let me get away with sticking my foot in it, though. Which was surprising. He could have really laid on the guilt." Piper chewed on her lip a moment. "Do I come across really spoiled?"

Her sister reached up under her red ball cap to scratch her temple. "We're both spoiled, Pipes, in the sense that we've been given everything we could want. But I don't like that word, because it implies you're . . . ruined. Like you have no good qualities. And you do." She frowned. "Did he call you spoiled?"

"It has been heavily implied."

Hannah sniffed. "I don't like him."

"Me either. Especially his muscles. Yuck."

"There were definitely muscles," Hannah agreed reluctantly. Then she hugged her middle and sighed, letting Piper know exactly whom she was thinking about. "He can't compete with Sergei, though. Nobody can."

Realizing her hands were greasy from the meat, Piper reached over to the sink, which was right there, thanks to the kitchen being all of four feet wide, and rinsed her hands. She dried them on a cloth and set it down, then went back to prodding the meat. It was getting pretty brown, so she tossed in the onion slices, congratulating herself on being the next Giada. "You've always gone for the starving-artist boys," she murmured to Hannah. "You like them tortured."

"Won't deny it." Hannah slipped off her hat and ran her fingers through her medium-length hair. Hair just as nice as Piper's, but worn down far less often. A crime, to Piper's way of thinking, but she'd realized a long time ago that Hannah was going to be Hannah—and she didn't want to change a single thing about her sister. "Sergei is different, though. He's not just pretending to be edgy, like the other directors I've worked with. His art is so bittersweet and moving and stark. Like an early Dylan song."

"Have you talked to him since we got here?"

"Only through the group Zoom meetings." Hannah went to the narrow refrigerator and took out a Diet Coke, twisting off the cap. "He was so understanding about the trip. I get to keep my job . . . and he gets to keep my heart," she said wistfully.

They traded a snort.

But the sound died in Piper's throat when flames leapt up from the counter.

The counter?

No, wait. The rag . . . the one she'd used to dry her hands.

It was on fire.

"Shit! Hannah!"

"Oh my God! *What the fuck?*"

"I don't know!" Operating on pure reflex, Piper threw the spatula at the fire. Not surprisingly, that did nothing to subdue the flames. The flaring orange fingers were only growing larger, and the counter's laminate was basically nonexistent. Could the counters themselves catch on fire, too? They were nothing more than brittle wood. "Is that the rag we used to clean?"

"Maybe . . . yeah, I think so. It was soaked in that lemon stuff." In Piper's periphery, Hannah danced on the balls of her feet. "I'm going to run downstairs and look for a fire extinguisher."

"I don't think there's time," Piper screeched—and it galled her that in this moment of certain death, she could almost hear Brendan laughing at her funeral. "Okay, okay. Water. We need water?"

"No, I think water makes it worse," Hannah returned anxiously.

The meat was now engulfed in flames, just like her short-lived cooking career. "Well, Jesus. I don't know what to do!" She spied a pair of tongs on the edge of the sink, grabbed them, hesitated a split second before pinching a corner of the flaming rag and dragging the whole burning mess into the pan, on top of the meat.

"What are you doing?" Hannah screamed.

"I don't know! We've established that! I'm just going to get it outside of this building before we burn the place down."

And then Piper was running down the stairs with a pan. A pan that held an inferno of meat and Pine-Sol-soaked cotton. She could hear Hannah sprinting down the stairs behind her but didn't catch a word of what her sister said, because she was one hundred percent focused on getting out of the building.

On her way through the bar, she found herself thinking of Mick Forrester's words from earlier that day. *Boy, your dad had a great laugh. Sometimes I swear I still hear it shaking the rafters of this place.* The remembrance slowed her step momentarily, had her glancing up at the ceiling, before she kicked open the front door and ran out onto the busy Westport street with a flaming frying pan, shouting for help.

Chapter Nine

Brendan went through the motions of looking over the chalkboard menu at the Red Buoy, even though he already knew damn well he'd be ordering the fish and chips. Every Monday night, he met Fox at the small Westport restaurant. An institution that had been standing since their grandfathers worked the fishing boats. Brendan had never failed to get the same thing. No sense in fixing something that wasn't broken, and the Red Buoy had the best damn fish in town.

Locals came and went, calling hellos to each other, most of them picking up takeout to bring home to their families, greasy bags tucked under their arms. Tonight, Brendan and Fox were making use of one of three tables in the place, waiting for their orders to be called. And if Fox noticed Brendan glancing too many times at No Name across the street, he hadn't mentioned it.

"You're even more quiet than usual," Fox remarked, leaning back so far in his chair, it was a wonder he didn't topple over. He wouldn't, though, Brendan knew. His best friend and relief skipper of the *Della Ray* rarely made a misstep. In that way, he lived up to his name. "You got crabs on the brain, Cap?"

Brendan grunted, looking across the street again.

If he didn't have crabs on the brain, he sure as shit needed to put them there. In a couple of weeks, they would be making the journey to the Bering Sea for the season. For two weeks after that, they'd be hunting in those frigid yet familiar waters, doing their best to fill the belly of the boat with enough crab to support their team of six until next year.

Every crew member and deckhand of the *Della Ray* had year-round fishing jobs working out of Westport Harbor in addition to participating in the season, but king crab was their payday, and Brendan's men counted on him to deliver.

"Been studying the maps," Brendan said finally, forcing himself to focus on the conversation and not the building across the way. "Got a feeling the Russians are going to set their pots where we dropped ours last year, figuring it's tried and true. But the season is earlier than ever this year, and the tides are more volatile. Nothing is surefire."

Fox considered that. "You're thinking of heading farther west?"

"North." They traded a knowing look, both of them aware of the rougher waters that lay in that direction. "Can't think of a crew that's had much luck up toward St. Lawrence Island in several years. But I've got a hunch."

"Hey. Your hunches have always made my bank account happy." He dropped forward, clinked his bottle of Bud against Brendan's. "Let's do the damn thing."

Brendan nodded, content to let the silence settle.

But he noticed that Fox seemed to be battling a smile. "You got something to say?" Brendan finally asked.

Fox's mouth spread into the smile that made him popular

with women. In fact, he hadn't been at No Name on Sunday night because he'd taken a trip to Seattle to see a woman he'd met online. Seeing as he'd spent two nights there, Brendan had to assume the date had been . . . successful, though he'd cut his tongue out before asking for details. That kind of thing was better off left private.

For some reason, the fact that his best friend was popular with women was annoying him today more than usual. He couldn't fathom why.

"I might have something to say," Fox answered, in a way that presumed he did. "Took a walk up to the harbor this morning. Heard we've got some LA transplants in old Westport. Word is you had a little battle of wills with one of them."

"Who said?"

His friend shrugged. "Don't worry about it."

"Someone on the crew, then. Sanders."

Fox was visibly enjoying himself. "You're staring a hole through the window of No Name, Cap." There was a stupid dimple in his relief skipper's cheek. Had it always been there? Did women like shit like that? "Heard she didn't back down from your death stare."

Brendan was disgusted. Mostly because he was right. Piper hadn't backed down from it. Not last night and not this morning. "You sound like a teenage girl gossiping at her first sleepover."

That got a laugh out of Fox. But his friend went back to drinking his beer for a moment, his smile losing some of its enthusiasm. "It's okay, you know," he said, keeping his voice low in deference to the other customers waiting for their orders. "It's been seven years, man."

"I know how long it's been."

"Okay." Fox relented, knowing him well enough to drop the subject. Not the subject of his wife. But the subject of . . . moving on. At some point, near or far. Even the glimmer of that conversation made him nervous. Like everything else in his life, he'd remained married in his mind since she'd passed, because it had become a habit. A routine. A comfort of sorts. So he wasn't welcoming the possibility.

Still, when they both rose to collect their orders a minute later and sat back down at the table, Brendan didn't start eating right away. Instead, he found his hand fisted on the table, to the right of his plate. Fox saw it, too, and waited.

"Don't go sniffing around the older one. Piper," Brendan muttered. "And don't ask me to explain why, either."

Fox dipped his chin, his mouth in a serious line but his eyes merry as fuck. "Not a single sniff. You've got my word . . ." Brendan's friend dropped the fork he'd just picked up, his attention riveted on something happening out in the street. "What in the sweet hell?"

Brendan's head jerked around and pieced the situation together in the space of a second, his captain's mind immediately searching for a solution. His life might run on schedules and routine, but that organized mentality was what made it easier for him to manage chaos. Problems arose, solutions presented themselves. Just another type of order.

But this . . .

He didn't feel like his usual self watching Piper barrel into the street wielding fire.

His body moved for him, though. He shot from the table and

shouted to the visor-wearing register girl, "Fire extinguisher. Now."

She turned as pale as a ghost, and dammit, he'd have to apologize for scaring her later, but right then, he was moving across the street at a fast clip, pulling the pin out of the fire extinguisher. For a few hellish seconds, he watched Piper turn in circles, looking for somewhere safe to set down the enflamed pan, before she had no choice but to throw it into the street.

"Move," Brendan ordered, aiming and dousing the flames in sodium bicarbonate. Left behind was a charred pan from the nineteenth century, by the look of it. He took a breath, realized his heart was sprinting in his chest. Without stopping to think, he dropped the extinguisher and grabbed Piper's wrists, turning her hands over to look for burn marks. "Did you get yourself?"

"No," she breathed, blinking up at him. "Thanks. Um . . . thanks for putting it out."

He dropped her hands, not sure he wanted to acknowledge the free fall of relief he felt over her being unharmed. Stepping back, he whipped off his beanie, letting a welcome rush of irritation snake its way into his belly. "Really, Piper?" Brendan shouted. "I was only joking about having the fire department on speed dial."

Until Hannah stepped between them, Brendan wasn't even aware the little sister had followed Piper out of the building. Oh, but she was there, she was pissed, and her anger was directed squarely at him. "Don't yell at her, you fucking bully."

Inwardly, he flinched. *Bully?*

Fox made a choking sound. Brendan turned to tell his friend

to keep his mouth shut and realized they were drawing a crowd. A curious one.

"Hannah, it's fine." Piper sighed, moving out from behind her sister. Face red from embarrassment, she used the hem of her shirt to pick up the frying pan. The move left almost her entire trim stomach exposed, and Brendan ground his molars together. If he couldn't help noticing the little mole to the right of her belly button, nobody else could, either. She wasn't wearing the sequined thing anymore, but in bike shorts, with loose hair and a dirt smudge on her nose, she wasn't any less beautiful. "Ignore him," Piper said, dismissing him with a flick of her hand. "Do you see a place I can throw this away?"

"*Ignore* him, the lady says," Fox said, amused.

"What are you, his pretty-boy sidekick?" Hannah waved off a stunned Fox with a suck of her teeth and refocused her wrath on Brendan. "The last thing she needs is another dude making her feel like garbage. Leave her alone."

"*Hannah*," Piper hissed sharply, walking past. "It's not worth getting upset over. Come help me."

But her sister wasn't finished. "And it was *my* fault. I left the cleaning rag on the kitchen counter, all soaked in chemicals. She's the one that saved the building from burning down." Hannah poked him in the middle of his chest. "Leave. Her. Alone."

Brendan was feeling shittier by the second. Something funny was stuck in his throat, and the appetite he'd left the house with had deserted him. He'd still been reeling over Hannah calling him a *bully* when she'd said, *The last thing she needs is another dude making her feel like garbage,* and now something hot and dangerous was simmering in his belly.

None of this was familiar. Women, especially ones half his size, didn't yell at him in the street. Or scare the shit out of him by nearly catching on fire. Part of him wanted to swipe a hand across the chessboard of the day and start over tomorrow, hoping and praying everything would be back to normal. But instead he found he wanted to . . . fix this situation with Piper more than he wanted to cling to the status quo. Maybe he was coming down with the goddamn flu or something, because when Piper tossed the pan into a trash can and sailed back toward her building, it was clear she intended to go home without saying another word to him. And for some reason, he just couldn't allow that to happen.

Leave her alone, the sister had said, and his apology got stuck in his throat.

Like he was a prize asshole who went around hurting women's feelings.

No. Just this one.

Why just this one?

Brendan cleared his throat hard. "Piper."

The woman in question paused with her hand on the door, gave an impatient hair toss that was way too sexy for a Monday night in Westport. Her expression said, *You again?*

Meanwhile, Hannah frowned up at him. "I said to leave my sister—"

"Listen up," Brendan said to the younger one. "I heard what you said. I respect you for saying it. You've got a nice, solid backbone for someone from Los Angeles. But I don't follow orders, I give them." He let that sink in. "I yelled at her because that's what people do when there's a close call." Over the top of Hannah's head, he met Piper's gaze. "I won't do it again."

A wrinkle appeared between Piper's brows, and damn, he was relieved. At least she no longer seemed indifferent about him. "It's okay, Hannah," Piper said, her hand dropping away from the door. "If you want to head back upstairs, I can go grab some takeout for dinner."

Hannah still wasn't budging. Neither was the crowd surrounding them. Brendan couldn't really blame the locals for being curious, either. These two girls were totally out of place in their small-fishing-town surroundings. Like two explosions of color.

Piper came forward and laid her head on her sister's shoulder. "I appreciate you defending me, Hanns, but you're a lover, not a fighter." She dropped a kiss on her cheek. "Go decompress. Your Radiohead albums are hiding in the secret pocket of my red quilted Chanel suitcase."

The younger sister gasped, whirling on Piper. "They wouldn't fit in any of my suitcases. You snuck them for me?"

"I was saving them for a rainy day." She bumped her hip to Hannah's. "Go. Fire up the turntable and listen as loud as you want."

"You a vinyl fan?" Fox piped up, reminding Brendan he was standing there in the first place. Hannah looked at Brendan's friend dubiously, but it only served to deepen that stupid dimple. He jerked a thumb in the direction of the harbor. "You know, there's a record store within walking distance. I could show you."

The younger Bellinger's eyes had gone wide as saucers.

"Fox," Brendan warned, taking his arm and pulling him aside.

"Oh, come on," Fox threw back, before he could say anything. "She's a kid."

"I'm not a kid," Hannah called. "I'm twenty-six!"

Fox dropped his voice another octave, moved in closer. "Jesus, she's cute, but she couldn't be further from my type. I'm just trying to buy you some alone time with Piper." He raised an eyebrow. "And who wouldn't want alone time with Piper. Good Christ, man. Sanders didn't do her justice."

"Shut the fuck up."

His friend laughed. "You really know how to make up for lost time, don't you?"

"I said, don't make me explain," Brendan gritted out.

"All right. All right. Just vouch for me," Fox muttered. "I'll have her back in twenty minutes, and I might even say some nice things about your grouchy ass. Wouldn't hurt."

Brendan hated admitting that Fox had a point. This was his third encounter with Piper, and he'd been a dick all three times. At first because she'd judged his town. Then he'd landed on the conclusion that she was an overindulged rich girl. After that, he could only blame being painfully rusty with the opposite sex. And this . . . being alone with a woman. It was a huge step. He could give her a simple apology now, go home, try to stop thinking about her. Yeah, he *could* do that. Just avoid this part of town for three months and stay the course of his routine.

She glanced up at him through her eyelashes. Not in a flirtatious way. More . . . inquisitive. As if she was wondering about him. And he found himself regretting the bad impressions he'd made. "He's my relief skipper. If he doesn't have her back in twenty minutes, I could drown him and make it look like an accident."

A smile teased her lips, and he wondered—couldn't help himself—what kind of man would get a kiss from a woman like that. "Take a picture of his ID, Hanns," Piper said, still looking at Brendan like he was a puzzle she wasn't sure she wanted to solve. "Text it to me first."

Sliding his wallet from his back pocket, Fox nodded. "I guess they grow them smart as well as beautiful in LA."

"Wow." Piper smiled at Fox. "A compliment. I was starting to think those were against the law in Westport."

Brendan turned a death glare on Fox. "What'd I say?"

Fox slid his ID to Hannah. "Sorry, Captain. The charm comes naturally."

The younger Bellinger snapped a picture of Fox's driver's license. A moment later, there was a *bing*, and Piper confirmed that she had the man's vital information. Fox gestured for Hannah to precede him down the sidewalk, and she did, arms crossed. But not before she mouthed a warning to Brendan.

Good Lord, what happened to him being well respected in this town?

If these two girls had had the proper tools, he was pretty damn sure he'd be tarred and feathered right about now. Maybe hanging from his toes in the harbor like a prize catch.

Brendan closed the distance between them, feeling like he was walking a plank. But he needn't have worried about being alone with Piper, because he swore half the damn town was still standing around, leaning in to see how he'd get out of the doghouse. "That fire ruin your dinner?"

She nodded, playing with the hem of her shirt. "I guess the

universe just couldn't allow something so perfect. You should have seen it. The meat barely looked like brains anymore."

He was caught off guard by the urge to smile. "I, uh . . ." He replaced his beanie, tried to scare off a few locals with a loud sniff, gratified when they scattered in all directions. "It was rude to shout before. I apologize." Lord, she was even prettier with the sunset in her eyes. That was probably why he added, "For this time and the other times."

Piper's mouth twisted and she ducked her head somewhat, like she was trying to camouflage her own smile. "Thank you. I accept."

Brendan grunted, dipped his chin toward the Red Buoy. "They called my number right before you ran out on fire. Go in there and eat it." When she blinked, he played back his demand and realized that's exactly what it had been. A demand. "If you'd like," he tacked on.

She hummed and slipped past him, her perfume reaching up and apparently doing something to his brain, because he followed in her wake without sending the order to his feet. Everyone turned and stared when they walked inside and sat down at the same table. Hell, the customers waiting for their orders didn't even attempt to disguise their interest.

He didn't want any of them to overhear their conversation. It was none of their business. That was the only reason he took the seat next to Piper and tugged her chair a little closer.

Brendan pushed the plate of fish and chips in front of her, then picked up the fork and put it in her hand.

"So . . ." She forked the smallest fry on the plate, and he frowned. "Your friend is your relief skipper. That makes you . . . the captain?"

Thank Christ. Something he could talk about.

"That's right. I captain the *Della Ray*."

"Oh." She tilted her head. "Where does that name come from?"

"I took the wheel from my father-in-law, Mick. It's named after his wife."

"How romantic." If bringing up his in-laws made for awkward conversation, she didn't let it show. Instead, her interest seemed piqued. "Me and Hannah walked up to the harbor this afternoon. So many boats are named after women. Is there a reason for that?"

He thought of Piper strutting along his harbor and wondered how many car accidents she'd caused. "Women are protective. Nurturing. A boat is given the name of a woman in the hopes that she'll protect the crew. And hopefully put a good word in with the other important woman in our lives, the ocean."

She took a bite of fish, chewing around a smile. "Have you ever had a woman on your crew?"

"Jesus Christ, no." There went the smile. "I'm trying *not* to sink."

Amusement danced across her face. "So the idea of women is comforting, but their actual presence would be a disaster."

"Yes."

"Well, that makes perfect sense." Her sarcasm was delivered with a wink. "My stepfather told us a little bit about king crab fishing. It's only a few weeks out of the year?"

"Changes every season, depending on the supply, the overall haul from the prior year."

Piper nodded. "What do you do the rest of the year? Besides yell at harmless women in the street."

"You planning on holding that over me for long?"

"I haven't decided."

"Fair enough." He sighed, noticed she'd stopped eating, and nudged her fork hand into action. When she'd put a decent-sized bite into her mouth, he continued. "In the summer, we fish for tuna. Those are the longer jobs. Four, five days out. In between those long hauls, we do overnight trips to bring in salmon, trout, cod."

Her eyebrows went up, and she angled her fork toward the plate. "Did you catch this?"

"Maybe."

She covered her mouth. "That's so weird."

Was it? He kind of liked sitting there while she ate something he'd brought back on his boat. He liked knowing most of the town either made money off his catches or fed them to their families, but it had never quite felt like the masculine pride hardening his chest right now. "You want me to put in an order for your sister? Or they can box up Fox's dinner, and he can fend for himself."

"She'll be happy with the other half of yours." She pushed Fox's plate toward him. "You should eat his, though. I don't know what it is, but it looks good."

Brendan grunted. "It's a potpie."

"Ohh." She waited, but he made no move to pick up his fork. "You don't like potpie?"

"It's not fish and chips."

"And that's bad."

"It's not bad, it's just not what I order." He shifted in his chair, wondering if the seats had always been so uncomfortable. "I always order the fish and chips."

Piper studied him in that way again, from beneath her long eyelashes—and he wished she wouldn't. Every time she did that, the zipper of his jeans felt tight. "You've never eaten anything else on the menu?"

"Nope. I like what I like."

"That's so boring, though."

"I call it safe."

"Oh no." A serious expression dawned on her face. "Do you think there is a female fisherman hiding in this pie, Brendan?"

His bark of laughter made her jump. Hell, it made *him* jump. Had anyone ever caught him off guard like that? No, he didn't think so. He turned slightly to find the employees of the Red Buoy and a half-dozen customers staring at him. When he turned back, Piper was holding out the fork. "Try the pie. I dare you."

"I won't like it."

"So?"

So? "I don't *try* things. If I make the decision to eat the pie, I'll have to eat the whole thing. I don't just go around sampling shit and moving on. That's indecisive."

"If Hannah was here, she'd tell you your problem is psychological."

Brendan sighed up at the ceiling. "Well, I didn't seem to have any damn problems until you two showed up and started pointing them out."

A beat passed. "Brendan."

He dropped his chin. "What?"

She held out the fork. "Try the pie. It's not going to kill you."

"Christ. If it's that important to you." Brendan snatched the fork out of her hand, careful not to graze her with the tines. As he held the fork above the pastry shell, she pressed her knuckles to her mouth and squealed a little. He shook his head, but some part of him was relieved she didn't seem to be having a terrible time. Even if her entertainment came at his expense. He reckoned he kind of owed her after the scene in the street, though, didn't he?

Yeah.

He stabbed the fork into the pie, pulled it out with some chicken, vegetables, and gravy attached. Put it in his mouth and chewed. "I hate it." Someone behind the counter gasped. "No offense," he called without turning around. "It's just not fish and chips."

Piper's hands dropped away from her face. "Well, that was disappointing."

He kept eating, even though the runniness of the gravy curled his upper lip.

"You're really going to eat the whole thing," she murmured, "aren't you?"

Another large bite went in. "Said I would."

They ate in silence for a couple of minutes until he noticed her attention drifting to the window, and he could see she was thinking about the frying pan incident. Another stab of guilt caught him in his middle for yelling at her. "You planning on trying to cook again?"

She considered her plate of food, which she'd hardly made a dent in. "I don't know. The goal was to make it through one night and go from there." She squinted an eye at him. "Maybe I'll have better luck if I give our stove a woman's name."

Brendan thought for a second. "Eris." She gave him an inquisitive head tilt. "The goddess of chaos."

"Ha-ha."

Piper laid her fork down, signaling she'd finished eating, and Brendan felt a kick of urgency. They'd been sitting there a good ten minutes, and he still didn't know anything about her. Nothing important, anyway. And he wouldn't mind making sense of her, this girl who came across pampered one minute and vulnerable the next. Hell, there was something fascinating about how she glimmered in one direction, then the other, delivering hints of something deeper, before dancing away. Had he really talked about fishing for most of dinner?

He *wanted* to ask what Hannah had meant when she said men treat Piper like garbage. That statement had been stuck in his craw since he'd heard it. "You never answered me this morning. Why exactly are you in Westport?" was what he asked instead. She'd been running fingers through her hair, but paused when she heard his question. "You said three months," he continued. "That's a pretty specific amount of time."

Beneath the table, her leg started to jiggle. "It's kind of an awkward story."

"Do you need a beer before telling it?"

Her lips twitched. "No." She closed her eyes and shivered. "It's more than awkward, actually. It's humiliating. I don't know if I should give you that ammunition."

Man, he'd really been a bastard. "I won't use it against you, Piper."

She speared him with those baby blues and seemed satisfied with whatever she saw. "Okay. Just keep an open mind." She blew out a breath. "I had a bad breakup. A public one. And I didn't want to be labeled social media pathetic, right? So I mass texted hundreds of people and broke us into the rooftop pool at the Mondrian. It got out of control. Like, police helicopters and fireworks and nudity out of control. So I got arrested and almost cost my stepfather the production money for his next film. He sent me here with barely any money to teach me a lesson . . . and force me into being self-sufficient. Hannah wouldn't let me come alone."

Brendan's fork had been suspended in the air for a good minute. He tried to piece it all together, but everything about this world she'd described was so far from his, it almost sounded like make-believe. "When was this?"

"A few weeks ago," she said on an exhale. "Wow, it sounds a lot worse when it's all strung together like that." Chewing her bottom lip, she searched his face. "What are you thinking? That you were right and I'm just some rich, spoiled brat?"

"Don't put words in my mouth. You're already making me eat this goddamn pie."

"No, I'm not!"

He shoveled in another bite of crap, his mind circling back to the bad breakup she'd mentioned. Why did his spine feel like it was getting ready to snap? "I'm thinking a lot of things," he said. "Mostly, I can't imagine you in jail."

"It wasn't so bad. The guard, Lina, was a doll. She let me use the regular bathroom."

"How'd you pull that off?"

"People like me." She looked down her adorable nose at him. "Most of the time."

He snorted. "Yeah, I can see that. Flirt."

She gasped. Then shrugged. "Yeah." A couple of seconds ticked past. "You didn't let me flirt with you. And then I thought you were married. My whole pattern got thrown off, and now I don't know how to act. Trying to flirt again seems pointless."

The hell it was. "Try it."

"No. I can't!" she sputtered. "The third wall is already down."

Was he sweating under his clothes? What the hell was wrong with him? "What is the next stage after flirting? Once you've settled in?"

"*Settled in?* Ew." She shrugged. "Also, I don't know. I've never gotten that far." She crossed her legs, drawing his gaze to the slide of her shorts along that smooth underside of her thigh. And there went his zipper again, confining things. "We've gotten way off the topic of my whole sordid story."

"No, we haven't," he responded. "I'm still digesting it all. Along with—"

"Don't you dare bring up the pie again." They each offered up half a smile. "Anyway, unless I can finagle a way back to Los Angeles, me and Hannah will be here until Halloween. I think my best bet is to spend less time cooking, more time figuring out how to finagle." She tapped a fingernail on the table. "Maybe if there was a way to prove I've learned how to be responsible, Daniel would let me come home."

Brendan was brooding over Piper being at a party that involved nudity—in what capacity, exactly? Had *she* been naked?—so he spoke more harshly than intended. "Here's an idea. Why don't you try and actually enjoy your time outside the ninth circle of hell that is Los Angeles?"

"Who said I'm not enjoying myself? Look at me, getting snipped at over fish and chips. If this isn't living it up, I've been doing it wrong." Smirking, she popped a fry into her mouth, and he tried not to watch her chew. "But you're right. I could try harder. Maybe I'll charm one of those cute fishermen up on the harbor into taking me fishing."

Something acidic burbled in his windpipe at the prospect of her on another man's boat. "You could. If you wanted a subpar experience."

"Are you saying you could deliver a better one?"

"Damn right."

Were they still talking about fishing? Brendan didn't know. But he was turned on . . . and she appeared to be waiting for something. For him to ask her out on his boat?

A breeze of panic kept his mouth shut a moment too long. Piper gave him an assessing look and visibly moved on, rising to her feet when her sister and Fox appeared outside the restaurant. "There they are. I'll grab a to-go box for the rest of this." She leaned down and kissed both of his cheeks, like they were in goddamn Paris or something. "Thanks for dinner, Captain. I promise to stay out of your hair."

As she dumped the remaining fish and chips into a container and bounced off to join her sister, Brendan wasn't sure if he wanted Piper out of his hair. If he didn't, he'd just missed a clear opening to ask her out. In the morning, he'd be leaving for a three-day fishing trip, so—assuming he *wanted* the opportunity to see more of the girl from Los Angeles—he'd have to wait for another one. And it might never come.

Fox dropped into the chair beside him, grinning ear to ear. "How'd it go, Cap?"

"Shut up."

Chapter Ten

*P*iper was stuck in a nightmare in which giant mice with twitchy little noses chased her through a maze while she wielded a flaming frying pan. So when she heard the knock on the door the following morning, her waking thought was *The mouse king has come for me.* She pinwheeled into a sitting position and soundly smacked her head on the top bunk.

"Ow," she complained, pushing her eye mask up to her forehead and testing the collision spot with a finger. Already sore.

A yawn came from above. "Did you hit your head again?"

"Yes," she grumbled, trying to piece together why she'd woken up in the first place. It wasn't like much sunlight *could* filter in through their window and the building next door. Not when a scant inch separated them and the neighboring wall. The apartment was all but black. It couldn't even be sunrise yet.

A fist rapped twice on the door, and she screamed, her hand flying to the center of her chest. "Mouse king," she gasped.

Hannah giggled. "What?"

"Nothing." Piper shook off the mental cobwebs and eyed the door warily. "Who's there?"

"It's Brendan."

"Oh." She glanced up and knew she was trading a frown with Hannah, even though they couldn't see each other. What did the grumpy boat captain need from her that couldn't wait until normal-people hours? Every time she thought they'd seen the last of each other, he seemed to be right there, front and center. Confusing her.

She hadn't been lying about not knowing how to act in his presence. It was usually easy to charm, flirt, flatter, and wrap men around her pinky. Until they got bored and moved on, which they seemed to do faster and faster these days. But that was beside the point. Brendan had robbed her deck of the pretty-girl trump card, and she couldn't get it back. He'd had too many peeks behind the curtain now. The first time they'd met, she'd been a drowned rat and offended his beloved Westport. Meeting two, she'd blasphemed his dead wife. Three, she'd almost burned this relic of a building down . . .

Although eating with him had been kind of . . . nice.

Maybe that wasn't the right word.

Different. Definitely different. She'd engaged in conversation with a man without constantly trying to present her best angle and laugh in just the right way. He'd *seemed* interested in what she had to say. Could he have been?

Obviously, he hadn't been instantly enraptured with her appearance. Her practiced come-hither glances only made him grumpier. So maybe he wanted to be friends! Like, based on her personality. Wouldn't that be something?

"Huh," she murmured through a yawn. "Friends."

Swinging her legs over the edge of the bed, she slipped her feet into her black velvet Dolce & Gabbana slippers and padded to the door. Before she opened it, she gave in to vanity and scrubbed away the sleep crusties in the corners of her eyes. She opened the door and craned her neck in order to look up into the face of the surly boat captain.

Piper started to say good morning, but Brendan cleared his throat hard and did a quarter turn, staring at the doorjamb. "I'll wait until you're dressed."

"Sorry . . . ?" Nose wrinkled, she looked down at her tank top and panties. "Oh."

"Here," Hannah called sleepily, tossing Piper a pillow.

"Thanks." She caught it, held it in front of herself like a puffy shield.

Hold on. Was this man she'd judged as little more than a bully . . . blushing?

"Oh, come on, Brendan," she chuckled. "There's a lot worse on my Instagram. Anyone's Instagram, really."

"Not mine," Hannah said, voice muffled. A second later, she was snoring softly.

For the first time, Piper noticed the tool kit at Brendan's feet. "What's all that for?"

Finally, Brendan allowed his attention to drift back to her, and a muscle wormed in his jaw. The pillow covered Piper from neck to upper thigh, but the curve of her panty-clad backside was still visible. Brendan's eyes traveled over that swell now, continuing up the line of her back, his Adam's apple bobbing in his throat. "I changed the lock on the door downstairs," he said hoarsely, his gaze ticking to hers. "Came to change this one, too. It'll only take a few minutes."

"Oh." Piper straightened. "Why?"

"We leave this morning for three nights. Last fishing trip

before crab season. I just . . ." He crouched down and started rooting through his box, metal clanging so she could barely hear him when he said, "Wanted to make sure this place was secure."

Piper's fingers tightened on the pillow. "That was really nice of you."

"Well." Tools in hand, he straightened once again to his full height. "I saw you hadn't done it. Even though you've had two days."

She shook her head. "You had to go and ruin the nice gesture, didn't you?"

Brendan grunted and set to work, apparently having decided to ignore her. Fine. Just to spite him, she let the pillow drop and went to make coffee. On her sister's trip to the record store with Fox, Hannah had found a mom-and-pop electronics shop, purchasing the kind of one-cup brewer you'd normally find in a hotel room. They'd been selling it for *ten dollars*. Who sold anything for ten dollars? They'd rejoiced over Hannah's bargain hunting the way Piper used to celebrate finding a four-thousand-dollar Balmain dress at a sample sale.

"Would you like a cup of coffee?" Piper asked Brendan.

"No, thanks. Already had one."

"Let me guess." After adding a mug of water, she lowered the lid on the maker and switched it on. "You never have more than a single cup."

Grunt. "Two on Sundays." His brows angled down and together. "What's that red mark on your head?"

"Oh." Her fingers lifted to prod the sore patch. "I'm not used to sleeping with another bed three feet above mine. I keep whacking my head on the top bunk."

He made a sound. Kept frowning.

His visible grumpiness made the corner of Piper's mouth edge up. "What are you going fishing for this time?"

"Halibut. Rockfish."

She rolled her eyes at his abrupt answer, leaned back against the chipped kitchen counter. "Well, Hannah and I talked it over and we're running with your suggestion." She picked up her finished coffee, stirring it with her finger and sipping. "We want to enjoy our time in Westport. Tell me where to go. What to do."

Brendan took another minute to finish up the lock. He tested it out and replaced his tools in the box before approaching her, digging something out of his back pocket. She caught a tingle on the soft inner flesh of her thighs and knew he was checking her out, but she pretended not to notice. Mostly because she didn't know how to feel about it. That familiar burn of a man's regard wasn't giving her the obligatory thrum of success. Brendan's attention made her kind of . . . fidgety. He'd have to be dead not to look. But actual interest was something else. She wasn't even sure what she would do if Brendan showed more than a passing notice of her hotness.

And he was still wearing his wedding ring.

Meaning, he was still hung up on his deceased wife.

So she and Brendan would be friends. Definitely *only* friends.

Brendan cleared his throat. "You're a five-minute walk to the lighthouse. And it's still warm enough for the beach. There's a small winery in town, too. My men are always complaining about having to go there on date nights. They have something called a selfie spot. So you should love it."

"That tracks."

"I also brought you some takeout menus," he said in a low voice, slapping them down on the counter, and with him standing so close, it was impossible not to register their major size difference. Or catch a whiff of his saltwater-and-no-nonsense deodorant.

Friends, she reminded herself.

A grieving widower was not fling material.

Swallowing, Piper looked down at the menus. He'd brought three of them.

She pursed her lips. "I guess it's too early to be insulted."

"This isn't me telling you not to cook. These are fallbacks." He opened the first folded menu, for a Chinese restaurant. "In each of them, I went ahead and circled what I order every time, so you'd know the best dish."

She hip-bumped him, although thanks to him being a foot taller, her hip landed somewhere near the top of his thigh. "You mean, the only one you've ever tried?"

A smile threatened to appear on his face. "They're one and the same."

"Bah."

"You have your phone handy?" Brendan asked.

Nodding, she turned on a heel, took two steps, and picked up the discarded pillow, holding it over her butt to end his suffering—and to let him know she'd gotten the friends-only message. She collected her cell from its place of honor beneath her pillow, then pivoted, transferring the pillow once again to block her front. When she turned around, Brendan was watching her curiously, but didn't comment on her sudden modesty.

"If you and your sister have any problems while I'm gone, call Mick." He dipped his chin. "That's my . . . my father-in-law."

"We met him yesterday," Piper said, smiling through the odd tension at the mention of Brendan having a father-in-law. "He's a sweetie."

Brendan seemed momentarily caught off guard. "Ah. Right. Well, he's not too far from here. Let me give you his contact info in case you need something."

"Yes, Captain." She clicked her bare heels together. "And after that, I'll swab the deck."

He snorted. "She uses a mop once . . ."

Piper beamed. "Oh, you noticed our spruce job, did you?"

"Yeah. Not bad," he commented, glancing around the apartment. "Ready?"

Piper humored him by programming Mick's number into her phone as he rattled it off. "Thanks—"

"Take mine, too," he said abruptly, suddenly fascinated by one of the menus. "I won't have reception on the water, but . . ."

"Take it in case I need cooking advice when you get back?"

He made an affirmative sound in his throat.

Piper pressed her lips together to hide a smile. She'd seen Brendan with his friend Fox. How they needled each other like brothers as a means of communication. It really shouldn't come as a surprise that making new friends didn't come naturally to him. "All right. Give me those digits, Captain."

He seemed relieved by her encouragement, reciting the number as she punched it into her phone. When she hit dial on his number, his head came up as if trying to figure out where the sound was coming from.

"That's your phone," she said, and laughed. "I'm calling you so you'll have my number, too."

"Oh." He nodded, the corner of his mouth tugging a little. "Right."

She cupped a hand around her mouth and whispered, "Should I be expecting nudes?"

"Jesus Christ, Piper," he grumped, straightening the takeout menus and signaling an end to the discussion. But he hesitated a second before striding for the door. "Now that I'm in your phone, does this mean next time you break into a rooftop pool, I'll be on the mass invite?"

Brendan winked to let her know he was joking. But she couldn't help grinning at the mental image of this earthy giant of a man walking through a sea of polished LA social climbers. "Oh yeah. You're in."

"Great."

After one more almost imperceptible sweep of her legs, Brendan coughed into his fist and turned again. He picked up his toolbox and started down the stairs. Just like that. His work was done and formalities were stupid. Piper followed, looking down at him from the top of the stairs. "Are we friends, Brendan?"

"No," he called back, without missing a beat.

Her mouth hung open, a laugh huffing out of her as she closed the door.

Hannah sat up and asked, "What the hell is going on there?"

Slowly, she shook her head. "I have no freaking idea."

Chapter Eleven

Brendan sat in the wheelhouse of the *Della Ray* stabbing at the screen of his phone.

He should have been helping the crew load groceries and the ice they would need to keep the fish fresh in the hold. But they'd be pushing off in ten minutes, and he needed to take advantage of the last remaining minutes of internet access, spotty though it was in the harbor.

He'd downloaded Instagram; now they were asking him for personal information. Did he have to be a member of this stupid thing to look at pictures? Chrissakes. He shouldn't be doing this. Even if Piper had volunteered the information that she was apparently half-naked on this fucking app, he shouldn't be looking. In fact, if he expected to concentrate worth a damn on this trip, he absolutely should not be adding to the treasure trove of Piper imagery already floating around in his head.

First and foremost was the memory of Piper answering the door in those little white panties. White. He wouldn't have figured on that. Maybe sparkly pink or peacock blue. But hell if the white cotton cupping her pussy, a contrast of innocent and sexy, had him sporting a semi an hour later and downloading apps like a goddamn teenager. He'd been grinding his back teeth since he walked out of No Name, bereft over his palms not sliding down the supple curve of her ass—and God, he had no business thinking about that.

Why had she covered herself with the pillow the second time?

Had he been so obviously turned on it made her uncomfortable?

Considering that, he frowned. He didn't like the idea of her being nervous.

Not around him. Not at all.

"All loaded. Ready to go," Fox said, swinging into the wheelhouse, his Mariners cap pulled down low over his eyes. But not low enough that Brendan could miss them lighting up. "You downloading Instagram, Cap?"

"Who's downloading Instagram?" Sanders asked, ducking his red curly head under the doorframe. "Who doesn't already have Instagram?"

"People who have better shit to do," Brendan growled, snapping both of their mouths shut. "They're asking me to make a username."

In came a third member of the crew, Deke, his dark brown fingers wrapped around a bottle of Coke as he took a sip. "Username for what?"

Brendan tipped his head back. "Jesus Christ."

"Instagram," Sanders said, filling in Deke.

"You're doing a little Piper recon, aren't you?" Fox asked, his expression one of pure, everlasting enjoyment. "Downloading a few pictures to keep you warm on the trip?"

"You can do that?" Brendan half shouted. "Anyone can just download pictures of her?"

"Or me, or you, or anyone," Deke said. "It's the internet, man."

Brendan stared at his phone with renewed disgust. As far as he was concerned, this was even more reason to get on this dumb app and see what's what. "It won't let me just use my own name as my username."

"Yeah, probably because about nine hundred Brendan Taggarts joined before you."

"So what should I use?"

"CaptainCutie69," Fox spat out.

"IGotCrabs4U," Deke supplied.

"SlipperyWhenWet."

Brendan stared. "You're all fired. Go home."

"All right, all right, we'll be serious," Fox said, holding up his hands. "Did you try CaptainBrendanTaggart?"

He grunted, punched it in with one blunt digit. It took him forever, because his finger was so big, he kept hitting erroneous characters. "Accepted," he grumbled finally, shifting in the captain's chair. "Now what?"

Deke settled in next to Sanders, like they were in the middle of goddamn gossip hour. "Search her name," he said, pulling out his own phone.

Brendan pointed at him. "You better not be looking."

The man pocketed his phone again without another word.

"The captain is a little sensitive about Piper," Fox explained, still wearing that shit-eating grin. "He doesn't know what to do with his confusing man feelings."

Brendan ignored his friend in favor of typing Piper's name

into the search bar, sighing when a whole list of options came up. "Does the blue check mark mean it's her?"

"Ooh." Sanders perked up. "She's got a check mark?"

"Is that good or bad?"

Deke polished off his Coke, letting out a belch that no one reacted to. It was merely a component of the fishing-boat soundtrack. "It means she's got a big following. Means she's internet famous, boss."

Making a low sound in his throat, Brendan punched the check mark . . . and Piper exploded across the screen of his phone. And Christ, he didn't know where the hell to look first. One little square had a picture of her kneeling in the surf at the beach, her back on display, wearing nothing but a thong bikini bottom. He could have stared at her gorgeous ass all day—and he'd definitely be coming back to it later when he was alone— but there was more. So much more. *Thousands* of pictures of Piper.

In another one, she had on a red dress, with lips to match, a martini in her hand, her foot kicking up playfully. More beautiful than anyone had the right to be. He zeroed in on a recent one, from a few weeks ago, and found his mouth dropping open at the spectacle. When she'd told him that story about how she'd gotten arrested and sent to Westport, he'd assumed she'd embellished a little.

Nope.

There she was, among the rowdy crowd, wreathed in smoke and fireworks, arms thrown up. Happy and alive. And was that the number of people who'd clicked the heart?

Over *three million*?

Brendan dragged a hand down his face.

Piper Bellinger was from a different, flashier planet.

She's out of your league.

Way out.

Remembering how he'd fed her fish and chips last night when she was obviously used to caviar and champagne, he was embarrassed. If he could go back in time and not bring her those stupid takeout menus, he would do it in a heartbeat. God, she must have been laughing at him.

"Well?" Fox prompted.

Brendan cleared his throat hard. "What does 'follow' mean?"

"Don't," Deke rushed to say. "Don't press it."

His thumb was already on the way back up. "Too late."

All three of his crew members surged to their feet. "No. Brendan, don't tell me you just tapped the blue button," Sanders groaned, hands on his mop of red hair. "She's going to see you followed her. She's going to know you internet stalked her."

"Can't I just unfollow now?" Brendan started to tap again.

Fox lunged forward. "No! No, that's even worse. If she already noticed you followed her, she's just going to think you're playing games."

"Jesus. I'm deleting the whole thing," Brendan said, throwing the offending device onto the dashboard, where it bashed up against the windshield. His crew stared back expectantly, waiting for him to put his money where his mouth was. "Later," he growled, firing up the motor. "Get to work."

As soon as the three men were out of sight, he picked the phone back up slowly. Weighing it in his hand for a moment, he opened the app again and scrolled through Piper's feed until one image stopped him. She was sitting beside Hannah on a diving board, both of them wrapped in the same towel, water droplets all over her face. This looked like the Piper he'd had dinner with last night. Was she *that* girl? Or the daring jet-setter?

The sheer number of photos of her glittering at parties, balls, even awards shows suggested she loved the spotlight, the wealth and luxury. Shit he knew nothing about. More than that, she clearly liked polished, manicured men, probably with bank accounts that matched her own. And that meant his interest in her wasn't only annoying, it was laughable. He was a set-in-his-ways fisherman. She was a rich, adventurous socialite. He couldn't even order something new at a restaurant, and she dined with celebrities. *Dated* them.

He'd just have to spend the next few months keeping his admiration of her to himself, lest he make himself look like a fucking fool.

With one last glance at the picture of her smiling on the diving board, he determinedly shoved his phone into the front pocket of his jeans and focused on what he knew.

Fishing.

Chapter Twelve

Obviously they visited the winery first.

Brendan was right about Piper loving the selfie spot—damn him—a jewel-toned wall painted to look like stained glass, vines crawling up the sides and wrapping around a neon VINO sign. Essentially an altar at which to worship the social media gods.

Hannah was not a drinker. Thanks to four glasses of wine, many attempts were made to get a non-blurry picture of Piper before an adequate one was selected.

Piper applied a filter before swiping over to Instagram. Automatically, she tapped her notifications. "Oh, look at that." Her pulse stuttered. "Brendan followed me." She tapped his profile and choked. "Oh. I'm the *only* one he's following. He just joined."

Hannah squished her cheeks together. "Oh boy. Rookie move."

"Yeah . . ." But it was a really, really endearing move, too.

How did she feel about Brendan looking at her plethora of side boob and booty? Even her most modest pictures were kind of provocative. What if her lack of modesty turned him off? Did he really create a profile *just* to follow her?

Maybe Hannah had a point about social media having too much ownership over her thoughts and enjoyment. Now she was going to spend the next three days wondering which pictures Brendan looked at and what he thought about them. Would he laugh at her captions? If this Instagram feed was his glimpse into Piper Bellinger's life, would it override the real-life impression she'd given him?

"You should have seen this little record shop, Pipes," Hannah said around a sip of wine. Leave it to her sister to wax poetic about a record store after too much to drink, instead of an ex-boyfriend or a crush. As far back as she could remember, Hannah had been hunkered down in headphones, her face buried in song lyrics. When she turned sixteen, Piper brought Hannah to her first concert—Mumford & Sons—and the poor girl had almost passed out from stimuli. Her soul was made of musical notes. "They had a poster for a 1993 Alice in Chains concert. Just tacked to the wall! Because they haven't had a chance to take it down!"

Piper smiled at her sister's enthusiasm. "Why didn't you buy anything?"

"I wanted to. There was a really nice *Purple Rain* LP, but they had it way underpriced. It would have felt like stealing."

"You're a good apple, kid." Piper had the niggling urge to scroll her Instagram feed and see everything through Brendan's eyes, but she determinedly ignored it. "So. What's Fox like?"

Hannah set down her glass. "Uh-uh. Don't ask me like that."

"What? He's cute."

"He's not my type."

"Not depressed and bitter enough?"

Her sister snorted. "His phone dinged like a hundred times in twenty minutes. That's either one passionate girl or several admirers, and my money is on the latter."

"Yeah," Piper admitted. "He did have that playboy look about him."

Hannah swung her feet. "Besides, I think he was just doing the wingman thing. He wasted no time extolling Brendan's virtues."

"Oh?" Piper took a too-casual gulp of wine. "What did Fox have to say about him? Just out of curiosity."

Her sister narrowed her eyes. "Tell me you're not interested in him."

"Whoa. I'm not. His wedding ring is like, welded onto his finger."

"And he's mean to you." Hannah shifted her weight on her stool, looking as if she was working up to saying something. "You've been tread on by some mean guys lately, all right? There was Adrian. The one before him who produced that sci-fi HBO pilot, whose name I can't remember. I just want to make sure you're not falling into a bad pattern."

Piper reared back a little. "A pattern where I pick men who'll make me feel shitty?"

"Well . . . yeah."

She replayed her last three relationships. Which didn't take that long, since collectively they'd lasted six weeks. "Shit. You might be onto something."

"I am?" Hannah's eyebrows shot up. "I mean . . . I know."

"Okay, I'll be more aware of it," Piper said, rubbing at the dull ache in the center of her chest. If her sister was right, why was she picking bad apples on purpose? Did the idea of a *good* relationship scare her? Because she didn't think she could pull one off? It was not only possible, but probable. Still, putting Brendan in the "bad apple" category didn't quite sit right. "None of those other guys were the type to apologize. They definitely weren't the kind of guys who'd pine for their dead wife. I think maybe I'm just curious about Brendan more than anything else. We don't grow them like him in LA."

"That is true."

"We had an actual conversation without sexual overtones. Neither one of us checked our phones even *once*. It was fucking weird. I'm probably just . . . fascinated."

"Well, be careful." Tongue tucked in the corner of her mouth, Hannah started folding a bar napkin into an airplane. "Or have some fun with Fox instead. Bet it would be way less complicated."

Piper couldn't even remember the guy's face. Only that she'd classified it as attractive.

Now, *Brendan's* face. She could recall crow's-feet fanning out at the corners of his eyes. The silver flecks dotting the green of his irises. His gigantic, weathered hands and the breadth of his shoulders.

She shook herself. They'd had a meal together yesterday.

Of course she recalled those things.

Can you even remember Adrian's voice?

"I think maybe I'll just stick to myself on this trip," Piper murmured.

Two hours later, they weaved down the sidewalk on the way

home. It was well past time to put her little sister to bed. At four o'clock in the afternoon, but who was keeping track?

Crossing the street toward home, Piper's step slowed. It appeared they had a visitor. A little old man with a toolbox and a smile like sunshine.

"Ma'am."

"Um, hi." Piper nudged Hannah into alertness, nodding at the man waiting outside No Name. Come to think of it, returning home to find a local at their door was beginning to be a habit. "Hi. Can I help you?"

"Actually, I'm here to help you." With his free hand, he plucked a slip of paper from the pocket of his shirt. "I own the hardware store down on West Pacific. My sons have the run of the place now, but they have little ones, so they don't make it in until later in the morning. When I opened up today, there was a note taped to my door."

He held it out to Piper. How could this possibly pertain to her? With a mental shrug, she took the note and scanned the four blunt lines with a burgeoning clog in her throat.

NO NAME BAR. UPSTAIRS APARTMENT. PIPER BELLINGER.
NEEDS PADDING INSTALLED ON THE BASE OF THE TOP BUNK.
SHE KEEPS HITTING HER HEAD.
CAPTAIN TAGGART

"Oh my," she breathed, fanning herself with the note. *Am I levitating?*

She'd just decided to be friends-only with the sea captain. *This* definitely wasn't going to help divert her rather irritating attraction to him.

"He left some cash to cover it," the man said, reaching out to pat her arm. "You're going to have to help me up the stairs once we're inside, I'm afraid. My legs decided they'd had enough living when I turned seventy, but the rest of me is still here."

"Sure. Of course. Let me take the tools." Grateful for something to distract her from Brendan's gesture, Piper claimed the dusty box. "Um. Hannah?"

"What?" Owlish eyes blinked back. "Oh."

Yawning, Hannah transferred her drunken weight onto the side of the building so Piper would be free to unlock the door. They all went inside, traveling in a comically slow-moving pack toward the stairs. Piper hooked her right arm through the old man's left, and they followed Hannah's uneven gait up toward the apartment. "I'm Piper, by the way. The girl from the note."

"I probably should have checked. My wife would have had some questions if I'd let some stranger squire me up to her apartment." She laughed, helping him up the fifth stair and the sixth, their pace slow and steady. "I'm Abe. I saw you walking yesterday in the harbor. I'm usually sitting outside the maritime museum reading my newspaper."

"*Yes.* That's how I recognize you."

He seemed pleased that she remembered. "I used to read the paper outside every day, but it's getting harder to climb the stairs to the porch. I'm only able to get up them on Wednesdays and Thursdays now. Those are my daughter's days off from the supermarket. She walks me over and helps me climb them, so I can sit in the shade. The other days, I sit on the lawn and pray the sun isn't too bright."

Keeping hold of Abe, Piper unlocked the apartment door.

Once they were inside and she'd shoved a bottle of water into Hannah's hands, Piper gestured to the bunk. "This is the one. You might be able to see the outline of my head on those boards by now."

Abe nodded and crouched down *very* slowly to access his toolbox. "Now that we're in the light, I can see that bruise you're sporting, too. Good thing we're getting this fixed."

While Abe got to work nailing memory foam to the top bunk with a nail gun, Piper tried to avoid Hannah's teasing pokes in her side. "Brendan no like Piper boo-boo. Brendan fix."

"Oh, shut up," she whispered, for her sister's ears alone. "This is just what people do in small towns like this. Maybe he's trying to rub LA's awfulness in my face."

"Nope. First the lock. Now this." Wow. She'd really slurred that *s*. "He's a real champ."

"I thought you didn't even like him. What happened to 'Leave my sister alone, you bully'?"

"At the time, I meant it," Hannah grumbled.

"Look, I'm just biding time until I can get back to my natural habitat. No distractions need apply."

"But—"

"You wouldn't be encouraging me to make time with a crab fisherman, would you?" She gave Hannah a once-over, followed by a sniff. "I'm telling Mom."

Hannah rolled her eyes and opened her mouth to deliver a rejoinder, but Abe interrupted with a jolly "All finished!"

God, how loud had they been at the end of that conversation?

Abe must have interpreted her worried expression, because he laughed. "I hope you don't mind me saying, it was nice listening to some bickering between sisters. Ours have grown up, gotten hitched, and moved out, you know. I spend a lot of time with my sons at the shop, but they have the nerve to get along."

Piper stooped down to help Abe put everything back in his toolbox. "So . . . um." She lowered her voice several octaves. "Do you know Captain Taggart well?"

Her sister snorted.

"Everyone knows the captain, but he does like to keep to himself. Doesn't do a lot of jawing, just comes into the shop and buys what he needs. In and out." Abe slapped his knee and stood. "He's downright focused."

"He is," Piper agreed, thinking a little too long and hard about those green-and-silver eyes. How they tried so hard to stay above her neck. When Abe cleared his throat, she realized she'd been staring into space. "Sorry. Let me help you down the stairs."

"I'll be on my way," Abe said when they'd reached the first level, a smile wreathing his mouth. "Say, have you gone to see Opal yet?"

Opal. Opal.

Piper rooted around her memory bank for that name. Hadn't Mick Forrester mentioned an Opal and written down the woman's address? Why did everyone think she would visit this person? Obviously, she needed to get some answers. "Um, no. Not just yet."

He seemed a little disappointed, but hid it quickly. "Right. Well, it was nice to meet you, Piper. Don't forget to give me a wave when you see me outside the museum."

"I won't." She handed him the toolbox carefully, making sure he could take the weight. While watching him head for the door, his feet shuffling, the stiffness in his legs obvious, an idea occurred. "Hey, Abe. I've got a pretty flexible schedule here, and the museum is only a quick walk. So . . . like, I don't know, if you wanted to sit outside and read your paper more than twice a week, I could walk over and help you climb the porch."

Why was she nervous this little old man was going to turn her down?

Is this what a man felt when he asked for her number?

Her nerves settled when Abe turned to her with a hopeful expression. "You would do that?"

"Sure," she said, surprised by how nice it felt to be useful. "Friday morning? I could meet you outside the hardware store after my run."

He winked. "It's a date."

Hannah had sworn off booze, so they avoided any more trips to the winery. Instead, they cleaned. Even put up some green-and-white striped curtains in the apartment. On Brendan's suggestion, they visited the lighthouse and took a day trip to the beach, although the abundance of rocks and the need for a sweatshirt by three P.M. made it nothing like the coastline in California. Still, Piper found herself relaxing, enjoying herself, and the rest of the week went by faster than expected.

She went out on her run Friday morning, finishing up outside the hardware store where Abe waited, a rolled-up newspaper tucked under his arm. He peppered her with questions about life in Los Angeles on the walk over to the maritime museum—he was yet another man who'd rarely ventured outside of Westport—and she left him in the Adirondack chair with a promise to meet him again tomorrow morning.

Piper walked down to the end of one of the docks in the harbor and dangled her feet over the side, looking out at the wide mouth of the Pacific.

What was Brendan doing at that very moment?

She'd kind of hoped distance and time would rid her of the adamant tingle she felt every time she thought of him. But three days had passed, and his image still popped into her mind with annoying regularity. This morning, she'd woken up with a start, jerked into an upright position, and the memory foam had blocked her forehead from ramming into the upper bunk. And she'd drifted back down to her pillow with an enamored sigh.

Was he thinking about her?

"Ugh, Piper." She surged to her feet at the end of the dock. "Get your life together." She needed another distraction. Another way to absorb some time, so her thoughts wouldn't keep drifting back to Brendan.

Maybe now was a good time to solve the mystery of this Opal character.

Piper had taken a picture of the address Mick gave her outside No Name, and she scrolled to it now, tapping it with her thumb. Distraction achieved. She'd told Mick she'd visit the woman, and with a whole day in front of her, there was no time like the present.

She punched the address into her map app, snorting to herself when she arrived after a mere two minutes of walking. Opal lived in an apartment building overlooking Grays Harbor, and it was kind of weird, buzzing someone's apartment without calling ahead of time, but the vestibule door unlocked immediately. With a shrug, Piper took the elevator to the fifth floor and knocked on the door of apartment 5F.

The door swung open and a woman Piper estimated to be in her late sixties leapt back, a hand flying to her throat. "Oh God, I thought you were my hairdresser, Barbara."

"Oh! Sorry!" Piper's cheeks burned. "I wondered why you buzzed me up so fast. You are Opal, right?"

"Yes. And I'm not buying anything."

"No, I'm not selling anything. I'm Piper. Bellinger." She put out her hand for a shake. "Mick told me I should come see you. I'm . . . Henry Cross's daughter?"

A different kind of tension gripped Opal's shoulders. "Oh my Lord," she breathed.

Something charged the air, causing the hair on the back of Piper's neck to stand up. "Did you . . . know me when I was a baby, or . . . ?"

"Yes. Yes. I did." Opal pressed a hand to her mouth, dropped it. "I'm Opal Cross. I'm your grandmother."

I'm your grandmother.

Those words sounded like they were meant for someone else.

People who got ugly knitted sweaters on Christmas morning or fell asleep in the back of a station wagon after a road trip to Bakersfield. Her mother's parents were living in Utah and communicated through sporadic phone calls, but Henry's . . . well, she'd stopped wondering about any extended family on her biological father's side so long ago, the possibility had faded into nothing.

But the woman hadn't. She was standing right there in front of Piper, looking as if she'd seen a ghost.

"I'm sorry," Piper whispered finally, after an extended silence. "Mick told me to come here. He assumed I knew who you were. But I . . . I'm so sorry to say I didn't."

Opal gathered herself and nodded. "That isn't too surprising. Your mother and I didn't end on the best terms, I'm afraid." She ran her eyes over Piper once more, shaking her head slightly and seeming at a loss for words. "Please come in. I . . . Barbara should be here for coffee soon, so I've got the table set up."

"Thank you." Piper walked into the apartment in a daze, her fingers twisting in the hem of her running shirt. She was meeting her long-lost grandmother in sweaty running clothes.

Classic.

"Well, I barely know where to start," Opal said, joining Piper in the small room just off the kitchen. "Sit down, please. Coffee?"

It was kind of disconcerting the way this woman looked at her as if she'd returned from the dead. It felt a little like she had. As if she'd walked into a play that was already in progress, and everyone knew the plot except her. "No, thank you." Piper gestured to the sliding glass door leading to a small balcony. "B-beautiful view."

"It is, isn't it?" Opal settled into her chair, picking up a half-finished mug of coffee. Setting it back down. "Originally, I wanted an apartment facing the harbor so I could feel close to Henry. But all these years later, it just seems like a sad reminder."

She winced. "I'm sorry. I don't mean to be so casual about it all. It helps me to be blunt."

"It's fine. You can be blunt," Piper assured her, even though she felt a little jarred. Not only by the sudden appearance of a grandmother, but by the way she spoke of Henry like he'd only passed yesterday, instead of twenty-four years ago. "I don't remember a lot about my father. Just small things. And I haven't been told much."

"Yes," Opal said, leaning back in her chair with a tightened jaw. "Your mother was determined to leave it all behind. Some of us find that harder to do." A beat passed. "I'd been a single mother since Henry was a little boy. His father was . . . well, a casual relationship that neither of us had a mind to pursue. Your father was all I had, besides my friends." She blew out a breath, visibly gathering herself. "What are you doing back in Westport?"

"My sister and I . . ." Piper trailed off before she could get to the part about confetti cannons and police helicopters. Apparently the need to make a good impression on one's grandmother was strong, even when meeting her as a fully grown adult. "We're just taking a vacation." For some reason, she added, "And doing a little digging into our roots while we're here."

Opal warmed, even appearing relieved. "It makes me very happy to hear that."

Piper shifted in her chair. Did she want her father to become a more . . . substantial presence in her life? A serious part of Piper didn't *want* sentimental attachment to Westport. It scared her to have this whole new aspect of her world, her existence opened up. What was she supposed to do with it?

She'd felt so little at the brass statue—what if the same happened now? What if her detachment from the past extended to Opal and she disappointed the woman? She had clearly been through enough already without Piper adding to it.

Still, it wouldn't exactly hurt to find out a *little* more about Henry Cross, this man who'd fathered her and Hannah. This man people spoke of with a hushed reverence. This man who'd been honored with a memorial up on the harbor. Would it? Just this morning during her run, she'd seen a wreath of flowers laid at its feet. Her mother had been right. He *was* Westport. And although she'd felt less emotion than expected the first time she visited the brass statue, she was definitely curious about him. "Do you . . . have anything of Henry's? Or maybe some pictures?"

"I was hoping you'd ask." Opal popped up, moving pretty damn quickly for a woman her age, crossed to the living room, and retrieved a box from a shelf under the television. She took her seat again and removed the top, leafing through a few pieces of paper before pulling out an envelope marked *Henry*. She slid it across the table to Piper. "Go ahead."

Piper turned the envelope over in her hands, hesitating momentarily before lifting the flap. Out spilled an old fisherman's license with a grainy picture of Henry in the laminated corner, most of his face obscured by water damage. There was a picture of Maureen, twenty-five years younger. And a small snapshot of Piper and Hannah, tape still attached to the back.

"Those were in his bunk on the *Della Ray*," Opal explained.

Pressure crowded into Piper's throat. "Oh," she managed, running her finger over the curled edges of the picture of her and Hannah. Henry Cross hadn't been some phantom; he'd been a flesh-and-blood man with a heart, and he'd loved them with it. Maureen, Piper, Hannah. Opal. Had they been a part of his final thoughts? Was it crazy to feel like they'd deserted him? Yes, he'd chosen to perform this dangerous job, but he still deserved to be remembered by the people he loved. He'd had Opal, but what about his immediate family?

"He was a determined man. Loved to debate. Loved to laugh when it was all over." Opal sighed. "Your father loved you to pieces. Called you his little first mate."

That feeling Piper had been missing at the memorial . . . it rode in now on a slow tide, and she had to blink back the sudden hot pressure behind her eyes.

"I'm sorry if this was too much," Opal said, laying a hesitant hand on Piper's wrist. "I don't get a lot of visitors, and most of my friends . . . Well, it's a complicated thing . . ."

Piper looked up from the picture of her and Hannah. "What is?"

"Well." Opal stared down into her coffee mug. "People tend to avoid the grieving. Grief, in general. And there's no one with more grief than a parent who has lost a child. At some point, I guess I decided to spare everyone my misery and started staying home. That's why I have my hair appointments here." She laughed. "Not that anyone gets to see the results."

"But . . . you're so lovely," Piper said, clearing her throat of the emotion wrought by the pictures. "There's no way people avoid you, Opal. You have to get out there. Go barhopping. Give the men in Westport hell."

Her grandmother's eyes sparkled with amusement. "I bet that's more your department."

Piper smiled. "You would be right."

Opal twisted her mug in a circle, seeming unsure. "I don't know. I've gotten used to being alone. This is the most I've talked to anyone besides Barbara in years. Maybe I've forgotten how to be social." She exhaled. "I'll think about it, though. I really will."

Offering a relationship to this woman wasn't a small thing. This was her grandmother. It wasn't just a passing acquaintance. It could be a lifelong commitment. A relationship with actual gravity. "Good. And when you're ready . . . I'm your wingwoman."

Opal swallowed hard and ducked her head. "It's a deal."

They sat in companionable silence for a moment, until Opal checked her watch and sighed. "I love Barbara to death, but the woman is flakier than a bowl of cereal."

Piper pursed her lips, studied the woman's close-cropped gray hair. "What were you planning on having her do?"

"Just a trim, like always."

"Or . . ." Piper stood, moving behind Opal. "May I?"

"Please!"

Piper slipped her fingers into Opal's hair and tested the texture. "You don't know this, Opal, but you're in the presence of a cosmetic genius." Her lips curved up. "Have you ever thought about rocking a faux hawk?"

Twenty minutes later, Piper had shaped Opal's hair into a slick, subtle hill down the center of her head, using the lack of a recent haircut to their advantage by twisting and spiking the gray strands. Then they'd broken out a Mary Kay makeup kit Opal had caved and purchased from a door-to-door saleslady—leading to her current suspicion of solicitors—and transformed her into a stunner.

Piper took a lot of pleasure in handing Opal the mirror. "So?"

Opal gasped. "Is that me?"

Piper scoffed. "Hell yes, it's you."

"Well." Her grandmother turned her head left and right. "Well, well, well."

"Considering that night out a little more seriously now, aren't we?"

"You bet I am." She looked at herself in the mirror again, then back to Piper. "Thank you for this." Opal took a long breath. "Will you . . . come back and see me again?"

"Of course. And I'll bring Hannah next time."

"Oh, I would just *love* that. She was so tiny last time I saw her."

Piper leaned down and kissed Opal on both cheeks, which she seemed to find inordinately funny, then left the small apartment, surprised to find herself feeling . . . light. Buoyant, even. She navigated the streets back to No Name without the use of her phone's map, recognizing landmarks as she went, no longer unfamiliar with the friendly smiles and circling seagulls.

The envelope holding Henry's possessions was tucked into her pocket, and that seemed to anchor her in this place. She stopped outside of No Name, taking a moment to look up at the faded building, and this time . . . she tried to really *see* it. To really think about the man who made his livelihood within its walls, once upon a time. To think about Maureen falling in love with that man, so much that she married and conceived two daughters with him.

She was one of those daughters. A product of that love. No matter what Piper felt for her past, it was real. And it wasn't something she could ignore or remain detached from. No matter how much it scared her.

Feeling thoughtful and a little restless, she went to find Hannah.

Piper and Hannah stared down at the phone, listening to their mother's voice through the speakerphone. "I reached out to Opal several times throughout the years," Maureen said. "She's as stubborn as your father was. She saw my leaving as a betrayal, and there was no fixing it. And . . . I was selfish. I just wanted to forget that whole life. The pain."

"You could have told me about her before I came," Piper intoned. "I was blindsided."

Maureen made a sound of distress. "I was right on the verge and . . ." Maureen sighed. "I guess I didn't want to see your faces when I told you I'd been holding on to something so important. I'm sorry."

Twenty minutes later, Piper paced the scuffed floor of No Name while Hannah sat cross-legged on a barrel eating French fries, a thousand-yard stare in her eyes. Her sister was still processing the news that they had a freaking grandmother, but she probably wouldn't reach full understanding until she could be alone with her records.

Reaching out to rub Hannah's shoulder comfortingly, Piper looked around and surveyed the space. Was she suffering an emotional upheaval from the shock of finding a long-lost family member . . . or was she starting to develop an interest in this place?

They'd been so young when Maureen moved them. It wasn't their fault they'd forgotten their father, but they couldn't very well ignore him now. Not with pieces of him everywhere. And this disheveled bar was the perfect representation of a forgotten legacy. Something that was once alive . . . and now corroded.

What if it could be brought back to life?

How would one even begin?

Piper caught her reflection in a section of broken glass peeking out from behind a piece of plywood. Her talent for finding the most flattering lighting could not be discounted, but there were only a couple of cobweb-covered bulbs, with no light fixtures. It was basically anyone over twenty-five's worst nightmare, because it highlighted every crevice in a person's face. The place had a certain speakeasy vibe that could really benefit from some soft, red lighting. Moody.

Hmm. She was no decorator. Maureen paid an interior designer to come in annually and refresh the house in Bel-Air, and that included their bedrooms. But Piper understood atmosphere. What inspired people to stay awhile.

Some men went to bars to watch sports. Or whatever. But what *packed* a bar full of men? Women. Appeal to the ladies, and men started coughing up cover charges just for a chance to shoot their shot.

Where would she even start with this place?

"Just for the sake of argument, let's say we wanted to pretty this place up. Considering we have limited funds, do you think we could make it worthwhile?"

Hannah appeared caught off guard. "Where is this coming from?"

"I don't know. When I was talking to Opal, I started thinking how unfair it is that Henry's own family never grieved him. Sure, it was mostly Mom's decision, but maybe this is a way to make amends. To . . . connect with him a little bit. To have a hand in the way he's remembered. Is that silly?"

"No." Hannah shook her head. "No, of course it's not. Just a lot to take in."

Piper tried a different tack. "At the very least, this could be a way to convince Daniel we're responsible and proactive citizens of the world. We could make over the bar, show him how dazzlingly capable we are, and get an early trip home to Los Angeles."

Hannah raised an eyebrow.

"That's not a bad idea. Not bad at all." With a blown-out breath, her younger sister hopped off the stool, wiping her hands on the seat of her jeans. "I mean, we'd need a DJ booth, obviously."

"Over there in the corner by the window?" Piper pointed. "I like it. People walking by would see MC Hannah spinning and trip over themselves to get inside."

The sisters had their backs to each other as they completed a revolution around the bar. "This place isn't big enough for a dance floor, but we could build a shelf along the wall for people to set their drinks. It could be standing room only."

"Ooh. That's totally an option for a new name. Standing Room Only."

"Love." Hannah pursed her lips. "We'd have to do a lot of cleaning."

They shared a groan.

"Do you think we could fix these chairs?" Piper asked, running her finger along the back of a lopsided seat. "Maybe polish the bar?"

Hannah snorted. "I mean, what the fuck else are we doing?"

"God, you're right. Can you believe it has only been *five days*?" Piper dug a knuckle into the corner of her eye. "What is the worst that can happen? We do a ton of work, spend all of our money, Daniel isn't impressed and forces us to finish out our sentence, which should really just be *my* sentence?"

"Don't split hairs. And the best that can happen is we go home early."

They traded a thoughtful yet noncommittal shrug.

In that moment, the final shard of sunset peeked in through the grimy window, illuminating the mirror behind the plywood. There was a white corner of something on the other side, and without thinking, Piper moved in that direction, stepping over empty bottles to scoot behind the bar and pinch the white protrusion between her fingers. She gave it a tug and out came a photograph. In it, two people she didn't recognize appeared to be singing in this very establishment, though a much cleaner version, their hair proclaiming them children of the eighties.

"Oh. A picture." Hannah craned her neck to get a better look at the area behind the plywood. "You think there's more?"

"We could pull this board down, but we're either going to end up with splinters or a herd of spiders is going to ride out on the backs of mice, holding pitchforks."

Hannah sighed. "After cleaning that upstairs toilet, I'm pretty desensitized to anything unpleasant. Let's do it."

Piper whimpered as she took hold of the plywood, Hannah's grip tightening alongside hers. "Okay. One, two, *three*!"

They threw the wood board on the ground and leapt back, waiting for the repercussions, but none came. Instead, they were left staring at a mirror covered in old pictures. They traded a frown and stepped closer at the same time, each of them peeling down a photograph and studying it. "This guy looks familiar . . ." Piper said quietly. "He's way younger in this shot, but I think he's the one who was in here Sunday night. He said he remembered Mom."

Hannah leaned over and looked. "Oh my gosh, that's totally him." Her laugh was disbelieving. "Damn, Gramps. He could get it back then."

Piper chuckled. "Recognize anyone in yours?"

"No." Hannah took down another. "Wait. Pipes."

She was busy scanning the faces looking back at her from the past, so she didn't immediately hear the hushed urgency in Hannah's tone. But when the silence stretched, she looked over to find Hannah's face pale, fingers shaking as she studied the photo. "What is it?" Piper asked, sidling up next to her sister. "Oh."

Her hand flew to her suddenly pumping heart.

Whereas the brass statue of Henry had been impersonal and the fishing license had been grainy, an unsmiling man making a standard pose, this photo had *life* in it. Henry was laughing, a white towel thrown over one shoulder, a mustache shadowing his upper lip. His eyes . . . they leapt right off the glossy photograph's surface, sparkling. So much like their own.

"That's our dad."

"Piper, he looks just like us."

"Yeah . . ." She was having trouble catching her breath. She took Hannah's hand, and they turned it over together. The handwriting was faded, but it was easy to make out the words, *Henry Cross*. And the year, *1991*.

Neither of them said anything for long moments.

And maybe Piper was just overwhelmed by the physical proof that their birth father had really existed, a picture discovered while standing in his bar, but she suddenly felt . . . as if fate had placed her in that very spot. Their life before Los Angeles had always been a fragmented, vague thing. But it felt real now. Something to explore. Something that maybe had even been missing, without her knowing enough to acknowledge it.

"We should pretty up the bar," Piper said. "We should do it. Not just so we can go home early, but . . . you know. Kind of a tribute."

"You read my mind, Pipes." Hannah laid her head on Piper's shoulder as they continued to stare down at the man who'd fathered them, his face smiling back from another time. "Let's do it."

Chapter Thirteen

℘rendan watched through his binoculars as Westport formed, reassuring and familiar, on the horizon.

His love for the ocean always made returning home bittersweet. There was nowhere he was more at ease than the wheelhouse, the engine humming under his feet. A radio within reach so he could give orders. His certainty that those commands would always be carried out, no questions asked. The *Della Ray* was a second layer of skin, and he slipped into it as often as possible, anxious for the rise and fall of the water, the slap of waves on the hull, the smell of salt and fish and possibilities.

But this homecoming didn't have the same feel as it usually did. He wasn't calculating the hours until he could get back out on the water. Or trying to ignore the emotions that clung to the inside of his throat when he got his crew home safe. There were only nerves this time. Jumpy, anxious, sweaty nerves.

His mind hadn't been focused for the last three days. Oh, they'd filled the belly of the ship with fish, done their damn job, as always. But a girl from Los Angeles had been occupying way too much headspace for his comfort.

God only knew, tonight was *not* the night for exploring that headspace, either.

As soon as they moored the boat and loaded the catches to bring to market, he was expected at the annual memorial dinner for Desiree. Every year, like clockwork, Mick organized the get-together at Blow the Man Down, and Brendan never failed to work his fishing schedule around it. Hell, he usually helped organize. This time, though . . . he wondered how he'd make it through the night knowing he'd been thinking of Piper nonstop for three days.

Didn't matter how many times he lamented her glamorous internet presence. Didn't matter how many times he reminded himself they were from two different worlds and she didn't plan to be a part of his for long. Still, he thought of her. Worried about her well-being while he was on the water. Worried she wasn't eating the right items off the menus he'd left. Hoped the hardware store had gotten his note and she was no longer bumping her head.

He thought of her body.

Thought of it to the point of distraction.

How soft she'd be beneath him, how high maintenance she'd probably be in the sack and how he'd deliver. Again and again, until she wrecked his back with her fingernails.

A lot of the men on board started checking their phones for reception as soon as the harbor was in sight, and Brendan normally rolled his eyes at them. But he had his phone in hand now, kept swiping and entering his password, wanting a look at her fucking Instagram. He'd barely been aware of the damn app a few days ago; now he had his thumb hovering over the icon, ready to get his fill of her image. He'd never been so hard up for relief that he beat off while on the boat, but it had been necessary the first damn night. And the second.

Three bars popped into the upper left-hand corner of his screen, and he tapped, holding his breath. The first thing he saw was the white outline of a head. Pressed it.

Piper had followed him back?

He grunted and looked over his shoulder before smiling.

There was one new picture in her feed, and he enlarged it, the damn organ in his chest picking up speed. She'd taken his suggestion and gone to the winery, and Jesus, she looked beautiful.

Making grape decisions.

He was chuckling over that caption when a text message popped up from Mick.

Call me was all it said.

Brendan's smile dropped, and he pushed to his feet, pulse missing a few beats as the call to his father-in-law connected. Dammit, Piper had gotten herself in trouble again, hadn't she? She'd probably started another fire or broken her neck falling down the stairs while trying to escape a mouse. Or—

"Yeah, hey, Brendan."

"What's wrong?" he demanded. "What happened?"

"Whoa, there." Mick laughed, music playing in the background. "Nothing happened. I just wanted to remind you about tonight."

Guilt twisted like a corkscrew in his gut. Here was this man preparing for a party to memorialize seven years without his daughter, and Brendan was worried about Piper. Could think of nothing *but* her. That wasn't right. Wasn't he a better man than that?

Brendan looked down at the wedding band around his finger and swallowed. Seven years. He could barely remember Desiree's voice, her face, or her laugh anymore. He wasn't the type to make a vow and easily move on from it, however. When a promise came out of his mouth, it was kept to the letter. She'd been woven into the fabric of his life in Westport so thoroughly, it was almost like she'd never really died. Which might account for him getting stuck on the *till death* part of his promise.

Remnants of her surrounded him here. Her parents, her annual memorial, people who'd come to their wedding. Taking the ring off had struck him as disrespectful, but now . . . now it was starting to feel even more wrong to keep it on.

Tonight was not the night to make big decisions, though.

He had a duty to be at the memorial and be mentally present, so he would be.

"I'll be there," Brendan said. "Of course I will."

The first few years after Desiree passed, the memorial potlucks had been reenactments of her funeral. No one smiling, everyone speaking in hushed tones. Hard not to feel disrespectful being anything but grief-stricken when Mick and Della plastered pictures of their daughter everywhere, brought a cake with her name in bright blue frosting. But as the years went on, the mood had lightened somewhat. Not completely, but at least nobody was crying tonight.

The venue probably didn't do much to cultivate an easy atmosphere. The basement of Blow the Man Down hadn't seen renovations like the upstairs. It was a throwback to the days of wood paneling and low, frosted lighting, and it reminded Brendan of the hull of his ship, so much so that he could almost feel the swell and dip of the ocean beneath his feet.

A collapsible table and chairs had been set up against the far wall, laden with covered dishes and a candlelit shrine to Desiree, right there next to the pasta salad. High tops and stools filled out the rest of the space, along with a small bar used only for parties, which was where Brendan stood with his relief skipper, trying to avoid small talk.

Brendan felt Fox studying him from the corner of his eye and ignored him, instead signaling the bartender for another beer. It was no secret how Fox viewed the yearly event. "I know what you're going to say." Brendan sighed. "I don't need to hear it again."

"Too bad. You're going to hear it." Apparently Fox had taken enough orders over the last three days and was good and finished. "This isn't fair to you. Dragging you back through this . . . loss every goddamn year. You deserve to move on."

"Nobody is dragging anyone."

"Sure." Fox twisted his bottle of beer in a circle on the bar. "She wouldn't want this for you. She wouldn't want to be shackling you like this."

"Drop it, Fox." He massaged the bridge of his nose. "It's just one night."

"It's not just one night." He kept his voice low, his gaze averted, so no one would pick up on their argument. "See, I know you. I know how you think. It's a yearly nudge to stay the course. Stay steady. To do what you think is honorable. When the hell is it enough?"

Goddammit, there was a part of him that agreed with Fox. As long as this memorial had remained on the calendar, Brendan kept thinking, *I owe her one more year. I owe her one more.* Until that refrain had turned into *I owe it one more year.* Or *I owe* Mick *one more.* For everything his father-in-law had done for Brendan. Making him captain of the *Della Ray.* Would that faith and trust go away if Brendan moved on?

Whatever the reason, at some point the grieving had stopped being about his actual marriage, but he had no idea when. Life was a series of days on land, followed by days at sea, then repeat. There wasn't time to think about himself or how he "felt." And he wasn't some selfish, fickle bastard.

"Look," Fox tried again, after a long pull of his beer. "You know I love Mick, but as far as he's concerned, you're still married to his daughter and that's a lot of pressure on y—"

"Hey, everyone!"

Brendan's drink paused halfway to his mouth. That was Piper's voice.

Piper was here?

He gripped his pint carefully and looked over his shoulder at the door. There she was. In sequins, obviously. Loud pink ones. And he couldn't deny that the first emotion to hit him was pleasure. To see her. Then relief that she hadn't gone back to LA already. Eagerness to talk to her, be near her.

Right on the heels of that reaction, though, the blood drained from his face.

No. This wasn't right. She shouldn't be there.

On one arm, she had that ridiculous lipstick-shaped purse. And cradled in her other arm was a tray of shots she'd obviously brought from the bar upstairs. She clicked through a sea of dumbfounded and spellbound guests, offering them what looked like tequila.

"Why the long faces?" She flipped her hair and laughed, taking a shot of her own. Jesus. This was all happening in slow motion. "Turn the music up! Let's get this party started, right?"

"Oh fuck," Fox muttered.

Brendan saw the exact moment Piper realized she'd just crashed a memorial for a dead woman. Her runway strut slowed, those huge blue eyes widening at the makeshift shrine next to the pasta salad, the giant poster-board picture of Desiree's senior photo, her name in script at the bottom. *Desiree Taggart.* Her mouth opened on a choked sound, and she fumbled the tray of shots, recovering just in time to keep them from crashing onto the floor. "Oh," she breathed. "I—I didn't . . . I didn't know."

She dropped the shots onto the closest table like they offended her—and that was when her eyes locked on Brendan, and his stomach plummeted at the utter humiliation there. "Piper."

"Sorry. I'm . . . Wow." She backed toward the exit, her hip ramming into a chair and sending it several inches across the floor, making her wince. "I'm so sorry."

As quickly as she'd arrived, she was gone, like someone had muted all sound and color in the room. Before and after Piper. And Brendan didn't think, he just dropped his beer onto the bar with a slosh and went after her. When he started up the stairs, she'd already cleared the top, so he picked up his pace, weaving in and out of the Friday-night crowd, grateful for his height so he could look for pink sequins.

Why did he feel like he'd been socked in the stomach?

She didn't need to see that, he kept thinking. *She didn't need to see that.*

Out of the corner of his eye, he caught a flash of pink cross-ing the street. There was Piper, in what appeared to be ice-pick heels, heading toward the harbor instead of back home. Some-one called his name from the bar, but he ignored them, push-ing outside and following in her wake. "Piper."

"Oh no. No no no." She reached the opposite sidewalk and turned, waving her hands at him, palms out. "Please, you have to go back. You cannot leave your wife's memorial to come af-ter the idiot who ruined it."

Even if he wanted to, he couldn't go back. His body physi-cally wouldn't allow it. Because as much as he hated her obvi-ous embarrassment, he would rather be out there chasing her in the street than in that basement. It was no contest. And yeah, he couldn't deny anymore that his priorities were shifting. As a creature of habit, that scared him, but he refused to simply let her walk away. "You didn't ruin anything."

She scoffed and kept walking.

He followed. "You're not going to outrun me in those heels."

"Brendan, *please*. Let me cringe to death in peace."

"No."

Still facing away from him, she slowed to a stop, arms lifting to hug her middle. "Pretty shortsighted of me to leave those shots behind. I could use about six of them right now."

He heard her sniffle, and bolts tightened in his chest. Crying women didn't necessarily scare him. That would make him kind of a pansy ass, wouldn't it? But he'd encountered very few of them in his lifetime, so he took a moment to consider the best course of action. She was hugging herself. So maybe . . . maybe one from him, too, wouldn't be a bad move?

Brendan came up behind Piper and cupped her smooth

shoulders with his hands, making sure she wasn't going to run if he touched her. Lord, they were so soft. What if he scratched her with his calluses? Her head turned slightly to look at his resting right hand, and he was pretty sure neither one of them breathed as he tugged her back against his chest, circling his arms around her slight frame. When she didn't tell him to fuck off, he took one more chance and propped his chin on top of her head.

A sound puffed out of her. "You really don't hate me?"

"Don't be ridiculous."

"I really didn't know. I'm so sorry."

"That's enough apologizing."

"They all must hate me, even if you don't. They have to." He started to tell her *that* assumption was silly, too, but she spoke over him, sounding so forlorn he had to tighten his hold. "God, I *am* an airhead, aren't I?"

He didn't like anything about that question. Not the question itself. And not the way it was phrased, as if someone had used that bullshit term to describe her. Brendan turned her in his arms and promptly forgot the process of breathing. She was gorgeous as hell with her damp eyes and cheeks pink with lingering embarrassment, all of her bathed in moonlight. He had to call on every iota of willpower not to lower his mouth to hers, but it wasn't the right time. There was a ghost between them and a ring on his finger, and all of it needed resolving first.

"Come on, let's sit down," Brendan said gruffly, taking her elbow and guiding her to one of the stone benches overlooking the nighttime harbor. She sat and crossed her legs in one fluid move, her expression bordering on lost. Lowering himself down beside her, Brendan took up the rest of the space on the bench, but she didn't seem to mind their hips and outer thighs together. "You aren't an airhead. Who said that to you?"

"It doesn't matter. It's true."

"It is *not* true," he barked.

"Oh yes, it is. I have left an endless trail of proof. I'm like a super-hot snail." She smacked her hands over her eyes. "Did I really say 'Why the long faces' at a memorial dinner? Oh my *God.*"

Unbelievably, Brendan felt a rumble of laughter building in his sternum. "You did say that. Right before you took a shot."

She punched him in the thigh. "Don't you dare laugh."

"Sorry." He forced his lips to stop twitching. "If it makes you feel better . . . that dinner needed a little levity. You did everyone a favor."

Brendan felt her studying his profile. "Tonight must have been hard for you."

"It was hard seven years ago. Six. Even five. Now it's just . . ." He searched for the right word. "It's respect. It's duty."

Piper was silent so long, he had to glance over, finding her with an expression of wonder. "Seven years?" She held up the appropriate number of fingers. "That many?"

He nodded.

She faced the harbor, letting out a rush of breath, but not before he saw her attention dip to his ring. "Wow. I thought it might have been a year. Maybe even less. She must have been really special."

Of course that was true. Brendan didn't know how to explain the convenience and . . . the practicality of his past marriage without it sounding disrespectful to a woman who could no longer speak for herself. Today, especially, he wouldn't do that. But he couldn't deny an urge to expose himself somewhat. It only seemed fair when she was sitting there, so vulnerable. He didn't want her to go it alone.

"I was away fishing when it happened. An aneurysm. She'd been out for a walk on the beach. Alone." He let out a slow breath. "She always went alone, even when I was home. I wasn't, uh . . . the best at being married. I didn't mold myself to fit new routines or different patterns—I'm sure you're shocked." She stayed quiet. "They say even if I'd been there, I couldn't have done anything, but I could have tried. I never tried. So this . . . year after year, this is me trying, I guess. After the fact."

Piper didn't respond right away. "I don't know a lot about marriage, but I think people mature and get better at it over time. You would have. You just didn't get a chance." She sighed into the night breeze. "I'm sorry that happened to you."

He nodded, hoping she would change the subject. Maybe Fox was right and he'd been serving a penance long enough, because dwelling on the past now just made him restless.

"My longest relationship was three weeks." She held up the right number of fingers. "This many. But in weeks."

Brendan hid a smile. Why did he kind of love knowing that there wasn't a single man in Los Angeles who could lock Piper down? And . . . what *would* it take? "Is he the one who called you an airhead?"

"You're hyperfocused on this." She pulled her shoulders back. "Yes, he was the one who said it. And I proved him right in the next breath by assuming he was ending things because I'd discussed the compatibility of our astrological signs with my therapist. I couldn't have sounded more like an LA bimbo if I tried."

"It pisses me off when you call yourself names."

She gasped. "Pissed off? That's a real switch for you."

The corner of Brendan's lips tugged. "I deserve that."

"No, you don't," she said, and sighed, falling silent for a few moments. "Since we got here, it has never been more obvious that I don't know what I'm doing. I'm really good at going to parties and taking pictures, and there's nothing wrong with that. But what if that's it? What if that's just *it*?" She looked at him, seeming to piece her thoughts together. "And you keep witnessing these huge fails of mine, but I can't hide behind a drink and a flirty smile here. It's just me."

He couldn't hide his confusion. "*Just* you?"

Once again, he was seeing flashes of insecurity beneath the seemingly perfect outer layer of Piper Bellinger, and they roused his protective instincts. He'd ridiculed her at the outset. Now he wanted to fight off anything that made her sad. Fucking hell, it was confusing.

Piper hadn't responded, quietly dabbing at her damp eyes—and he'd been okay with the crying for a while, but he should have been able to dry her tears by now. What was he doing wrong here? Remembering how the hug had at least gotten her to stop running away, he put his left arm around her shoulders and tucked her into his side. Maybe a distraction was the way to go. "What did you do while I was gone?"

"You mean, besides enjoying harbor tours from all the local fishermen?"

Despite her teasing tone, something hot poked him in the jugular. "Funny."

Her lips twitched, but over the course of a few seconds, she sobered. "A lot has happened since you left, actually. I met my grandmother, Opal."

Brendan started a little. "You didn't know her at all before this trip? No phone calls, or—"

"No." Her cheeks colored slightly. "I *never* would have known about her, either, if we hadn't come here. She's just been sitting in her apartment all this time, grieving my father. Knowing that kind of makes my life in LA feel like make-believe. Blissful ignorance." A beat passed. "She had some differences of opinion with my mother. We didn't get into it too deeply, but I'm guessing my mother wanted to put it all behind her, and Opal wanted to . . ."

"Live in the fallout."

"'Fallout' is a nice way of saying 'the real world,' but you're right." She looked down at her lap. "Me and Hannah went to see the memorial for Henry, and I didn't know what I was supposed to feel, but I didn't think it would be just *nothing*. It stayed that way right up until today when we found a whole collage of pictures in the bar. Behind some plywood. He was laughing in one of the photos, and that's when . . . there was finally recognition."

Brendan studied her. This girl he'd pegged as a silly flirt on day one. And he found himself pulling her closer, needing to offer comfort. Wanting her to lean on him for it. "What does the recognition feel like?"

"Scary," she said on an exhale. "But I have some guilt over ignoring this place, the past, even if it's not entirely my fault. It's causing me to lean into the scary, I guess. In my own way. So I gave Opal a faux hawk, and we're giving Henry's bar a makeover, starting tomorrow. If there are two things I know, it's hair and partying."

When had his thumb started tracing the line of her shoulder? He ordered himself to quit it. Even if it felt so fucking good.

"You're dealing with a whole lot of new information in your own way," he said gruffly. "Nothing wrong with that. You're adjusting. I wish I had more of that mentality."

Piper looked up at him, her eyes soft and a little grateful, turning his pulse up to a higher setting. They stared at each other three beats too long, before both of them diverted their gaze quickly. Sensing they were in need of a distraction from the building tension between them, Brendan coughed. "Hey, remember that time you were the only one I followed on Instagram?"

She burst out laughing, such a bright, beautiful thing, that he could only marvel. "What were you thinking?"

"I was just hitting buttons, honey."

More laughter. This time she actually pressed her forehead into his shoulder. "It makes me feel better about the world that someone out there isn't playing games." She drummed her fingers on her bare knee. "So which pictures did you look at?"

He blew out a long breath. "A lot of them."

She bit her bottom lip and ducked her head.

They sat in silence for a few moments. "Which girl are you? The girl in the pictures or the one sitting next to me?"

"Both, I think," she said after a pause. "I like dressing to the nines and being admired. And I like shopping and dancing and being pampered and complimented. Does that make me a bad person?"

He'd never met anyone like her. These luxuries weren't part

of his world. He'd never had to think about anything but fishing, working hard, and meeting quotas, but he wanted to get the answer right because it was important to her. "I've been on a lot of boats with a lot of men that do too much talking about women. And it seems to me that most people like being admired and complimented, they're just not as honest about it. That doesn't make you a bad person, it makes you truthful."

She blinked up at him. "Huh."

"Let me finish." He palmed her head and tucked it back against his shoulder. "I didn't think you'd survive one night in that apartment. Piper, *I* wouldn't even have stayed there, and I've slept in bunks with unwashed men for weeks on end. But you stuck it out. And you smiled at me when I was being a bastard. You're a good sister, too. I figure all of that has to balance out your carrying around that ugly purse."

Piper sat straight up and sputtered through a laugh, "Do you have any idea how much this ugly purse cost?"

"Probably less than I'd pay to have it burned," he drawled.

"But I love it."

He sighed, pushed a hand through his hair. "I guess I wouldn't burn it, then."

She was looking at him with soft eyes and a lush mouth, and if it were any other night, if the timing was better, he'd have kissed her and done his best to bring her home. To his bed. But he couldn't yet. So even though it pained him, he stood and helped Piper to her feet. "Come on, I'll make sure you get home all right."

"Yes. Oh my gosh, yes." She let him help her up. "You should get back. And Hannah will be wondering where I am."

"Why didn't she come tonight?"

"My sister is not a party person. All those genes landed on me. Plus, she's still a little scarred from her winery hangover."

"Ah."

Side by side, they started back, taking a different side street to avoid Blow the Man Down. When she rubbed her arms, he cursed the fact that he didn't take the time to grab his jacket when coming after her, because he would have given anything to wrap her in it at that very moment. Collect it tomorrow with her scent on the collar.

"You did it," she murmured, after they'd been walking for two blocks. "I'm still embarrassed about crashing the party. But I feel . . . better." She squinted an eye up at him. "Brendan, I think this means we're friends."

They arrived at her door and he waited for her to unlock it. "Piper, I don't just go putting my arms around girls."

She paused in the doorway. Looked back. "What does that mean?"

He gave in to just a touch of temptation, tucking a wind-tangled strand of hair behind her ear. *Soft.* "It means I'll be around."

Knowing if he stood there a second longer, he'd try to taste her mouth, Brendan backed away a couple of steps, then turned, the image of her stunned—and definitely wary—expression burned into his mind the whole way back to Blow the Man Down.

Later that night, Brendan stood in front of his dresser, twisting the gold band around his finger. Wearing it had always felt right and good. Honorable. Once something was a part of him, once he made promises, they stuck. He stuck. A fisherman's life was rooted in tradition and he'd always taken comfort in that. Protocols might change, but the rhythm of the ocean didn't. The songs remained the same, sunsets were reliable and eternal, the tides would always shift and pull.

He'd given no thought to where his life would go next. Or if it *could* go in a different direction. There was only routine, maintaining an even keel, working, moving, keeping the customs he'd been taught alive. Ironically, it had been those same qualities that made him a distracted husband. An absent one. He'd never learned to shift. To allow for new things. New possibilities.

Now, though. For the first time since he could remember, Brendan felt a pull to deviate from his habits. He'd sat on the harbor tonight with his arm around Piper, and it wasn't where he was *supposed* to be.

But he hadn't wanted to be anywhere else. Not serving penance for being a shit husband. Not paying respect to his in-laws, who still lived as if their daughter had died yesterday. Not even plotting courses or hauling pots onto his boat.

No, he'd wanted to be sitting there with the girl from Los Angeles.

With that truth admitted to himself, wearing the ring was no longer right.

It made him fraudulent, and he couldn't allow that. Not for another day.

The tide had changed, and he wouldn't make the same mistakes twice. He wouldn't stay so firmly rooted in his practices and routines that a good thing would come along and slip away.

As he slid off the gold band and tucked it into a safe place in his sock drawer, he said good-bye and apologized a final time. Then he turned off the light.

Chapter Fourteen

Deciding to make over the bar and actually *doing* it were two very different things.

The sisters quickly decided there was no way to salvage the floor in the bar. But thanks to an abundance of foot-sized holes in the hardwood, they could see the concrete beneath, and thus, their industrial-meets-nautical-chic vision was born.

Ripping up floorboards was easier said than done. It was filthy, sweaty, nasty work, especially because neither one of them could manage to pry open the windows, adding stagnant air into the mix. They were making progress, though, and by noon on Saturday, they'd managed to fill an entire industrial-sized garbage bag with No Name's former flooring.

Piper tied up the end of the bag with a flourish, trying desperately not to shed tears over the abysmal state of her manicure, and dragged it toward the curb. Or she tried to drag it, anyway. The damn thing wouldn't budge. "Hey, Hanns, help me get this thing outside."

Her sister dropped the crowbar she'd bought that morning

at the hardware store, shouldered up beside Piper, and took hold. "One, two, *three*."

Nothing.

Piper stepped back, swiping her wrist across her forehead with a grimace. "I didn't stop to think about the part where we actually had to move it."

"Me either, but whatever. We can just disperse it among a few bags that won't be so hard to carry."

A whimper bubbled out of Piper's lips. "How did this happen? How am I spending my Saturday dividing up garbage?"

"Reckless behavior. A night in jail . . ."

"Rude." Piper sniffed.

"You know I love you." Hannah peeled off her gloves. "Want to break for lunch?"

"*Yes.*" They took two steps and slumped onto side-by-side stools. As exhausting and difficult as this bar makeover was shaping up to be, with a little distance, the amount of work they'd done in just a few hours was kind of . . . satisfying. "I wonder if we could paint the floor. Like a really deep ocean blue. Do they make paint for floors?"

"Don't ask me. I'm just the DJ."

Now that the idea was in Piper's head, she was interested in getting the answers. "Maybe I'll go with you to the hardware store next time. Sniff around."

Hannah smiled but didn't look over. "Okay."

A minute of silence passed. "Did I tell you I crashed a memorial party for Brendan's wife last night? Walked in with a tray of shots like it was spring break in Miami."

Her sister turned her head slowly. "Are you shitting me?"

"Nope." She pulled an imaginary conductor's wire. "The Piper train rolls on."

To Hannah's credit, it took her a full fifteen seconds to start laughing. "Oh my God, I'm not laughing at . . . I mean, it's a sad thing, the memorial. But, oh, Piper. Just, oh my God."

"Yeah." She smacked some dust off her yoga pants. "Do you think my lipstick purse is ugly?"

"Uhhh . . ."

Hannah was saved from having to answer when the front door of No Name opened. In walked Brendan with a tray of coffees in his hand, a white, rolled-up bakery bag in the other. There was something different about him this morning, but Piper couldn't figure it out. Not right away. He was wearing his signature sweatshirt, beanie, and jeans trifecta as usual, looking worn in and earthy and in charge, carrying in with him the scent of the ocean and coffee and sugar. His silver-green eyes found Piper's and held long enough to cause a disturbing flutter in her belly, before he scanned the room and their progress.

"Hey," he said, in that raspy baritone.

"Hey back," Piper murmured.

Piper, I don't just go putting my arms around girls.

She'd lain awake half the night dissecting that statement. Pulling it apart and coming at it from different angles, all of which had led to roughly the same conclusion. Brendan didn't put his arms around girls, so it meant something that he'd put them around her. Probably just that he wanted to have sex with her, right? And she was . . . interested in that, it seemed, based on how her nipples had turned to painful little points the second he ducked into No Name with his big gladiator thighs and thick black beard. Oh yeah. She was interested, all right. But not in the usual way she was interested in men.

Because Brendan came with a whole roll of caution tape around him.

He wasn't a casual-hookup guy. So what did that make him? What else even *was* there? Apart from her stepfather, she'd come across very few serious-relationship types. Was he one of them? What did he want with *her*?

There was a good chance she was reading him wrong, too. This could very well just be a friendship, and since she'd never had a genuine friendship with a man, platonic intentions might be unrecognizable to her. This was a small town. People were kind. They tipped hats.

She'd probably been in LA too long, and it had turned her cynical. He'd just put his arms around her last night to be decent. *Relax, Piper.*

"Is that coffee for us?" Hannah asked hopefully.

"Yeah." He crossed the scant distance and set the tray down on the barrel in front of the sisters. "There's some sugar and whatnot in the bag." He tossed the white sack down, rubbed at the back of his neck. "Didn't know how you took it."

"Our hero," Piper said, opening the bag and giving a dreamy sigh at the donuts inside. But first, caffeine. She plucked out a Splenda and one of the non-dairy creamers, doctoring the coffee. When she glanced up at Brendan, he was following her actions closely, a line between his brows. Memorizing how she took her coffee? No way.

She swallowed hard.

"Thank you. This was really thoughtful."

"Yes, thank you," Hannah chimed in after taking a sip of hers, black, then riffling through the white bag for a donut. "It's not even made out of cauliflower. We really aren't in LA anymore, Pipes."

"Cauliflower? Jesus Christ." Brendan pulled his own coffee out of the tray—and that's when Piper realized what was actually different about him this morning.

He'd taken off his wedding ring.

After seven years.

Piper's gaze traveled to Brendan's. He knew she'd seen. And there was some silent communication happening between them, but she didn't understand the language. Had never spoken it or been around a man who could convey so much without saying a single word. She couldn't translate what passed between them, or maybe she just wasn't ready to decipher his meaning.

A drop of sweat slid down her spine, and she could suddenly hear her own shallow breaths. No one had ever looked her in the eye this long. It was like he could read her mind, knew everything about her, and liked it all. Wanted some of it for himself.

And then she knew, by the determined set of his jaw and his confident energy, that Brendan Taggart did not think of her as a friend.

"This donut is incredible," Hannah said, her words muffled by the dough in her mouth. "There's caramel in this glaze. Pipes, you have to try—" She cut herself off, her gaze bouncing back and forth between Piper and Brendan. "What's happening here?"

"N-nothing," Piper said in a high-pitched voice. "I don't know. Um. Brendan, do you know if it's, like, possible to paint concrete?"

Her flustered state seemed to amuse him. "It is."

"Oh good, good, good." Exasperated with her own awkwardness, she hopped off the stool. Then she knocked into another one in an attempt to give Brendan a wide berth. "We've decided to go with an industrial-meets-nautical theme. Kind of a chic warehouse vibe, but with like, fisherman-y stuff."

"Fisherman-y stuff," he repeated, sipping his coffee. "Like what?"

"Well, we're going with darker colors, blacks and steels and grays and reds, but we're going to distress everything a little. Most of the boats in the harbor have those muted, weathered tones, right? Then I was kind of thinking we could integrate new and old by hanging nets from the ceiling, but I could spray-paint them gold or black, so it's cohesive. I'm just rattling all of this off, though. It might be . . ." Her hands fluttered at her waist. "Like, I might have to rethink everything . . ."

Brendan's expression had gone from amused to thoughtful. Or maybe . . . disapproving? She couldn't tell. It seemed like weeks had passed since the first night she'd walked through the doors and he'd made it clear No Name belonged to the locals. So he probably hated her ideas and the fact that she wanted to change anything in the first place.

"Right," he said, rolling the word around his mouth. "Well, if you want nautical, you're not going to overpay for anything in the tourist shops up at the harbor. There's a fishing supply store in Aberdeen where they throw in netting for free with most purchases and everything doesn't have a goddamn starfish glued onto it." His lips twisted around a sip of coffee. "I can't help you with gold spray paint."

"Oh." Piper let out a breath she wasn't aware she'd been holding. "Thanks. We're on a budget, especially after our little trip to the winery, so that's helpful."

He grunted and walked past her, stepping over the gap in the floorboards. It seemed like he was heading toward the back staircase, so Piper frowned when he continued past that, stopping in front of yet another piece of plywood that had been nailed over holes in the wall. Only, when he ripped off the wood with one hand and tossed it away, there was a door behind it instead.

Piper's mouth fell open. "Where does that lead?"

Brendan set down his coffee on the closest surface, then tried the rusted knob. It turned, but the door didn't open. Not until he put his big shoulder against it and shoved . . .

And Piper saw the sky.

A fallen tree and, of course, more spiderwebs, but there was sky. "An outdoor space?"

Hannah hopped up, mouth agape. "No way. Like a patio?"

Brendan nodded. "Boarded it up during a storm a few years ago. Wasn't getting much use anyway, with all the rain." He braced a hand on the doorjamb. "You want this cleared out."

The sisters nodded along. "Yeah. How do we do that?"

He didn't answer. "Once the tree is gone, you'll see the patio is a decent size. Dark gray pavers, so I guess that's in keeping with . . . What is it, your theme? There's a stone hearth back in the corner." He jerked his chin. "You want to put up a pergola, get a waterproof cover. Even in damp weather, you'll be able to use it with a fire going."

What he was describing sounded cozy and rustic and *way* outside their capabilities.

Piper laughed under her breath. "I mean, that sounds amazing, but . . ."

"We're not leaving for crab season until next Saturday. I'll work on it." He turned and strode for the exit, pausing beside the impossible-to-lift trash bag. "You want this on the curb?"

"Yes, please," Piper responded.

With seemingly zero effort, he tossed it over his right shoulder and walked out, taking the smell of salt water and unapologetic maleness with him. Piper and Hannah stared at the door for several long minutes, the wind coming in from the patio cooling their sweaty necks. "I think that was it," Hannah finally said on a laugh. "I don't think he's coming back."

Brendan *did* come back . . . the next day, with Fox, Sanders, and a man named Deke in tow. The four of them hauled the tree out through the front of the bar, and with an indecipherable look in Piper's direction, Brendan promptly left again.

Bright and early on Monday morning, he was back. Just strolled in like not a moment had passed since his last dramatic exit, this time with a toolbox.

Piper and Hannah, who were in the process of prying sheetrock off the perfectly good brick wall, glanced through the front door to see a pickup truck loaded with lumber. One trip at a time, Brendan brought the wood through the bar to the back patio, along with a table saw, while Piper and Hannah observed him with their heads on a swivel, as if watching a tennis match.

"Wait, I think . . ." Hannah whispered. "I think he's building you that freaking pergola."

"You mean *us*?" Piper whispered back.

"No. I mean *you*."

"That's crazy. If he liked me, why wouldn't he just ask me out?"

They traded a mystified look.

Hannah sucked in a breath. "Do you think he's, like, courting you?"

Piper laughed. "*What? No.*" She had to press a hand to her abdomen to keep a weird, gooey sensation at bay. "Okay, but if he is, what if it's working?"

"Is it?"

"I don't know. No one's ever built me anything!" They hopped back as Brendan stomped through the bar again, long wooden boards balanced on his wide shoulder. When he set the lumber down, he grabbed the rear neck of his sweatshirt and stripped it off, bringing the T-shirt underneath along with it, and sweet mother of God, Piper only caught a hint of a deep groove over his hip and a slice of packed stomach muscles before the shirt fell back into place, but it was enough to make her clench where it counted. "Oh yeah," Piper said throatily. "It's working." She sighed. "Shit."

"Why 'shit'?" Hannah gave her a knowing smirk. "Because Mom made that ominous warning about fishermen?" She made a spooky woo-woo sound. "It's not like you'd let it get serious. You'd keep it casual."

Yes. She would.

But would Brendan?

Builds a Pergola Guy didn't seem like the casual type. And his lack of a wedding ring was almost more a presence than the actual ring had been. Every time their eyes met, a hot shiver roared down her spine, because there was a promise there, but also . . . patience. Maturity.

Had she ever dated a real man before? Or had they all been boys?

It was Wednesday afternoon during their lunch break. Brendan, Deke, Fox, and Sanders ate sandwiches from paper wrappers, while Hannah and Piper mostly listened to the crew pitch theories about their upcoming crabbing haul—and that's when it hit Piper.

She pulled out her phone just to be sure, blowing sawdust off the screen.

And decided the oversight couldn't stand for another moment.

"Brendan," she called, during a break in the crab conversation. "You still haven't posted your first picture on Instagram."

His sandwich paused halfway to his mouth. "That's not required, is it?"

Fox gave her an exaggerated nod behind the captain's back, urging her to lie. "It's totally required. They'll delete your account otherwise." She studied her phone, pretending to scroll. "I'm shocked they haven't already."

"Can't look at pictures if your account is gone, boss," Deke said, so nonchalantly Piper could only imagine how accustomed these guys were to pranking each other. "Just saying."

Brendan flicked a look at Piper. If she wasn't mistaken, being called out for stalking her Instagram account had turned the very tips of his ears a little red. "I can put up a picture of anything, right? Even this sandwich?"

How far could they take this without him calling bullshit? Already it was an unspoken game. Get the captain to post a picture on the internet by any means necessary. "Has to be your face the first time," Hannah chimed in, scrubbing at the hair beneath her baseball cap. "You know, facial recognition technology."

"Yup." Sanders pointed his sandwich at Hannah. "What she said."

"The light is perfect right now." Piper stood and crossed the floor of No Name toward Brendan, wiggling her phone in the air. "Come on, I can pose you."

"*Pose* me?" He tugged on his beanie. "Uh-uh."

"Just give in. We all do it, man," Sanders said. "You know those engagement photos I took last year? Two hours of posing. On a goddamn *horse*."

"See? You only have to pose with a *saw*horse." Piper put a hand on Brendan's melon-sized bicep and squeezed, loosing an unmistakable flutter in her belly. "It'll be fun."

"Maybe we don't have the same idea of fun," he said dubiously.

"No?" Aware she was playing with fire but unable to stop herself, Piper leaned down and murmured in his ear, "I can think of a few fun things we'd both enjoy."

Brendan swallowed. A vein ticced in his temple. "One picture."

"Fabulous."

Piper pulled Brendan to his feet, tugging the reluctant giant outside, his boots crunching through the construction debris. A rapid shuffling of barrels told her Hannah and the crew were following them to the patio, eager to catch this rare, sparkling moment in time.

"Everyone is going to remember where they were when Brendan took his first picture for the gram," Deke said with mock gravity.

"First and last," corrected the captain.

"Who knows, you might form a habit," Piper said, coming up beside Brendan where he stood behind the sawhorse. "Okay, so shirt on? Or off?"

Brendan looked at her like she was insane. "On."

Piper wrinkled her nose at him. "Fine, but can I just . . ." She pinched the sleeve of his sweaty red T-shirt between her fingers and tugged it up, revealing the deep cut of his triceps. "Ooh. That'll work."

He grunted, seeming annoyed at himself for being flattered.

But he *definitely* flexed that tricep a little.

Piper hid her smile and moved to stand a short distance away, phone at the ready in portrait mode. "Okay, left hand on the sawhorse, pick up the drill in your right."

"Big tools!" Hannah called. "Yay, symbolism."

"This is ridiculous." He looked around. "It's obvious I'm not drilling anything."

"Distract them with your smile," Hannah said, in between long sips of her fountain soda. "Show them those pearly whites."

"Who is *them*?" Brendan wanted to know. "Piper is the only one following me."

Everyone ignored that.

"Post some content and I'll consider it." Sanders sniffed.

"Smile like we're hauling in a hundred crabs per pot," Fox suggested.

"We *have* done that. Do you remember me smiling then?"

"That's a valid point," said Deke. "Maybe Cap's just got resting asshole face."

Finally, Piper took pity on Brendan and approached the sawhorse. "I forgot to tell you something. It's kind of a secret." She crooked her finger at the man, gratified when he leaned down as if compelled. His sweaty warmth coasted over her, and she went up on her toes, eager to get closer. Maybe even requiring the added proximity. "I've been ordering your suggested dishes off the takeout menus, and you were right. They're the best ones."

She caught his smile up close with the tap of the screen.

"Look at that," she whispered, turning the phone in his direction. "You're a natural."

The corner of his lips tugged, taking his beard along with it. "Are you going to tap the heart on it?"

"Mmm-hmm." Oh, she was openly flirting with the captain now. Did that mean the third wall was back up? Or was she in some undiscovered flirting territory that lay on the other side of the rubble? "I'd tap it twice if I could."

He made a sound in his throat, leaned in a little closer. "I know they don't require a picture to keep your account active. This was about making you smile, not me." His gaze fell to her mouth, taking its time finding her eyes again. "Well worth it." With that, he set down the drill and pinned his crew with a look. "Back to work."

All Piper could do was stare at the spot he'd just vacated.

Goose bumps. He'd given her goose bumps.

Throughout the course of the week, as Brendan constructed the pergola over the back patio, it was impossible for Piper not to feel a growing sense of . . . importance. There was a warmth in her middle working its way outward with every whirr of the saw, every swing of his hammer. She'd thought nothing could make her feel sexier than a pair of Louboutins, but this man building her something by hand not only turned her on, it made her feel coveted. Wanted. In a way that wasn't superficial, but durable.

So. That was terrifying.

But it wasn't just Brendan's work making her feel positive, it was her own persistence. Piper and Hannah came down the stairs every morning and got started, hauling debris, hammering up the sagging crown molding, sanding the window frames and giving them fresh coats of paint, and organizing the storage spaces behind the bar. A warm glow of pride settled in and made itself at home with the completion of each new project.

On Thursday, in the late afternoon, the sounds of construction ceased on the back patio, the hammer and saw falling silent. Hannah had gone to spend the afternoon with Opal, so it was only Piper and Brendan in No Name. She was sanding down some shelves behind the bar when his boots scuffed over the threshold, the skin of her neck heating under his regard.

"It's finished," Brendan said in that low timbre. "You want to come look?"

Piper's nerves jangled, but she set down her sandpaper and

stood. He watched her approach, his height and breadth filling the doorway, his gaze only dipping to the neckline of her tank top briefly. But it was enough for his pupils to expand, his jaw to tighten.

She was a dusty mess. Had been for the last six days. And it hadn't seemed to matter at all. In dirty jogging pants or sequins, she was still pergola worthy. Had he busted his hump simply because he liked *her* and not just how she looked? The possibility that he'd shown up to see her, help her, without anything in return, made her comfortable in her own skin—ironically, without any of her usual beautifying trappings.

At the last second, he moved so she could slide through the doorway, and it took all of her self-control not to run her hands up Muscle Mountain. Or lean in and take a hearty drag of real, actual male exertion. God, with every passing day, she was growing less and less enamored of the groomed and coiffed men of her acquaintance. She'd like to see *them* try to operate a table saw.

Piper stepped outside and looked up, startled pleasure leaving her mouth in the form of a halting laugh. "What? You . . . Brendan, you just *built* this?" Face tipped back, she turned in a slow circle. "This is beautiful. Amazing. This patio was a jungle on Sunday. Now look at it." She clutched her hands together between her breasts. "Thank you."

Brendan cleaned the dirt off his hands with a rag, but he watched her steadily from beneath the dark band of his beanie. "Glad you like it."

"No. I *love* it."

He grunted. "You ready?"

"Ready for what?"

"For me to ask you to dinner yet."

Her pulse tripped all over itself. Got up. Tripped again. "Did you think you needed to build a pergola to convince me?"

"No. I, uh . . ." He tossed down the rag, shoved his hands into his pockets. "I needed something to keep me busy while I worked up the nerve to ask."

Oh.

Oh *no*. That worrisome little flurry in her belly went wild, flying in a dozen directions and careening into important inside parts. She needed to do something about this before . . . what? She didn't know what *happened* with serious men. Men who courted her and didn't just go putting their arms around women all willy-nilly. "Wow. I—I don't know what to say. Except . . . I will absolutely have dinner with you, Brendan. I'd love to."

He averted his gaze, nodded firmly, a smile teasing one corner of his mouth. "All right."

"But . . ." She swallowed hard when those intense green eyes zipped back in her direction. "Well. I like you, Brendan. But I just want to be up front and say, you know . . . that I'm going back to LA. Part of the reason we're fixing up the bar is to impress Daniel, our stepfather. We're hoping the display of ingenuity will be a ticket home early." She smiled. "So we both know this dinner is casual. Friendly, even. Right? We both know that." She laughed nervously, tucking some hair into her ponytail. "I'm just stating the obvious."

His cheek ticced. "Sure."

Piper pursed her lips. "So . . . we're agreeing on that."

A beat passed as he considered her. "Look, we both know I like to put things into neat little boxes, but I . . . haven't been able to do that with you. Let's just see what happens."

Panic tickled her throat. "But . . ."

He just went along packing up his tools. "I'll pick you up tomorrow night. Seven."

Without waiting for a response, he turned and walked into the bar, toward the exit.

She took a moment to internally sputter, then trotted along after him. "But, Brendan—"

One second he was holding the toolbox, the next it was on the ground and he was turning. Piper's momentum brought her up against Brendan's body, *hard*, and his boat captain forearm wrapped around her lower back, lifting her just enough that her toes brushed the concrete. And then he bowed her backward on that steel arm, stamping his mouth down onto hers in an epic kiss. It was like a movie poster, with the male lead curling his big, hunky body over the swooning, feminine lady and taking his fill.

What?

What was she thinking? Her brain was clearly compromised—and it was no wonder. The mouth that found hers was tender and hungry, all at once. Worshipful, but restraining an appetite like she'd never encountered. As soon as their lips connected and held, her fingers curled into the neck of his T-shirt, and that arm at the small of her back levered her upright, flattening the fronts of their bodies, and oh God, he just devoured her. His lips pushed hers wide, his workingman's fingers plowed into her hair, and his tongue snuck in deep, invading and setting off flares in her erogenous zones.

And he *moaned*.

This huge, gritty badass of a man moaned like he'd never tasted anything so good in all his life and he needed to get more. He brought them up for a simultaneous gasp of air, then he went right back to work, his tongue stroking over hers relentlessly until she was using her grip on his collar to climb him, her mouth just as eager, just as needy.

Oh God, oh God, oh God.

They were going to have sex, right then and there. That was the only place a kiss like this could lead. With him moaning for an entirely different reason, those sturdy hips of his holding her thighs apart to take his thrusts. How had they been orbiting each other for over a week without this happening? With every slant of his hard mouth, she was losing her mind—

The door to No Name opened, letting in the distant sounds of the harbor.

"Oh! I'm sorry . . ." Hannah said sheepishly. "Um, I'll just . . ."

Brendan had broken the kiss, his breathing harsh, eyes glittering. He stared at her mouth for a few long moments while Piper's brain struggled to play catch-up, his hand eventually dropping away from her hair. *No,* she almost whined. *Come back.* "Tomorrow night," he rasped. "Seven."

He kept his eyes on Piper until the last possible second before disappearing out the door. At which point, she staggered behind the bar and uncapped a beer from the cooler. Thank God they'd had the foresight to fill it with ice. Piper drank deeply, trying to get her libido back in check, but it was no dice. The seam of her panties was damp, her nipples stiff and achy, her fingers itching to be twisted once again in Brendan's shirt.

"I'm going to need your help, Hanns," she said finally. "Like, a lot of it."

Her sister stared back, wide-eyed, never having seen Piper knocked sideways by a man. "Help with what?"

"Remembering that whatever happens with Brendan . . . it's temporary."

"Will do, sis." Hannah came around the bar, opened her own beer, and stood shoulder to shoulder with Piper. "Jesus. I've never seen you this worked up. Who knew your kink was outdoor living spaces?"

Piper's snort turned into a full-fledged laugh. "We have a date in approximately twenty-four hours. You know what that means?"

"You have to start getting ready now?"

"Yup."

Hannah laughed. "Go. I'll clean up here."

Piper kissed her sister's temple and jogged up the back stairs, going straight to her closet. She pressed the mouth of the beer bottle to her lips and perused her choices, wondering which dress said *I'm not the settling-down type.*

Because she wasn't.

Especially not in Westport. She just needed to remind Brendan of that.

With a firm nod, she chose the emerald-green Alexander Wang fit-and-flare velvet minidress. If she was just here to have fun, she'd have the *most* fun. And try to forget how involved her heart had been in that kiss.

Chapter Fifteen

Brendan adjusted the silverware on his dining room table, trying to remember the last time he'd had reason to use more than one set. If Fox or some of the crew came over, they ate with their hands or plastic forks. Piper would be used to better, but that couldn't be helped. Instead of dipping his toe back into dating after a seven-year hiatus from all things female, he'd plunged right into the deep end with a woman who might be impossible to impress.

Sure, he was intimidated by the level of luxury Piper was used to, but he couldn't let making an effort scare him.

Trying was the least he could do, because . . . Piper Bellinger got to him.

He'd soaked up every second watching her work in No Name all week—and he'd come to find the high-maintenance-socialite aspect of her personality . . . well, adorable. She owned it. Wasn't apologetic about hating manual labor or her love of overpriced shoes and selfies. And fuck, every time she cringed about the dirt under her fingernails, he wanted to lay her on a silk pillow and do all the work for her, so she wouldn't have to. *He* wanted to do the spoiling. Badly.

It was obvious that she hated construction, yet she showed up every day with a brave smile and got it done. Furthermore, she made time in the afternoons to bring Hannah to see Opal, and he witnessed her growing comfort, day in and day out, with the fact that she had a grandparent. Noticed the way she'd begun weaving Opal into conversations without sounding stilted or awkward. She was trying new things and succeeding.

If she could do it, so could he.

Brendan opened the fridge and checked the champagne again, hoping the high price meant it was halfway decent. He'd tasted her unbelievable mouth yesterday evening, and his pride demanded only the best on her tongue. He'd have to stretch beyond his normal capabilities for this woman. She wasn't going to be happy with beer and burgers and a ball game at Blow the Man Down. Not always. She'd make him work to keep her content, and he *wanted* that challenge.

It hadn't been like this the first and only other time he'd dated a woman. There'd been no urgency or anticipation or raw hunger that never let up. There had been acceptance, understanding. All of it quiet.

But the thump of his heart as he climbed into his truck was not quiet.

No Name was within walking distance, but Piper would probably be wearing some ridiculous shoes, so he'd drive her to and from his house. Leaving home at this hour was not part of his usual routine, and everyone who saw his truck raised their eyebrows, waving hesitantly. They knew he'd be leaving tomorrow morning for crab season and probably wondered why he wasn't heading to bed early with two weeks of treacherous sea in his future.

There was a woman to see to first. That was why.

Brendan parked at the curb outside of No Name. He tried the front entrance and found it unlocked, so he went in and climbed the stairs to her door. It wasn't the first time he'd seen her dressed to kill a man, so he shouldn't have been surprised when she answered with a flirty smile and smelling exotic, like smoke. In a dress so short, he'd see everything if he went down two steps.

He almost swallowed his fucking tongue.

"Hey there, sailor."

"Piper." Brendan exhaled hard, doing everything he could to prevent his instant hard-on from growing unmanageable. Jesus, the date hadn't even started yet, and he needed to adjust himself. "You know we're just going to my house, right?"

"Mmm-hmm." She pouted at him. "You don't like my dress?"

And in that moment, Brendan saw right through her. Saw what she was doing. Making tonight about sex. Trying to keep things casual. Categorizing him as a friend with benefits. With a less determined man, she would have succeeded, too. Easily. She was paradise on legs, and probably a lot of weak-willed bastards wouldn't be able to stop themselves from taking *anything* she was willing to give.

But he remembered their kiss. Would likely remember it for the rest of his life. She'd hidden nothing while their mouths were touching. She'd been scared, surprised, turned on, and scared again. He could relate. And while he had no idea if he could offer this woman enough to make her happy, he wasn't letting Piper classify him as a casual hookup. Because what she made him feel wasn't casual. Not one bit.

"You know I love it, Piper. You look beautiful."

Her cheeks flushed at the compliment. "And you're not wearing your beanie." She reached out and ran her fingers through his hair, her nails lightly grazing his scalp. "I can't believe you've been hiding all of this from me."

Christ. He was in danger of swallowing his tongue again.

It wasn't just that he hadn't been touched by a woman in seven years. It was that *this* woman was the one doing the touching. "There's a chill in the air. Do you have a jacket or do you want to borrow mine?"

Hannah appeared behind her sister in the doorway, headphones looped around her neck. She dropped a black sweater over Piper's shoulders and sniffed. "Have her home at a reasonable hour, please."

Brendan shook his head at the younger one and offered his hand to Piper. "Not much choice. We leave for Alaska in the morning."

Hannah hummed for a second, singing a song under her breath about the bottom of the deep blue sea, but he didn't recognize it. Seemingly caught up in the words, Hannah patted her sister on the shoulder and closed the door.

Sliding her hand into Brendan's, Piper made an amused sound. "She's probably already making you a sailing-themed playlist for the trip. She can't help herself."

"If we're not setting traps or pulling them up, we're trying to get a few hours of sleep. Not a lot of time for listening to music." He cleared his throat. "I won't tell her that, though."

He opened the front door, and Piper smiled at him as she

passed through. There were a few customers waiting outside the Red Buoy across the street. When they saw him helping Piper into his truck—and sure enough, she was wearing those ice-pick heels again—they elbowed each other, one of them even running inside to relay the gossip. He'd been prepared for a reaction. Didn't mind it at all, especially with him going out of town for two weeks. Right or wrong, it would ease his mind if the town knew she was spoken for.

Even if Piper wasn't aware of it yet.

They drove the three minutes to Brendan's house, and he pulled into the driveway, coming around the front bumper to help her out. He didn't have a hope in hell of keeping his eyes off her legs when she turned all ladylike in the seat, using his shoulders for balance as she descended from the passenger side of his truck.

"Thank you," she whispered, running a finger down the center of his chest. "Such a gentleman."

"That's right." He tipped her chin up. "That's exactly what I'm going to be, Piper."

Her bravado slipped a little. "I guess we'll see about that."

"I guess we will."

She took her chin out of his hand and strutted up the walkway, which was just playing dirty. The clingy green material of her dress stretched and shifted over her ass, immediately making him question whether being a gentleman was overrated.

Yeah, he wanted to take her to bed more than he could remember wanting anything. Every muscle in his body was strung tight at the sight of her gorgeous legs in the darkness outside his front door. But he couldn't shake the intuition that going too fast with Piper would be a mistake. Maybe she even wanted him to give in, just so she could put him in a box labeled *Fling.*

Worst part of it was . . . maybe he *was* only fling material for her. Tonight, she looked more suited to gliding around a Hollywood mansion than eating a homemade meal at his bachelor pad. He might be delusional trying to shoot his shot. If she was determined to go back to LA, there was no way he could stop her. But something inside him, some intuition, wouldn't allow him to give Piper anything but his best effort.

Brendan unlocked the door, flipped on the lights, and turned to watch her reaction. She'd be able to see most of it at first glance. The downstairs was an open concept, with the living room on the right, kitchen and dining room on the left. It wasn't full of knickknacks or cluttered with pictures. Everything was simple, modern, but what furniture he did have was handmade locally with driftwood—and he liked that. Liked that his home was a representation of what the people of his town could do with wood from the ocean.

"Oh." She let out a rush of breath, a dimple popping up in her cheek. "Brendan . . . you set the table already."

"Yeah." Remembering his manners, he went to the kitchen and took the bottle of champagne out of the fridge. She came to stand by the dining table, seeming a little dumbfounded as she watched him pop the cork and pour. "You'll have to tell me if this is any good. They only had two kinds at the liquor store, and the other one came in a can."

She laughed, set her purse down, and removed the sweater in a slow, sensual movement that nearly caused his composure to falter. "Why don't you have some with me?"

"I drink beer. No champagne."

Piper edged a hip up onto the table, and he almost over-flowed the glass. "I bet I'll convince you to have some by the end of the night."

Jesus, she probably could convince him to do a lot of things if she put her mind to it, but he reckoned he should keep that to himself. He handed her the champagne flute he'd purchased that very afternoon, watched her take a sip, and the memory of their kiss rolled through him hard.

"It's fantastic," she said with a sigh.

Relief settled in next to need. He ignored the latter. For now. "Just going to put the fish in the oven, then I want to show you something."

"Okay."

Brendan opened the fridge and took out the foil-covered baking dish. He'd already prepared the sole, drizzled it with lemon juice, salt, and pepper. In Westport, you learned young how to make a fish dinner, even if you never honed another skill in the kitchen. It was necessary, and he thanked God for that knowledge now. As he turned on the oven and slid in the dish, he decided his kitchen would forever look boring without Piper standing in it. She was something out of another world, posed to seduce with her killer body angled just right, elbow on hip, wrist lazily swirling her champagne.

"Come on." Before he could give in to temptation and lift her onto the table, forget about dinner altogether, he snagged her free hand, guiding her through the living room toward the back of the house. He slapped on the light leading to his back patio and opened the door, gesturing for her to precede him. "Thought I'd show you what's possible with the outdoor space at the bar, if you wanted to add some greenery." It occurred to him then that maybe gardening wasn't exactly a sexy trait for a man to have. "I just needed something to do on my days off—"

Her gasp cut him off. "Wow. Oh my God, Brendan. It's magical out here." She walked through the roughly cut stone pathway, somehow not tripping in her heels. The ferns, which he really needed to get around to trimming, grazed her hips as she passed. The trickling sound from the stone water feature seemed to be calling her, and she stopped in front of it, trailing a finger along the surface. There was a single wrought-iron chair angled in the corner where he sat sometimes with a beer after a long trip, trying to get his equilibrium back. "I wouldn't have pegged you for a gardener, but now I can see it. You love your roots." She glanced back at him over her shoulder. "You've got everything carved out just the way you like it."

Do I?

He would have thought so until recently.

His going through the motions, doing the same thing over and over again, had become less . . . satisfying. No denying it.

"I do love this place," he said slowly. "Westport."

"You'd never think of leaving." A statement, not a question.

"No," he answered anyway, resisting the urge to qualify that definite *no* somehow.

She leaned down to smell one of the blooms on his purple aster bush. "What about a vacation? Do you ever take them?"

He rubbed at the back of his neck. "When I was a kid, my parents used to bring me camping on Whidbey Island. They moved down to Eugene, Oregon, a while back to be closer to my mother's family."

"No leisure trips since childhood? Nothing at all?"

Brendan shook his head, chuckling when Piper gave him a scandalized look. "People take trips to see the ocean. I don't need to go anywhere for that. She's right here in my backyard."

Piper came closer, amusement dancing in her eyes. "My mother warned me all about you king crab fishermen and your love affairs with the sea. I thought she was being dramatic, but you really can't resist the pull of the water, can you?" She searched his face. "You're in a serious relationship."

Something shifted in his stomach. "What do you mean, she warned you?"

Her shoulder lifted and dropped. "She loves her husband, Daniel. But . . . I think there was some unprocessed grief talking. Because of what happened to Henry." She stared off into the distance, as if trying to recall the conversation. "She told me and Hannah that fishermen always choose the sea. They go back over and over again, even if it scares their loved ones. Based on that, I'm guessing she wanted Henry to quit and . . . you know the rest."

This wasn't a conversation he'd planned on. Would he ever give up the more dangerous aspects of his job? No. No, battling the tides, the current, the waves was his life's work. There was salt water running through his veins. Making it clear that he would always choose the ocean, no matter what, put him at a deficit with Piper already—and they hadn't even eaten yet.

But when she turned her face up to the moonlight, and he saw only honest curiosity there, he felt compelled to make her understand.

"Every year, I get a couple of greenhorns on the boat. First-time crabbers. Most of them are young kids trying to make some quick cash, and they never make it longer than the first season. But once in a while, there's one . . . I can see it from the wheelhouse. The bond he's forming with the sea. And I know he'll never get away from her."

She smiled. "Like you."

A voice whispered in the back of his head, *You're screwing yourself.* He was an honest man, though, often to a fault. "Yeah. Like me." He searched her hairline. "That bruise on your head is finally gone."

She reached up and rubbed the spot. "It is. Did I ever thank you properly for sending Abe to pad the upper bunk?"

"No thanks necessary."

Piper eliminated the remaining distance between them, stopping just shy of her tits touching his chest. She was soft, graceful, feminine. So much smaller than him. With her this close, he felt like a tamed giant, holding his breath and waiting, waiting to see what the beautiful girl would do next. "You could have just kissed it and made it all better."

His exhale came out hard, thanks to all the blood in his body rushing south to his cock. "You told me your flirt was broken with me. It doesn't seem like that's the case tonight."

Her lips curved. "Maybe because I came dressed in body armor."

Brendan tilted his head and let his gaze sweep across her bare shoulders, legs, and back to her low, tight neckline. "That armor couldn't protect you from anything."

Something flickered in her eyes. "Couldn't it?"

She sailed into the house, leaving her seductive scent in her wake.

Brendan had always thought battling the ocean would forever be his biggest challenge. But that was before he met Piper. Maybe he didn't know the how or the what of this thing between them yet, but his gut never lied. He'd never lost a battle with the water when listening to his instincts, and he hoped like hell those same instincts wouldn't fail him now.

Chapter Sixteen

$\mathcal{P}$iper watched Brendan take a seat on the opposite side of the table and frowned.

The boat captain didn't appear to be easily seduced. When she'd picked this dress out, she hadn't even expected them to make it through the front door, but here they were, sitting in his charmingly masculine dining room, preparing to eat food *he made himself.*

And he'd bought her champagne.

Men had bought her jewelry, taken her to nice restaurants—one eager beaver had even bought her a Rolls for her twenty-second birthday. She'd made no bones about liking nice things. But none of those gifts had ever made her feel as special as this homemade meal.

She didn't want to feel special around Brendan, though. Did she?

Since arriving in Westport, she'd had more frank conversations with Brendan than anyone in her life, save Hannah. She wanted to know more about him, to reveal more of herself in return, and *that* was intensely scary.

Because what could come of this?

She was only in Westport for three months, almost two weeks down already. Tomorrow *he'd* leave for two weeks. Then back in and out to sea, three days at a time. This had all the makings of a temporary hookup. But his refusal to put a label on this thing between them left the door of possibilities swinging wide open.

She actually didn't even know how to *be* more than a temporary hookup.

That impossible-to-ignore white tan line around his ring finger and the fact that she was his first date since taking it off? It was overwhelming for someone whose longest relationship had only been three weeks and had ended with her confidence shot full of holes. Whatever he expected to happen between them . . . she couldn't deliver on that.

And maybe that was the real problem.

The burly sea captain waited in silence for her to take the first bite, his elbows on the table, totally unpracticed at being on a date. A muscle ticced in his cheek, telling her Brendan was nervous about her reaction to his cooking. But every thought in her head must have been showing on her face, because he raised an eyebrow at her. She rolled the tension out of her shoulders and dug her fork into the flaky white fish, adding a potato, too, and pushing it between her lips. Chewing. "Oh. Wow, this is great."

"Yeah?"

"Totally." She took another bite, and he finally started eating his own meal. "Do you cook for yourself a lot?"

"Yes." He ate the way he did everything else. No pussyfooting around. Insert fork, put food in mouth, repeat. No pausing. "Except for Monday nights."

"Oh, the Red Buoy is a scheduled weekly event. I should have known." She laughed. "I make fun of you for your routines, but they're probably what make you a good captain."

He made a sound. "Haven't been in my routines this week, have I?"

"No." She considered him. Even warned herself against delving too deeply into why he'd changed things up. But her curiosity got the best of her. "Why is that? I mean, what made you decide to"—*take off your ring?*—"rearrange your schedule?"

Brendan seemed to choose his words. "I'll never be impulsive. Consistency equals safety on the water, and I got comfortable abiding by rules at all times. It makes me worthy to have lives in my hands, you know? Or that was my reasoning in the beginning, and it just stuck. For a long time. But recently, here on land . . . someone kept throwing wrenches in my routines, and the world didn't end." He studied her, as if to judge her reaction and whether or not to continue. "It was kind of like I'd been waiting for a shoe to drop. Then it dropped, and instead of chaos, I just, uh . . ." A beat passed. "Saw the potential for a new course."

Piper swallowed hard. "The shoe dropped, but it was a peep-toe stiletto?"

"Something like that."

"I *can* harness my chaos for good. I might need you as a character witness at a future trial." Her words didn't quite convey the levity she was hoping for, mostly because she sounded breathless over his admission. Piper Bellinger had had a positive effect on someone. He'd admitted it out loud. "But it's not just me that forced the change," she said, and laughed, desperate to dull the throb in her chest. "There had to be other factors."

Brendan started to say something and stopped.

Since meeting this man, she'd suspected he never said anything without a reason. If he was holding back, she could only imagine how important it must be. She found herself setting down her fork, wanting to give him her undivided attention. "What is it?"

He cleared his throat. "I'm purchasing a second boat for next season. It's being built now. I'm going to check on the progress while I'm in Dutch Harbor—that's the port in Alaska where we'll wait a week after setting our traps."

"That's exciting." Her brow wrinkled. "How are you going to captain two ships?"

"I'm not. I'm going to put Fox in the wheelhouse of the *Della Ray*."

Piper smiled into a sip of champagne. "Does he know yet?"

"No. I can't give him time to talk himself out of it."

"Would he? He seems . . . confident."

"That's a nice way of saying he's a cocky asshole. And he is. But he's smarter than he thinks." Brendan paused, looking down with a knitted brow. "Maybe handing over the *Della Ray* is a good way to distance myself from the past."

Piper stayed very still. "Why do you want to distance yourself?"

"Apart from it being time? I think . . . a part of me feels obligated to remain in the past as long as I'm captaining Mick's boat." He scrubbed a hand down his face, laughing without humor. "I can't believe I'm saying it out loud when normally I'd just bury it. Maybe I *should* bury it."

"Don't." Her mouth was dry over this man opening up to her. Looking at her across the table with rare male vulnerability, as if he truly valued her response. "You don't have to feel guilty about wanting some space after seven years, Brendan," she said quietly. "That's a lot more than most people would give. The fact that you feel guilty at all just proves you're a quality human. Even if you wear a beanie at the dinner table."

The green of his eyes warmed. "Thank you. For not judging me."

Sensing his need to move on from the subject, Piper looked around the dining room. "Who am I to judge anyone? Especially someone who has a cool house his parents don't own. Two boats and a life plan. It's intimidating, actually."

He frowned. "You're intimidated by *me*?"

"Not so much you. More like your work ethic. I don't even know if I'm pronouncing that right. That's how *not* often I've said 'work ethic' out loud." She felt the need to even the playing field, to reward his honesty with some of her own. His confessions made it easy to confess her own sins. "My friend Kirby and I started a lipstick line called Pucker Up, maybe three years back. Once the launch party was over and we realized how much work we had to do, we gave away our inventory to friends and went to Saint-Tropez. Because we were tired."

"Maybe it wasn't the right career path."

"Yeah, well." Her lips twitched. "Professional napper was my fallback, and I nailed that. That's partially why I'm here. But *also* because my friend Kirby ratted me out to the cops."

"She didn't," he said, his expression darkening.

"She did! Fingered me as the ringleader from the shallow end of the pool. Appropriately." Piper waved a hand around. "It's fine, though. We're still friends. I just can't trust her or tell her anything important."

He seemed to be concentrating hard on what she was saying. "Do you have a lot of friends like that?"

"Yes." She drew a circle on the side of the champagne flute. "It's more for image than anything, I guess. Influence. Being seen. But it's weird, you know. I've only been out of Los Angeles for two weeks, and it's like I was never there. None of my friends have texted or messaged me. They're on to bigger and better things." She shook her head. "Meanwhile people still leave flowers at Henry's memorial after twenty-four years. So . . . how real or substantial is an image if everything it earns someone can all go away in two weeks?"

"*You* haven't gone away, though. You're sitting right there."

"I am. I'm here. At this table. In Westport." She swallowed. "Trying to figure out what to do when no one is watching. And wondering if maybe that's the stuff that actually matters." Her laugh came out a little unsteady. "That probably sounds amateurish to someone who would build a freaking *boat* and not tell a soul about it."

"No, it doesn't." He waited until she met his eyes. "It sounds like you've been uprooted and dropped somewhere unfamiliar. Do you think I'd cope as well if I was shipped off someplace where I knew no one, had no trade?"

She gasped. "How would you get your fish and chips on Monday nights?"

A corner of his lips jumped. "You're doing just fine, honey."

It was the gruff *honey* that did it. Her legs snuck together under the table and squeezed, her toes flexing in her shoes. She wanted Brendan's hands on her. All over. But she was also scared of going to him, because once again, the sexy smoke screen she'd been hiding behind had dissipated, leaving only her. Brendan was looking at her with a combination of heat and tenderness, and she needed to turn up the dial on the former.

This was all going too far, too fast, and she was starting to like him too much.

She might be having an existential crisis, but she still wanted Los Angeles back and all the glittery trappings that came with it. Didn't she? Sure, after weeks with no contact from her friends, the call of LA had quieted slightly. She'd actually started to enjoy not checking her notifications every ten seconds. But fame waxing and waning was part of the deal, right? That rush of recognition and adoration she'd stopped craving of late would come back. It always did. There was no other option but going home, and if anything, her time in Westport would make her appreciate her privilege this time around. Wasn't that the lesson she'd been sent to learn?

Yes.

Bottom line, she'd spent twenty-eight years building this image and couldn't just start over from scratch.

Could she have Brendan tonight and still keep her eye on that reality?

Of course she could.

Ignoring the notch in her throat, Piper pushed back from the table and stood, champagne in hand. She rounded the piece of furniture slowly, gratified when his throat worked in a heavy swallow. His eyes and chin were stubborn, though.

Well, if he was going to be obstinate, she'd have to play to win.

Piper slipped between Brendan and the table, scooting it back a little so she could stand comfortably in the V of his thighs. His eyes were all but black with hunger, lighting on her cleavage, her thighs and hips, her mouth. As soon as she raked the fingers of her free hand into his hair, that big chest started to heave, his eyelids drifting shut. "Piper," he said hoarsely. "This isn't why I invited you to dinner."

She took her hand back, set down the champagne being held in the other, and tucked her fingers under the straps of her dress. "Maybe it's not the only reason," she murmured, peeling down the green velvet bodice, leaving her breasts bare mere inches from his mouth. "But it's one of them, isn't it?"

Brendan opened his eyes, and a shudder racked him, his hands flying up to grip her hips. "Oh Jesus fucking Christ, they're so pretty, baby." He leaned in, pressing his open mouth to the smooth path of skin between her breasts, breathing heavily, using his hold on her hips to pull her closer, like he couldn't help it. "This is where you put that perfume, isn't it? Right here between your sexy little tits."

The desperation in his hands, the chafe of velvet on flesh, turned her nipples to points. "I put it there for you tonight," she whispered into his hair. "All for you."

He moaned, turned his head slightly so he could breathe against her nipple. "I know what you're doing. You want to make this about fucking."

Her pulse skittered in her ears. "Stop overthinking it and touch me."

Still, he hesitated, that jaw about to shatter.

Piper reached back and picked up the champagne flute, taking a slow sip. She swallowed most of the bubbly liquid, but left a trace of it on her tongue, bringing it to Brendan's lips. Licking the champagne into his mouth. "Told you I'd get you to try it," she murmured, teasing the tip of his tongue with her own. "Want more?"

That big body swayed closer, lines of strain appearing around his mouth. "Please . . ."

"You don't have to beg," Piper said, bringing the champagne flute to her breasts, tipping the glass and letting the champagne trickle out over one nipple, then the next, and Brendan started to pant. "Not for something we both want. Touch me, Brendan. Taste me. Please?"

"Christ, I have to." He traced his mouth to her left nipple, pressed his bared teeth against it, before rubbing his tongue against the stiff bud, yanking her hips forward, the move arching her back so she had to use his hair for balance, taking two big handfuls. Her mouth was in an O, watching him savor her, manhandle her body. No games. Just need.

His mouth raced down to her belly button, licking that hollow where some of the dripping champagne had ended up, before rising again to the opposite breast, suckling harder now. Devouring. She'd intended to be in control here, but his mouth was delivering the most incredible texture and suction, and her ass bumped back against the table clumsily, a sob ripping from her throat. "Brendan," she gasped. "*Brendan*."

"I know, baby. Can I put my hands up your dress?" he rasped, his palms already kneading the backs of her thighs, his beard stroking back and forth over her distended nipple, and sending a rush of wet to the apex of her thighs. "*Piper.*"

"What?" she breathed, head spinning. "Whatever you said. Yes. Yes."

Those busy hands moved faster than lightning, clutching her ass so roughly, the air evacuated her lungs. He drew her forward so he could pant directly against her belly, his hands never ceasing to massage, squeeze, and lift the flesh of her bottom, his calloused fingers tangling in her thong in his haste to touch, to mold.

"Y-you're an ass man, I guess," she stammered.

He shook his head. "No, Piper. I'm a *this*-ass man."

"Oh," she simpered.

That was oddly romantic. And possessive. And she liked both of those qualities too much. She needed to regain control somehow, because she'd severely miscalculated how quickly Brendan could pull her under. This attraction was even more dangerous than she'd originally thought. "Brendan," she managed, taking hold of his broad shoulders and using every ounce of her strength to push him back into his chair. "W-wait, I . . ."

"I'm sorry," he said between breaths. "It's not just that it's been so long for me, it's that you had to be the sexiest woman on the fucking planet."

Had Piper heard him right? She shook her head to clear it, though most of the lust fog remained in place. "Wait, I know you wore the ring, but . . . no sex? At all? Knowing you, I should have assumed that, but . . ." Her gaze traveled down the front of his body, stopping when she reached the outline of his painful-looking erection. It protruded against the fly of his jeans, large and heavy. His own hand crept toward it, his sexual frustration obvious in every harsh line of his face.

There was a way to wrestle back control of this push and pull between them *and* make him feel good—and she suddenly couldn't help herself. "Oh, Brendan." She went down on her knees and pressed a kiss to the thick bulge. "We need to take care of this, don't we?"

His head fell back, chest lifting and plummeting. "Piper, you don't need to."

She cupped his big arousal, massaged him through his jeans, and he moaned through his teeth. "I want to," she whispered. "I want to make you feel so good."

She flicked open the button at the top of his fly and lowered the zipper carefully, sucking in a breath when his shaft grew impossibly larger inside his briefs in the absence of confinement. Brendan's knuckles were white on the arms of the chair, but he stopped breathing altogether as she drew down the waistband of his briefs and saw his erection up close. *Male.* There was no other way to describe the unapologetic weight and steel of him, the thick black hair at the base, the heavy sac. He was long and smooth and broad, veins wrapped around him like lines on a road map, and wow. Yes. She'd been telling the truth. She really did want to make him feel good. So badly, her inner thighs were turning slick with her own need. *Wanted* to be on her knees, giving pleasure to this man who'd been celibate so long. This man who'd treated her with care and respect and got nervous about her tasting his cooking.

Furthermore, she could establish up front that this was just sex.

Just sex.

"Look at you, Piper," Brendan said hoarsely. "Christ, I didn't stand a chance, did I?"

With a sympathetic pout, she gave his shaft a tight pump. And another one. Waited until his eyes started to glaze over, then she dragged her tongue up the meaty underside of him, closed her mouth over the velvet helmet on top. Making her tongue flat and stiff, she teased the salty slit, the sensitive ridges, before tunneling him in deep, deep, right up to the point where tears pricked her eyelids. God, he pulsed on her tongue, great, quick surges of life that her femininity started to echo, making her groan around his hard flesh.

"Goddamn, baby, that mouth," he groaned, one of his hands fisting her hair, urging her faster, even as he barked, "Stop. *Stop.* I'm going to come."

Piper let him slide from her mouth with a swirl of her tongue, her right hand working him, thickening him with every stroke of her fist. Yeah, he wasn't going to last much longer, and there was something so hot about it. How much he'd needed the relief. "Where do you want to give it to me?" she whispered, taking his sac in her hand and juggling him gently, leaning in to curl her tongue around the purpling tip. "Anywhere you want, Captain."

"*Fuck,*" he gritted out, his thighs starting to vibrate. Instead of answering her pretty, pressing question, he closed his eyes, nostrils flaring as he took in a drag of air. "No."

Then the unexpected happened.

Right on the verge of his well-deserved orgasm, Brendan surged forward, wrapping his hands around her waist and lifting her up onto the dining room table. She teetered, dizzy from the rapid ascent, but she snapped back to reality when Brendan dropped to his own knees and stripped off his shirt. "Ohhh," she said in slow motion. "Heyyy, looook aaaat thaaaat."

Dude was *yoked.*

She'd known, on some level, that Brendan was built like a motherfucker. His arms always tested the seams of his sweatshirts, his chest ridged with muscle, but she'd been unaware of the definition. The chiseled planes of his pecs ended in a tight drop-off; then it was a mountain range of abs. But not the obnoxious kind. They had meat on them. And hair. All of him did. He looked like a real man who worked in the wild, because that's exactly what he was. And not a single tattoo, which was so Brendan, it made her throat feel weird. Of course he wouldn't want to deal with the fuss of all that or waste his time getting one done.

Come back to earth, Piper.

"Wait, I was . . ." She pointed at his erection. "You were—"

"Don't worry about me," he rasped, dragging her to the edge of the table. "Open your thighs and let me see it, Piper."

Her inner walls clenched, delighting in his bluntness. "But—"

"You think I'm going to get sucked off and leave town for two weeks? Not going to happen. You're getting off, baby, or nobody is getting off."

As if on autopilot, her thighs squeaked wide on the table. Oh, this wasn't good. She didn't even know which part of her was in command. Her head, her heart, her lady business. Or maybe they all were, three bitches hitting the switches of her control panel. She only knew Brendan needed to stop revealing positive sides of himself.

Now they were adding *generous* to the mix?

The hem of her delicate dress in his boat captain's hands made her whimper. He lifted it, and God only knew what he was seeing. Her thong was sheer to begin with, but she'd never been this wet in her ever-loving life. Not to mention, his impatient hands on her butt had tugged it askew.

He stared hard at her juncture, the grip on her knees flexing, a curse issuing unsteadily from his mouth. "Yeah, I have to be an idiot leaving you without my attention for two weeks."

She panted. "Are you calling me high maintenance?"

"Are you denying it?" He tugged aside the strip of material shielding her core, which thankfully she'd waxed clean as a whistle right before leaving LA. "Fuck me. You can be as high maintenance as you want, honey. But I'm the only one who does the maintenance." He ran his thumb down the seam of her sex. "Understood?"

Piper nodded, as if in a trance.

What was the use of saying no? At least this one verbal agreement was about sex. Nothing emotional. And she wasn't going to pretend like someone in this town might come along and interest her even a fraction of the amount that Brendan did. She might have to travel pretty far to find that, come to think of it.

His lips ghosted up her inner thigh, blunt fingers hooking in the sides of her panties. "Lift up," he rumbled, nipping at her sensitive skin with his teeth. "Want them off."

Oh great. His voice could get even deeper? It resonated all the way up to her clit, and she fell back on her elbows, inching her hips up enough for Brendan to peel the thong down her legs. She watched this man, who grew more exciting by the moment, expecting him to drop the underwear on the floor. He wrapped the thin black material around his shaft instead, pressing his mouth and nose up against her wetness, groaning as he choked himself up and down in a tight fist.

"Holy . . ." Piper breathed, momentarily blacking out.

"See this, baby?" He rubbed his mouth side to side, parting the damp folds of her femininity, that hand jerking roughly between his thighs. "You're still getting me off, too."

When had her back hit the table?

One second she was looking down at Brendan's head, the

next she was staring wide-eyed up at the ceiling. Brendan's tongue snaked down slowly through the valley of her sex, and her fingers clawed their way into his hair, the move involuntary, but if he stopped, if he *stopped*, she was going to die.

"Good, Piper. Pull me in tight. Show me how bad you want my tongue."

No no no. His voice was like sandpaper now. Could she come from that baritone alone?

"Brendan." She lifted her legs, hooked them over his shoulders, earning a growl, another rough jerk of her hips to the edge of the table. "Please, please. *Please.*"

She'd never begged for anything sexual in her life. Especially not oral. Men always made it seem like they were doing a woman a favor. Or maybe she'd just been detached and projecting an explanation that would keep her that way. She couldn't remain detached now, and this . . . oh, it was definitely not a hardship for Brendan—and he let her know it. His forearm came down on her hips, pinning them to the table, and he growled into that second lick, dragging the tip over her clit, teasing it, the rippling flex of his shoulder telling Piper that his hand was moving feverishly just out of sight. With the use of her panties.

He was the most consistent man she'd ever met, and she thanked God for that now because he sealed his upper lip to the very top of her slit, his tongue never quitting or changing pace. It was perfect, perfect, lavishing her swelling clit with friction and pressure, and she was actually going to get there because of it. Oh my God, she was going to have an orgasm. Like a real, authentic orgasm. She wasn't going to fake it to stroke his ego. This was happening.

"Please don't stop, Brendan. It's perfect. It's . . . oh God, oh Jesus."

Her thighs started to tremor uncontrollably, and she could see nothing but sparks dancing in front of her eyes. The fingers she'd plowed into his hair drew him closer, legs wrapping around his head, her hips lifting, seeking, lower body twisting. And she still didn't dislodge him from that magical spot, and maybe he was Jesus. She didn't know. Knew nothing but the intense pleasure bearing down on her. But then he took his forearm off her hips and pressed the heel of his hand to her weeping entrance and rotated it—hard—and she screamed. She fucking screamed. And she didn't stop when he slid a thick finger inside of her, searched and found her G-spot, adding firm pressure.

She climaxed. Which was a pitiful word for traveling to a distant plane where fairies danced and gumdrops rained from the sky. When her back protested, she realized it had arched off the table involuntarily. She stared at her elevated hips in a daze, the endless relief coursing through her, tightening her muscles and letting them go. Wow. Oh wow.

Brendan moved over her slumped body, and his face, it was almost unrecognizable for the lust bracketing his mouth, the fever making his eyes bright. That huge part of him was still hard, his hand twisting up and down the length, one side of her panties wrapped around his shaft, the other around his fist. "Can I rub it here, baby?" Brendan rasped the question, his bare chest heaving, a fine sheen of sweat on those work-honed muscles. "Just want to rub it where I made you come."

"Yes."

He all but fell on her, his face landing in the crook of her neck, his fist positioning his stiffness between her thighs, right over that uber-sensitive flesh. "One day soon, Piper, I'm going to fuck you so goddamn hard." He alternated between dragging his swollen tip through her saturated folds and stroking himself. "Going to fuck the word 'friend' right out of your beautiful mouth. You'll forget how to say anything but my name. Real quick, honey."

Her clit hummed again, unbelievably, and that buzz of connection, of more promised pleasure had to be the reason she turned her head slightly, whispering in his ear, "Promise?"

With a strangled growl of her name, he hit his peak, shooting moisture onto her belly, his hand moving in a blur, his teeth bared against the side of her throat. "Piper. *Piper.*"

The power, the exhilaration of Brendan saying her name as he orgasmed was so incredible, she couldn't hold still. She raked her tongue up and down his straining neck, rubbed the insides of her thighs up and down his heaving rib cage, scraped her fingernails over his shoulders and down his back. When his heavy body collapsed on her, she kept going, some instinct she'd never had before urging her to soothe, to whisper words of praise that she actually, literally meant. She could have laid there straight through to tomorrow, just existing under the reassuring weight of him—and that complacency brought back her senses.

Okay, they gave good sex.

Or . . . *almost* sex, anyway.

Better than any actual intercourse she'd ever had, though. By leaps and bounds.

Because you like him. A lot. For who he is, not what he can do for you.

That realization smacked her hard in the face. *God*. She'd never thought of her past actions in those terms before, but they fit. Shallow. So shallow. Who was she to accept the sweet gestures this man offered? He should have waited to take his wedding ring off for some selfless local girl who would be content waving him off to sea for the rest of her life.

A pang caught Piper in the chest, and she tried to sit up but couldn't move because Brendan had her pinned to the table. His head lifted, eyes narrowing like he could already sense her building tension. "Piper."

"What?" she whispered, winded from her thoughts.

"Get out of your head."

With a sardonic smile, she rolled her eyes. "Aye, aye, Captain." With some effort, she tried to do as he asked. Tried to set aside her worries for later. He was leaving for two weeks tomorrow morning, after all. That would be plenty of time to pull her stupid head out of the clouds. "That was . . . wow." *Keep it light. Sexy.* "Really, really good."

Brendan grunted. He dropped his head and smiled into the valley between her breasts, making her heart flutter. "Good?" he snorted, kissing her breasts in turn and standing, visibly reluctant to leave her. After zipping his still semi-hard erection back into his jeans, he took some napkins out of the holder on the table and cleaned Piper of his spend, wiping efficiently like he did everything else, shaking his head slowly at her appearance. "I'm going to starve to death without the taste of you."

Despite the languidness of her muscles, she managed to sit up and fix her dress, blinking at the panties sitting in a wet heap on the floor, memories of the last half hour flooding in. Wow. She'd been so . . . present. Inside every second with him.

When she'd been intimate in the past, she spent the whole time obsessing about her appearance, what the guy was thinking, if she was meeting expectations. None of those anxieties had taken hold with Brendan. None. Because . . . he liked *her*. Not her image. Her actual personality and opinions. With Brendan's hands on her, she'd had no walls, no boundaries. Tonight had been all *about* boundaries, but instead of setting them, the line kept getting pushed further and further out.

She hopped off the table, landing on the heels she still wore, and gave him a flirty hip-check. "Maybe I'll give you another taste when you get back."

"Maybe, huh?" He caught her arm and spun her around, backing her up against the refrigerator, pinning her there with his rugged frame. Piper's traitorous body melted immediately, eager to be supported by his superior strength, her head lolling back. Brendan's hard mouth found hers with lips already opening, his tongue delving deep, carrying the light flavor of her climax, giving it to her with thorough strokes, a low growl of satisfaction simmering in his throat. When he pulled back, his silver-green eyes searched her face, one hand cradling her jaw. "Does that taste like 'maybe' to you?"

In other words, she'd be back for more.

"Somebody's cocky all of a sudden," Piper huffed.

"Not cocky, honey." He kissed her mouth again, softly this time. "Determined."

She sputtered. Determined to do what?

Oh man, she needed to get out of there.

"I have an early morning," she blurted. "And so do you, right? So."

"So." He seemed to be fighting a smile, and it was galling.

Still not wearing a shirt, he gathered Piper's cardigan and helped her put it on, before handing over her purse. At the very last second, he threw on his own shirt and picked up his car keys. "I'm going to have mercy on you this time, Piper, and drive you home." He threaded their fingers together and tugged her toward the door. "This just had to be the year crab season gets slotted early, didn't it? Otherwise I'd spend about a week getting inside your head—"

"It would take longer than that."

"But dammit." He jerked open the front door. "It'll have to wait until I'm back."

Ha. No way. There would be no getting in anyone's head. Two weeks was like, a million years. They wouldn't even remember each other's names by then. They'd pass each other on the street and vaguely recall a fish dinner and an oral-sex fest.

You're lying to yourself.

And she kept right on doing it the whole ride home. Kept lying to reassure herself when Brendan walked her up the stairs to her apartment. But the pretense shattered at her feet when he kissed her like he'd never see her again, his mouth moving over hers with such tenderness, her knees turned to rubber and she had to hold on to his collar to stay upright.

"Here," he said, exhaling shakily and pulling the keys out of his pocket. "I'm giving you a spare key to my place, all right? Just in case you and your sister need somewhere to go while I'm out of town."

Piper stared at the object with dawning horror. "A *key?*"

"It's going to get cooler in the next couple of weeks, and the heat in this place probably isn't great." He folded her hand around it, kissed her forehead. "Stop freaking out."

She uttered a string of gibberish.

Did he think she would actually use this thing?

Because she wouldn't.

He chuckled at her expression and turned to go—and she panicked. A different kind of panic than the variety she felt at being handed the key. She thought of the brass statue on the harbor and Opal emptying the contents of an envelope onto the table.

"Brendan!"

Slowing, he turned with a raised eyebrow.

"Please be careful," she whispered.

Warmth fused into his eyes, and he checked her out, head to toe, before continuing on his way, the door downstairs closing behind him, followed by silence.

Much later, she realized what Brendan was really doing when he catalogued her features, her hands, her cocked hip.

Memorizing the sight of her.

Just in case?

Chapter Seventeen

The storm started thirteen days later.

Piper had fallen into a daily routine by then. Run along the harbor just after sunrise. Walk Abe to the maritime museum in the morning, visit Opal on her way home, often with Hannah in tow. Work on the bar until dinnertime, then collapse. They'd made a ton of progress on No Name and were going to start decorating next week, as soon as they installed the crisp white cornice and gave the concrete another coat of industrial paint.

They'd taken an Uber to the fishing supply store last week, thanks to Brendan's suggestion, and gotten most of what they needed to achieve the nautical theme, then ordered more accoutrements for cheap online. And to their utter astonishment, Abe's sons had shown up last week to drop off some handcrafted bar stools and chairs as a thank-you for walking their father to the museum every morning. Piper told them it wasn't necessary, but they'd refused to take no for an answer, thank God, because they had actual furniture now!

Piper and Hannah were applying slow strokes of lacquer to

the antique bar when a boom of thunder outside made them both jump.

"Whoa," Hannah said, using the back of her wrist to wipe her forehead. "That sounded like cannon fire."

"Yeah." Piper tucked a stray piece of hair into her ponytail and crossed the bar to look out the window. A shudder went down her spine when she saw the Red Buoy closing early. Same with the bait shop two doors down. Was there going to be a really bad storm or something?

Brendan.

No, Westport was far enough from the Bering Sea that he wouldn't get hit with the same storm, right? She had no earthly idea. She was from Southern freaking California, where the sun shined and, other than fog, weather was just a vague entity people in other states had to worry about.

He'd be okay.

Piper pressed a hand to the center of her chest to find her heart racing. "Hey, can you call the record store and ask if they're closing early?"

Over the last two weeks, Hannah had become a regular fixture at the shop. Once she'd revealed her expertise in all things music related, they'd asked her to help give the place an update. While it had cut into Hannah's time working on the bar, Piper hadn't been able to deny her sister this most epic opportunity to flaunt her music snobbery. Hannah was now an unofficial employee of Disc N Dat and had even made some local friends who went and drank coffee together after hours.

"Yeah, sure," Hannah said, whipping her cell out of her back pocket. "I'll text Shauna."

"'Kay."

Piper took a deep breath, but the pressure in her chest wouldn't abate. Brendan was supposed to return the day after tomorrow, and she'd been mentally coaching herself to keep things between them strings-free. But with a storm darkening the sky, she couldn't seem to think straight, much less remember why her relationship with Brendan had to remain casual. She needed to, though, right? No Name was almost finished, and they were super close to nailing down a grand reopening date, at which time they would call Daniel and invite him. Providing this plan to impress Daniel worked, they could be in the homestretch. LA bound. She couldn't afford to get caught up with the boat captain, even if she missed him. Even if she looked for him around every street corner in Westport, just in case he'd gotten home earlier.

"I'm going to run over to the Red Buoy and see if they know what's going on."

Hannah saluted Piper on her way out the door. As soon as she stepped out onto the street, the wind knocked her sideways two steps, her hair blowing free of its ponytail and whipping around her face in a cloud, obscuring her vision. Quickly, she gathered the mane in a fist and looked up at the sky, finding big gray billowing clouds staring back at her. Her stomach dropped, and a wave of fear rolled through her belly.

This seemed like a big deal.

Unable to swallow, she jogged across the street, catching the girl who worked the register on her way out, her head buried in the hood of a rain slicker.

"Hey, um . . . is there going to be a pretty bad storm . . . or something?" Piper asked, clearly the most California girl who ever California'd.

The girl laughed like Piper was joking, sobered when she realized she wasn't. "We've got a typhoon closing in."

What the hell was a typhoon? She resisted the urge to get her phone out and google it. "Oh, but it's, like, contained to the Washington coast, right? Or is it bigger?"

"No, it's coming toward us from Alaska, actually. That's how we know it's going to be a bad motherfucker, excuse my language."

"Alaska," Piper croaked, her fingers turning numb. "Okay, thanks."

The girl scurried off, climbing into a waiting truck right as the first raindrops started to fall. Piper barely remembered walking back across the street and taking shelter in the door- way of No Name. She got her phone out and searched "ty- phoon" with trembling fingers.

The first two words that came up were "tropical cyclone."

Then, "a rotating, organized system of clouds and thunder- storms that originates over tropical or subtropical waters."

"Oh my God."

She had to breathe in and out slowly so she wouldn't throw up.

Brendan was very good at his job. Smart. The most capable, confident man she'd ever met. There was no way something could happen to him. Or Fox and Deke and Sanders. They were big, strong, God-fearing fishermen. There was no way, right?

Henry's laughing face sprung to her mind. Right on its heels, Mick's voice filtered through her thoughts. *And that Ber- ing Sea water is so damn frigid, there's only a minute's window before it sucks the breath right out of a man's lungs.*

Not Brendan. It wouldn't happen to Brendan.

Getting her legs to carry her into No Name required effort,

but she made it, leaning back weakly against the wall. It took her a moment to realize Hannah was throwing on a sweat-shirt. "Hey, Shauna asked if I could pop down really fast and help close up the shop. I should be back in ten minutes." She stopped short when she saw Piper's face. "Are you okay?"

"It's a typhoon. Coming in from Alaska."

Hannah laughed as she threw her messenger bag across her chest. "You sound like a meteorologist. What even is a typhoon?"

"A tropical cyclone," Piper said robotically. "A rotating, or-ganized system of clouds and thunderstorms that originates over tropical or subtropical waters."

"Oh shit." Understanding dawned in Hannah's eyes. "Ohhh. Shit."

"He's going to be fine. They're going to be fine."

"Of course they will." Hannah hesitated, then started to take off her bag. "I'm going to stay here with you—"

"No. Go go go." Her laugh was high-pitched. "I think I can handle ten minutes."

Her sister was dubious. "Are you sure?"

"Totally."

Neither one of them had any idea how bad a storm could get in ten minutes.

Rain lashed the window so hard, Piper moved to the center of the bar for her own safety. The wind sounded like it was inside with her. With a growing sense of dread, she watched more and more people run for cover in the street, eventually clearing it completely. Thunder rocked the ground, followed closely by jagged twists of lightning in the sky.

Piper fumbled her phone in her hands, finding Hannah in

her favorites and dialing. "Hey," she said as soon as her sister picked up. "I think you should stay where you are, okay?"

"Shauna says the same. How'd it pick up so fast?"

"I don't know." She closed her eyes. Brendan had been in this same storm. Fast. Furious. "I'm fine here. Just stay in a safe place and don't move until it lightens up. All right, Hanns?"

"Okay."

Piper hung up and paced a moment, her stride hitching when the electricity went out.

She stood there in near darkness and acted on one of the most foolish instincts in her life—and Jesus *Christ*, that was saying something. But she couldn't stand there and think and worry and speculate. She had to move . . . and she wanted to be near Brendan the only way she could. So she locked the door of No Name behind her and started running in the direction of his house. It was only a three-minute drive. She'd be there in five if she sprinted. And then she'd be safe. And maybe being close to him would keep *him* safe, too, which was a ridiculous notion, but she clung to it hard and pounded the pavement.

Thunder boomed at her back, propelling her on, her sneakers sodden after only two blocks thanks to the rain coming down in torrents now. She turned two corners and ran down a narrow street that seemed semi-familiar? On the night of their date, she'd been too preoccupied to notice any of the street names. But then, there it was. Brendan's truck, parked in front of his house, looking as sturdy and dependable as its owner.

Relief swamped her, and she kicked into a fast sprint, the teeth of his house key biting into her palm. She ran up the path and unlocked the door with pale fingers, her teeth chattering, and fell over the threshold in a heap, kicking the door closed behind her. And then the storm was nothing more than muffled rumblings, her own harsh pants drowning it out.

"Hello?" Piper sat up and called out, because it seemed like the thing to do. Maybe he'd gotten back early and just hadn't come to see her yet. "Brendan?"

There was no answer.

She used the hem of her shirt to dry the rain from her face and stood, moving through the still, warm house while wind whipped against the windowpanes, rattling them. Was this a stalker move? That worry had her chewing her lip, but he'd given her a key, right? Plus, there was something so inviting about the house, almost as if it had been expecting her. His scent lingered in the air of the living room, saltwater and man.

Piper kicked off her shoes and walked barefoot to the kitchen and turned on his coffee machine, desperate to get rid of the chill. When a mug had been prepared, she opened the refrigerator to take out the milk—and an unopened bottle of champagne rolled toward her in the crisper drawer. Her half-drunk one was still wedged in the door, but . . . he'd bought two? Just in case she stopped over while he was gone?

Her throat ached as she carried the mug of coffee up the stairs, trying not to acknowledge how natural it felt to set her coffee on the sink in his bathroom and strip off her soaked clothes, hanging them over the towel rack. She brought the coffee into the shower and drank it while the water stole the chill from her bones. She lathered herself in his body wash, and his scent carried up to her on the wafting steam, making her nipples stiffen. Making her close her eyes, press her forehead to the tile wall, and ask God, very politely, to bring the stubborn man home safely.

Wrapped in a towel minutes later, she walked into Brendan's bedroom, turned on a lamp on his bedside table, and sighed. So practical. Navy blue and beiges everywhere, no-nonsense white walls, creaky floorboards that reminded her of the decks of ships she'd seen in the harbor. A window directly in front of his bed faced the harbor. The ocean beyond. The love of his life. As if he needed to see it first thing in the morning.

She sent a text to Hannah to make sure her sister was all right, then slumped sideways in the center of the bed, Brendan's pillow hugged to her chest, praying that when she woke up everything would be fine. That he'd walk through the door.

God must have been busy answering someone else's prayers.

Brendan tuned out the endless chatter coming in through the radio from the coast guard, his single-minded focus where it needed to be. Pulling pots. This wasn't their first typhoon, and it wouldn't be the last. They were par for the course this time of year in the Bering Sea and the neighboring Pacific. This job was dangerous for a reason, and they had no choice but to ride it out, finish retrieving this string, and make it back to Dutch. So he trained his eyes on the water ahead, searching for out-of-the-ordinary swells while keeping tabs on the busy deck below.

His crew moved like a well-oiled machine, although after a week of hauling pots, they were showing signs of fatigue. The next buoy appeared alongside the ship, and in a practiced movement, Sanders threw out his hook, dragging in the line and attaching it to the winch. Deke joined him on the other side to engage the hydraulic system, raising the pot. An exultant cheer went up from the men on the deck, though it was muffled by the storm raging around the boat, the burr of the engine below.

Half-full. If this pot didn't put them at their quota, it would bring them close, providing the crabs were male and they wouldn't be required to throw the lot of them back. It was against regulation to take females from the sea, as they kept the population growing.

He waited for Fox to signal a number through the window of the wheelhouse.

Seventy.

Brendan made a note of the number in his log, his mouth moving as he did the math. Their quota issued by the wildlife commission was eighty thousand pounds of crab for the season. They were at 99 percent with five pots left to collect. But with the storm howling outside and the men growing weary, it wasn't worth continuing. Especially not if he could beat the Russians to market and get a stronger price for what they'd caught.

He signaled Fox to wrap up the operation, secure the gear on deck, and get everyone below. They were heading back to Dutch early. And the fucking relief that gripped him around the throat was so much stronger than usual, he had to take several bracing breaths, his fingers flexing around the wheel as he waited for a break in the swells to start executing the turn.

Had this storm made landfall yet back home?

Where was she?

Would she be waiting for him?

Brendan braced his body against the side of the wheelhouse as the *Della Ray* carried over a three-story swell and slapped back down into a black pit of churning seawater. Goddamn this storm. It wasn't any fiercer than the ones they'd worked through in the past, but this time . . . the boat didn't seem quite as substantial under his feet. Was the wheel vibrating with too much force in his hands?

His life felt too easily snatched away.

These were worries he hadn't acknowledged since being a greenhorn, and it was because he'd never wanted to get home so badly. Not once in his fucking life.

A crew crabbing not too far from them had lost a member yesterday when his foot had gotten tangled in a rope, dragging him straight down to the bottom of the drink. Another boat had gone missing entirely, seven men on board. A bad season. More loss than usual. So easily, it could have been one of his crew. Could have been him.

Whitewater, high and downward-sloping, broke out of the corner of Brendan's eye, and he grabbed the radio, shouting down to the deck to brace for impact. *Rogue wave.* And for once, Brendan resented the wild rush he got from the danger. From taking on nature and winning. At that moment, it was just the thing keeping him from Piper.

The wave hit, and the boat groaned, tilting sideways. For long moments, the violent wave rained down on the wheelhouse and obscured his view of the deck. And with his world on its side, all he could hear was Piper's voice telling him to be careful.

The coast guard shouted through the radio, interspersed with static, and he prayed.

He prayed like he never had before.

Just let me go home and see her.

But the Bering Sea chose that moment to remind him exactly who was in control.

Chapter Eighteen

$\mathcal{P}$iper woke up to her phone ringing.

She blinked at the device, then at her surroundings. White walls, navy bedspread, beige chair angled in the corner by a lamp. No storm sounds. Was it over?

The world was almost eerily quiet around her, save the jangling notes of her ringtone, but she ignored the winding sensation in her stomach. There was a glow on the horizon that told her it was very early in the morning. Everything had to be fine now, right?

Taking one final inhale of Brendan's pillow, she answered her sister's call. "Hey, Hanns. Are you all right?"

"Yeah, I'm fine. I just got back to the building. Where are you?"

Piper's cheeks fused with heat. "Brendan's," she said sheepishly.

"Oh." There was a long pause. "Piper . . ."

Suddenly alert, she sat up, shoving the fall of hair out of her face. "What?"

"I don't know any of the details, okay? But I ran into one of the crew members' wives on the way back. Sanders? All she said was . . . there's been an accident."

Her lungs filled with ice. "What?" She pressed a hand between her breasts, pushing down, trying to slow the rollicking pace of her heart. "What kind of accident?"

"She didn't say. But she was upset. She was leaving for the hospital."

"Which . . . ? What?" Piper scrambled off the bed, naked, the towel having loosened overnight. "Did she say anything about Brendan?"

"Just that he's at the hospital."

"*What?*"

"I'm sure he's fine, Piper. Like . . . he's built like a semitruck."

"Yeah, but he's up against a body of fucking water and a cyclone. A *cyclone!*" She was screeching now, off the bed and turning in circles, trying to figure out what to do. Where to start. "Okay, okay, I'm not his girlfriend. I can't just go to the hospital, can I?"

"Pipes, I'd like to see someone try and stop you."

She was already nodding. As usual, her little sister was right. If she stayed there and waited for news, she would go absolutely insane. "Did she say which hospital?"

"Grays Harbor Community. I already mapped it and it's half an hour away. They were brought to a hospital in Alaska first, then flown back here."

Piper yanked open a middle drawer in Brendan's dresser and grabbed the first shirt she could find, then ran for the bathroom. "In a helicopter? Oh my God, this is bad." She met her own wild eyes in the mirror over the sink. "I have to go. I'll call you in a while."

"Wait! How are you going to get there?"

"I'm stealing Brendan's truck. There has to be a spare key around here somewhere. He's such a spare-key guy." Her hand shook around the phone. "I'll call you. Bye."

It took her five minutes to put on Brendan's shirt and her hang-dried yoga pants from the day before. She found a spare toothbrush under the sink, used it in record time, and ran down the stairs while finger-combing her hair. After shoving her feet into her still-soaked sneakers, she began her search for the truck's spare key. It wasn't in any of the junk drawers or hanging from any convenient pegs. Where would Brendan put it?

Trying desperately not to dwell on the image of him in a hospital bed somewhere, unconscious and gravely injured, she jogged to the kitchen and climbed up on the counter, running her hand along the top of the cabinets. Jackpot.

She was out the door a few seconds later, sitting in the driver's seat of Brendan's big-ass truck. And dammit, his scent was there, too. So strong that she had to concentrate on punching the hospital name into her map app, cursing autocorrect every time it swapped out right letters for the wrong ones. "Come on," she whined. "Not today, Satan."

Finally, she was on her way, flooring it down the quiet, empty, debris-strewn streets of Westport and onto an unfamiliar highway. There was no one on the roads, and she hated that. It made last night's storm seem even more serious. More likely to cause casualties.

Please, please, please. Not Brendan.

Okay, fine. She wasn't planning on getting serious with the man, but she really, *really* needed him to be alive. If someone that vital and enduring and stubborn could be wiped off the face of the earth, what hope did the rest of them have?

She used her shoulder to wipe away the moisture dripping down her cheeks.

Not getting serious about Brendan.

Right.

It took her twenty-five minutes to reach the hospital, and it was as quiet as the roads. There were a couple of cars parked outside and a sleepy administrator manning the front desk. "Sanders. Taggart," she blurted.

The woman didn't look up from her computer screen as she directed Piper to the fourth floor, nodding toward the elevator bank across the lobby. Upon entering the elevator, her fingers paused over the button.

The fourth floor was the ICU.

No. No. No.

After pressing the button, she closed her eyes and breathed, in and out, in and out, all but throwing herself through the doors when they opened. More lack of activity greeted her. Shouldn't doctors and nurses be rushing around trying to save Brendan? Her wet sneakers squelched on the linoleum floor of the dim hallway as she made her way to the information desk. There was nobody there. Should she wait or just start checking rooms?

A nurse left one room and ran to another, a clipboard in her hand.

Going to see Brendan? Was something wrong?

Heart in her throat, she crept toward the room where the nurse had gone—

"Piper?"

She whirled at the sound of Brendan's deep voice. And there he was in his signature jeans, beanie, and sweatshirt, the sleeves pushed up to his elbows. Above his head, the hallway light flickered, and briefly, she wondered if that meant he was a ghost. But no. No, there was his scent, the furrow of his dark brow, that baritone. He was there. Alive alive alive. Thank God. His eyes were so green. Had she ever noticed how beautiful a shade they were? They were ringed with dark circles, but they were incredible. "Oh good," she croaked, his image rapidly blurring. "Y-you're okay." She tried to be subtle about swiping the tears from her eyes. "They just said there'd been an accident, so I . . . I just thought I would come check. To be neighborly and all."

"Neighborly."

His raspy voice sent a hot shiver down her spine. "Yes. I even brought you your truck."

Brendan took a step closer, his eyes looking less and less tired by the moment. "You were at my house?"

She nodded, backed up, narrowly missing a supply cart.

His chest rose and fell, and he stepped forward again. "Is that my shirt, honey?"

Honey. Why'd he have to go and call her that? "No, I have one just like it."

"Piper."

"Mmm?"

"Please. Please come here."

Brendan's heart hammered, the tendons in his hands aching from the strain of not reaching for her. She'd come to the hospital. In his clothes. Did she realize tears were spilling down her cheeks and she was shaking, head to toe? No, she didn't. Based on her flirty shoulder shrugs and attempts to wink, she thought she was playing it cool, and it made his chest burn.

This girl. He'd be keeping her. There was no way around it.

There had been a moment last night when he'd thought his luck might have run out, and there'd just been images of her, flashing back to back, and he'd railed at the unfairness of meeting Piper but not being given enough time to be with her. If they weren't at the outset of something real here, his gut was a filthy liar. If he was honest with himself, it had been trying to tell him Piper would be important from the second he saw her in her floppy hat through the window of No Name.

"Piper."

"Mmm?"

"Please. Please come here."

She shook her head, stopped trying to put on a brave smile. "Why? So you can put me in the recharging station? You have the most dangerous job in the *country*, Brendan." Her lower lip wobbled. "I don't want your hugs."

His brow arched. "Recharging station?"

"That's what I call it . . ." Still backing away from him, she flipped her hair back, sniffed. "Never mind."

"When I hug you?" *Fuck*. His heart was turning over and over like a car engine. "My hugs are your recharging station?"

"Stop assigning meaning to my words."

An obstruction formed in his throat, and he had a feeling he'd never be able to swallow it. Not as long as she looked up at him, all beauty and strength and vulnerability and confusion and complications. "I should have called, but I left my phone on the boat and it's been hectic transporting him here on the helicopter. I didn't have time to find another phone, and then I worried you'd be sleeping." He paused. "Can you be mad at me while I kiss you, baby? It's all I've wanted to do for the last two weeks."

"Yeah, okay," she whispered, reversing directions and coming toward him. She jogged the final step and leapt. He made a gruff sound, wrapping his arms around her as tight as possible, and lifted her off the ground when her trembles increased.

"No, honey. No shaking." He planted kisses in hair that smelled suspiciously like his shampoo. "I'm fine. I'm right here."

Her face pressed into the crook of his neck. "What happened?"

"Sanders has a concussion. Bad one. A wave sent him sliding down the deck, and he clocked himself on one of the steel traps. We got back to Dutch and took him to the hospital." He rubbed circles on her back. "I left Fox in charge of bringing the crab to market and flew back with Sanders this morning."

"Is he going to be okay?"

"Yeah. He is."

She nodded, wrapped her arms tighter around his neck. "And the hydraulic system worked well the whole trip? No problems with the oil pressure?"

With an exhaled laugh, he angled his head back to meet her eyes. "Did you do a little googling while I was gone?"

"Maybe a little," she said, burying her face farther into his neck. "Are you sure you want to kiss me with my eyes all red and puffy?"

He fisted her hair gently, tugging until they were nose to nose. "I especially want to kiss you with your eyes all red and puffy."

The moment their mouths collided, Brendan knew he'd made a mistake. He should have waited to kiss her until they were home in his bed, because the uncertainty of the last eleven days reared back and punched him. It did the same to Piper—he could feel it.

She gave a broken moan and opened her sweet mouth for him, her breath coming in short pants almost immediately, just like his. He'd barely slid his tongue between her lips when she gripped his shoulders, drew herself high against his chest, and slung her legs around his waist. And Jesus, he'd already been halfway to hard, but his cock surged against his fly now, swelling like a motherfucker when she settled the warm give of her sex on top of him, the drag of friction making him curse. Making him wish they were anywhere but a hospital hallway, half an hour from his house.

Still, he couldn't keep from kissing her like he'd been dreaming of doing every night since he'd left, roughly, hungrily, using his hold on her hair to guide her left, right, meeting her lips with wide slants of his own, swallowing down her little whimpers like they were his last meal. God. God, she tasted so fucking good. Better than any port after a storm.

Home. He'd made it.

"Piper," he growled, taking two steps and flattening her against the closest wall, his mouth raking down her delicious neck, his left hand sliding up to cup her tits. "I can't fuck you here, baby. But that's exactly what I'm going to do if we keep at it like this."

Dazed blue eyes met his, her mouth wet from kissing. "I need you now," she said hoarsely, tugging on the collar of his shirt. "Now, now, Brendan. Please, I can't wait."

He learned something about himself in that moment. If this woman tacked the word "please" onto any request, he would find a way to fulfill it.

Build me a palace, please.

How many floors, baby?

Brendan was already carrying her to the darker end of the hospital corridor before she finished phrasing her demand. Thank Christ the floor was mostly empty, because nothing was going to stop him from getting inside her now. Not when she was scoring his neck with her teeth, her thighs clinging to his hips like ivy. He stopped in front of the farthest door from the mild action in Sanders's room, looked through the glass to make sure there was nobody occupying it, then brought her inside, capturing her mouth in a kiss as he walked them to the far side of the room. She rode her pussy up and down the rigid length of him, mewling into his mouth and pulling at his shirt, and Jesus, he was so turned on, their surroundings were inconsequential in comparison. Still, he wouldn't have someone walking in and seeing Piper in a private moment—that was for his eyes only—so he forced himself to focus. Just long enough to make it right.

He set Piper down on her feet and called on his willpower to tear himself away from her mouth. "Don't move," he said, propping her against the wall—yes, propped. Her legs didn't appear to be working, and hell if he wasn't gratified to know he wasn't so far out of practice that he couldn't get Piper hot and bothered. Thank God.

Wanting to get his hands back on her as soon as possible, he charged to the door and shoved a chair under the handle. On his return to the far side of the room, he yanked the curtain that would block them from view, in case anyone walked past. Then he was in front of Piper, framing her face in his hands, marveling over the feverish urgency in her eyes. For him. Less than twelve hours ago, he'd been sure his luck had run out, but he'd been wrong. It overflowed.

She ran her hands up under his sweatshirt, her fingernails dragging through his chest hair. "Will you take your shirt off for me?" she whispered, scrubbing the ridges of his abdomen with the heels of her hands. "Please? I love your body."

"That's my line," he said unevenly, rocked by her confession. Yeah, he took care of himself and the work kept his body strong and able, but he was a damn long way from perfect. Not like her. But as he'd already discovered, if Piper said please, he would comply, and he did so now, tugging off the sweatshirt in one quick move, finding her mouth as soon as his head was free of the collar.

Lips seeking and wet, their kiss escalated to the point of no return again. They both wrestled with the waistband of her yoga pants, shoving them down past her hips, lower until she could kick them away. And then she was back to climbing him, her lithe thighs skimming up to his waist, his hips punching forward to get his cock up against her softness, pinning her to the wall in the process.

"Noticed we didn't have to get any panties off," he said in between kisses, finding her incredible ass with both hands and kneading her buns almost angrily, because Jesus, this thing drove him fucking crazy. "You drive here in my truck with a bare pussy, Piper?"

She bit his bottom lip, tugged. "Slept in your bed with it, too."

"Christ." A rumble started in his chest, didn't stop until he'd drawn off the borrowed shirt she wore, dropping it to the ground, leaving her completely, blessedly naked. Naked and wrapped around him, all messy morning hair and eyes puffy from crying over him. If his cock wasn't throbbing with pain, he might have gotten down on his knees and worshiped her. All those moments on the boat, begging to see her one more time, had been well founded. If anything, he should have begged harder, because she was a siren, an angel of mercy, and a horny woman all rolled into one. A fucking dream.

And she was trying like hell to get the fly of his jeans open.

Brendan aided her, undoing the top snap, wincing as he lowered the zipper and his cock surged, filling with even more pressure now that it had room to breathe. It crowded into the notch between her legs, and she whimpered, digging her heels into his ass to bring him closer—and he came, grinding against her slippery flesh. One thrust and he'd be home.

That's when the worst possible thing occurred to him.

"Goddammit, Piper." His life flashed before his eyes. "I don't have a condom."

She paused in the act of laying kisses on his neck, her breath hitching. "You're lying. Please tell me you're lying."

"I'm not. I don't carry them." Her head fell back on a sob, and he couldn't stop himself from licking the sexy line of her throat, catching his teeth on her earlobe. "I didn't think I'd see you . . ."

Their heads turned at the same time, another kiss pulling them deep deep deep, and his hips pumped involuntarily, moving in the act of fucking, his shaft sliding up and back through the smooth lips of her sex without breaching her entrance.

"Brendan," she panted.

"Yes, baby."

"I had a physical. Right before I left." They breathed hard against each other's mouths. "I'm all clear and I'm on the shot and I just need you so bad. So bad."

He dropped his face into her neck and growled, reached between them to fist his erection. "I'm all clear, too. Piper, Jesus, are you going to let me fuck you bare?"

"Yes. Yes."

She purred that second "yes," and his balls cinched up painfully, making him grit his teeth, mentally ordering himself not to come too fast. But when he notched his first few inches inside of her wet heat, it became obvious what a challenge that would be. "God, baby. God." He rocked deeper, and she gasped. "You're tighter than sin."

By the time he filled her completely, she was shaking like a fucking leaf, and he had to focus, focus on staying still. Just long enough to organize his lust, garner some semblance of control, or he'd just take her in a frenzy. He just needed a minute. Just a minute.

"Rough," she sobbed, her back arching off the wall. "Want you rough."

There went his minute.

Brendan's first upward thrust drove her up the wall, and she choked on a scream, those beautiful blue eyes glazing over. He clapped a palm over her mouth and pumped again, harder, their eyes meeting over the curve of his hand. There was a coiling in the dead center of his chest, and it must have registered on his face because something flared in her gaze. A ripple of panic in the lake of her lust.

She pushed his hand away slowly, her expression changing. Her eyelids dropped to half-mast, and she looked up at him through the veil of them, biting her lip. "Does this feel good?" Rhythmically, she squeezed him with the walls of her pussy, humming in her throat, killing him slowly. "Are my thighs open wide enough for you, Captain?"

His legs almost gave out, but he held on. Held on, even though part of him was so starved for release that he was tempted to let her make this just about sex. Even though she'd slept in his bed, worried for him enough to show up at the hospital crying. But he would fight this battle with her as many times as it took. Until she realized he wasn't falling for it and there was more here. A hell of a lot more.

Brendan glued his mouth to her ear and started to fuck—hard—her legs jostling around his hips with every vicious thrust. "Came here to be neighborly, Piper? Is there anything neighborly about the way I'm giving you this cock?"

God, he loved the way she whined his name in response.

"I was out in the middle of a fucking storm thinking about you. Thinking about how pretty you look in my garden. Thinking about you waiting for me at the end of my dock, in my harbor. Standing there in the sunset so I can touch you before I even touch land." He opened his lips on the pulse at her neck, razing the spot with his teeth, his hips moving in hard punches. "I thought about your mouth and your eyes and your legs and your pussy. I never stopped. Now you knock that phony shit off, baby, and tell me you missed me."

She inhaled hard, her fingers curling on his shoulders. "I missed you."

A balm spread over his heart, even as his need, his urgency, wrenched higher, hotter. "You can wrap me as tight as you want around that little finger, but I won't play games about what this is. Get me, Piper?"

Their eyes locked just before their mouths did. They knew the battle of wills was far from over, but their hunger was going to eclipse it for now. He took hold of her ass and hefted her higher against the wall, jerking her knees up and propping them on his hips. He angled himself deep, inward and up, so he could hit that spot inside of her—and he went at her hard. Her throaty whimpers told him to stay right there, keep delivering, and he did. He put a lock on the hot seed inside of him dying to get loose and focused on the way her face changed every time he increased his pace. It went from optimistic to astonished to desperate.

"Oh my God, Brendan, don't s-stop." Her eyes lost focus, her nails digging into the skin of his shoulders. "Harder. Harder. You're going to . . . you're going to make me . . ."

"Every time, Piper." Out on the water, he'd replayed Piper having an orgasm while he licked her clit on his kitchen table about a thousand times, but feeling it happen around his cock flipped some primal switch inside of him, and he let loose, pressing their foreheads together and drilling into her sweet, snug channel that was already starting to convulse. "Come on, baby. Let's have it. Show me what I do to that high-maintenance pussy."

Her mouth formed an O, and she tightened up, her hands slapping at his shoulders—and then she crashed, her flesh rippling around him. She writhed between him and the wall, fighting the pleasure and requiring it at the same time, her eyes wide and seeing nothing. "Brendan. Jesus Christ. Jesus Christ. *Brendan.*"

Hearing his name on her lips pushed him past his breaking point, and the seal ripped off his resistance. The bottom of his spine twisted, molten lust impacting him low, hard, more urgently than he'd ever felt anything. Piper's legs went limp right as he came, but she held on to him tight as he bucked. Lifting her feet off the floor until the last of the unbelievable pressure left him. And he collapsed against her.

"*Holy . . .*" she breathed into his neck. "Holy shit."

His heart pounded in his jugular. "Couldn't agree more."

She puffed a dazed laugh.

He kissed her temple, pulled back to search her eyes. "Don't tense up on me, Piper."

"I'm not sure I'll ever be tense again," she whispered, her lids falling.

With a chest full of pride, Brendan kissed her forehead, cheeks, mouth, then knelt down and kissed her belly, picking up her borrowed shirt before straightening. He dropped it over her head, helping her put both arms through the holes, and zipped himself back into his jeans. With Piper still leaning against the wall in a stupor that he definitely didn't mind, he found a box of tissues, plucked out a handful, and cleaned his spend off the insides of her thighs.

That last part woke her up. "I can do that," she said, reaching for the tissue box.

He caught her wrist. "I like doing it."

"Brendan . . ." Her swallow was audible. "Just because I missed you . . ."

There it was. "Yeah?"

"Well . . ." She stooped down and collected her pants, dragging them up her legs with trembling hands. "I—I'm worried I'm leading you on—"

"Jesus." He laughed without humor, took a moment to pull his sweatshirt over his head, and ignored the pinch in his chest. "I can only imagine what kind of idiots you've dated, Piper. But I'm not one of them. I'm a grown-ass man, and I know where we stand. I know you're going to make me work for you, and I'm not scared of it."

Her eyes went momentarily dreamy, but she snapped out of it fast. "Work for me? There's nothing to work for!"

"What the hell does that mean?" he barked.

"It means . . ." She wrung her hands. "I'm . . . I'm not available to be your girlfriend."

Brendan sighed. Was he annoyed? Yes. Did he want to be anywhere else in the world? No. And that was fucking confusing, but apparently it was what he enjoyed now. Being confused and charmed and pulled apart over this woman. "What do you want to call this, Piper? Let's compromise."

"Friends with benefits?"

"No."

"Why?"

He reached out, cupped her pussy roughly through the Lycra of her yoga pants, teasing the seam with his middle finger. "This is a hell of a lot more than a benefit."

Piper swayed.

He removed his hand quickly and caught her, gathering her up against his chest. "How about we call ourselves 'more than friends'?"

"That's too broad. It could mean anything." She rubbed absent circles on his chest while he counted her eyelashes. "Married people are more than friends."

It was too soon to examine why he liked the word "married" on her lips so much, right? "We'll go with 'more than friends,'" he rumbled, kissing her before she could protest. It took her a few seconds to participate, but their mouths quickly turned breathless. He backed her against the wall once more, Piper's palm molding to the front of his jeans where his cock rose again, ready, desperate for more of her—

"Brendan Taggart, please make your way to the fourth-floor information desk," came a tired voice over the PA system, repeating itself twice while they remained frozen mid-kiss.

"Fuck," he ground out, breathing through his nose and willing his hard-on to subside. There was no way it was happening, though, so he adjusted himself to be as inconspicuous as possible, then took Piper's hand and tugged her toward the door. "Come with me."

"Oh." He looked back over his shoulder to find Piper patting her haphazard hair in a way he found adorable. "Um. Okay."

Brendan moved the chair he'd braced under the door handle, and they walked side by side into the dim hospital hallway. He looked down at her, trying to puzzle together how she felt about the label "more than friends." This conversation, this war, was far from over, but he couldn't help but feel like he'd won a battle, just getting her to hold his hand as if it was the natural thing to do. *You're not getting rid of me, Piper.*

"Brendan?"

The sound of his father-in-law's voice caused a hitch in his stride. Brendan tore his attention off of Piper to find Mick loitering by the information desk. "Mick."

His father-in-law went still, dismay marring his features as he split a look between Brendan and Piper. Their joined hands. Piper's messy hair. And for a few seconds, Brendan couldn't stave off the guilt. Not completely. But only because he should have gone to Mick, told the man about his feelings for Piper. Blindsiding him like this was the last thing Brendan wanted to do. He'd never seen Brendan with anyone but his daughter, and the shock had to bite.

Distracted by his regrets, he didn't react quickly enough to Piper pulling her hand away.

He tried to get it back, but it was too late.

"Hey, Mick," she said quietly, wetting her lips.

Mick didn't respond. In fact, he blatantly ignored Piper, and Brendan felt a surge of anger. This was his fault, though. He'd missed a crucial step, and now here they were, in this awkward situation that could have been avoided. And dammit, the last thing he needed was to hand Piper another reason to keep distance between them.

"Oh good," said a smiling nurse, stepping behind the desk. "You found him."

"Just came to check on Sanders," Mick mumbled, jerking his thumb at nowhere in particular.

"Oh, um. I'm going to . . ." Piper started. "I, um . . . You can get a ride back with Mick, right?" She wouldn't look at him, was already edging toward the elevators. "Hannah is probably wondering where I am. I should head home."

Brendan followed Piper, catching her by the elbow before she could hit the call button. "Stay. We'll drive home together."

"Stop." She batted his chest playfully, falling back on flirting. "You totally have to stay here and make sure Sanders is okay. I'll just see you later!"

"Piper."

"Brendan," she echoed, mimicking his serious face while her finger desperately punched the elevator button. "It's fine, okay?" When he still hesitated to let go of her elbow, she lost her bravado and begged him with her eyes. "Please."

With a stiff nod, he watched her disappear behind the doors of the elevator, already missing the weight of her hand inside his. He wanted to go after her, at least kiss her before she drove home, but had a feeling she needed space. He just hoped the headway they'd made this morning on the journey to "more than friends" hadn't been erased in a matter of minutes.

Duty and respect pulled at him, so while he vowed to make things right with Piper later, he turned on a heel and went to face his father-in-law.

Mick put up a hand as Brendan reached him. "You don't have to explain, Brendan. I know you're a young man with oats to sow." He rubbed at the back of his neck. "Not a lot of fellas who'd be able to ignore a girl like that."

"No. She's . . . impossible to ignore." He'd made it all of one day, hadn't he? Less? Before she'd started feeling . . . inevitable. Brendan couldn't help glancing back at the elevator. When he turned around, Mick was fixated on his ring finger. The lack of hardware surrounding it, rather. The lines around Mick's eyes turned stark white and a sheen filled them.

Brendan hated the feeling of disloyalty that burrowed under

his skin. Logically, he knew there was nothing disloyal about him pursuing Piper. Not at all. But this man who'd taken Brendan under his wing, made him the captain of his boat, and been a damn good friend and father figure . . . shit, disappointing him burned. It was right there on the tip of his tongue to explain that he was serious about Piper, not sowing oats, but Mick seeing he'd finally taken off his wedding ring was enough for one day. He didn't need to hit the man over the head. Not when he probably saw the lack of Brendan's ring as one more piece of his daughter being chipped away.

He clapped Mick on the shoulder. "Let's go check on Sanders, all right?"

Mick, obviously grateful for the change of subject, nodded, and they walked side by side to the wing where Sanders was healing.

Chapter Nineteen

$\mathcal{P}$iper dragged herself up the steps to the apartment and unlocked the door. Out of concern for her growling stomach, she'd stopped for coffee and breakfast on the ride home, making it close to noon. She'd already texted Hannah to let her know Brendan and the crew were fine, then promptly ignored all the follow-up questions about how things went at the hospital. Because . . . how *did* things go at the hospital?

Still not in possession of concrete answers, she trudged into the apartment carrying a cinnamon dolce latte for Hannah, half expecting her sister to be working at the record shop, but Hannah was lying on the top bunk, obligatory headphones over her ears, wailing about a simple twist of fate.

Piper knocked on the frame of the bunk bed, and Hannah yelped, shooting up into a sitting position and knocking the headphones onto the cradle of her neck. Her startled expression turned quickly to delight. "Oooh. For me?"

Piper handed her sister the cup. "Hmm."

Hannah raised an eyebrow while taking a sip. "You look . . . different today."

"I took a shower last night and slept with wet hair," Piper murmured absently, sitting down on the bottom bunk. She stared at the far wall of the apartment—which was actually quite *near*—and tried to process the last few hours.

Her sister hopped down from the top bunk. "Piper." She snuggled close, nudging Piper in the ribs with an elbow. "You're too quiet. Talk to me."

Piper pressed her lips together and said nothing.

"Oh, come on."

Silence.

"Start small. Something innocuous. How was the drive?"

"I don't remember." Unable to keep a certain piece of news to herself any longer, though she would probably regret sharing at a later date, Piper reached over and clutched Hannah's knee. "Hannah, he . . . he gave me a vaginal orgasm."

Her sister almost dropped her coffee. "What? Like . . . you climaxed just from penetration?"

"Yes," Piper whispered, fanning her face. "It was like, I thought . . . maybe? And then . . . no way. But then, yes. Yes, yes, fucking *yes*. Against a wall. *A wall*, Hanns." She closed her eyes and added, "It was the most wonderful sex of my life. And he didn't even break a sweat."

"Oh, Piper." Hannah shook her head. "You are so fucked."

"No." Piper threw her shoulders back. "No, I escaped without too much damage. He got me to admit we're more than friends, but there was minimal cuddling and we have no plans to see each other again. I'll just avoid him for a while."

Hannah lunged to her feet and turned on Piper. "What are you scared of?"

Piper snorted. "I'm not scared."

And she wasn't. Was she? This constant weight in her belly was totally normal. As was the certainty that Brendan would eventually realize there were a thousand other girls just like Piper Bellinger; she was definitely not the kind of girl for whom a man kept a ring on for seven years, that's for sure!

She was just an exotic bird in this small, uneventful town, and he'd realize that eventually.

Or he wouldn't.

That was even *more* terrifying.

What if his feelings for her were actually genuine? She couldn't fight her own much longer. They were getting worse by the day. She'd driven like a bat out of hell to the hospital, already half in mourning. Sick with it. And the *joy* when he'd arrived, hale and hearty. My God, she was almost exhausted thinking about the gymnastics her heart had done.

If these feelings got deeper and deeper on both sides . . . then what?

She stayed in Westport?

"Ha!"

Hannah uncapped her coffee and took a long swig, swallowing. "You realize you're having a conversation inside your own head, right? I can't hear it."

"I'm not staying here," Piper breathed, her heart feathering in her throat. "He can't make me." She yanked her phone out of her pocket, tapping until she arrived at Instagram, scanning her colorful feed. These pictures and the effortless lifestyle they represented seemed almost foreign now—trite—and that was scary. Did it mean she was actually considering a *new* path? One she didn't document for the sake of adoration, albeit phony? Her daily life in Westport was fulfilling in a way she never expected, but she was still an outsider here. In LA, her fit was seamless, at least outwardly. She was good at being Piper Bellinger, socialite. Whether Piper could be a fixture in Westport remained to be seen.

She held up her phone, facing the stream of pictures toward Hannah. "For better or worse, this girl is who I am, right? I'm getting so far away from this Piper. So fast."

"Okay," Hannah said slowly. "Does Brendan make you feel like you need to change?"

Piper thought about it. "No. He even called my pussy high maintenance, like in a good way. I think he *likes* me like this. It's horrible."

"Yeah, it sounds like the worst. What is the real problem, Piper?"

Piper exploded. "Hannah, I was scared shitless last night!"

Her sister nodded, sobering. "I know."

"And he's not even my boyfriend."

"Yet."

"Rude." She brandished her phone. "This girl is not . . . strong enough. To worry like this all the time. To love someone and lose them, like Mom and Opal lost Henry. I'm not cut from that cloth, Hannah. I go to fucking parties and push bathing suit brands. I don't know who I *am* in Westport."

Hannah closed the distance between them, wrapping her arms around Piper. "Wow. A vaginal orgasm and a psychological breakthrough in the same day. You must be tapped."

"I am. I'm exhausted." She returned Hannah's hug, dropping her forehead unceremoniously into her sister's neck. She thought of Mick's face when he saw her holding Brendan's hand and cringed inwardly. Honestly, she wasn't even ready to tell Hannah about that moment. How low she'd felt. Not necessarily a home-wrecker, but . . . an interloper. An outsider. *Who does this LA party girl think she is, coming in here and trying to fill the shoes of a born-and-bred fisherman's wife?*

Piper's phone dinged.

Who was that?

It couldn't be Brendan. He'd left his phone on the boat. And none of her friends had reached out with so much as a hello since she'd left the Bel-Air zip code.

She held up the screen, and a smile bloomed across her face. "Oh, this is excellent news."

Hannah dropped her arms away from Piper's neck. "What is it?"

"It's Friday night and our grandmother is finally ready to party."

Never one to take partying lightly, Piper wasted no time.

She showered, coiffed until her hair looked presentable, carefully applied her makeup, and ventured purposefully toward the harbor with a garment bag containing a selection of dresses, including one for herself. Opal was petite, and with a little last-minute stitching, Piper would have her looking like a boss bitch in no time.

The second Opal opened the door—wearing a seriously cute lavender shortie robe—Piper could tell she was having second thoughts. "Nope." Piper cut her off with a kiss, right on the mouth. "Everyone gets pre-party jitters, Opal. You hear me? Everyone. But we don't let that stop us, do we? No. We persevere. And we get drunk until we feel nothing."

Visibly bolstered, Opal nodded, then went straight to shaking her head. "I'm a lightweight. I've been drinking nothing but coffee since the nineties."

"Sad. But that's why we use the Bellinger method. One glass of water between each alcoholic drink. Then a piece of toast and two Advil before bedtime. Soaks it right up. You'll be able to run a marathon tomorrow morning."

"I can't run one now."

"I know. That's how well it works."

Opal guffawed. "Since you started visiting me, Piper, I've laughed more than I have in decades. Hannah wasn't able to make it?"

"No, she had a shift at the record shop. But she sends a kiss."

Her grandmother nodded and transferred her attention to the garment bag, missing the unexpected moisture that danced in Piper's eyes. "Well, darling. Let's see what you got."

It only took three hours to transform Opal from grieving semi-hermit to a lady about town. After Piper added some styling mousse to the older woman's hair and did her makeup, Opal chose her dress.

Clearly, she had taste, because she went straight for the puff-sleeved Versace.

"The student has become the master, Grandma."

Opal started a little at the title, and Piper held her breath, too. It had slipped out unplanned, but felt oddly natural. Finally, Opal surged forward and wrapped Piper in a hug, holding tight a few moments before stepping back to study her. "Thank you."

Piper could only nod, thanks to the log jammed in her throat, watching Opal as she swept off to the bedroom to change. Surprised to find her fingers trembling, Piper sloughed off the leggings and sweater she'd worn for the trip over, zipping herself into a green-and-black zebra-striped minidress from Balmain. Muscle memory kicked in, and she lifted her phone to take a selfie, noticing with a start that she had a text from Brendan.

Want to see you tonight.

Wave after wave of flutters coursed through her midsection. God, she loved how he got right to the point. No games. No beating around the bush. Just *This is what I want, baby. Now it's your turn.*

Did she want to see Brendan? Yes. Undeniably yes. More than that, she wanted to be seen by him looking like this. Wanted to watch male appreciation draw his features tight and know with absolute conviction he was thinking about having sex with her. And it would be so much easier to play it cool in her battle armor, surrounded by witnesses in a bar. Westport's nightlife might not be *exactly* what Piper was used to, but it was closer to her environment than a bar under construction or a hospital with bad lighting.

She needed to feel like herself. Needed a reminder of her old life.

The life she was going back to. Sooner rather than later.

Too often lately she'd been thrown off-kilter by her feelings. Or the situation she found herself in, over a thousand miles from home. Friendless, a fish out of water.

Brendan, since she'd met him, had made it impossible for her to keep up a pretense. She'd never been able to be anything but honest with him. Scarily honest. But he wasn't standing in front of her now, brimming with all that intensity, was he? And LA Piper was rattling her hinges, demanding to be appeased. *That* Piper wouldn't text back that she wanted to see him tonight, too. Uh-uh. She'd leave a bread crumb and dance off in a flash of strobe lights.

Heading out for the night. Maybe catch you later in Blow the Man Down. xo

Three little dots popped up, letting her know Brendan was writing back.

Then they went away.

She pressed a hand to her stomach to counteract a kick of excitement.

Opal walked out of the bathroom looking like a certified snack.

"Well?"

"Well?" Piper gave a low whistle. "Look out, Westport. There's a stone-cold fox on the loose."

Piper's one and only experience in Blow the Man Down had been less than stellar and walking through the door again was nerve-racking. But tonight wasn't just about reminding herself of old Piper; it was about bringing this woman she'd really come to like out of her shell.

Opal had her arm linked through Piper's as they entered the noisy bar. Fishermen occupied the long row of stools near the entrance, toasting another week completed out on the water. And the survival of last night's storm seemed to give the atmosphere an added buoyancy. Bartenders dropped pints in front of mostly older men, their friends and wives. No one was smoking, but the scent of cigarettes drifted in from outside and clung to clothes. Neil Young's voice wove through the conversations and laughter.

Opal balked as soon as they stepped over the threshold, but Piper patted her arm, guiding her through the more boisterous section of the bar, toward the seating area in the back. Last time, she'd only stood at the bar long enough to order that fateful tray of shots, but it had been enough time to get the lay of the land. And she was relieved to see the tables in the rear of Blow the Man Down were occupied by women again tonight. Some of them were Opal's age, others were closer to Piper's, and they were all talking at once.

A couple of the older women nudged each other at Opal's appearance. One by one, the dozen or so ladies started to notice her. For long moments, they stared at her with mouths agape—and then they all ambushed her at once.

"Opal," said a kind-looking woman with a red bob, rising to her feet. "You're out!"

"And looking like hot shit!" inserted another.

Laughter rippled over the tables, and Piper could sense Opal's pleasure. "Well, I have a fancy stylist now," Opal told them, squeezing Piper's arm. "My granddaughter."

Westport was a small town, and it was obvious some of the women already knew the Bellinger sisters had taken up residence, as well as their familial connection to Opal, while others were visibly connecting the dots and marveling. Either way, the group as a whole seemed surprised to see them out together and looking so close.

"Is there . . . room for two more?" Opal asked.

Everyone shuffled at once, dragging chairs over from other tables. Opal's eyes held a suspicious luster when she looked up at Piper and let out a breath. "It's like I never left."

Piper leaned over and kissed her cheek. "Why don't you go sit down. I'll go grab us some drinks. Tequila for you, right?"

"Oh, stop." Opal tapped her arm playfully. "Stoli and Seven with two limes, please."

"Damn," Piper muttered with a smile, as Opal walked off. The older woman claimed a chair and was immediately heaped with well-deserved attention. "I have a feeling you'll be just fine."

Piper bought a round of drinks for her and Opal, taking a seat beside her. After half an hour of easy conversation, the evening appeared to be shaping up as a low-key lady hangout. Until one of the twentysomething girls bought Piper a drink in exchange for a beauty consultation. Really, the drink hadn't been necessary. She was happy to dole out advice based on the girl's skin tone and oval face shape . . . but then another girl slapped down a shot in front of Piper, wanting to know her beauty regimen. Another traded a lemon drop for tips on dressing sexy when it was always "balls-ass cold and raining" in the winter.

And then it all went downhill from there.

"It's all about swagger," Piper shouted over the music an hour later, an eye squinted so she would only see one set of people, instead of two.

Unless there were two sets? When did they get there?

She tried to remember what she'd been saying in the first place. Had all of it been a slurred mess? But no, the girls who'd pushed tables to the side to create a runway down the back of Blow the Man Down were listening to her with rapt focus. *Deliver, Piper.* "You, me, all of us, ladies. We wield the power." She threw out a finger aimed at the bar full of men. "They know it. They know we know it. The secret is to show them we know that they know that we know. Does that make sense?"

A chorus of yeses went up, followed by the clinking of glasses.

"Watch me walk," Piper said, pushing her hair back over her shoulders and strutting along the floorboards, turning on a dime at the end of her makeshift runway. Not her best work, but pretty decent after four, maybe eight drinks. "Look at my face. It's like, I don't have time for *your* shit. I'm busy. I'm living!"

"Is this going to get me laid?" one girl asked.

Piper grabbed the girl's face and stared into her soul. "Yes."

"I believe you."

"Hey, Piper." Another girl stumbled into view. Or was she twins? "Labor Day is coming up. We should have a party and try out the makeup tips."

"Oh my gosh," Piper breathed, the best/worst idea breaking through her delightful drunkenness. "I should throw the party. I own a *bar.*"

"Hey, everyone! Piper is throwing a Labor Day party!"

The cheers were deafening.

"Show us the walk again!"

Piper took a shot someone offered her. "Screw that! Let's dance!"

Chapter Twenty

$\mathcal{B}$rendan leaned against the wall of Blow the Man Down, arms crossed, a quiet smile on his face as he watched Piper weave her magic over everyone in her vicinity.

She was shit-faced—and adorable.

Everyone who spoke to Piper got her undivided attention and walked away like she'd just imparted the secrets of the universe. She forged connections to people, damn near instantaneously, and they loved her. Did she realize she was doing it?

Someone shouted at the bartender to play Beyoncé, and tables were shoved even farther out of the way, transforming the space from Piper's personal runway to a dance floor, and all he could do was stand there and watch her, his pulse thickening—along with another part of his anatomy—at the way she worked her hips, arms loose and careless over her head, eyes dreamy. She was drawing attention from a lot of men at the bar, and frankly, he didn't like it, but Piper was the girl he'd fallen for. Being jealous came with the territory.

Piper went still on the dance floor, a frown marring her forehead, and, as if she'd finally sensed his presence, turned to look directly at him. And when her face transformed with pure joy and she waved enthusiastically, Brendan knew he loved her.

God knew, it had happened fast, but he'd been incapable of putting the brakes on.

Not when she was the destination.

His mouth turned dry, but he managed to wave back.

This wasn't any emotion he'd experienced before. Not like the simple companionship of his marriage. Not like the love/hate bond he had with the ocean. What he felt for Piper turned him into a young man in the throes of his first infatuation, while also calling on the deepest roots of his maturity. In other words, to keep this woman, he'd step up and do whatever it took, but his fucking heart would be racing the whole time.

He could put every ounce of his effort into keeping Piper, and she still might leave. Could dance off into the sunset at a moment's notice and go back to her extravagant life, leaving him reeling. And that terrified him the most.

But Brendan determinedly set aside those dark thoughts. Because she was coming toward him now, all flushed from liquor and dancing, and he simply opened his arms, trusting she'd walk straight into them. His eyes closed automatically when she did, his mouth tracing her hairline, planting kisses. Christ, she fit against him in a way that made him feel protective, ready to act as her shield, while also making him hard, hungry.

"You're here," she murmured happily, going up on her toes to sniff his neck.

"Of course I'm here, baby."

"Sanders is okay? The crew made it back?"

"Sanders is home," he burred against her ear, warmed by

her worry for his men. "The rest of them, too. They reached the harbor just a little while ago."

"I'm so glad." She sent an accusatory look over her shoulder. "These unscrupulous local women made me drunk."

"I can see that." His lips twitched, his hand rubbing circles in the center of her back. "You want to dance some more, or can I bring you home?"

"Where is home?"

"With me."

"Mmmm." She looked up at him through one eye. "I don't have my wits about me, Brendan. You can't use anything I say tonight against me. It's all a wash."

"Okay, I promise."

"Good, because I missed you. Again." She kissed his chin, worked her way around to his ear, whined against it in a way that made his cock stiffen. "This morning with you was the best, best, best sex of my life."

She said it right as the music cut out.

Everyone at the bar heard it.

A couple of men saluted Brendan with their pints, but thankfully drunk Piper was none the wiser about her public confession. And hell, having Piper effectively tell everyone in Westport they were sleeping together—and that so far he'd been great at it—was one way to appease his jealousy.

The music started again, but she didn't seem compelled to do anything but stand there and hug him, which suited him down to the ground. "Here I am, once again, in the *recharg*-ing station!" Piper sang, giggling to herself. "I like it here. It's so warm. You're a big hard teddy bear from the sea. Like tuna from the sea, but with a bear."

Brendan's laugh turned heads. "I like drunk Piper."

"You should. I have zero inhibitions right now." She smelled his neck again, kissed it once, twice. "Or whatever number is less than zero."

He ran a hand down her hair. "All I'm doing to you tonight is putting you in bed."

"Ooh, do I get to sleep in the recharging station?"

His heart was living in his throat. "Yeah, honey. You can sleep in it every night."

She sighed contentedly.

"On my way over, I saw Hannah walking home and stopped off to grab you an overnight bag."

"That was nice of you." In an instant, her expression went from swoony to worried. "But Brendan, what if I'm potpie?"

"What?"

"You took a bite of me, and even if you decide you don't really like me, you're going to be noble and eat the whole thing. You can't do anything halfway. It's all or nothing. If I'm potpie, you have to tell me. You can't just keep eating and eating and . . . I'm drunker than I thought."

Yeah, she might be drunk, but her worry was genuine. Her forlorn tone of voice made that obvious, and it troubled him. Not because there was even a chance it might be valid—she was a woman, not a fucking pie. Her worry bothered him because she didn't feel secure. Yet. And he needed to find a way to fix it.

"Let's go home," he said.

"Okay. Let me just make sure Opal has a ride."

Piper trotted off to confer with a group of woman, hugging each of them multiple times before making her way back to his side. Brendan wrapped an arm around her shoulders and guided her out of the bar. He'd parked his truck near the entrance, and he unlocked it now, boosting Piper into the passenger side and buckling her in. When he climbed into the driver's side, her head was lolling on the seat, and she was studying him. "We're going to talk about what you said. In the morning. When you're clearheaded and you'll remember what I say back."

"That's probably a good idea. I'm feeling very share-y right now."

"I'm tempted to let you share, so I know what I'm up against. But I don't want you telling me things and regretting it tomorrow."

She was silent as he pulled onto the road and took the first right. "You talk about being with me like it's a battle."

"It is, in a way. But I'm grateful I'm the one fighting it."

He could feel her studying his profile. "You're worth fighting for, too. If you got banished to LA for three months, I would pull out all the stops to keep you there." She paused. "Nothing would work, though. It's not real enough for you. You'd hate it."

"'Hate' is a strong word, honey. You would be there."

"Eh." She waved a hand. "There are thousands of me there."

Brendan snorted at her joke. And then he realized she was serious.

"Piper, there is *nobody* like you."

She smiled like she was humoring him.

"*Piper.*"

She looked startled by his tone. "Whoa. What?"

He pulled the car onto the side of the road, slammed on the

brakes, and threw it into park. "Did you hear me?" He reached over to tilt up her chin. "There is nobody like you."

"Why are you getting so worked up?"

"Because I . . ." He raked a hand through his hair. "I thought I was an intuitive man. A smart man. But I keep finding out new ways I'm flying blind when it comes to something so important. You. *You* are important. And I thought you were just scared of commitment. Or didn't think you could belong in Westport. But it's more than that, isn't it? You think I have some kind of passing interest in you? Like it could just change like the wind?"

"Everyone else does!" Her eyes flashed. With pain, with irritation. "Not just guys. My friends, my stepfather. I'm this season's color, in demand today, on the sales rack in Marshalls tomorrow. I'm just . . . momentary."

"Not to me." God, he wanted to shake her, kiss her, shake her some more. "Not to me."

She jerked her chin out of his grip, flounced back against the seat. "Can we just talk about this tomorrow, like you said?"

Brendan slammed the car back into drive. "Oh, we're going to talk about it."

"Good! Maybe I'll put together some talking points."

"Me too, baby."

They drove past No Name, and she made a small sound. Sniffed.

"What?" he asked, softening his tone.

"I was remembering the time you sent Abe to nail the memory foam to the top bunk. You're actually really thoughtful and wonderful, and I don't want to argue with you."

He almost blurted out *I love you*, right then and there, but buttoned it up at the last second. The moment was too volatile to throw that confession into the mix, but he didn't think he'd be able to keep it inside much longer. "I don't want to argue with you either, Piper. All I want to do is bring you home, put you in one of my shirts, and find out if you snore."

She gasped, some of the humor returning to her eyes. "I don't."

"We'll see."

"Do you have toast and Advil?"

"Yes."

They pulled into his driveway a moment later. Brendan got out and rounded the front bumper to Piper's side, smiling when she melted out into his arms. He held her and swayed for a few beats in the darkness, in what he thought might be a silent, mutual apology for shouting at each other on the drive home. And he wanted to do this for the rest of his life. Collect her from a night out with the girls, have her soft and pliant against him, be her man.

"You're not even going to make out with me tonight, are you?" Piper said, her voice muffled by his shoulder. "You probably think you'd be taking advantage of me."

Brendan sighed. "You've got it right."

She pouted up at him. "That's romantic and I hate it."

"How about I promise to make up for it tomorrow?"

"Can we negotiate a kiss good night?"

"I think I can manage that."

Appeased, she let him bring her inside. While he made her toast, she sat perched on his kitchen counter with a glass of water, looking so beautiful, he had to keep glancing over his shoulder, checking to see if she was real. That he hadn't dreamed her up.

"What are you thinking about?" she asked after swallowing a bite.

"That I like you being here." He braced his hands on the counter, dropped his mouth to her bare knees, and kissed them, in turn. "That I liked going into my bedroom today and finding a Piper-sized indent on my comforter." A thought occurred to him. "When did you come over?"

She gulped. Didn't answer.

"Not with that storm going on." His right eye was beginning to tic. "Right?"

Piper set down her toast, laid the back of her hand against her forehead. Wobbled dramatically. "I feel kind of faint, Brendan. I think I'm fading."

With a growl, he drew her off the counter. And with her legs hooked around his waist, he left the kitchen and carried her up the stairs. "I'll add it to my list of talking points for tomorrow."

She groaned, her fingers playing with the ends of his hair. "Tomorrow sounds like it's going to be a super-sexy good time."

"We'll get to that after."

"Before."

"After."

"Before *and* after."

Brendan set Piper down on the end of his bed, rocked by the rightness of having her there. Emotion crammed into his chest, but he turned away before she could see it. "Take off that dress." He opened his drawer, took out one of his favorites—a white, worn-in T-shirt with GRAYS HARBOR written in script in the middle. "Speaking of which, do you even own a pair of jeans—" He turned back around to find Piper sprawled out on his bed in a neon-purple thong. And nothing else. "That can't be comfortable to sleep in," he said hoarsely, already regretting his vow to give her a good-night kiss and nothing more.

She raised her knees. "I guess you have to come over here and take it off."

"Christ." The flesh in his jeans swelled, curving against his zipper, and he blew out an uneven breath. "If the ocean doesn't kill me, you will."

Just like that, her knees dropped back down, her arms coming up to cross over her breasts. And maybe he shouldn't have been shocked when tears rushed into her eyes, but he was. They made his throat constrict.

"God," he said thickly. "That was a stupid thing to say."

"It's okay."

"No, it's not." He lifted her up and pulled the T-shirt down over her head, holding her tight to his chest. "It's not okay. I'm sorry."

"We can add it to the talking points for tomorrow," she said, looking him in the eye long enough to make his heart beat triple time, then tugging him down into the pillows. "Want my kiss," she murmured against his lips, pulling him under with a slow, wet complication of tongues, her smooth, bare legs winding through his, her fingers pulling him closer by the waistband of his jeans until their lower bodies were locked together, soft against hard, man against woman. "Maybe we're a little more than more than friends," she whispered, tucking her head under his chin. "Good night, Brendan."

His eyelids fell like shutters, his arms pulling her closer.

I love you, he mouthed over her head.

He didn't fall asleep for hours.

Chapter Twenty-One

Homey sounds came from somewhere. Drawers opening and thudding softly, bare feet on a floor, the sputtering of a coffee maker. Piper cracked an eye open but didn't move. She couldn't, because she'd lose the sweet spot of warmth and fluffy bedclothes and the scent of Brendan. Best sleep of her life, hands down. She'd woken up at some point during the night having to pee and found herself locked into the recharging station, Brendan's soft breaths against the back of her neck. And she'd decided to hold it.

What did she say last night?

Something about potpies.

She also remembered trying to seduce him and failing. Womp.

Some shouting on the ride home.

No sex.

She'd just have to gauge his mood to find out if she'd said or done anything irredeemably embarrassing. There was a good chance she had, because otherwise he would still be in bed, right? Like, hello. Horny lady. *Right* here.

Piper's bladder screamed at her, and she sat up, grateful the Bellinger Method had worked, and padded to the bathroom. She ignored the gooey, melting sensation in her belly when she found her toothbrush from the morning before waiting beside Brendan's in the medicine cabinet. Where else was he supposed to put it?

With the toothbrush in her mouth, she picked up an unused bottle of cologne and sniffed. But it wasn't him at all, and she couldn't imagine him using it. Other than that, there was only his razor, some shaving cream, and deodorant. Her medicine cabinet at home would probably make him break out in a rash, it was so jam-packed.

She finished brushing her teeth, splashed some water on her face, finger-combed her hair, and headed downstairs . . . and . . . and jackpot.

Brendan was standing in the kitchen in nothing but black boxer briefs.

Piper crowded against the wall so she could observe him without being discovered. He was hunched over the kitchen counter reading a newspaper, and good gravy, the thick, masculine ropes of back muscles were all she wanted for breakfast. How dare he with those thighs? Did he use them to anchor the boat? They were generous and ripped and—

"You want coffee?" he asked without looking up.

"*Aherm?*" Piper blurted loudly, coming the rest of the way down the stairs, very aware that he was in underwear while she wore nothing but his T-shirt and a thong. And then he pushed up from the counter and scratched his happy trail, and yes, she was very aware of that, too. "Um, yes? Coffee, sure. Sure."

He half grinned. "Okay."

She wrinkled her nose at him. "What is this extra cockiness you have going on?"

Brendan poured her a cup of coffee, preparing it exactly how she liked it. "You might have told me last night in the bar that I was the best, best, best sex of your life."

Heat climbed her cheeks. "I said 'best' three times, hmm?"

After handing her the coffee, he leaned back against the counter and crossed his ankles. "You sure did."

She hid her wan smile in a sip of coffee. "I think I might have also become a professional beauty consultant last night. One who gets paid in drinks." More and more memories knitted together. "And, oh God, I volunteered to throw a party on Labor Day at the bar."

"Whoops."

"I can't wait to tell Hannah." She cupped her hands around the mug, enjoying the warmth. Not just from the drink itself, but from Brendan's kitchen. The way he looked at her with affection, not a rush in the world to move or hurry. When had she started liking those things? The silence between them didn't need to be filled, but she was thinking too much, so she did it anyway. "Who would buy you cologne?"

His brow arched. "You mean the one in my cabinet? Birthday gift from Sanders. His wife picked it out. Obviously. He didn't even know what it was until I opened it—and the guys, they ragged on him for months. I probably just keep it because it makes me laugh."

"You're so close with them. Your crew."

"Have to be. Our lives—" He cut himself off, taking an abrupt sip of coffee.

"Are in one another's hands?" When she said it, the memory of her crying in his bed last night came rolling back in on a tide. This was probably it, then. No more smoke screens or hiding or flirting her way to safety with this man. Even if she couldn't recall every single second of last night, she could feel that the layers had been stripped away. By his hands. His words. His presence.

"Anyway, it's not the scent I would pick for you."

Interest lit his expression. "What would you pick?"

"Nothing. You already have the ocean on your skin. And it's not like you to embellish what's already working." Something heated in his eyes at her words. At the proof she'd been cataloguing his finer details? "But if I had to pick a scent . . . something, like, rainy and mossy. To remind me of your garden. How earthy you are. How substantial." Her attention meandered down the line of black hair disappearing into his briefs. "How male."

His chest rose and fell on a shudder. "You're really messing up my plans for the morning, Piper."

"What were your plans?"

"To take you out on the *Della Ray*."

The smile blasted across her face. "*What?* Are you serious?"

"Uh-huh. Being out on the water is good for talking."

"Oh, right." She rocked back on her heels, her initial excitement tempered by the reminder that the reckoning had arrived. "Talking points."

"That's right." He raked her with a blistering look that turned her nipples to tingling peaks. "Now I just want to take you back to bed, though."

Her breathing went shallow. "Can't we do both?"

His regret was obvious when he shook his head. "Next time I fuck you, I want to be sure you're not going to pull away from me afterward."

"And I can't escape on a boat?"

"That might have crossed my mind."

She huffed a laugh. He was really serious about her. And she'd gone home with him last night knowing it. As natural as could be, like she did it all the time. That's how it felt being collected by Brendan and sleeping in his arms. Expected. Inevitable.

Damn him.

There was a chance she might be serious about Brendan, too.

How had this happened?

"Just so we're clear," she said, setting down her coffee mug. "You are withholding sex."

"No, I'm not." His jaw flexed. "I'll fuck you facedown over that counter, Piper. If sex is all you want, I'll give it to you. But I want more." His voice brooked no nonsense. "You do, too, or you wouldn't have come here in the middle of a storm and slept in my bed. Don't *ever* do that again, by the way. I need to know you'll be safe when I'm not here."

"I'm a strong runner!"

He gave a dubious grunt.

"Fine," she said, voice irregular. "We'll talk!"

"Good. Whenever you're ready."

Lost in a sea of emotional vulnerability, she utilized her best physical weapon, stripping off his shirt and tossing it to him. Then she marched out of the kitchen and up the stairs in nothing but her thong, knowing full well he'd watch her the whole way. If he was going to demand she let him in completely, she'd all of her defenses, she'd make sure it was a long day for them both.

As the *Della Ray* backed out of its slip into the mouth of the harbor, it became obvious to Piper that the boat was an extension of Brendan himself. And the time he spent on land was just filler. He sat in the captain's chair with easy command, confident in every movement, the wheel sliding through his ready hands, his eyes vigilant. Framed in the hazy sunlight, he could have been from past or present. A man and the ocean. Timeless.

Piper watched him from the relief skipper's seat, her cheek pressed to the wood paneling of the wheelhouse, never having felt safer in her life. Physically, anyway. The hum of the engine beneath posed an ominous warning to the trembling organ in her chest.

"How far out are we going to go?"

"Five or six miles," he said. "I'll drop the anchors and give you a tour. Sound good?"

She nodded, finding herself looking forward to it. Watching this man move in his natural habitat. It had the makings of capability porn all over it. And maybe if she asked enough questions, they could avoid having the talk of all talks.

Yeah, right. There was no getting out of this. The set of his jaw said a resolution was imminent, and he had way less of a hangover than she did. Also, he was in a sexy boat captain mode. It did not bode well.

"Hey," Brendan said, his bearded chin giving a persuasive jerk. "Come steer this thing."

"Me?" She stood slowly. "Are you sure? Based on my track record, I will find the one parking meter in the middle of the ocean and back into it."

Laugh lines appeared around his eyes—and then he patted his big, sturdy thigh. Oh yeah, like she was going to pass that up. "Get over here."

She feigned one more moment of indecision, then climbed onto his left thigh, mentally praising Hannah for packing her a skirt so she could feel the denim of Brendan's jeans against the backs of her legs. The shift of muscle.

Brendan took an old captain's hat off a peg on the wall and dropped it onto her head. Then he wrapped his left arm around her middle and tugged her back more securely against his chest. "See this dial? Just keep the arrow right about here. Northwest." He took her hands and placed them on the wheel, making sure they were steady before letting go. "How's that?"

"Cool." She laughed breathily, fascinated by the vibrations that started in her palms and traveled up to her elbows. "Really cool."

"Yeah. It is."

Feeling almost giddily light and kind of . . . unrestrained, she pointed out at the horizon. "Mermaid off the port bow!"

He snorted in her ear. "Phew. I've gotten the *Little Mermaid* reference out of my system. I was going to explode."

"I don't know how I feel about my boat making you think of a Disney movie."

"Aw, don't be jealous of Prince Eric, we—" She turned her head and found him a breath away, those vivid green eyes trained on her mouth. Not on the water, where she expected them to be. The arm around her belly flexed, his palm molding to her rib cage. Heat slicked up the insides of her thighs, her skin sensitizing all over. "Don't you dare look at me like that," she said choppily. "You're the one who wanted to talk first."

He exhaled hard. "And then you ran up my stairs in a purple string. It had an impact."

"You live, you learn," she chirped.

A growl kindled in his throat. "You're going to punish me all day, aren't you?"

"Count on it. I bet you're second-guessing wanting a high-maintenance girlfri—" She cut herself off just in time. "I'm holding your livelihood in my hands, Brendan. Let me focus."

They drove the boat for another fifteen minutes before Brendan eased the throttle into an upright position. He pressed a series of buttons, and a steady rumble followed, which he explained was the anchors going down. And then it was quiet. Just the lapping of water against the side of the boat, and the gentle groans of the ship compensating for the rise and fall of the ocean. They sat in the captain's chair with her head leaned back against his shoulder, his fingers trailing up and down her bare arm.

"Come on," he said gruffly. "I'll bring you out on deck."

Nodding, she followed Brendan down the stairs of the wheelhouse and out onto the wide floating platform that made up the deck. The vessel bobbed beneath them, but he moved like it was stationary, his legs easily compensating for the dips and lifts. She tried to copy his effortlessness and thought she looked only slightly drunk.

"Last week, there were seventy steel traps stacked on this end." He gestured to the end of the deck nearest the wheelhouse, then stooped down to show her a covered portal. "When we're on the crab, this is where we put the keepers. Males over a certain weight. We send them below to processing, then on to the freezer hold."

"What if you're fishing?"

"Same hold. But we pack it full of ice. No water."

She squinted up at the large cranes overhead, the spotlights and antennas secured to the top, and a chill caught her off guard. "Those lights are to help you see in the dark? Or see if there's a wave coming?"

Brendan came to stand beside her, dropped a kiss onto her shoulder. "Yeah. I can see when they're coming, baby."

"Did you know . . . that's how Henry died?" Why was she whispering? "A rogue wave just knocked him right overboard. Mick told me."

"Yeah, I knew." He didn't say anything for a moment. "I'm not going to pretend things like that don't still happen, Piper, but it happens a hell of a lot less these days. Training to be on deck is more comprehensive, the machinery we have leaves less room for human error. Boats are better designed for safety now, and with all of the recent updates, mine is one of the safest."

Piper looked up at him. "Is this why you brought me out here?" she asked quietly. "To show me why I don't have to worry when you're gone?"

"It's one of the reasons. I don't like you crying."

She swallowed a sharp object in her throat. "When I heard there was an accident, I just kept thinking of the boat flipping over. Can that happen?"

"Rarely. Very rarely. Especially for one this large." Brendan studied her face for a beat, then moved behind her, wrapping his arms around her shoulders. "Close your eyes."

She forced herself to relax. "Okay."

"Just feel the way the boat moves like it's part of the water. That's how it's designed, to compensate for waves. Like an airplane going over turbulence. There are bumps, but they never stop you from moving." His hand snuck around the front to lift her chin. "You see how low the railings are on this boat? And those openings at the base? That's so the water can just pass right over and through. It can't hold water from a wave or make the weight uneven."

"But . . . because they're so low, isn't it easy for a man to go over the side?"

"It hasn't happened yet to anyone on my team." He let go of her chin and pulled her closer. "I can tell you when I worked on the crew, before I was a captain, my legs became part of the boat. You learn to balance. You learn to read the water, to brace, to loosen. I'm in the wheelhouse, so it's near impossible for me to go overboard, but I'm responsible for five men, not just myself anymore."

"Which is harder?"

"Responsibility."

Absently, she reached up and stroked his beard. "They're right to trust you."

She felt him swallow against the back of her head. "Do you . . . feel any better?"

"A little. Standing on the boat makes it seem more substantial."

It's a clear day, though. Not a rain cloud in sight. Storms are a different story.

He was making such a sweet effort to allay her fears that she kept silent.

"What else do you worry about?" Brendan asked against her ear.

Piper shrugged but didn't answer. One wrong move, and they could veer into dangerous territory. Maybe she should make another *Little Mermaid* reference—

"Piper."

"Oh yes?"

"What else do you worry about?"

Her sigh allowed the truth to sneak up her throat, but she played it off like her concern was minor. When it was definitely not. In fact, she was starting to think it was the kernel center of the whole piece of popcorn. "I'm not, um . . . built for this whole worrying business, Brendan. Keeping the home fires burning. Wrapping a cardigan around my shoulders and pacing the docks, clutching a locket or something? Does that sound like me? No. You *know* I'm too high maintenance for that. I'm . . ."

He stayed quiet, just held her.

Which was bad, because she started to ramble.

"You know. Just hypothetically speaking. Once a year, you go out to catch crab, sure. But all the time? Going to bed thinking you might not come back, night after night? Uh-uh. I'm not . . ." She squeezed her eyes closed. "I'm not strong enough for that."

"Yes, you are. I know it asks a lot, but yes, you are."

"No. I'm not. Not every woman can do this. She—" Ugh. Piper rolled her eyes at herself. How truly pathetic she was being, bringing up another woman. But as soon as the words started to flow, a pressure in her chest started to lessen, like a brick had been sitting on top of it. "You had a fisherman's wife. She was born here, and this was normal to her. You can't really expect *me* to live up to that. I will . . ." *Disappoint you. Disappoint myself. Disappoint Henry.* "A little less than a month ago, I had no responsibilities. No worries. And now, now . . . this huge one. It's huge. This guy I care about a lot, like, *a lot*, has the most dangerous job in the universe. And I don't have a job *at all.* I don't even live here. Not permanently. Like, we are *not* a fit, Brendan. It won't work, so stop—"

"Stop what, Piper? Thinking about you every second of the day? Missing you so much I climb the fucking walls? Stop being hungry for you? I can't turn any of that off and I don't want to." When he turned Piper around, she saw he was visibly concerned by what she'd revealed. *Well, welcome to the party, bucko.* "Okay, let's start from the beginning. We're going to talk about my marriage. Not how she died, but what it was like."

She took a breath. "I don't know if I want to."

"Can you trust me, honey? I'm just trying to get to the light. Get to *you.*" He waited for her nod, then did that wide-stance, settling-in thing and crossed his arms. As if letting her know he was immovable. "I knew Desiree my whole life, but not well. She was a girl a year above me in school. Quiet. I didn't really get to know her until I started working for Mick. Right around the time my parents moved out of town, he took me under his wing and became kind of a . . . guide. He showed me this thing I love. Fishing. How to do it well. And over time, I guess she became family, too. I never felt . . ." He lowered his voice. "There wasn't an attraction like I have for you. I'm not just talking about sex. We were friends, in a way. She was always trying to meet her father's expectations, and so was I, after he gave me the *Della Ray.* He obviously thought we'd make a good match, so I asked her out, and I think . . . both of us just wanted to make Mick happy. That's what we had in common. So we just went through the motions, even when it didn't feel right. When she died, I kept the ring on, kept my vows, to keep him healed as much as possible. Then you showed up, Piper. Then you. And it felt wrong having *ever* given those vows to anyone else.

"Was she strong? Was she comfortable waving off me and Mick every time we left the harbor? Yeah. I guess she was. But she had decades to get there. It's been a month for you, Piper. Less, if you count the time we spent pretending we didn't want each other. So that comparison is unfair. You're unfair to yourself."

There was no doubt Brendan believed everything he was saying. And it was hard not to believe him, too, when he stood a foot above her, a sea captain in his domain with a voice full of conviction. He was huge in that moment. So intense she had to remind herself to breath. Was she happy his marriage hadn't been full of passion? No. This man deserved that. So had Desiree. But that part of his life had been a shadowy corner, and it helped to have the mysterious aspects of it gone. "Thank you for telling me."

"I'm not done."

"Wow. Once you get going, there's no slowing you down."

Brendan stepped closer, seized her by the elbows. "Last night, you said a couple of things that bothered me, and now we're going to work through those." He leaned down and kissed her forehead, her nose, her mouth. "Don't ever tell me again there are a thousand others like you, because that's the biggest pile of bullshit I've ever heard. And someday, trust me, I hope I meet the person who told you that. A person doesn't rebuild a legacy for a dead man unless they have character and can accept responsibilities." He kissed her temple hard. "Last night, I watched you in the bar, how you immediately made everyone your best friend. Made them count. And do you know what it meant to me having you show up at the hospital?" He didn't speak for a moment. "You have perseverance, character, and a huge heart. I think you might still be finding your way, but so am I. Me and my stupid routines. I thought I had it all figured out until you made me start breaking them. I want to keep breaking them with you."

As he'd been speaking, Piper had turned into a limp linguini noodle in his arms. The tip of her nose was red, and she had to blink up at the sky to keep from tearing up. Warmth and a sense of belonging reached all the way down to her toes, curling them in her ballet flats. "This is a lot to process," she whispered.

"I understand—"

"I mean, we're boyfriend and girlfriend now. I guess you got what you wanted."

A rush of his breath passed over the crown of her head. His arms were crushing her to that burly chest now. "Damn right I did." A beat passed. "About you going back to LA . . ."

"Can we put that one part off?" She pressed her nose to the collar of his shirt and inhaled his centering scent. "Just for now?"

He sighed, but she felt him nod. "Yeah. For now."

They stayed like that for a little while, Piper locked in the safety of his embrace while the boat carried high and low on the ocean, sunbeams warming her back.

He'd given her a lot to think about. Maybe it was time to

examine herself. Or, more importantly, how she viewed herself. But one thing she didn't have to overthink was making these moments with Brendan count.

She kissed his chin and eased back, lacing their fingers together and enjoying the way his gaze meandered down the front of her body. "Do I get the rest of the tour?"

"Yeah." He cleared his throat and pulled her back in the direction of the wheelhouse. "Come on."

Piper tilted her head while staring at Brendan's rippling back, wondering if he realized how hard he was about to get laid.

He'd woken up with a plan to try to slay her dragons . . . and he'd executed it. Nothing stood in his way. He'd even passed on sex so they could dig to the root of their issues, and God, that wasn't just commendable. It was hot.

Captain Brendan Taggart was a man. A real one.

Her first.

And she could admit now that staying with him would mean giving up Los Angeles and the life she knew. But there was one root he hadn't found despite all his digging: Who the hell would Piper Bellinger be if she stayed in Westport?

That was a problem for another time, though.

Hold her calls. Right now, she was one hundred percent sex brained.

First, Brendan showed her the engine room, and she nodded prettily while he explained what a thruster was for, commending herself for not giggling once. Then they went back upstairs to the crew room, the galley where they ate while on the water, and finally the bunk room. "Wow," she murmured, observing the narrow beds tucked in tight against the walls. "Close quarters." There were nine total, the majority of them stacked two beds high. Kind of like the bunk she shared with Hannah, but the boat's beds were attached to the wall. Most of them had snapshots taped up beside them. Kids, women, smiling men holding giant fish in their hands. One had a slightly inappropriate calendar that made her snort.

"Sorry about that," Brendan grumbled, rubbing at the back of his neck. "It's not mine."

She rolled her eyes at him. "Duh." She tapped her lips with a finger and did a revolution around the small room, stopping in front of a bunk along the far wall, as separate from the others as one could get in such tight quarters. It was the only one that didn't have a bed above it. "No, yours is this one. The bed without any pictures, isn't it?"

He grunted in the affirmative.

"Do you . . . want a picture of m—"

"Yes."

"Oh." Was she blushing? "Okay. That can be arranged."

"Thank you."

Piper approached her new boyfriend slowly, letting him see the intent in her eyes, and the green of his own deepened drastically, a muscle sliding vertically in his strong throat. She let just the tips of her breasts meet his chest. "Do you ever get alone time on the boat?"

"If I need time alone, I make it," he rasped. "I've needed a lot of it lately."

Which was as good as an admission that he'd masturbated on board while thinking of her. Feminine pleasure turned to slickness between her thighs. "Then, what about private pictures? Just for you." She rubbed her breasts side to side, and his breath stuttered. "Would you like some of those?"

His eyelids went to half-mast. "God, yes."

She bit her lip, stepped back. "Take out your phone."

Brendan reached back and removed his cell from his back pocket, not taking his eyes off Piper once while opening his camera. Then he nodded once to let her know he was ready.

She'd always liked being the center of attention, but having this man's undivided focus was thrilling in an entirely new way. Because her heart was involved.

Heavily, apparently.

It knocked impatiently against her ribs, echoing in her ears as she shrugged off the jacket she'd worn and hung it neatly on one corner of Brendan's bed. The boat groaned and sighed beneath their feet as she skimmed her palms up the front of her body, over her breasts, squeezing, then coasting back down to collect the hem, slowly easing the garment up and off, leaving her clad in just a red denim skirt and ballet flats. She stacked her hands behind her head, dropped a hip, dragged her lower lip through her teeth. Let it go with a pop.

He exhaled a pained laugh, shook his head. *"Fuck."*

"We'll get to that."

Brendan's nostrils flared as he lifted the phone and set off the electronic shutter.

Click.

She unbuttoned her skirt next, turning around while lowering the zipper. With a flirty look over her shoulder, she let the red bottoms drop. Hannah had been pretty hilarious, not packing Piper underwear or a bra, but Brendan's reaction to her bare backside was definitely worth any chafing that had occurred. Yeah, it was all forgiven when he took an involuntary step forward, his chest heaving. *Click. Click. Click.*

She braced a hand on the wall and leaned forward slightly, arching her back and swinging her hips to pop that booty out—*CLICK*—and that was all she wrote.

Brendan dropped the phone and crossed to her in one lunge.

He stooped down and picked her up, tossing her with a bounce onto his bed, covering her naked body with his fully clothed one, and slamming his mouth down on top of hers. And oh Lord, oh Lord, that contrast fired off flamethrowers in her blood. She was vulnerable and coveted and lusted after, and it was everything. Everything.

"This bed isn't strong enough to survive what I'm going to do to you," Brendan growled against her mouth, capturing her lips again in a kiss fraught with male sexual frustration. It let her know in no uncertain terms that she was the source and he'd be exacting revenge.

Take it. Take it.

Without breaking contact with her mouth, Brendan's hand wedged down between them and wrestled his zipper down, the desperation of his jerky movements exciting her like nothing else, dampening the folds between her legs. "Hurry," she begged, biting at his lips. "Hurry."

"Goddammit, Piper, you make me so fucking hard." They both pushed down the waistband of his boxer briefs, hands colliding, tongues stroking into each other's mouths, Piper teasing, Brendan aggressing. Finally, his shaft was free, and he winced, sucked in a breath, wrapping a fist around the thickness of it. "Tell me you're wet. Tell me to put it in."

"I'm so wet," she moaned, lifting her hips, running the insides of her knees up and down his heaving rib cage. "I'm ready. I need you. Rough as you can."

That full, smooth dome pressed up against her entrance, and she braced, one hand flying to his shoulder, the other to the wooden bunk rail. And still she wasn't prepared for the savagery of that first thrust. With a hoarse roar, his hips drove Piper up the narrow bed, his thickness invading all available space within her, and without allowing her time to acclimate, he was already pumping feverishly, rocking the bed with staccato squeaks.

Piper's mouth was permanently wide open against his shoulder, her eyes watering with the force of pleasure. Pleasure from having his hard sex smacking through her wetness like it owned the joint, his calloused hands shoving her knees down, opening her wider for his convenience. Pleasure from having brought this vital man to his proverbial knees with need. God help her, she loved that. Knew he loved being challenged. Knew he loved that she loved challenging him. Perfect, perfect, perfect.

"Scream for it, baby," he panted, raking her ear with his open mouth. "Whine for my cock. No one can hear us."

A lid came off inside of her, whatever was left of her inhibitions hopping out and running wild on tiny legs. She choked on her first attempts to call his name, because the force he was exerting on top of her was so intense, his huge body surging between her legs without cease—and still fully clothed while she remained bare. Why was that so sinfully hot?

"Brendan," she gasped. Then louder, "Brendan. You're so good. It's *so good.*"

"I'll never lie in this bed again without having to jerk off." His hand came up to frame her jaw, applying just enough pressure while looking her square in the eye that another rush of wetness coated her sex, aiding him in his destruction of her senses. "You love knowing that, don't you? You love making me fucking crazy."

She bit her lip and nodded. "Sure you want to be my boyfriend?"

"*Yes,*" he growled, and slammed into her, holding still, deep, his pained face dropping into the crook of her neck. "And don't call me that right now or I'm going to come."

Oh. Jesus. That confession sent a contracting ripple through Piper's core, and she let out a strangled sob, her hands flying to Brendan's ass inside his loosened jeans, fingernails sinking in and yanking him, scraping pathways into his flesh. "Oh my God. N-now. Now."

"*Fuck,*" he ground out, picking up his blistering pace again, the sound of wet slaps echoing in the tiny room. "Fuck it. I can't stop." She milked him with her intimate muscles, and he moaned, pumped harder, rattling the bed beneath them. "That make you hot, baby? Hearing how being your man is going to get me off? Get your boyfriend off? Say it again."

She ran her nails down his hard, flexing butt and dug them in, whispering, "My boyfriend fucks me so right, I let him come inside me whenever he wants." A smile, dazed and wicked, curved her lips when she snuck her middle finger down the split of his backside and cinched it inside the puckered entrance. "He knows just how to earn it."

Piper had been hovering right on the edge of her own orgasm when she purred those last three words, but Brendan's reaction pushed her even closer to oblivion. She watched through an opaque cloud of gathering bliss as he barked a shocked curse, his hips punching forward and back in desperation, neck tendons looking ready to snap. "Christ, I'm done. I'm done. And you better fucking come with me, Piper," he rasped, reaching down and fondling her clit with his thumb. "I satisfy my girl-friend's pussy every time."

And, oh God—*boom*—she fired out of the cannon. Her knees shot up and hugged his body, back arching as she screamed, shook, slapped at his shoulders, all while tears rolled down her temples. It wouldn't end. The hot, grinding pulsations wouldn't end, especially when Brendan drove deep, deep inside of her, stilled and then shuddered violently, his hips moving in dis-jointed patterns, the volume of his moans rivaling her scream that still lingered in the air. She writhed underneath him, try-ing to find the bottom of the pleasure well, but until his mouth landed on hers, anchoring her, she didn't realize . . . didn't re-alize the bottom of the well wasn't physical. She needed their emotional connection to calm herself down. Needed him, his heart, his Brendan-ness. As soon as their lips met, her heart sighed happily and rolled over, languidness traveling through her limbs and making her go boneless.

"Shhh, honey." He breathed hard, his fingers shaking as they stroked the side of her face. "I've got you. I've always got you."

She didn't look away. "I know."

Satisfaction filtered into his silver-green eyes. "Good."

Brendan eased off of Piper and disappeared into the bath-room, coming back with zipped jeans and paper towels, wip-ing off the insides of her thighs and kissing sensitive spots as he cleaned. Then he joined her in the bed, both of them turning onto their sides, her back up against his chest, a possessive arm wrapped around her waist.

Piper was slipping into a drowsy slumber when Brendan rumbled the question in her ear. "So are we going to just *not* talk about the finger thing?"

The boat rocked steadily in the sunshine as they laughed and laughed some more. And five miles from land, it was easy to pretend no hard decisions would have to be made.

Sooner rather than later.

Chapter Twenty-Two

They pulled into Grays Harbor that evening. Brendan had planned to be back earlier, but Piper had fallen asleep on his chest, and a bulldozer couldn't have moved him.

There she went again, changing his plans. Taking a red pen to his routines.

As he parked his truck in front of No Name and glanced across the console at Piper, he thought back to the conversation on the boat. They'd managed to clarify a lot of unspoken issues between them. His marriage, her fears about his profession, and most important, the way she viewed herself. All that talk, all that clearing the air, led to her staying in Westport, whether she was willing to discuss it yet or not. What would it take for her to consider it?

He was asking for a lot of sacrifice on Piper's part. She would have to leave her home, her friends, and everything she'd ever known.

Hannah, too, eventually, when she went back to LA.

Simply breaking free of his patterns didn't even come close to what he was asking of Piper. Compared to what—to *whom*—he would get in return, that was nothing.

And that bothered him. A lot.

Made him feel like a selfish bastard.

"Hey." Piper leaned across to the driver's seat and kissed his shoulder. "What's with the scary frown?"

He shook his head, debating whether or not to be honest. There had been a lot of honesty between them on the boat, and it had cleared their most pressing obstacles. Made the apprehension of what was to come feel mitigated. Manageable. But he couldn't bring himself to remind her of the unbalanced scales. Didn't want her thinking about it or considering the issue too closely. Not yet, when he hadn't been given enough time to find a solution.

Was there a fucking solution?

"I was just thinking about not having you in my bed tonight," Brendan said finally, glad he didn't need to lie. Not completely. "I want you there."

"Me too." She had the nerve to blush and avert her eyes after what they'd done on the boat? Goddamn. This woman. He wanted to spend decade upon decade deciphering all the little components that made her up. "But it's not fair to Hannah. She's in Westport because of me and I can't keep leaving her alone."

"I know," he grumbled.

"I'll text you," she coaxed. "And don't forget about your shiny new nudes."

"Piper, even when I'm dead I won't forget them."

She shimmied her shoulders, pleased. "Okay, well. Good. So, I guess this is where we do the big, dramatic boyfriend-girlfriend kiss and act like we won't see each other for a year."

Brendan sighed. "I always thought it was ridiculous, the way the guys can't peel themselves off their wives and girlfriends at the dock. Pissed they're making us late." He regarded his beautiful girlfriend stonily. "I'll be surprised if I don't try and carry you over my shoulder onto the boat next time. Take you with me."

"Really?" She sat up straighter. "Would you?"

"Hell no. What if there was a storm or you got hurt?" Why was he suddenly sweating? His pulse wasn't functioning the way it was supposed to, speeding up and tripping all over itself. "I'd lose my shit, Piper."

"Hannah would call this a double standard."

"She can call it whatever she wants," he said gruffly. "You stay on land unless it's a short trip like today. And *I'm* with you. Please."

Piper was battling a smile. "Well, since you said please, I guess I'll turn down all of my fishing boat invitations."

Even though she was being sarcastic, Brendan grunted, satisfied. "You said something about a big dramatic kiss," he reminded her, reaching over to unbuckle her seat belt, brushing a knuckle over her nipples, one at a time, as he took his hand back. They puckered under his gaze, her hips shifting on the seat. She cut off his miserable groan by leaning over, tugging his beard until he met her halfway, and kissing him. Lightly at first, then they surged together and sank into a long, wet sampling of lips and tongues, their breaths shuddering out between them.

They broke apart with reluctant sighs. "Mmmm." She blinked up at him, slid back into her seat, and pushed open the door. "Bye, Captain."

Brendan watched her disappear into the building and dragged a hand down his face.

If Piper Bellinger was going to kill him, he'd die a happy man.

He started to drive home but found himself turning toward Fox's place instead. His best friend lived in an apartment near the harbor, a stone's throw from the water, and where Brendan's house had an air of stability, Fox's was as temporary as it got. Cursory paint job, basic furniture, and a huge-ass television. In other words, a single man's dwelling. Brendan didn't tend to visit Fox at home very often, since they saw each other for days—often weeks—at a time on the boat. Not to mention, Brendan had his routines, and they didn't involve going to bars or meeting women or any of the things Fox did with his spare time.

But this whole business of Piper sacrificing everything while he gave very little? It was pushing up under his skin like tree roots. Turning the problem over and over in his mind wasn't solving it. Maybe he needed to address his worries out loud, just in case he was missing something. An easy solution. Hell, it was worth a shot. Better than going home and stewing about it alone.

Fox opened the door in sweatpants and bare feet, a bottle of beer in his hand. The sounds of a baseball game drifted into the breezeway from behind his skipper. "Cap." His brow was knitted. "What's up? Something wrong?"

"No. Move." He pushed past Fox into the apartment, tipping his head at the beer. "You got another one of those?"

"Got a dozen or so. Help yourself. Fridge."

Brendan grunted. He took a beer from the fridge and twisted the cap off with his hand, joining Fox in front of the baseball game, putting the men on opposite sides of the couch. He tried to focus on what was happening on the screen, but his problem-solver brain wasn't having it. Five or so minutes passed before Fox said anything.

"You going to tell me why you're chewing nails over there?" Fox held up a hand. "I mean, chewing nails is kind of your default, but you don't usually do it on my couch."

"You have company coming over or something?"

"Jesus, no." His friend snorted. "You know I don't date local."

"Yeah," Brendan said. "Speaking of which, you usually head to Seattle after a payday like the one we just had. What are you doing here?"

Fox shrugged, stared at the TV. "Don't know. Just wasn't feeling the trip this time."

Brendan waited for his friend to elaborate. When he didn't seem inclined to, Brendan guessed there was no point in putting off the reason for his visit anymore. "These women you meet in Seattle. You've never been . . . serious about any of them, right?"

"I think you're missing the point of leaving Westport to meet women." He saluted with his beer bottle. "Sorry, sweetheart. Just in town for the night. Take it or leave it." He tipped the drink to his mouth. "They always take it, in case that wasn't obvious."

"Congratulations."

"Thank you." Fox laughed. "Anyway, why are you asking me about—" He cut himself off with an expression of dawning comprehension. "Did you come here for advice on women?"

Brendan scoffed. "That's a stretch."

"You did, didn't you? Son of a bitch." Fox grinned. "Piper still giving you a problem?"

"Who ever said she was a problem?" Brendan shouted.

"Relax, Cap. I meant . . ." Fox searched the ceiling for the correct wording. "Have you gotten her out of your system?"

As though such a thing was possible? "No."

"You haven't slept with her?"

Fuck. He didn't like talking about this. What happened between him and Piper should be private. "I'm not answering that," he growled.

Fox looked impressed. "You have, then. So what is the problem?"

Brendan stared. "I think the problem might be that I came to you for advice."

His friend waved off the insult. "Just ask me what you want to know. I'm actually pretty fucking flattered that you came to me. I know two things: fishing and women. And those two things have a lot of similarities. When you're fishing, you use bait, right?" He pointed at his smile. "I've got your woman bait right here."

"Jesus Christ."

"Next you've got the hook. That's your opening line."

A hole opened in the center of Brendan's stomach. "My opening line to Piper was basically telling her to go home."

"Yeah, I'm pretty surprised that worked myself." He rubbed at the line between his brows. "Where was I with my analogy?"

"You were done."

"No, I wasn't. Once she's hooked, you just have to reel her in." He leaned forward and braced his forearms on his knees.

"Sounds like you've already done all that, though. Unless . . . Wait, the goal was just sex, right?"

"I didn't have a fucking goal. Not at the beginning. Or I probably wouldn't have shouted at her, called her purse ugly, and strongly suggested she go home." Suddenly sick to his stomach, Brendan slapped down the beer bottle and pushed to his feet. "God, I'm lucky she's giving me the time of day *at all*. Now I have the nerve to try and make her stay here for me? Am I insane?"

Fox gave a low whistle. "Okay, things have progressed a lot since the last time we talked." His friend's bemusement was alarming. "You want *that* girl to stay in *this* town?"

Brendan massaged the pressure in his chest. "Don't say it like that."

A beat of silence passed. "I'm out of my depth on this one, Cap. I don't have any advice on how to actually keep the fish *in* the boat. I usually just let them swim off again."

"Fuck sake. Stop with the analogy."

"It's a good one and you know it."

Brendan sat back down, clasped his hands between his knees. "If she went back to LA, I'd have no choice but to let her. My job is here. A crew who depends on me."

"Not to mention, you'd go crazy there. It's not you. You . . . *are* Westport."

"So that leaves Piper to give up everything." His voice sounded bleak. "How can I ask her to do that?"

Fox shook his head. "I don't know. But she'd be gaining you." He shrugged. "It's probably not a *total* shit trade."

"Thanks," Brendan said drily, before sobering. "If she's happy, she won't leave. That stands to reason, right? But what do women like? What makes them happy?"

Fox pointed to his crotch.

Brendan shook his head slowly. "You're an idiot."

The man chuckled. "What do women *like*?" This time, he seemed to actually consider the question. "I don't think there's any one thing. It depends on the woman." He jerked a shoulder, went back to looking at the ball game. "Take Piper's sister, for example. Hannah. She likes records, right? If I wanted to make her happy, I'd bring her to Seattle tomorrow. There's a vinyl expo happening at the convention center."

"How the hell do you know that?"

"It just popped up on the internet. I don't know," Fox explained, a little too quickly. "The point is, you have to think about the specific woman. They don't all like flowers and chocolate."

"Right."

Fox started to say something else, but a series of notes filled the room. It took Brendan a moment to realize his phone was ringing. He shifted on the couch and tugged it out of his back pocket. "Piper," he said, hitting the answer button immediately, trying not to be obvious that just the promise of hearing her voice sent his pulse into chaos. "Everything okay?"

"Yes. The building is still intact." She sounded breezy, relaxed, totally unaware that he was across town trying to unlock whatever magic would give them a chance for a future. "Um, would it be a lot to ask to borrow your truck tomorrow? There is this amazing, artsy chick on Marketplace selling a shabby chic chandelier that we need, like, absolutely need, for the bar. For *forty bucks*. But we have to pick it up. She's located between here and Seattle."

"About an hour drive," he heard Hannah call in the background.

"About an hour drive," Piper repeated. "We were trying to figure out the cost of an Uber, but then I remembered I have a hot boyfriend with a truck." She paused. "This wouldn't mess with any of your routines, would it?"

His gut kicked.

Routines.

Asking Piper to remain in Westport would require her to have a lot of faith in him. To take a major leap. Showing Piper how far he'd come in terms of bucking his habits might make a difference when it came time for her to decide whether or not to return to LA. If he could give her some of what she was missing in LA, he'd close the gap on that leap he'd eventually ask for.

Brendan could be spontaneous.

He could surprise her. Make her happy. Provide her with what she loved.

Couldn't he?

Yeah. He could. Actually, he was looking forward to it.

"Why don't we pick up your chandelier and keep driving to Seattle? We could stay the night and head back to Westport on Monday."

Brendan lifted an eyebrow at Fox. Fox nodded, impressed.

"Really?" Piper breathed a laugh. "What would we do in Seattle?"

No hesitation. "There's a vinyl expo at the convention center. Hannah might like it."

"A vinyl expo?" Hannah yelped in the background, followed by the sound of feet pounding closer on the wood floor. "Oh, um . . . yeah, safe to say she's interested." A beat passed. "How did you even know this expo was taking place?"

Piper's question must have been loud enough to hear through the receiver, because Fox was already shaking his head. "Fox mentioned it." Brendan gave him the finger. "He's going."

The look of betrayal on his friend's face was almost enough to shame Brendan. Almost. The chance to spend more time with his girlfriend trumped his own dishonor. God knew Piper was a distraction, and he didn't want Hannah to be unsafe in a strange city. Piper wouldn't, either.

"So we'd all go together?" Piper asked, sounding amused and excited all at once.

"Yeah."

She laughed. "Okay. It sounds fun! We'll see you tomorrow." Her voice dropped a few octaves, emerged sounding a little hesitant. "Brendan . . . I miss you."

His heart climbed up into his throat. "I miss you, too."

They hung up.

Fox jabbed the air with a finger. "You owe me. Big time."

"You're right. I do." Brendan headed for the door, ready for a night of planning. "How about I give you the *Della Ray*?"

He closed the door on his friend's stupefied expression.

Chapter Twenty-Three

$\mathcal{P}$iper had butterflies in her stomach.

Good ones.

She was going out of town today with her boyfriend. It didn't matter if she was a little suspicious of the circumstances. Nor did it matter that, by agreeing to be his girlfriend and traveling together, she was sinking deeper into a relationship. One that might not stand the test of time, depending on whether she went back to Los Angeles sooner or later. But none of that was happening today. Or tomorrow. So she was going to kick back, relax, and enjoy the ride. And Brendan would be enjoying a few rides himself.

Piper zipped her toothbrush into her overnight bag and snickered at her own innuendo, but she shut it down when Hannah gave her a questioning look. *Rein it in, horny toad.*

Seriously. It was damn near uncomfortable how sexually charged she'd become over the last couple of days. Vaginal orgasms were ruining her for regular life. Even the most casual mention of Brendan and her pussy started pumping out a slow jam.

Speaking of which. "I think I'll get waxed while we're in civilization," Piper said, trying to decide if she'd forgotten to pack anything. "You want to come with me?"

"Sure." Hannah slung her stuffed backpack over one shoulder. "Just in case we go to the hotel pool or something."

"As soon as I find out where we're staying, I'll schedule us." Piper clapped her hands together. "Sisters wax date!"

"It's all so thrilling," Hannah deadpanned, leaning a hip against the side of the bunk bed. "Hey, Fox isn't coming along to, like . . . babysit me. Right?"

Piper's nose wrinkled. "Brendan said he was already going."

"Yeah, except he didn't know the difference between a forty-five and a seventy-eight that day at the record shop." She narrowed her eyes. "I smell something fishy."

"Welcome to Westport. It's the official town aroma." Piper braced her hands on Hannah's shoulders. "He's not coming to babysit you. You're twenty-six. Anyway, why would you need a babysitter? Me and Brendan will be with you the whole time."

Hannah's mouth fell open. "Piper, you can't be this naive."

"What do you mean?"

"When I asked if Fox was coming to babysit me, I meant, is he coming to distract me so Brendan can have time alone with you and your freshly waxed box?" Now it was Piper's mouth's turn to fall open. "Because I definitely don't mind that. At all. I will be among my people, and I can browse records until the cows come home. But I don't want Fox to feel obligated to entertain me. That would kind of ruin the experience, you know?"

"I get what you're saying." Piper squeezed Hannah's shoulders. "Do you trust me?"

"Of course I do."

"Good. If one of us gets the sense they're trying to divide and conquer, we'll split. Okay? If both of us aren't having a good time, it's not worth it."

Hannah nodded, gave a small smile. "Deal."

"Sealed." Piper wet her lips. "Hey, before they get here, I have something to ask you." She blew out a slow breath. "How do you feel about having the grand opening of the new-and-improved bar on Labor Day?"

Her sister's lips moved, counting silently. "That's eight days from now! A week!"

Piper laughed prettily. "Doable, though?"

"You volunteered to throw a party, didn't you?"

Piper groaned, dropping her hands away from her sister's shoulders. "How did you know that?"

"I know *you*. Planning parties is what you do."

"I can't help it." Her voice dropped to a whisper. "They're so fun."

Hannah fought a smile and won. "Pipes, we haven't even invited Daniel yet." She studied Piper. "Are you even planning on inviting him anymore? Or do you want to stay the full three months?"

"Of course I plan on inviting him!" Piper said automatically. Something sharp twisted in her middle the moment she said those words. But she couldn't take them back.

It didn't hurt to have a fail-safe, though, right? Daniel could always agree to let Piper come home early, and she could turn down the offer. Even if their stepfather was lenient, she didn't have to get on a plane the same day. Her options just needed to stay open.

The more time she spent with Brendan, though, the less inclined she was going to be to give herself an out. And she was not even *close* to ready to make the decision to stay in Westport. How could she be? She might have made friends at Blow the Man Down. Might have started forging connections with people like Abe and Opal and the girls at the Red Buoy. And the hardware store owners and some of the locals who milled around all day at the harbor. So what if she liked stopping to chat with them? So what if she didn't feel as out of place now as she had upon arriving? That didn't spell forever.

She thought of Brendan stroking her hair while they napped in his bunk on the *Della Ray*. Thought of the gentle rocking of the water and the sound of his even breathing. And she had to force out her next words.

"I'll call and invite Daniel right now."

Just to be safe.

Hannah arched a brow. "Really?"

"Yeah." Piper reached for her phone, ignoring the weird stab of foreboding in her tummy, and dialed. Her stepfather answered on the second ring. "Hey, Daniel!"

"Piper." He sounded nervous. "Everything okay?"

She giggled, trying to dispel the coldness in her chest. "Why does everyone answer my calls this way? Am I that much of a disaster?"

"No." Liar. "No, it's just that you haven't called in a while. I expected you to be begging to come back to LA long before now."

Yeah, well. Who could have predicted a big bruiser of a sea captain who gave vaginal orgasms and made her forget how to breathe?

"Uh . . ." She tucked some hair behind her ear and gave

Hannah a reassuring look. "We've been a little distracted, actually. That's what I'm calling to talk to you about. Me and Hannah decided to give the bar a little face-lift."

Silence. "Really."

She couldn't tell if he was impressed or skeptical. "Really. And we're having the grand opening on Labor Day. Do you think . . . ? Would you come? Please?"

After a moment, Daniel sighed. "Piper, I'm busy as hell with this new project."

Was that relief she was feeling? God, if so, it was unnerving. "Oh. Well . . ."

"Labor Day, you said?" She heard him clicking a few buttons on his computer. Probably opening up his calendar. "I have to admit I'm a little curious to see what you call a face-lift." He sounded a little dry, but she tried not to get offended. She hadn't exactly given him a reason to suspect she would be DIY-gifted, unless she counted that bong she'd made out of an eggplant during her senior year of high school. "I could probably swing it. How far away is Seattle?"

A weight sunk low in her stomach. He was coming.

Piper forced a smile. This was a good thing. This was what she and Hannah needed.

Options. Just in case.

"Two hours, give or take. I'm sure I can find you a hotel near Westport—"

Daniel snorted. "No, thanks. I'll have my assistant find me something in Seattle." He sighed. "Well, it's on the calendar. I guess I'll see you girls soon."

"Great!" Piper's smile faltered. "What about Mom?"

He started to say something and changed track. "She isn't

interested in going back. But I'll represent us both. Sound good?" More key punching. "I have to go now. Good talking to you. Hugs to you and Hannah."

"Okay, bye, Daniel." Piper hung up and fused her features with optimism, staunchly ignoring the bonfire taking place in her stomach. God, why did she feel so guilty? Having her step-father come to Westport in the hopes of cutting their sabbatical short had been the plan all along. "All set!"

Hannah nodded slowly. "Okay."

"Okay! And he said to give you a hug." Piper crushed her sister to her chest, rocking her maniacally. "There you go." She picked up her bag. "Shall we?"

When the sisters walked outside, Brendan and Fox were leaning against the running truck wearing identical scowls, as if they'd been arguing. Upon seeing Piper, Brendan's face cleared, heat flaring in his eyes. "Good morning, Piper," he greeted her gruffly.

"Good morning, Brendan."

Piper couldn't help but notice that Fox looked almost . . . nervous when he saw Hannah, his rangy frame pushing off the truck to reach for her backpack.

"Morning," he said. "Take that for you?"

"No, thanks," Hannah said, skirting past him and throwing it through the open window of the truck's backseat. "I'll hang on to it."

Piper laughed. "My sister doesn't part with her headphones." She let Brendan take her bag and caught the lapel of his flannel, tugging him down for a kiss. He came eagerly, slanting their lips together and giving her the faint taste of his morning coffee. And in a move she found old school and endearing, he tugged off his beanie and used it to shield their faces from view. "Missed you," she whispered, pulling away and giving him a meaningful look.

Brendan's chest rumbled in response, and he damn near ripped the passenger-side door off the hinges, stepping back to help her inside. Fox and Hannah climbed into the rear cab, sitting as far apart as possible. Hannah's backpack rested on the seat between them, making Piper wonder if there was some tension there her sister hadn't told her about. Had she been so wrapped up in her own love life that she'd missed something important happening with Hannah? She vowed to remedy that at the earliest opportunity.

They were driving for five minutes before Piper noticed the address on the navigation screen. It included the name of a very upscale hotel. "Wait. That's not where we're staying, is it?"

Brendan grunted, turned onto the highway.

Marble bathtubs, Egyptian cotton, white fluffy robes, and flattering mood lighting danced in her head. "It is?" she breathed.

"Uh-oh. Someone is breaking out the big guns." Hannah chuckled in the backseat. "Well played, Brendan." Her voice changed. "Wait, but . . . how many rooms did you book?"

"I'm staying with Hannah," Piper said preemptively, passing her sister an I-got-you-bitch look over the cab divider.

"Of course you are," Brendan said easily. "I got three rooms. Fox and I will have our own. He gets enough of my snoring on the boat."

Three rooms? A month ago, she wouldn't even have considered the cost of staying the night at a luxury hotel. But she mentally calculated the price of *everything* now, right down to a cup of afternoon coffee. Three rooms at this hotel would be pricey. Well into the thousands. How much money did fishermen make, anyway? That hadn't been part of her research.

She'd worry about it later. Right now, she was too busy being turned on by the thought of a room service cheese plate and complimentary slippers.

The captain really did have her figured out, didn't he?

"I made a road-trip playlist," Hannah said, leaning forward and handing Piper her phone. "I named it 'Seattle Bound.' Just hit shuffle, Pipes."

"Yes, ma'am." She plugged it into Brendan's outlet. "I never question the DJ."

"The Passenger" by Iggy Pop came on first. "That's Bowie's voice joining in on the chorus," Hannah called over the music. "This song is about their friendship. Driving around together, taking journeys." She sighed wistfully. "Can you imagine them pulling up next to you at a stoplight?"

"Is that what you'll be shopping for at the expo?" Fox asked her. "Bowie?"

"Maybe. The beauty of record shopping is never knowing what you'll leave with." Animated by her favorite topic, Hannah sat forward, turning in the seat to face Fox. "They have to speak to you. More importantly, you have to listen."

From behind her sunglasses, Piper watched the conversation with interest via the rearview mirror.

"Records are kind of like fine wine. Some studios had better production years than others. It's not just the band, it's the pressing. You can be as sentimental as you want about an album, but there's a quality aspect, too." She grinned. "And if you get a perfect pressing of an album you love, there's nothing like that first note when the needle touches down."

"Have you had that?" Fox asked quietly after a moment.

Hannah nodded solemnly. "'A Case of You' by Joni Mitchell. It was the first song I played on her *Blue* album. I've never been the same."

"Fast Car" by Tracy Chapman came up next on the playlist.

Piper's sister hummed a few bars. "Mood is also a factor. If I'm happy, I might shop for Weezer. If I'm homesick, I'll look for Tom Petty . . ."

Fox's lips twitched. "Do you listen to anything from your own generation?"

"Sometimes. Mostly no."

"My Hannah is an old soul," Piper called back.

Brendan's friend nodded, regarding Hannah. "So you have songs for every mood."

"I have *hundreds* of songs for every mood," Hannah breathed, unzipping her backpack and yanking out her headphones and jam-packed iPod, pressing them to her chest. "What kind of mood are you in right now?"

"I don't know. Uh . . ." Fox exhaled up at the ceiling, that smile still playing around the edges of his lips. "Glad."

Glad, Hannah mouthed. "Why?"

Fox didn't respond right away. "Because I don't have to share a room with Brendan. Obviously." He nodded at Hannah's headphones. "What do you got for that?"

Looking superior, Hannah handed him the headset.

Fox put them on.

A moment later, he let out a crack of laughter.

Piper turned in the seat. "What song did you play him?"

"'No Scrubs.'"

Even Brendan laughed at that, his rusted-motor laugh making Piper want to crawl up into his lap and nuzzle his beard. Probably best to wait until they weren't driving for that.

Over the course of the two-hour trip, Fox and Hannah inched closer together in the backseat until they were eventually sharing the set of headphones, taking turns choosing songs to play each other and arguing over whose picks were better. And while Piper hadn't liked the tension between Fox and her sister, she wasn't sure she liked *this* any better. She'd gone on enough dates with players to spot one a mile away—and unless she was wildly mistaken, Fox had playboy royalty written all over him.

After a quick stop to pick up the chandelier and cover it with a tarp in the back of Brendan's truck, they arrived at the hotel before lunchtime. Piper was given precious few minutes to enjoy the lobby waterfall and soothing piano music before they were headed for the elevators.

"I asked them to put us as close as possible, so we're all on the sixteenth floor," Brendan said, passing out room keys, so casually in charge, Piper had to bite down on her lip. "The expo starts at noon. You want to meet in the lobby then and walk over?"

"Sounds good," said both sisters.

Although *I want to jump you* is what Piper was thinking.

They reached the sixteenth floor and headed in different directions—and Piper was grateful to have half an hour alone with her sister. "Hey, getting a little cozy with Fox there, eh?" she whispered, tapping the room key against the sensor, releasing the lock.

Hannah snorted. "What? No. We were just listening to music."

"Yeah, except music is like sex for you—" Piper broke off on a gasp, running the rest of the way into the room. It was magnificent. Muted sunlight. A view of the water. A white fluffy comforter on the king-sized bed, complete with mirrored headboard and mood lighting. Elegant creams and golds and marble. A seating area with a plush ottoman and tasseled throw pillows. Vintage *Vogue* covers even served as the artwork. "Oh, Hannah." Piper turned in a circle, arms outstretched. "I'm home."

"The captain done good."

"He done real good." Piper trailed her fingertips along a cloudlike pillow. "But we're still talking about Fox. What's going on there?"

Hannah plopped onto the love seat, backpack in her lap. "It's dumb."

"What is dumb?"

Her sister grumbled. "That day we walked to the record shop, I might have thought he was cute. We were having a good conversation—deeper than I expected, actually. And then . . . his phone just starts pinging nonstop. Multiple girl names coming up on the screen. Tina. Josie. Mika. It made me feel kind of stupid for looking at him that way. Like there was even . . . potential." She set aside her backpack with a shudder. "I think maybe the cleaning products we'd set on fire went to my head or something. But it was a momentary lapse. I'm all about Sergei. *All* about him. Even if he treats me like a kid sister."

"So . . . no gooey feelings for Fox?"

"No, actually." Hannah seemed pleased with herself. "I think

I like him as a friend, though. He's fun. Smart. It was natural for me to notice he's good-looking. I mean, who wouldn't? But it's all aboard the platonic train. Toot, toot. Friends only."

"You're sure, Hanns?" Piper eyeballed her sister. "Pretty obvious he's a lady's man. I wouldn't want you to get hurt or—"

"Pipes. I'm not interested." Hannah appeared to be telling the truth. "Swear to God."

"Okay."

"In fact, I'm cool hanging out with him today. There's no babysitting vibe." She made a shooing motion with her hand. "You and Brendan can go do couple-y things."

"What? No way! I want to browse vinyls, too."

"No, you don't. But you're cute for pretending."

Piper pouted, then brightened. "We will have our sisters wax date!" She gasped. "You know what? I booked it at a place closer to the convention center, because I assumed that's where we'd be staying. But I'm going to cancel it. I bet they have in-room waxing here. Let's splurge."

"Location doesn't matter to me. Hair is getting ripped out either way."

Piper lunged for the phone. "That's the spirit!"

Chapter Twenty-Four

Brendan had been hoping to get a lot of time alone with Piper while in Seattle. He hadn't expected to get it so soon, but he sure as hell wasn't going to complain. As the four of them stood in the lavish hotel lobby getting ready to part ways, he did his best not to feel underdressed in jeans, flannel, and boots. He'd taken off the beanie as soon as he'd gotten to his room, kind of dumbfounded by the level of extravagance. The price of their stay had tipped him off that it would be fancy, but he was going to spend the whole time worried about leaving boot prints on the carpet.

This is what she's used to.

This is what you'll give her.

Piper was laughing at Hannah's disgruntled expression. "Is it that bad?"

"She didn't even warn me. Just *rip.*"

"Who didn't warn you?" Fox asked, splitting a curious look between the women. "Jesus. What happened since we left you?"

"We got waxed," Piper explained breezily. "In the room."

Hannah poked her sister in the ribs. *"Piper."*

Piper paused in the act of fluffing her hair. "What? It's like a basic human function."

"Not for everyone." Hannah laughed, red-faced. "Oh my God. I should go before my sister embarrasses me any more." She turned to Fox, raised an eyebrow. "Ready?"

For once, Brendan's best friend appeared to be at a loss for words. "Uh, yeah." He coughed into his fist. "Let's go record shopping."

"Meet back here at six for dinner," Brendan said.

Fox saluted lazily and followed Hannah toward the exit.

They were almost to the revolving door when Piper tugged on Brendan's shirt, making him look down. "They worry me a little. She says they're just friendly, but I don't want my sister to get her heart broken."

Brendan wouldn't say it out loud, but he'd been worried about the same thing. Fox didn't have female friends. He had one-night stands. "I'll talk to him."

Piper nodded, though she cast one more worried glance at her sister's and Fox's retreating backs. "So . . ." She turned on a heel and gave Brendan her full attention. "It's just the two of us. For the whole afternoon. Should we go sightseeing?"

"No."

"No?" Her eyes were playful. "What did you have in mind?"

She obviously thought he was going to throw her over his shoulder and bring her back up to the room. And goddamn, he was tempted to spend the whole day fucking a bare-naked Piper on that ridiculous bed, but being predictable wouldn't serve him. He needed to use his time with her wisely. "I'm taking you shopping."

Her smile collapsed. A sheen coated her eyes.

A trembling hand pressed to her throat. "Y-you are?" she whispered.

He tucked a fall of hair behind her ear. "Yes."

"But . . . really? Now?"

"Yes."

She fanned her face. "For what?"

"Whatever you want."

Those blue eyes blinked. Blinked again. A line formed between her brows. "I can't . . . I can't think of a single thing I want right now."

"Maybe once you start looking—"

"No." She wet her lips, seeming almost surprised by the words coming out of her mouth. "Brendan, I will always love shopping and fancy hotels. Like, *love* them. But I don't need them. I don't need you to do"—she encompassed the lobby with a sweeping gesture—"all of this in order to make me happy." Her cheek pressed to his chest. "Can you let me into the recharging station, please?"

Without delay, his arms were wrapped around Piper, his mouth pressed to the crown of her head. Until she said the words and relief settled over him, he didn't know how badly he needed to hear them. He might be able to afford places like this, but he couldn't deny the need to be enough on his own. Oddly, now that she'd erased that worry, he found himself wanting to treat her to a day of her favorite things even more. "I'm taking you shopping, honey."

"No."

"Yes, I am."

"No, Brendan. This isn't necessary. I'd be just as happy watching them throw fish at Pike Place Market with you, and oh my God, I really mean that." She snuggled in closer, her hand fisting in his flannel. "I really, actually do."

"Piper." He dropped his mouth to her ear. "Spoiling you makes my dick hard."

"Why didn't you say so?" She grabbed his hand and tugged him toward the exit. "Let's go shopping!"

"Jeans?"

Piper lifted her chin. "You said whatever I want."

Enjoying the hell out of himself, Brendan followed Piper through the aisles of the classy Pacific Place shop, watching her ass punch side to side in her pink skirt. She was so in her element among the mannequins and racks of clothes, he was glad as hell he'd pushed to go shopping. As soon as they'd walked through the doors, salesgirls had descended on his girlfriend and they were already on a first-name basis, running off to retrieve a stack of jeans in Piper's size.

"Of course, you can get whatever you want," he said, trying to keep from knocking over racks with his wide shoulders. "I just figured you'd go straight for the dresses."

"I might have." She sent him a haughty look over her shoulder. "If I didn't remember you sarcastically asking me if I owned a pair of jeans."

"The night you went dancing at Blow the Man Down?" He thought back. "I didn't think you recalled half that night."

"Oh, only the important parts," she said. "Like backhanded slights against my wardrobe."

"I like your . . . wardrobe." All right, then. He used the word "wardrobe" now. With a straight face, too, apparently. "In the beginning, I thought it was . . ."

"Ridiculous?"

"Impractical," he corrected her firmly. "But I've changed my mind."

"You just like my clothes now because you get to take them off."

"That doesn't hurt. But mainly, they're you. That's the real reason." He watched the salesgirl approach with an armload of jeans and just barely stopped himself from barking at her to go away. "I like the things that make you Piper. Don't go changing them now."

"I'm not changing anything, Brendan," she said, and laughed, pulling him into the dressing-room area. "But I can only get away with dresses for so long. It's going to be fall soon, in the Pacific Northwest."

The salesgirl breezed in behind them and ushered Piper away, putting her in the closest dressing room with a half-dozen pairs of jeans of various colors and styles. Then she pointed at a tiny, feminine chair, wordlessly implying that Brendan should sit—and he did, awkwardly, feeling a lot like Gulliver. "Is this what it's like when you go shopping in LA?" he asked Piper through the curtain.

"Mmmm. Not exactly." She peeked out at him and winked. "I typically don't have a six-foot-four sea captain along for the ride."

He made an amused sound. "Does that make it better or worse?"

"Better. Way better." She pushed back the curtain and walked out in a pair of light-blue painted-on jeans and a black see-through bra. "Ooh, not a fan." She turned and looked at her butt in the full-length mirror. "Thoughts?"

Brendan dragged his jaw up off the fucking floor. "I'm sorry. How are you not a fan?"

She made a face. "The stitching is weird."

"The . . . what?" He leaned in for a closer look and immediately got distracted by the ass. "Who gives a shit?"

The salesgirl walked in and tilted her head. "Oh yeah. No. Pass on those."

Piper nodded. "That's what I thought."

"Are you two playing a joke on me? They're perfect."

Both women laughed. Out went the salesgirl. Piper retreated to the changing room. And Brendan was left wondering if he'd taken crazy pills. "Yeah, safe to say this is definitely different than shopping with my friends back in LA. I'm pretty sure half the time they tell me something looks great even when it doesn't. There's always a sense of competition. Trying to get the edge." A zipper went up and he watched her feet turn right, left, right under the curtain, smiling at the sparkly polish on her toes. It was so Piper. "I think maybe shopping hasn't been fun for a while and I didn't even realize it. Don't get me wrong, I adore the clothes. But when I think of going dress hunting with Kirby now, I can't remember feeling anything. I spent all of that time trying to give myself that first euphoric rush. But . . . I was more excited to get a deal on a fishing net at the harbor supply shop than I was buying my last Chanel bag."

She gasped.

Alarm snapped Brendan's spine straight. "What?"

"I think Daniel's lesson worked." She pushed aside the curtain, revealing her shocked expression. "I think I might appreciate money now, Brendan."

If he wasn't supposed to find her utterly fucking adorable, he was failing miserably.

"That's great, Piper," he said gruffly, ordering himself not to smile.

"Yeah." She pointed down at a pair of dark jeans that molded indecently to her mouthwatering hips. "These are a no, right?"

"They're a *yes.*"

She shook her head and closed the curtain again. "And they're a hundred dollars. I looked at the price tag!" Then she mumbled, "I *think* that's a lot?"

His head tipped back. "I make more than that on one crab, Piper."

"What? No. How many crabs do you catch?"

"In a season? If I hit the quota? Eighty thousand pounds."

When she opened the curtain again, she had the calculator pulled up on her phone. With her mouth in an O, she slowly turned the screen to show him all the zeroes. "Brendan, this is like, *millions* of dollars."

He just looked at her.

"Oh no," she said after a beat, shaking her head. "This is bad."

Brendan frowned. "How is this bad?"

"I just learned the value of money. Now I find out I have a rich boyfriend?" She sighed sadly, closed the curtain. "We have to break up, Brendan. For my own good."

"*What?*" Panic gave him immediate, searing heartburn. No. No, this wasn't happening. He'd heard her wrong. But if he hadn't misheard, they weren't leaving this fucking dressing room until she changed her mind. He lunged to his feet and ripped the curtain open, only to find Piper laughing into her cupped palm, her sides shaking. Relief washed through him, as if an overhead sprinkler system had been engaged. "That wasn't funny," he said raggedly.

"It was." She giggled. "You know it was."

"Do you see me laughing?"

She pressed her lips together to get rid of the smile, but her eyes were still sparkling with laughter. But he couldn't be mad at her, especially when she crossed her wrists behind his neck, pressed her soft body up against his hard one, and coaxed his mouth into a winding kiss. "I'm sorry." She licked gently at his tongue. "I didn't think you'd buy it so easily."

He grunted, annoyed at himself for enjoying the way Piper was trying to get back in his good graces. Her fingers twisted the ends of his hair, her eyes were contrite. All of it was oddly soothing. Christ, being in love was doing a number on him. He was a goner.

"Will you forgive me if I let you pick out my jeans?" she murmured against his lips.

Brendan smoothed his palms back and forth along her waist. "I'm not mad. I can't be. Not at you."

She dropped her hands away from his neck and handed him the next pair of jeans in the stack. As he watched, she unzipped the ones she was wearing and peeled them down her legs. Good God almighty, Piper was bent over in front of the mirror, her ass nearly brushing the glass—and looking down from above, he could see everything. The mint-green strip of fabric tucked up between her supple cheeks, the suggestion of a tan line peeking out.

By the time she straightened, her face was flushed, and Brendan's cock was straining against his zipper. "Put them on for me?"

Christ. It didn't matter that the salesgirl could come in at any minute. Arrested as he was by those big, blue bedroom eyes, nothing mattered but her. Hell, maybe that would always be the case. Brendan let out a shuddering breath and went down on his knees. He started to open the waistband so she could step into them, but the little triangle of her panties absorbed his attention when he remembered she'd gotten waxed that morning.

Truthfully, he'd never given a thought to women's . . . landscaping before. But ever since the first time he'd eaten Piper's pussy, he'd craved *hers*. The way it looked, felt, tasted, the smooth succulence of her.

"Can I see?"

Almost shyly, she nodded.

Brendan tucked a finger in the center of her thong's front waistband and tugged it down, revealing that teasing little split, the nub of flesh *just* pushing her lips apart. He swayed forward with a growl, pressing his face to the lush flesh and inhaling deeply. "This is mine."

Her stomach hollowed on an intake of breath. "Yes."

"Going to spoil you with my credit card now." He kissed the top of her slit. "Then have you sit on my face and spoil you fucking rotten with my tongue later."

"*Brendan.*"

He banded his arms around her knees when they dipped, using his upper body to lean her back against the dressing room wall. When he'd made sure she was stable, he urged her without words to step into the legs, one at a time. His hands scooted the denim up her calves, knees, and thighs, his mouth leaving kisses on the disappearing skin as he went. It hurt to drag the zipper up and hide her pussy away, but he did it, swirling his tongue around her belly button while engaging the snap.

He stood, turning Piper around so she was facing the mirror. He tugged her ass back into his lap so she could feel his hard-on, making her lips puff open, her neck go limp.

Through dazed eyes, she scanned her reflection, her attention on Brendan's hand as it traveled down her stomach, his long fingers delving into the front waistband to grip her pussy roughly, earning him a shocked whimper. "Keepers. Definitely."

"Y-yes, we'll get these," she said in a rush. Brendan tightened his grip again, lifted, and she went up on her toes, her lips falling open on a gasp. "Yes, yes, yes."

Brendan planted a kiss on the side of her neck, biting down on the spot and slowly sliding his hand out of her jeans. When she stopped swaying, he left her flushed in front of the mirror and edged out into the waiting area. "Good girl."

"You know," she panted through the curtain. "Shopping is more about the journey than the destination."

He gestured to the salesgirl as she walked in. "She'll take them all."

Chapter Twenty-Five

$\mathcal{P}$iper sniffed Brendan's neck and pursed her lips thoughtfully. "Nope, it's not the right one yet. Too citrusy."

Brendan leaned an elbow on the glass counter, half amused, half impatient. "Piper, you're going to run out of places to spray me."

It was getting later in the afternoon, and after lunch downtown—during which Brendan tried his first tiramisu and *liked* it!—they were back at the hotel. Her boyfriend had seemed quite inclined to get her upstairs as fast as possible, but she'd dragged him into a men's shop just off the lobby to see if they could find him a signature scent.

Was she stalling? Maybe a little.

For some reason, her nerves were popping.

Which was crazy. So they were going upstairs to get it on. They'd done that twice before, right? There was no reason for the extra race of bubbles in her bloodstream. Except a new torrent of them was set loose every time Brendan kissed her knuckles or put an arm around her shoulder. And even in the air conditioning, the skin of her neck flamed, and she found herself taking deep, deep breaths, attempting to still her sprinting heart.

If she could just focus on finding him the perfect cologne, that would give her enough time to relax. Or at least figure out why she couldn't.

She leaned across the glass to pluck up a square, sage-colored bottle, and Brendan splayed a hand on the small of her back. Casually. But her pulse spiked like she was taking a lie detector test and being questioned about her past spending habits. Mentally shaking herself, she lifted the bottle and took a sniff. "Oh," she whispered, smelling it again to be sure. "This is it. This is your scent."

And maybe it was the craziest thing, but finding that elusive essence of Brendan, holding it right there in her hand and having it flood her senses . . . it dropped that final veil that had been obscuring her feelings. She was hopelessly, irrevocably in love with this man.

The change in their surroundings made it impossible not to acknowledge every little reason she gravitated toward him. His honor, his patience, his dependability and steadfast nature. How he could lead and be respected without being power hungry. His love of nature and tradition and *home*. The way he so delicately handled his father-in-law's feelings even got to her.

As soon as she acknowledged the depth of her feelings, those three little words threatened to trip out of her mouth. *That* was the source of her nerves. Because where would that leave her? In a relationship. A permanent one. Not *only* with this man but with Westport.

"Piper," Brendan said urgently. "Are you okay?"

"Of course I am," she responded, far too brightly. "I—I found it. It's perfect."

His eyebrow raise was skeptical as he turned the bottle around. "Splendid Wood?"

"See? You were made for each other." She stared into his eyes like a lovesick puppy for several too-long seconds, before breaking the spell. "Um, we have to smell it on you, though."

Brendan was regarding her with a puckered brow, practically confirming that her behavior was off. "You've already sprayed my wrists and both sides of my neck," he said. "There's nothing left."

"Your chest?" She looked around the small men's shop. The clerk was busy on the other side with another customer. "Just a quick sniff test. So we don't waste money." She beamed. "Oh, listen to me, Brendan! I'm practically cutting coupons here."

Affection flashed in his face. "Be quick," he growled, unbuttoning the top three buttons of his flannel. "I'm going to need three showers to get this stuff off."

Piper danced in place, excited by the imminent breakthrough. This was going to be perfect. She just knew it. With an effort, she held back her squeal and released a puff of mist into Brendan's chest hair while he held open the flannel. She leaned in, burying her nose there, inhaling the combination of the earthiness and Brendan's salt water . . . and oh Lord, yes, she was in love all right. Her brain sighed with total contentment and joy at having captured him, found a way to breathe him in anytime she wanted. She must have stayed there in a dreamlike state, exhaling gustily, for long moments, because Brendan finally chuckled, and she opened her eyes.

"What are you thinking about down there?"

That if I'm not careful, there are going to be little sea captain babies scampering around.

And how bad did that sound, anyway?

Not bad at all. Kind of amazing, actually.

"I was thinking that I'm proud of you," she finally answered, rebuttoning his shirt. "You tried tiramisu today. And . . . and you just plan trips to Seattle now. On a whim. You're like a new man. And I was thinking . . ."

How she'd changed a lot, too, since coming to Westport. Since meeting Brendan. What she'd thought before was living life to the fullest had actually been living life for other people to watch. To gawk at. She wouldn't lie to herself and pretend one month had completely cured her of her deeply rooted yen for attention. For praise. For what she'd once interpreted as love. Now, though? She was participating in her own life. Not just posing and pretending. The world was so much bigger than her, and she was really seeing it now. She was really looking.

In the dressing room while trying on jeans, it didn't even occur to her to snap a selfie in the mirror. She just wanted to be there, in the moment, with this man. Because the way he made her feel was three million times better than the way three million strangers made her feel.

Holy God. Was she going to tell Brendan she loved him?

Yeah.

Yeah, she was.

If she thought breaking into a rooftop pool and summoning the police department was crazy, this felt a million times riskier. This was like rappelling down the side of that LA hotel with sticks of dynamite poking out of her ears. Because she was new at this, and the road to finding out exactly where she fit into her new place was a long one.

What if, ultimately, she didn't fit at all?

The way she'd felt when Adrian cut her loose would be laughable compared to disappointing Brendan. He knew exactly who he was (commander of a vessel), what he wanted (a fleet of boats), and how to get it (apparently make millions of dollars and just have boats built??). Meanwhile, she'd spent a week trying to find a chandelier with the right vibe.

This could be a disaster.

But she looked into his eyes now and heard his words echo back from the deck of the *Della Ray*. *You have perseverance, character, and a huge heart.*

And she chose to believe him.

She chose to believe in herself.

"Brendan, I—"

Her phone went nuts in her purse. Loud, scattered notes that she didn't immediately place because it had been so long since hearing them.

"Oh." She reared back a little. "That's Kirby's ringtone."

"Kirby." His brows snuck together. "The girl who turned you in to the police?"

"The one and only. She hasn't called me since I left." Something told her not to, but she unzipped her purse and took out the phone anyway, weighing it in her hand. "I wonder if something is wrong. Maybe I should answer."

Brendan said nothing, just studied her face.

Her indecision lasted too long, and the phone stopped screaming.

She blew out a breath of relief, glad the decision had been

taken out of her hands—and then the phone started blowing up. It wasn't just Kirby calling again; it was text messages from names she vaguely recognized, email pings . . . and now another number with an LA area code was calling on the other line. What was going on?

"I guess I should take this," she muttered, frowning. "Can I meet you by the elevators?"

"Yeah," Brendan said after a moment, seeming like he wanted to say more.

"It's just a phone call."

When that statement came out sounding like she was trying to reassure herself, too, she cut her losses and left the shop. Was it just a phone call, though? Her finger hovered over the green answer button. This was the first time her LA life had touched her since coming to Washington. She hadn't even answered yet, but it felt like someone was shaking her in bed, trying to wake her up from a dream.

"You're being ridiculous," she scolded herself quietly, hitting talk. "Hey, Kirby. Really stretched that apology window, didn't you, babe?"

Piper frowned at her reflection in the steel elevator bank. Was it her imagination or did she sound completely different talking to her LA friends?

"Piper! I did apologize! Didn't I? Oh my God, if not, I am, like, down on my knees. Seriously. I was such a terrible friend. I just couldn't afford for my dad to cut me off."

Why, oh, why did she answer the call? "Yeah, neither could I." It might have something to do with the endless dings and vibrations happening against her ear. "Look, it's fine, Kirby. I don't hold it against you. What's up?"

"What's *up*? Are you serious?" A few honks fired off in the background, the sound of a bus motoring past. "Have you seen the cover of *LA Weekly*?"

"No," she said slowly.

"You are on it—and looking like a smoke show, bitch. Oh my God, *the headline*, Piper. 'A Party Princess's Vanishing Act.' Everyone is freaking out."

Her temples started to pound. "I don't understand."

"Go look at their Instagram. The post is blowing up." She squealed. "The gist of the article is that you threw the party of the decade and then disappeared. It's like a giant mystery, Piper. You're like, fucking *Banksy* or something. Everyone wants to know why you went from Wilshire Boulevard to some random harbor. You didn't even tag your location! People are dying for details."

"Really?" She found a bench and fell onto it, trying to puzzle through the unexpected news. "No one cared yesterday."

Kirby ignored that. "More importantly, they want to know when you'll come back and reclaim your throne! Which brings me to the main point of my phone call." She exhaled sharply. "Let me throw you a welcome back party. I've already got the venue lined up. Exclusive invites only. The Party Princess Returns. I might have leaked the idea to a few designers, some beverage companies, and they are offering to pay you, Piper. A whole lot of money to walk out in their dress, drink their shit on camera. I'm talking about six figures. Let's do this. Let's make you a fucking legend."

A prickle climbed Piper's arm, and she looked up to find Brendan standing a few yards away, holding her bag of jeans and a smaller one, which she assumed contained the cologne.

He wasn't close enough to hear the conversation, but his expression told her he sensed the gravity of the phone call.

Was the phone call that important, though? This rise in popularity would be fleeting, fast. She'd have to ride the wave as far as possible, then immediately start trying to find a fresh way to be relevant. Compared to the man she loved being out on a boat in a storm . . . or a wave coming out of nowhere and snatching someone off the deck . . . a trip back into the limelight didn't seem that significant.

A month ago, this unexpected windfall of notoriety would have been the greatest thing that ever happened in her life.

Now it mostly left her hollow.

Was there a nagging part of Piper that wanted to fall back into this lifestyle she was guaranteed to be good at? Yes, she'd be lying if she said there wasn't. It would be second nature to strut into a dark club to the perfect song and be applauded for accomplishing absolutely nothing but being pretty and rich and photogenic.

"Piper. Are you there?"

"Yeah," she croaked, her eyes still locked with Brendan's. "I can't commit."

"Yes, you can," Kirby said, exasperated. "Look, I heard Daniel slashed your funds, but if you do this party, you'll have enough cash to move out, do your own thing. Maybe we could even revamp Pucker Up now that you have some extra clout! I'll buy you the plane ticket back to LA, all right? You can stay in my guest room. Done and done. I booked the venue for September seventh. Everywhere was already taken for Labor Day."

"September seventh?" Piper massaged the center of her forehead. "Isn't that a Tuesday?"

"So? What are you, forty?"

God. This was her best friend? "Kirby, I have to go. I'll think about it."

"Are you insane? There is nothing to think about. Paris is on my short list to DJ this thing—and she's at the *bottom*. This is the one we'll be talking about for the rest of our lives."

Brendan was coming closer, his gaze laser-focused on her face.

I can't tell him.

She didn't want to tell him about any of this. *LA Weekly*. The party being planned in her honor. Her splashy new title. Any of it.

If she made a pro/con list of LA versus Westport, *Piper loves Brendan* would be in the pro-Westport column and that outweighed *any* con. They couldn't discuss a potential return to LA without Piper revealing her feelings, and then . . . how could she do anything but turn the opportunity down after telling him those three words? But she wasn't one hundred percent ready to say no to Kirby. Not just yet. If she said no to this triumphant return to the scene she'd lived for the last decade, she'd be saying yes to Westport. Yes to being with this man who endangered himself as a matter of course. Yes to starting over from scratch.

Kirby was rambling in her ear about a Burberry-inspired color scheme and a signature drink called the Horny Heiress.

"Okay, thanks, Kirby. I miss you, too. Have to go. Bye."

"Don't you dare hang—"

Piper hung up quickly and powered down her phone, hopping to her feet. "Hey." She directed her most winning and hopefully distracting smile at Brendan. "You bought the co-logne? I wanted to get it for you as a gift."

"If it makes you want to smell me in public, I'll consider it an investment." He paused, nodding at her phone. "Everything okay?"

"What? Yes." *Stop fluttering your hands.* "Just some gossip that Kirby thought was urgent. Spoiler: it's not. Let's go up-stairs, right?"

Piper sprung forward and hit the call button, praising the saints when an empty car to their immediate left opened. She took Brendan's thick wrist, grateful when he allowed himself to be dragged inside. And then she pushed him up against the elevator wall and utilized two of her favorite skills—avoidance and distraction—to keep him from asking any more questions.

Questions she didn't want to ask herself, either.

Chapter Twenty-Six

$\mathcal{B}$rendan couldn't shake the sense that Piper had just slipped out of his reach—and it fucking terrified him.

While cologne shopping, she'd looked up at him in a way she hadn't before. Like she was getting ready to lay down her weapons and surrender. He'd never had anyone look at him like that. Scared and hopeful all at once. Beautifully exposed. And he couldn't *wait* to reward that trust. To make her glad she'd taken the leap, because he'd catch her. Couldn't wait to tell her that life before she'd shown up in Westport had been lacking all color and light and optimism.

Her hands smoothed down his chest now. Lower, to his abdomen.

She leaned in and buried her nose in his chest, inhaling, moaning softly . . .

Tracing the outline of his cock with her knuckle.

That touch, obviously meant to distract, trapped him between need and irritation. He didn't want Piper when her mind was obviously elsewhere. He wanted those barriers gone. Wanted all of her, every fucking ounce. But there was a part of him that was nervous, too. Nervous as hell that he wasn't equipped to fight whatever unseen foe he was up against.

The latter accounted for his harshness when he caught her wrist, holding it away from his distended fly. "Tell me what the phone call was really about."

She flinched at his tone, pushed away from him. "I *did* tell you. It was nothing."

"Are you really going to lie to me?"

God, she looked literally and figuratively cornered, stuck in the elevator with nowhere to run. Not that she didn't look for an exit, even on the ceiling. "I don't have to tell you every single thing," she stammered finally, punching the OPEN DOOR button repeatedly, even though they were only midway to the sixteenth floor. "Are you planning on being this domineering all the time?" Her laugh was high-pitched, panicky, and it burned a hole in his chest. "Because it's a little much."

Nope. Not taking that bait. "Piper. Come here and look at me."

"No."

"Why not?"

She rolled her eyes. "I don't want to be interrogated."

"Good," he ground out. "I want the truth without having to ask you for it."

He caught her audible swallow just before the elevator door opened, and she was off like a shot, speed-walking in the opposite direction of his room, which was where the hell she was going to end up, if he had anything to say about it. Brendan caught up with her right before she could swipe into her own room, wrapping an arm around her middle and hauling her back up against his chest.

"Enough."

"Don't talk to me like a child."

"You're acting like one."

She gasped. *"You're the one—"*

"Christ. If you tell me I'm the one who wanted a high-maintenance girlfriend, you're going to piss me off, Piper." He gripped her chin and tipped her head back until it met his shoulder. "I want *you*. However you are, whatever you are, I want *you*. And I'll fight to get inside that head as many times as it takes. Over and over and over. Don't you dare doubt me."

Her body heaved with two deep breaths.

"Kirby called to tell me I'm on the cover of *LA Weekly. Okay?* 'A Party Princess's Vanishing Act.' There's a whole story and . . . now I guess, ta-dah, I'm interesting again. After a month of silence, everyone suddenly wants to know where I've gone." She broke free of his grip and pushed away, her posture defensive. "Kirby wants to throw me a big, over-the-top coming-home party. And I didn't want to tell you because now you're going to bear down on me until I magically produce answers about what I want—and *I don't know!*"

Brendan's pulse ricocheted around his veins, his nerves escalating to full-on fear. *LA Weekly.* Over-the-top party. Did he stand a fucking chance against any of that? "What *do* you know, Piper?" he managed, hoarsely.

Her eyes closed. "I know I love you, Brendan. I know I love you and that's it."

The world went momentarily soundless, devoid of noise except for the sound of his heart tendons stretching, on the verge of snapping under the pressure of the wonder she'd just stuffed inside of it. She loved him. This woman loved *him*.

"How can you say 'that's it'?" He took a giant step and scooped her into his arms, rejoicing when she came easily, looping her legs around his waist, burying her face in his neck. "How can you say that's it when it's the best thing that's ever happened to me?" He kissed her hair, her cheek, pressed his mouth to her ear. "I love you, baby. Goddammit, I love you back. As long as that's the case, everything will be fine—and it will *always* be the case. We'll work on the details. Okay?"

"Okay." She lifted her head and nodded, laughed in a dazed way. "Yes. Okay."

"We love each other, Piper." He turned and strode toward his room, grateful he already had the key in his hand, because he wouldn't have been able to take his attention off her to search for it. "I won't let anything or anybody fuck with that."

Jesus. She'd been . . . unlocked. Her eyes were soft and trusting and beautiful and, most important, confident. In him. In them. He'd done the right thing pushing, hard as it had been to see her scared. But it was all right now, thank God. Thank *God*.

He slapped the room key over the sensor and kicked the door open, his sole mission in life to give this woman an orgasm. To see those softened blue eyes go blind and know his body was responsible. Would *always* be responsible for meeting her needs.

"I need you so bad," she sobbed, tugging at his collar, moving her hips in desperate little circles. "Oh my God, I'm *aching*."

"You know I'm going to handle it." He bit the side of her neck, thrust his hips up roughly, and listened to her breath catch. "Don't you?"

"Yes. *Yes*."

Brendan set Piper on her feet and spun her around, then

yanked her skirt up above her hips. "Maybe someday we'll be able to wait long enough to get undressed at the same time," he rasped, stripping her panties down to her ankles, before attacking his zipper with shaking hands. "But it's not going to be today. Get both knees on the edge of the bed."

God, he loved Piper when she was a shameless flirt. When she was pissed. When she was being a tease or making him work his ass off. But he loved her most as she was now. Honest. Hiding nothing. Hot and needy and real. Clambering onto the very edge of the bed and tilting her hips, begging. "Please, Brendan. Will you, please, will you, *please* . . ."

There was no way he couldn't take a moment to admire the work of art that was Piper. The lithe lines of her parted thighs, the ass that made his life heaven and hell. He gripped the cheeks now and kneaded them, spreading the flesh so he could see what was waiting for him in between. "Ah, baby. I should always be the one saying 'please,'" he said hoarsely, leaning down and stroking his tongue over the tight, gathered skin of her back entrance. She huffed his name, then moaned it hesitantly, hopefully, and yeah, he couldn't stop himself from yanking her sexy backside closer, burying his mouth in the valley between and tonguing her roughly.

"Oh wow," she breathed, pushing back against him. "What are you—*oh my God.*"

He brought his hand around her hip, trailing two fingers between her soft folds, and enjoyed the act of getting her pussy wet as hell by licking something else entirely. Enjoying her initial shyness and the way she eventually couldn't help but slide her knees even wider on the bed, her hips undulating in time with the hungry strokes of his tongue. By the time he let his tongue travel down and around to her sex, her clit was so swollen; he batted the nub with his tongue a few times, rubbed the sensitive button with his thumb, and she broke apart, hiccupping into the comforter, her delicious wetness coating her inner thighs, his mouth.

She was panting as he rose, dropped his chest down onto her back and pushed his cock inside of her still-contracting pussy. *"Mine,"* he gritted, the tightness of her cinching his balls up painfully, firing every ounce of his blood with possessiveness. "I'm taking what's mine now."

A movement ahead of them on the bed reminded Brendan of the mirrored headboard, and he almost came, caught off guard by the erotic sight of her slack jaw and tits that bounced along with every pump of his hips. His body loomed behind her, damn near twice her size, his lips peeled back from his teeth like he might very well devour her whole. Who wouldn't? Who wouldn't want to gather every part of this woman as close as possible? To consume her fire? Who wouldn't die trying to earn her loyalty?

"Christ, you're so beautiful," he groaned, falling on top of her, pinning her to the bed and bucking, filling her like she was filling his chest, his mind. All of him. Completing him just by breathing. He took her hair in a fist, using it to pull her head back, locking their gazes in the mirror. She gasped, jolted around his cock, her walls telling him she was as turned on by the movie they were starring in as he was. "Yeah, you like being admired and complimented, don't you, Piper? No better compliment than how hard you make my cock, is there? How rough you make me give it to you? Can't even get my goddamn jeans down." Her breath hitched, and she started to squirm underneath him, her fingers clawing at the comforter as she gave a closed-mouth scream of his name. "Go on. Give me that second one, baby. Want to turn you fucking limp."

Her blue eyes went blind, and she moaned hoarsely, her hips twitching beneath him, spasms racking her pussy and plunging him over the edge. He rocked into her hot channel one more time, spearing deep, looking her in the eyes as he growled her name, letting loose the excruciating pressure between his legs, panting against the side of her head.

"I love you," she gasped, the words seeming to catch her off guard, alarm her, and Brendan wondered if it was possible for his heart to explode out of his chest. How was he going to survive her? Every time he thought his feelings for her had finally reached their apex, she proved him wrong, and his chest grew another size. How could he continue at this rate for the next fifty, sixty years?

"Piper, I love you, too. *I love you*." Still pressing her down into the bed, he left slow kisses on her temple, her shoulder, her neck, before finally rolling off her to one side, drawing her tight to the place she called the recharging station. And he'd laughed at that name, but when she found her place in his arms, her features relaxed and she sighed, as if being held by him truly made everything okay. Jesus Christ, that privilege humbled him.

"I've never said it to anyone before," she murmured, resting her head on his bicep. "It didn't feel like I always thought it would."

He ran his hand down her hair. "How did you think it would feel?"

She thought about it. "Getting it over with. Like ripping off a Band-Aid."

"And how did it feel instead?"

"The reverse. Like putting a bandage on. Wrapping it tight." She studied his chin a moment, then ticked her eyes up to his. "I think because I trust you. I completely trust you. That's a huge part of love, isn't it?"

"Yeah. I reckon it has to be." He swallowed around the lump in his throat. "But I'm not an expert, baby. I've never loved like this."

It took a moment for her to speak. "I'll never keep anything from you again." Her exhale was rocky. "Oh wow. Big post-coital declarations happening here. But I mean it. No more keeping things to myself. Not even for the length of an elevator ride. I won't make you fight to get into my head. I don't want that. I don't want to be constant work for you, Brendan. Not when you make it so easy to love you."

He crushed her against him, no other choice, unless he wanted to splinter apart from the sheer fucking emotion she produced inside of him. "Constant work, Piper? No. You misunderstand me." He tipped her chin up and kissed her mouth. "When the reward is as perfect as you, as perfect as this, the work is a fucking honor."

Brendan rolled Piper onto her back as their kisses escalated, his cock growing stiff again in a matter of seconds, swelling painfully when she begged him to take off his shirt. He complied, somehow finding a way to kick off his jeans and boxers before stripping her clean of any clothing, too. Satisfied sounds burst from their mouths when their naked bodies finally twined together, skin on skin, not a single barrier in sight.

Piper's lips curved with humor beneath his. "So are we just *not* going to talk about the tongue thing?"

Their laughter turned to sighs and eventually to moans, the bedsprings groaning beneath them. And it seemed like nothing could touch the perfection of them. Not after such hard-fought confessions. Not when they couldn't seem to breathe without each other.

But if Brendan had learned one thing as a captain, it was this: Just when it seemed like the storm was beginning to break and daylight spread across the calm waters? That's when the biggest wave hit.

And forgetting that lesson could very well cost him everything.

Chapter Twenty-Seven

The rest of their time in Seattle was a dream.

Hannah and Fox met them in the hotel lobby at the designated time, loaded down with secondhand records. And while Piper still wanted Brendan to speak to Fox about Hannah being off-limits, her fears were temporarily put to rest by the genuine friendship that seemed to have sprouted between the two. One afternoon together and they were finishing each other's sentences. They had inside jokes and everything. Not that it surprised Piper. Her sister was a goddess with a pure, romantic spirit, and it was about time people flocked to her.

As long as certain appendages remained in their pants.

At dinner, Brendan and Fox told them about life on the boat. Piper's favorite story was about a crab claw getting fastened to Deke's nipple, requiring Brendan to give him stitches. She made them tell it twice while she laughed herself into a wine-aided stupor. Halfway through the meal, Fox brought up last week's storm, and Piper watched Brendan stiffen, his gaze flying to hers, gauging if she could handle it. She was surprised to find that while her nerves bubbled up ominously, she was able to calm them with a few deep breaths. Apparently Brendan was so happy about Piper encouraging Fox to finish the story, he pulled her over onto his lap, and that's where she happily remained for the rest of the evening.

They slept in their assigned rooms that night, although some naughty texts had been exchanged between herself and Brendan, and the next morning they piled into the truck to head back to Westport.

With her hand clasped tightly in Brendan's on the console and Hannah's road-trip mix drifting from the speakers, Piper found herself . . . looking forward to going home. She'd called Abe this morning to let him know she would be late for their walk, followed by a quick call to Opal to arrange coffee later in the week.

There were over a hundred text messages and countless emails on her phone from LA acquaintances, club owners, and Kirby, but she was ignoring them for now, not wanting anything to steal the lingering beauty of the Seattle trip.

Apart from those increasingly urgent messages about September 7, Piper was delighted to have two texts from girls she'd met in Blow the Man Down. They wanted to meet up and help plan the Labor Day party. And how would she feel about a group makeup tutorial?

Good. She felt . . . *really* good about it. With her growing number of friends and the grand opening on the horizon, Piper suddenly had a packed schedule.

What if she could actually belong in Westport?

Yes, Brendan made her feel like she already did. But he had his livelihood here. A community he'd known since birth. The last thing she wanted was to be dependent on him. If she stayed in Westport, she needed to make her own way. To be a person independent of their relationship, as well as a member of it. And for the first time, that didn't seem like a far-fetched possibility.

When they arrived in Westport, Brendan dropped Fox off at his apartment first, then completed the five-minute drive to Piper and Hannah's. His expression could only be described as surly as he shoved the truck into park, visibly reluctant to say good-bye to her. She could relate. But there was no way she'd make it a habit to leave Hannah alone.

Her sister leaned over the front seat now, chin propped on her hands. "All right, Brendan," she said drily. "Piper was singing 'Natural Woman' at the top of her lungs in the shower this morning—"

"Hannah!" Piper sputtered.

"And since I like seeing her happy, I'm going to do you a solid."

Brendan turned his head slightly, his interest piqued. "What's that?"

"Okay. I'm assuming you have a guest room at your place," Hannah said.

Piper's boyfriend grunted in the affirmative.

"Well . . ." Hannah drew out. "I could come stay in it. That would alleviate Piper's sister guilt and she could stay in the captain's quarters."

"Go pack," Brendan responded, no hesitation. "I'll wait."

"Hold on. What?" Piper turned on the seat, splitting an incredulous look between these two crazy people she loved. "I'm not—we're not—just going to move into your house, Brendan. That requires a-a . . . at the very least, a serious conversation."

"I'll let you chat," Hannah said merrily, hopping out of the truck.

"Brendan . . ." Piper started.

"Piper." He reached over the console, brushed his thumb along her cheekbone. "You belong in my bed. There's nothing to discuss."

She puffed a laugh. "How can you say that? I've never lived with anyone, but I'm pretty sure a significant portion of time is spent with no makeup and . . . laundry! Have you taken dirty clothes into consideration? Where will I put mine? I've managed to maintain a certain air of mystique—"

"Mystique," he repeated, lips twitching.

"Yes, that's right." She batted away his touch. "What's going to happen when there is no more . . . mystery left?"

"I don't want any mysteries when it comes to you. And we have to leave on a fishing trip on Saturday. Two nights away." *Just a few days from now.* "I want every second I can get with you until I pull out of the harbor."

"Saturday." This was news to her, although she'd known at some point he would be going back out on the water. Usually the turnaround was even tighter, but they'd taken a full week off after crab season. "Do you think you'll be back for the grand opening on Labor Day?"

"Damn right I will. I wouldn't miss it." He raised a casual eyebrow, as if he hadn't just made her pulse thrum with undiluted joy. "Will separate laundry baskets sway you?"

"Maybe." She chewed her lip. "There would have to be a no-kissing-until-I've-brushed-my-teeth rule."

"Nah, fuck that." His gaze dropped to the hem of her skirt.

"I want to push right into sleepy Piper and make her legs shake first thing in the morning."

"Fine," she blurted. "I'll go pack, then."

His expression became a mixture of triumph and affection. "Good."

Frowning at her boyfriend, even though her heart was tap-dancing, she pushed open the door of the truck. Before she could close it behind her, she remembered her promise to meet Abe and walk him to the museum. "How about we come over around dinnertime?" she said to Brendan. "We'll get groceries on the way. Maybe you can give me a cooking lesson."

"I'll have my extinguisher handy."

"Har-har." Was it normal for one's face to actually ache from smiling? "I'll see you tonight, Captain."

His silver-green eyes smoked with promise. "Tonight."

Piper jogged to the hardware store and walked Abe to the maritime museum, chatting with him for a while before continuing her run to Opal's house for coffee. Walking back to No Name, she tapped out replies to her new friends, Patty and Val, arranging a time to plan for Labor Day. She and Hannah would have to kick their productivity into hyperdrive to have the bar ready in time— they didn't even have a new sign yet—but with some determination, they could do it.

That evening, the sisters packed enough clothes for a couple of nights and walked to the market with their backpacks, buying ingredients identical to the ones Brendan dropped into her handcart that first morning in Westport.

Butterfly wings swept her stomach when she knocked on his door, but the strokes turned languid and comforting the moment his extra-large frame appeared in the entrance . . . in gray sweatpants and a T-shirt.

And *o-kay*. Just like that, the advantages of this living arrangement were already making themselves known.

"Don't look at my boyfriend's dick print," Piper whispered to Hannah as they followed him into the house, sending her sister into doubled-over laughter.

Brendan cocked—ha—an eyebrow at them over his shoulder, but continued on until they reached the guest bedroom, carrying the groceries they'd brought in one hand. The room he led them to was small and just off the kitchen, but it had a nice view of the garden and the bed looked infinitely more comfortable than the bunk back at No Name.

"Thanks, this is perfect," Hannah said, dropping her backpack on the floor. She turned in a circle to observe the rest of the room and sucked in a breath, her hand flying up to cover her mouth. "What is . . . what is that?"

Puzzled by her sister's change in demeanor, Piper's gaze traveled from Brendan's sweatpants to the object that had elicited the reaction. There on the desk was a record player. Dusty and heavy-looking. "I remembered my parents gave me theirs before they moved," Brendan said, crossing his arms, nodding at it. "Went and got it out of the basement."

"This is a vintage Pioneer," Hannah breathed, running her finger along the glass top. She turned wide eyes on Brendan. "I can use it?"

He nodded once. "That's why I brought it up." As if he hadn't just made Hannah's life, he jerked his chin at the closet. "Put whatever records I could find in there. Might be nothing."

"Anything will sound like something on this." Hannah's knees dipped, and she leapt up, doing an excited dance. "I don't even care if you unearthed this specifically to drown out the sex noises. *Thank you.*"

Brendan's ears deepened slightly in color, and Piper somehow fell further in love with him. Doing something nice for her sister had earned her everlasting devotion. And when he said, in his gruff, reserved way, "No. Thanks for, uh . . . letting me have Piper here," she almost fainted dead away. "I'll take that."

He eased the backpack off Piper's shoulders, kissed her forehead, and abruptly left the room. They observed his departure like seagulls watching a full slice of bread sailing through the air—and thanks to her harbor jogs, Piper knew what that looked like now. Reverent.

You have to marry him, Hannah mouthed.

I know, Piper mouthed back. *What the fuck?*

Still no actual sound came out of Hannah's mouth. *Ask him first. Do it now.*

I might. Oh God. I might.

Hannah carefully draped herself over the record player. "You can go on double dates with me and my record player. Piper, *look* at it." She slumped into the desk chair. "At the expo, I had my eye on this perfect, perfect Fleetwood Mac forty-five. It was too expensive. But if I'd known I had this Pioneer to play it on, I would have splurged."

"Oh no. It spoke to you?"

"Loud and clear." Hannah sighed, waving off her sadness. "It's fine. If it was meant to be, I'll run into it again one day." She pushed to her feet. "Let's go make dinner. I'm starved."

The three of them fell into a happy pattern.

In the mornings, Brendan woke Piper up with fingertips trailing up and down her belly, which led to her backside teasing his lap. Sometimes he rolled her over facedown and yanked her up onto her knees, taking her fast and furiously, her hands clinging to the headboard for purchase. Other times, he tossed her knees up over his muscular shoulders and rocked into her slowly, whispering gruff praise into the crook of her neck, the thick push and pull of his shaft between her legs as reliable as the tide, never failing to leave her limp and trembling, her cries lingering in the cool, dim air of his bedroom.

After she'd floated back down to earth from their intense lovemaking, she dressed for her jog and went to meet Abe, helping him up the stairs of the museum before continuing on her way. She'd return home and shower, then have breakfast with Brendan and Hannah before heading to No Name for work in his truck. Apart from the sign, the bar just needed décor and a few final touches. Brendan hung the chandelier, laughing at the way Piper squealed in victory, declaring it perfect. They arranged high top tables and stools, hung strings of lights on the back patio, and cleaned sawdust off everything.

"I've been thinking about the name," Piper said one afternoon, waiting until her sister looked at her. "Um . . . how do you feel about Cross and Daughters?"

A sound rushed out of Hannah, her eyes taking on a sheen. "I love it, Pipes."

Brendan came up behind her, planting a hard kiss on her shoulder. "It's perfect."

"I wish we had a little more time," Hannah said. "That name deserves a great sign."

"It does. But I think . . . maybe what's perfect about this place is that it's not. It's personal, not flawless. Right?" Piper laughed. "Let's paint it ourselves. It'll mean more that way."

Hannah's phone rang, and she left the room to answer, leaving Piper and Brendan alone. She turned to find him scrutinizing her in this way he'd been doing often lately. With love. Attentiveness. But there was more happening behind those eyes, too. He said he wouldn't pressure her for a decision, but the longer she left him hanging, the more anxious he grew.

They painted the sign on Thursday with big, sloppy buckets of sky-blue paint. Brendan had spent the morning sanding down a long piece of plywood and trimming the edges into an oval shape with his table saw. Once Piper made a rough outline of the letters with a pencil, they were off to the races, applying the blue paint with playful curves and tilting lines. Some might've said it looked unprofessional, but all she saw was character. An addition to Westport that fit like an acorn in a squirrel's cheek. After the paint dried, Brendan stood by anxiously, prepared to catch them if they fell off the ladders they'd been loaned from the hardware store. Now they affixed it over the faded original sign with his nail gun, Brendan instructing them patiently from the ground. When the sign was nailed on all sides, the two sisters climbed down and hugged in the street.

She couldn't say for certain how Hannah felt about having the bar completed, but in that moment, something clicked into place inside Piper. Something that hadn't even existed before she landed in this northwest corner of the map. It was the welcome home Henry Cross had deserved but never got. It was a proper burial, an apology for deserting him, and it soothed the jagged edges that had appeared on her heart the more she'd learned about her father.

"Now all we need is beer," Hannah said, stepping back and wiping her eyes. "And ice."

"Yeah, time to call the wholesaler, I guess. Wow. That was fast." She peered up at the sign, warmed by the curlicue at the end of "Daughters." "If we want to serve spirits eventually, we'll need a liquor license."

"If *you* want to, Pipes," Hannah said softly, putting an arm around her shoulder. "Leaving you is going to suck, but I can't be here forever. I've got my job with Sergei waiting. If you decide to stay . . ."

"I know," Piper managed, the sign blurring.

"Are you? Staying for sure?"

Through the window, they watched Brendan inside the bar where he screwed a light bulb into the chandelier. So capable and reassuring and familiar now, her heart drew up tight, lodging in her throat. "Yeah. I'm staying."

"Shit," Hannah breathed. "I'm torn between happy and sad."

Piper swiped at her eyes, probably smearing blue paint all over her face but not caring one bit. "I swear to God, you better visit."

Her sister snorted. "Who else is going to bail you out when all this goes south?"

Chapter Twenty-Eight

Things were too good to be true.

On the water, that usually meant Brendan was missing something. That he'd forgotten to flush out a fuel line or replace a rusting winch. There was no such thing as smooth sailing on a boat, not for long. And since he'd long lived his life in the same manner he captained the *Della Ray*, he couldn't help but anticipate a time bomb going off.

He had this woman. This once-in-a-hundred-lifetimes woman who could walk into a room and rob him of fucking breath. She was courageous, sweet, clever, seductive, adventurous, kind, guileless one moment, mischievous the next. So beautiful that a smile from her could make him whisper a prayer. And she loved him. Showed him exactly how much in new ways every day—like when he'd caught her spraying his cologne onto her nighttime shirt, holding it to her nose like it could heal all ills. She whispered her love into his ear every morning and every night. She asked him about fishing and googled questions to fill in the blanks, which Brendan knew because she was always leaving her laptop browser open on the kitchen counter.

Too good to be true.

He was missing something.

A line was going to snap.

It was hard to imagine anything bad happening at the moment, however, while cooking in the kitchen with Piper. With her hair over her shoulder in a loose braid, she was barefoot in yoga pants and a clingy sweater, humming between him and the stove, absently stirring pasta sauce with one hand. They'd cooked it three nights in a row, and he didn't have the heart to tell her he was sick of Italian, because she was so proud of herself for learning to make sauce. He'd eat it for a decade straight as long as she held her breath for the first bite and clapped when he gave her a thumbs-up.

Brendan had his chin on top of Piper's head, arms looped around her waist, swaying side to side to the music drifting from Hannah's room. In these quiet moments, he continually had to stop himself from asking for a decision. Was she going back to LA for the party? Or at all?

This party in her honor made him nervous for a lot of reasons. What if she went home and was reminded of all the reasons she loved it there? What if she decided that being celebrated and revered by millions was preferable to being with a fisherman who left her on a weekly basis? Because, Jesus, that wouldn't be such a fucking stretch. If she would just tell him Westport was her home, he'd believe her. He'd let the fear drop. But every day came and went with them dancing around the elephant in the room.

Despite his refusal to pressure her, the unknown, the lack of a plan, was getting to him.

He'd never compare his relationship with Piper to his marriage, but after the typhoon and Piper's subsequent race to the hospital—not to mention the tears she'd shed in his bed afterward—a new anxiety had taken root.

Bad things happen when I leave. When I'm not here to do anything about them.

He'd returned home once to find himself a widower.

It felt like just yesterday that he'd scared the hell out of Piper. Sent her running through a dangerous storm and driving to reach him in a state of panic.

What if he came home next time to find her gone? Without an answer in regard to the future, the upcoming trip loomed ominously, impatience scraping at him.

"Who cooks when you're on the *Della Ray*?" she asked, leaning her head back against his chest.

Brendan shook off his unwanted thoughts, trying his best to be present. To take the perfection she was giving him and be grateful for every second. "We take turns, but it's usually Deke, since he likes doing it."

She sighed. "I'm sorry you'll never be able to enjoy anything as much as my sauce."

"You're right." He kissed her neck. "Nothing will ever compare."

"I'll have some ready when you get home. *Two* servings."

"Just have yourself ready," he rumbled, running a finger along the waistband of her pants.

Piper tipped her head back, and their mouths met in a slow kiss that made him anxious for later, when they could be alone in bed together. Anxious to hear those sobs of urgency in his ears. Anxious to memorize them so he could bring them on the boat tomorrow. "Brendan?"

"Yeah?"

She bit off a laugh. "How long are you going to eat this sauce before you admit you're sick of it? I'm going to lose my bet with Hannah."

He laughed so hard she dropped the spoon into the sauce.

"Oh!" Piper tried to fish the utensil out of the bubbling sauce with her fingers, but yanked them out with a yelp. "Oh crap! Ouch!"

His laughter died immediately, and he turned her around, swiftly using a kitchen towel to clean off her burned fingers and kissing them. "You okay, baby?"

"Yes," she gasped, her petite frame starting to shake with laughter against him. "I guess losing a couple of fingers is the price of winning the bet."

"I love the sauce." Curious, he shifted. "How long did Hannah think it would take to . . ."

"Admit you were sick of my sauce? Eternity."

"That's how long it should have taken," Brendan growled, pissed at himself. "You should have lost. And you should have assumed it would take an eternity, too."

Her lips twitched. "I'm not mad." She laid her cheek against the center of his chest. "I got to hear that big, beautiful laugh. I'm a double winner."

"I love the damn sauce," he grumbled into the crown of her head, deciding to give voice to another one of the worries that had been needling him. "Are you going to be all right when I leave tomorrow?"

"Yes." She looked up at him with a furrow between her brows. "Don't worry about me when you're out there, please. I need to know you're focused and safe."

"I am, Piper." He brushed her cheek with his knuckles. "I will be."

Her body relaxed a little more against him. "Brendan . . ." With his name lingering in the air, she seemed to come out of a trance, starting to turn away from him. "We should order pizza—"

He kept her from turning. "What were you going to say?"

Based on the way she squared her shoulders, she was remembering her promise not to keep anything locked in her head. Away from him. A mixture of dread and curiosity rippled in his stomach, but he stayed silent. This was good. The openness between them was coming easier and easier, because of trust. "I was going to ask if you wanted kids someday. And I realize that sounds like . . . like I'm asking if you want them with *me*, which . . ." Color suffused her cheeks. "Anyway. It's just that we never talked about it, and kids seem like something you'd have a firm plan on—"

Her phone started vibrating on the kitchen counter. "Leave it."

Piper nodded. Her phone had been unusually active since they returned from Seattle, which was another reason he'd been on edge. But just like when they'd been in the hotel lobby shopping for cologne, the phone wouldn't quiet, dancing and jangling on the counter. "Let me just silence it," she murmured, reaching for the device. Pausing. "Oh. It's Daniel." Her eyes widened a little, as if maybe she'd just remembered something. "I—I'll call him back later."

Brendan wanted nothing more than to get back to the conversation at hand, but when he told her that yes, he wanted kids, he didn't need her distracted. "It's fine. Answer it."

She shook her head vigorously and put the phone on silent, but the unsteadiness of her hands caused it to slip. When she caught it, the pad of her finger hit the answer button by mistake. "Piper?" came a man's voice over the speakerphone.

"Daniel," she choked out, holding the phone awkwardly between her chest and Brendan's. "Hey. Hi!"

"Hi, Piper," he said formally. "Before I book this flight, I just want to make sure the grand opening is still on. You're not exactly famous for your reliability."

Brendan stiffened, alarm and betrayal turning his blood cold.

Here it was. The other shoe dropping.

Piper closed her eyes. "Yes," she said quietly. "It's still on. Six o'clock."

"That'll do fine, then," her stepfather responded briskly. "There's a flight that gets in a few hours before. Is there anything I can bring you from home?"

"Just yourself," she said with false brightness.

Daniel hummed. "Very well. Have to run. Your mother sends her love."

"Same to her. Bye."

When she hung up the phone, she wouldn't look at him. And maybe that was a good thing, because he was too winded to hide any of the dread and anxiety that had taken hold of his system. "Daniel is coming." He swallowed the nails in his throat. "You're still planning on impressing him with the bar. So he'll let you come back to LA early."

"Well . . ." She threaded unsteady fingers through her hair.

"That was the original plan, yes. And then everything started moving so fast with us . . . and I forgot. I just forgot."

"You forgot?" Brendan's voice was flat, anger flickering to life in his chest. Anger and fear, the fear of her slipping away. Goddammit. Just when he thought they were being honest with each other. "We've been doing nothing but work on Cross and Daughters for the last week, and the reason you started renovating it in the first place slipped your mind? Do you expect me to believe that?"

"Yes," she whispered, extending a hand toward him.

Brendan moved out of her reach, immediately regretting the action when she flinched and dropped her hand. But he was too fucking worried and shot through with holes to apologize and reach for her. His arms were leaden anyway. Impossible to lift. "You didn't keep Daniel's visit as a safety net?"

Her color deepened, speaking volumes. "Well, I d-did, but that was—"

His laughter was humorless. "And your friend Kirby? Have you told her you're not planning on flying to LA for the party?"

Piper's mouth snapped into a straight line.

"No, I didn't think so," he rasped, a sharp object lancing through his ribs. "You've got all kinds of safety nets, don't you, Piper?"

"I wasn't going to go," she wheezed, hugging her middle. "Brendan, stop being like this."

But he was past hearing her. Past anything but weathering the battering waves. Trying to keep the whole ship from getting sucked down into the eddy. This was it. This was the storm he'd felt coming. Felt in his fucking bones. Had he ever really had a chance with Piper, or had he been a delusional idiot? "Jesus, what the hell is wrong with me?" he said, turning and leaving the kitchen. "You were never going to stay, were you?"

Piper jogged after him. "Oh my God. Would you just stop and *listen* to me?"

Brendan's legs took the stairs two at a time, seeing nothing in front of him. Just moving on autopilot. "I was right here, ready to listen this whole time, Piper."

She followed. "You're not being fair! Everything is new to me. This town. Being in a relationship. I'm . . . I'm sorry it took me longer than it should have to let it all go, but letting everything go is a lot to ask."

"I know that, goddammit. I do. But if you weren't even considering this, *us*, you shouldn't have kept stringing me along like one of your followers when you were just plotting your exit behind my back."

Reaching the bedroom, he glanced back over his shoulder to find her looking stricken. And his stomach bottomed out, his heart protesting anything and everything but making her happy. Soothing her. Keeping her in his arms at all times.

What the hell was wrong with him? He hated himself for the tears in her eyes, for the insecurity in her posture. God, he *loathed* himself. But the fear of losing her was winning out over common sense. Over his instinct to comfort Piper, tell her he loved her a thousand times. Making him want to rage, to protect himself from being gutted like a fish.

"Look, Piper," he said unevenly, pulling his packed gym bag out from beneath the bed. "You just need to think about what you actually want. Maybe you can't do that when I'm constantly in your face."

"Brendan." She sounded panicked. "Stop! You're being ridiculous. I wasn't going to leave. Put the bag away. Put it away."

His hands shook with the need to do as she pleaded. "You never told me you were staying. You wanted an out. A fail-safe. Whether you think so or not."

"It's a big decision," she breathed. "But I was—"

"You're right. It is a big decision." He swallowed the urge to rage some more. To rage against her potentially leaving. To rage at the awful possibility of coming home from the trip and finding her unhappy. Or gone. Or regretful. But all he could do was face it head-on and hope he'd done enough to make her stay. All he could do was hope his love was sufficient. "I'm going to spend the night on the boat," he managed, though his throat was closing. "Think about what you want to do. Really think. I can't handle this will-she-or-won't-she bullshit anymore, Piper. I can't handle it."

She stayed frozen as he went down the stairs, past a wide-eyed Hannah.

"I'll be at the dock in the morning," Piper shouted, coming down the stairs, her expression now determined—and he loved her so goddamn hard in that moment. Loved every layer, every facet, every mood, every complication. "I already know what I want, Brendan. I want you. And I'll be at the dock to kiss you good-bye in the morning. Okay? You want to storm out? Fine. Go. I'll be the strong one this time."

He couldn't speak for a moment. "And if you're not there in the morning?"

Piper threw out a belligerent hand. "Then I'm falling back on my safety nets. Is that what you want me to say? You have to have it in black and white?"

"That's who I am."

"I know and I love who you are." Temper crackled in her beautiful eyes. "Fine, if I'm not there tomorrow morning, I guess you'll know my decision. But I *will* be there." She blinked several times against the moisture in her eyes. "Please . . . don't doubt me, Brendan. Not you. Have faith in me. Okay?"

With his heart in his mouth, he turned to go. Before he reached for Piper and forgot the argument and lost himself in her. But the same problems would exist in the morning, and he needed them solved once and for all. He needed the mystery gone. Needed to know if he'd have a lifetime with her or a lifetime of emptiness. The suspense was eating him alive.

He took one last look at her through the windshield of his truck before backing out of the driveway—and he almost shut off the ignition and climbed out. Almost.

Chapter Twenty-Nine

$\mathcal{P}$iper went to sleep pissed and woke up even pissier.

She rocketed out of bed toward the dresser drawers Brendan had designated for her, snatching out a black sports bra and red (the color of anger) running pants, along with some ankle socks.

As soon as she completed a quick run and walked Abe over to the museum, she was going to strut down that dock like it was a fashion week runway and kiss the captain's stupid mouth. She'd leave him hard and panting and feeling like a massive jerk, then she'd sashay home.

Home. To Brendan's house.

She stomped down the stairs, bringing a sleepy-eyed Hannah out of her room. "Are you ready to talk yet?"

Piper shoved an AirPod into her ear. "No."

Hannah propped a hip against the couch and waited.

"I am laser-focused on burying him in regrets right now."

"Sounds like the start to a healthy relationship."

"He left." Piper fell onto her butt and started to lace up her running shoes. "He's not supposed to leave! He's supposed to be the patient and reasonable one!"

"You're the only one who is allowed to be irrational?"

"Yes!" Something got stuck in her throat. "And he's obviously already sick of my shit. It's all downhill from here. I don't even know why I'm bothering with going to the dock."

"Because you love him."

"Exactly. Look at what I've opened myself up to." She yanked her laces taut. "I would relive being dumped by Adrian a thousand times to avoid Brendan walking out *once*. The way he did last night. It *hurts*."

Hannah sat down cross-legged in front of her. "I think that means the good times are worth a little struggling, don't you?" She ducked her head to meet Piper's eyes. "Come on. Put yourself in his shoes. What if he walked out last night without the intention of ever coming back? That's what he's afraid you're going to do."

"If he'd just listened—"

"Yeah, I know. You're telling us you're going to stay. But, Pipes. He's a hard-proof guy. And you left the loopholes."

Piper fell back flat onto the hardwood floor. "I would have closed them. He's supposed to be understanding with me."

"Yeah, but you have to be understanding with him, too." Hannah chuckled, laid down beside her sister. "Piper, the man looks at you like . . . he's full of cracks and you're the glue. He just wanted to give you some space, you know? It's a big decision you're making." She turned on her side. "And also, let's account for the fact that he's a man and there are balls and pride and testosterone in the mix. It's a deadly concoction."

"Truth." Piper took in a deep breath and let it out. "Even if I forgive him, can I still march down there like a righteous bitch and make him rue?"

"I would be disappointed if you didn't."

"Okay." Piper sat up and climbed to her feet, helping Hannah up after. "Thanks for the talk, O wise one. Promise I can call you on the phone anytime I want for your sage advice?"

"Anytime."

Piper left for her run with more than enough time to squire Abe to the museum and make it down to the dock to wish Brendan bon voyage. Still, she was anxious to see Brendan and reassure both of them they were solid, so she set a quick pace. Abe was waiting in his usual spot outside the hardware store when she arrived, newspaper rolled up under his arm.

He waved warmly as she approached. "Morning, Miss Piper."

"Morning, Abe," she said, slowing to a stop beside him. "How are you today?"

"Well as can be expected."

They fell into an easy pace, and Piper lifted her face to the sky, grateful for the calm weather, the lack of storm clouds. "I've been meaning to tell you, we're throwing a grand opening party at Cross and Daughters on Labor Day."

He quirked a white brow. "Cross and Daughters? Is that what you decided to call it?"

"Yeah." She cut him a look. "What do you think?"

"I think it's perfect. A nod to the new and the old."

"That's what I thought—" Abe's toe caught on an uneven crack in the sidewalk, and he went down. Hard. Piper grabbed for him, but it was too late, and his temple landed on the pavement with an ominous thud. "Oh my God! Abe!" The sudden rapid fire of Piper's pulse buckled her knees, and she dropped to the ground beside him, hands fluttering over his prone form, no idea what to do. "Oh Jesus. *Jesus.* Are you okay?" She was already pulling out her phone with trembling hands. "I'm going to call an ambulance, and then I'll call your sons. It's going to be all right."

His hand came up and stopped her from dialing. "No ambulance," he said weakly. "It's not as bad as all that."

She leaned over and saw the blood trickling from his temple. Was it a lot? Too much? "I— Are you sure? I really think I should."

"Help me sit up." She did, carefully, swallowing a spike when the blood traveled down to his neck. "Just call my sons. No ambulance, kiddo. Please. I don't want to give everyone a scare by being taken to the hospital. My phone is in my pocket. Call Todd."

"Okay," she managed, scrolling through his phone. "Okay."

By the time Piper pulled up the contact and hit dial, a woman had rushed out of the deli with a wadded-up fistful of paper towels for Abe to press to his wound. He was still speaking in complete sentences and his eyes were clear, which had to be a good thing, right? *Oh God, please don't let anything happen to this sweet man.*

Todd answered on the fourth ring, but he was at school dropping off his kids and couldn't be there for fifteen minutes, and that . . . that was when Piper realized she was going to miss the *Della Ray* leaving. It was scheduled to leave two minutes ago. Her heartbeat slammed in her eardrums, and her movements turned sluggish. Brendan wouldn't leave, though. He would wait for her. He would know she was coming. And if she didn't show up, she had to believe he would come find her.

But she couldn't leave Abe. She couldn't. She had to make sure he was going to be all right.

She called Brendan, but it went straight to voicemail. Twice. The third time she called, the line disconnected. Fingers unsteady, she pounded out a text message, her panic increasing when he didn't answer immediately. God, this couldn't be happening. She'd found out early on how terrible cell reception was in certain parts of Westport, especially the harbor, but technology couldn't be failing her so completely right now. Not when it was this crucial.

Todd didn't make it there in fifteen minutes. It took him twenty.

By that time, they'd gotten Abe to his feet and moved him to a bench. He seemed tired and slightly embarrassed about the fall, so she told him about the time she'd tried to slide down a stripper pole after six shots of tequila and ended up with a sprained wrist. That made him laugh at least. Todd arrived in his truck looking concerned, and Piper helped Abe into the passenger side, wads of balled-up paper towels pressed to her chest. She made him promise to give her a call later, and off they went, disappearing around the corner of the block.

Piper was almost scared to look at her phone, but she gathered her courage and checked the time. Oh God. Half an hour. Half an hour late.

She started running.

She ran as fast as her feet would carry her toward the harbor, trying to hold on to the faith. Trying to ignore the voice whispering in the back of her head that Brendan kept a tight schedule. Or that he'd given up on her. *Please, please, don't let that be the case.*

At Westhaven Drive, she whipped a right and almost knocked over a restaurant's specials board set out on the sidewalk. But she kept running. Kept going until she saw the *Della Ray* in the distance, traveling out to sea, leaving a trail of white, sloshing wake, and she stopped like she'd hit an invisible wall.

A deafening buzz started in her ears.

He'd left.

He was gone.

She'd missed him and now . . .

Brendan thought she'd chosen LA.

A great hiccupping sob rose up in her chest. Her feet carried her toward the docks, even though going there was useless now. She just wanted to make it there. Making it was all she had, even if she would have nothing to show for it. No kiss. No reassurance. No Brendan.

Her eyes were overflowing with tears by the time she reached the slip of the *Della Ray*, her surroundings so blurry, she almost didn't notice the other women standing around, obviously fresh from waving off the boat. She vaguely recognized Sanders's wife from the first night she and Hannah had walked into No Name. Another woman's age hinted at her being the mother of one of the crew members, rather than a significant other.

Piper wanted to greet them in some way, but her hands were heavy at her sides, her vocal cords atrophied.

"It's Piper, right?" Sanders's wife approached but recoiled a little when she spotted the tears coursing down Piper's numb face. "Oh. Honey, no. You're going to have to be a lot tougher than that."

The older woman laughed. "It's a good thing you didn't show up here with that face, making your man feel guilty." She stepped over a rope and headed toward the street. "Distracted men make mistakes."

"She's right," Sanders's wife said, still looking uncomfortable around Piper's steady waterfall of tears. The boat was just a dot now. "Especially if you're going to be with the captain. You need to be reliable. Hardy. They don't like to admit it, but a lot of their confidence comes from us. Sending them off isn't an easy thing to do, week after week, but we do what's necessary, yeah?"

Piper didn't know how long she stood and stared out at the water, watching a buoy bob on the roll of waves, the wind drying the tears on her face and making it stiff. Fishermen wove their way around her, guiding tourists to their boats, but she couldn't bring her feet to move. There was a hollow ache in her stomach that felt like a living thing, the pain spreading until she worried it would swallow her whole.

But it wasn't the end of the world, right?

"It's not," she whispered to herself. "He'll be back. You'll explain."

Piper filled her lungs slowly and ambled off the dock on stiff legs, ignoring the questioning looks of the people she passed. Okay, fine. She'd missed the boat. That sucked. Really, really bad. It made her sick to think he'd be under the assumption that their relationship was over for two days. It wasn't, though. And if she had to scream and beg when Brendan got home, she would. He'd listen. He'd understand, wouldn't he?

She ended up outside of Cross and Daughters but didn't remember any part of the walk. It hurt to be there when so much of Brendan filled the space. His pergola. The chandelier he'd hung. His scent. It was still there from the day before.

Pressure crowded her throat again, but she swallowed it determinedly.

She had to call distributors and confirm deliveries for Monday's grand opening. She didn't even have an outfit yet, and then there was the meeting this afternoon with Patty and Val. To help plan the party. She was up for exactly none of it, but she'd soldier on. She could make it through the next two days. Her heart would just have to deal.

That afternoon, Piper and Hannah met Patty and Val in Blow the Man Down, and they divvied up responsibilities. Hannah was, of course, the DJ and already had an end-of-summer soundtrack ready to fire up. Patty offered to bring firework cupcakes and Val suggested raffling off prizes from local vendors. Mostly they day drank and talked about makeup, and that helped numb some of Piper's heaviest anxieties that Brendan was lost to her. That he'd already given up.

Have faith.

Have faith.

It was noon on Labor Day when Daniel called to cancel.

Piper was busy stocking the bins behind the bar with ice, so Hannah answered the phone—and one look at her sister's face told Piper everything she needed to know. Hannah put the call on speaker, and Piper listened with her hands unmoving in the ice.

"Girls, I can't make it. I'm so sorry. We're having some last-minute casting issues, and I have to fly to New York for a face-to-face with a talent rep and his client."

Piper should have been used to this. Should have been prepared for their stepfather to flake at the last possible second. In his line of work, there were always flights to New York or Miami or London at the eleventh hour. Until that moment, she hadn't realized how badly she was looking forward to showing Daniel what they'd accomplished with Cross and Daughters. For better or worse, Daniel was the man who'd raised her, given her everything. She'd just wanted to show him it hadn't been for nothing. That she could create something worthwhile if given the opportunity. But she wouldn't get that chance now.

After Brendan left without a good-bye, her stepfather's cancellation was another blow to the midsection. Neither one of them believed in her. Or had any faith.

She had faith in herself, though. Didn't she? Even if it was beginning to fray around the edges and unravel the closer it came to grand-opening time. But Brendan would be back tonight and the certainty of that calmed her. Maybe he'd return angry with her or disappointed, but he'd be back on solid ground and she'd fight to make him listen. She'd keep fighting until his belief in her returned.

That plan helped center Piper, and she worked, stocking beer and setting out coasters, napkins, straws, pint glasses, orange wedges for the wheat beer. She and Hannah did some last-minute cleaning and hung the GRAND OPENING banner they'd painted the previous night outside. And then they stood in the center of the bar and surveyed what they'd done, both of them kind of dumbstruck at the transformation. When they'd arrived over a month ago, the place had been nothing but dust bunnies and barrels. It was still kind of a dive, but hell if it wasn't chic and a lot more welcoming.

At least to them.

But by six thirty, no one had darkened the door of Cross and Daughters.

Hannah sat in the DJ booth shuffling through her summer mix, and Piper stood behind the bar wringing her hands and obsessively checking the time on her phone. She had nine new messages from Kirby, all since this morning, demanding she get her ass on a plane back to Los Angeles. Piper had let the invitation hang for way too long, and now she didn't know how to turn down the party. And *under duress*, she could admit . . . she'd peeked at some of Kirby's emails detailing the guest list and the designer dress options.

If she was going, she'd pick the black Monique Lhuillier with the plunging neckline.

She really did need to let Kirby know she couldn't make it tomorrow night, but for some reason, Piper couldn't bring herself to send the text. To sever that final tie when she was still so shaken up from Brendan walking out. From having that steady, dependable presence ripped away when she needed it most. And the thing about LA parties was, if she didn't show up, no one would *really* care. There would be five minutes of speculation and some fleeting disappointment before everyone went back to doing lines and guzzling vodka.

Still, she'd send the text soon.

Piper had worn one of the pairs of jeans Brendan bought her. The more time dragged on without a single customer, the more Piper felt like an imposter in the soft denim, so unlike her usual dresses or skirts. Seven o'clock came and went. Seven thirty. Patty and Val still weren't there. No Abe or Opal.

No Brendan.

She ignored the worried looks Hannah kept sending her from the DJ booth, her stomach starting to sink. The locals had liked No Name. They didn't want this place prettied up by two outsiders. This was their way of letting the sisters know it.

Finally, just before eight o'clock, the door creaked open.

Mick walked in with a hesitant smile on his face.

Piper's palms started to sweat at the appearance of Desiree's father. The last time she'd seen him was in the hospital, right after she'd been with Brendan for the first time. Before that, she'd crashed his daughter's memorial dinner. They might have gotten off on the right foot, but that footing wasn't so solid anymore. There was something about the way he looked at her, even now, that measured her up and found her lacking. Or, if not lacking, she was not his daughter. With Mick sauntering toward her to take a seat at the bar, Piper's stomach started to churn. Brendan had obliterated her insecurities over Desiree, but right now, standing in the painfully empty bar, they crept back in, making the back of her neck feel hot. The lack of customers was a judgment. Mick's gaze was a judgment. And she wasn't passing.

"Hi there," Mick muttered, shifting on his stool. "Guess I'm early."

It was a lie for her benefit, and the generosity of it made Piper relax a little bit.

Momentarily, anyway.

"Would you like a beer, Mick?"

"Sure would. Bud should do it."

"Oh, we have some local IPAs." She nodded at the chalkboard mounted overhead. "There's the list. If you're a Bud drinker, I recommend the—"

He laughed nervously, as if overwhelmed by the list of five beers, their descriptions painstakingly hand-lettered by Hannah. "Oh. I . . . I'll just sit awhile, then." He turned in his stool, surveyed the bar. "Not a lot of interest in flashy changes around here, looks like."

A weight sunk in Piper's belly.

He wasn't just talking about Cross and Daughters, that much was clear.

His daughter was the old. She was the new. The sorely lacking replacement.

Westport was small. By now, Mick had probably heard about Piper crying like a baby on the docks, watching the *Della Ray* blur into the horizon. And now this. Now no one had arrived at the grand opening, and she was standing there like a certified idiot. She'd been an *idiot*. Not only to believe she could win over everyone in this close-knit place by making over the bar, but by believing her stepfather would give a shit. She'd been an idiot to keep important things from Brendan, whether or not the omissions had been intentional, and he'd lost faith in her. Lost trust.

I don't belong here.

I never did.

Brendan wasn't coming tonight. Nobody was. Cross and Daughters was empty and hollow, and she felt the same way, standing there on two shaky legs, just wanting to disappear.

The universe was sending her a loud-and-clear message.

Piper jolted when Mick laid a hand on top of hers, patting it. "Now, Piper . . ." He sighed, seeming genuinely sympathetic. "Don't you go feeling bad or anything. It's a tough place to crack. You have to be strong to stay afloat."

Words from Sanders's wife came drifting back.

Oh. Honey, no. You're going to have to be a lot tougher than that.

Then her first conversation with Mick.

Wives of fishermen come from tough stock. They have nerves of steel. My wife has them, passed them on to my daughter, Desiree.

She thought of running into Brendan in the market on her first morning in Westport.

You wouldn't understand the character it takes to make this place run. The persistence.

In her heart, she knew his mind had changed since then, but maybe he'd been right.

Maybe she didn't understand how to make anything last. Not a relationship, not a bar, nothing. Henry Cross's legacy didn't belong to her, it belonged to this town. How ridiculous of her to swoop in and try to claim it.

Mick patted her hand again, seeming a little worried by whatever he saw in her expression. "I better get on," he said quickly. "Best of luck, Piper."

Piper stared down into the luminous wood of the bar, swiping the rag over it again and again in a pretense of cleaning, but she stopped when Hannah circled a hand around her wrist.

"You okay, Pipes? People probably just got the time wrong."

"They didn't get it wrong."

Her sister frowned, leaned across the bar to study Piper's face. "Hey . . . you're *not* okay."

"I'm fine."

"No, you're not," Hannah argued. "Your Piper sparkle is gone."

She laughed without humor. "My what?"

"Your Piper sparkle," her sister repeated, looking increasingly worried. "You always have it, no matter what. Even when you've been arrested or Daniel is being a jerk, you always have this, like, optimism lighting you up. Brightness. But it's gone now, and I don't like it. What did Mick say to you?"

Piper closed her eyes. "Who cares?"

Hannah huffed a sound at Piper's uncharacteristic response. "What is going to make you feel better right now? Tell me what it is and we'll do it. I don't like seeing you like this."

Brendan walking through the door and pulling her into the recharging station would cure a lot of ills, but that wasn't going to happen. She could feel it. How badly she'd messed up by keeping safety nets in place without telling Brendan. How badly she'd hurt him by doing so. Badly enough that even the most steadfast man on earth had reached the end of his patience with her. "I don't know. God, I just want to blink and be a million miles away."

More than that, she wanted to feel like her old self again.

The old Piper might have been lacking in direction, but she'd been happy, right? When people judged the old Piper, it was from the other side of an iPhone screen, not to her face. She didn't *have* to try and fail, because she'd never tried in the first place, and God, it had been easy. Just then, she wanted to slip back into that identity and drop out, so she wouldn't have to feel this uncomfortable disappointment in herself. Wouldn't have to acknowledge the proof that she wasn't tough. Wasn't capable. Didn't belong.

Her phone buzzed on the bar. Another message from Kirby.

Piper opened the text and sighed over the Tom Ford peep-toe pumps on her screen. White with gold chains to serve as the ankle strap. Kirby was playing hardball now. Putting on those shoes and a killer dress and walking into a sea of photo-snapping strangers would be like taking a painkiller right now. She wouldn't have to feel a thing.

"Go home, Pipes."

She looked up sharply. "What?"

Hannah seemed to be wrestling with something. "You know I think your LA friends are phonies and you're way too good for them, right?" She sighed. "But maybe you need to go to Kirby's party. I can see you want to."

Piper set down her phone firmly. "No. After all this work? No."

"You can always come back."

Would she, though? Once she walked back into that fog of dancing and selfies and sleeping until noon, was it realistic that she would return to Westport and face her shortcomings? Especially if she made enough money on endorsements to-morrow night to get her out of Daniel's pocket? "I can't. I can't just . . ."

But why couldn't she?

Look around. What was stopping her?

"Well . . ." A tremble of excitement coursed up her finger-tips. "You'll come with me, right, Hanns? If I'm not here, you don't have to be either."

Her sister shook her head. "Shauna has me opening the rec-ord shop tomorrow and Wednesday. I can ask her to find a replacement, but until then, I have to stick around." Hannah reached out and took the sides of Piper's face in her hands. "I'll only be a couple of days behind you. Go. It's like you've flatlined and I hate it."

"Go right *now*? But . . ." She gestured weakly. "The bar. We did this for Henry."

Hannah shrugged. "Henry Cross belongs to this place. Maybe turning it back over to them is what he would have wanted. It was the spirit behind it that counted, Piper. I'm proud of us no matter what." She surveyed the line of empty stools. "And I think I can handle the rest of this shift alone. Text Kirby. Tell her you're coming."

"Hannah, are you sure? I really don't like leaving you here."

Her sister snorted. "Stop it. I'm fine. I'll go crash at Shauna's if it makes you feel better."

Piper's breath started to come faster. "Am I really doing this?"

"Go," Hannah ordered, pointing at the staircase. "I'll get you an Uber."

Oh wow, this was really happening. She was leaving Westport.

Returning to something she could do and do well.

Easy. Just easy.

Avoid this despair and disappointment. Just sink back in and never look back. Forget about this place that didn't want her and the man who didn't trust her.

Ignoring Brendan's clear, beloved image in her head, his deep voice telling her to stay, Piper ran up the stairs and started shoving her belongings into suitcases.

Chapter Thirty

Brendan stood on the deck of the *Della Ray*, staring off in the direction of Westport. The direction they were headed now. He saw none of the seemingly endless water in front of him. Saw none of the men pulling lines and fixing lures around him, the low blare of Black Sabbath coming from the wheelhouse speakers. He'd been locked in a sedated state since Saturday morning when they'd left the harbor.

She didn't show up.

He'd given Piper time to think, and she'd realized that being with him required too much sacrifice, and she'd made her decision. He'd known it was too good to be real. That she would give up everything, her whole life, just for him. His jugular ached from supporting his heart. That's where it sat now, every minute of the day; having Piper in his life had been so painfully sweet. So much better than he knew life could be.

It just hadn't gone both ways.

Over a decade as a fisherman and he'd never once been seasick, but his stomach roiled now ominously. He'd been able to distract himself from the devastating blow, the memory of the empty dock, for the last two days, pushing the men and himself hard, poring over digital maps, and even working in the engine room while Fox manned the wheelhouse. If he stopped moving or thinking, there she was, and Jesus, he'd fucking lost her.

No. He'd never earned the right to her in the first place.

That was the problem.

It was Monday afternoon. Labor Day. Piper would be getting ready to open the bar. Did she still expect him there? Or would she assume he'd stay away now that she'd decided to move on? To leverage the new bar into a trip home. If he showed up at Cross and Daughters, he might be in her way. She may not want him there.

Brendan dug the knuckles of his index fingers into both eyes, images of Piper slaughtering him. Mussed-up, grumpy morning Piper. Confused in the grocery store Piper. Holding a flaming frying pan, crying over him in the hospital, moaning into his pillow Piper. Each and every incarnation of her was a stab to the chest, until he swore going overboard and sinking to the bottom of the icy fucking ocean sounded preferable to living with the memories . . . and not having the actual woman.

But she'd done the right thing for herself. Hadn't she?

Didn't he have to respect that?

Respect that this woman he wanted for his wife was leaving?

Jesus Christ. He might never hold her again.

A drizzle started, but he made no move to go inside to grab his slicker. Getting soaked and dying from pneumonia sounded like a pretty good plan at present. A moment later, though, Sanders passed by and handed the rain jacket to Brendan. Simply to have something to do with his hands, he put it on and slid both hands into the pockets.

Something glossy slipped between his fingers.

He drew it out—and there was Piper smiling back at him.

A picture of them. One he hadn't been aware of her taking.

She'd taken a selfie behind his back while he held her in the recharging station. And her eyes were sex-drowsed and blissful. Happy. In love.

With an ax splitting his jugular in half, Brendan turned over the picture and saw she'd written a loopy, feminine message.

For your bunk, Captain.
Come back to me safely.
I love you so much, Piper.

The wind had been knocked out of him.

A wave rocked the boat, and he could barely make his legs compensate. All functioning power had deserted his body, because his heart required all of it to pound so furiously. He closed his eyes and clutched the picture to his chest, his mind picking through a million memories of Piper to find the one of her standing in his doorway. The last time he'd seen her.

Please . . . don't doubt me, Brendan. Not you. Have faith in me. Okay?

But hadn't he done exactly that by leaving?

He'd left her. After demanding over and over again she take a leap of faith, he'd walked out and ruined her tenuous trust. For God's sake, she'd only been in town for what? Five weeks? What did he want from her?

Everything, that's what. He'd asked for everything—and that hadn't been fair.

So she'd kept a few safety nets. *Good.* As the man who loved her, that's exactly what he should have been encouraging. Piper's safety. What the hell had he done instead?

Punished her for it.

No wonder she hadn't shown up at the dock. He hadn't deserved to see her there, much less stand there praying for her to show up, begging God to make her appear, when he now realized full well . . . that she *shouldn't* have come.

And now, when it was too late, the obvious solution to keeping her, to deserving her, bore down on him like a meteor. She didn't have to give up everything. He loved her enough to find solutions. That's what he did. There was no inconvenience or obstacle he wouldn't face if it meant having her in his life, so he'd fucking face them. He'd adapt, like Piper had.

"I made a mistake," he rasped, razor wire wrapping around his heart and pulling taut. "Jesus, I made a fucking mistake."

But if there was a chance he could fix it, he'd cling to that hope.

Otherwise he'd go insane.

Brendan whipped around on a heel and ran for the wheelhouse, only to find Fox looking concerned while he spoke to the coast guard over the radio.

"What is it?"

Fox ended the transmission and put the radio back in place. "Nothing too bad. They're just advising us to adjust our route south. Drilling rig caught fire about six miles ahead and there's some bad visibility, but it should only set us back about two hours."

Two hours.

Brendan checked the time. It was four o'clock. Originally,

they were scheduled to make it back at six thirty. By the time the boat was unloaded and they'd taken the fish to market, he was looking at goddamn ten or eleven o'clock before he'd make it to Cross and Daughters.

Now, on top of his inexcusable fuckup, he was going to break his promise to be at the grand opening.

Helplessness clawed at the inside of Brendan's throat. He looked down at the picture of Piper he still held, as if trying to communicate with her.

I'm sorry I failed you, baby.

Just give me one more chance.

The text message popped up on his phone the second they pulled into the harbor.

I'm coming. I had an emergency. Wait for me. I love you.

Those words almost dropped Brendan to his knees.

She'd tried to come? She'd wanted to see him off?

Oh God. What emergency? Had she hurt herself or needed him?

If so, if he'd left when she was in trouble, he would never recover.

After that, his ears roared and he saw nothing but his feet pounding the pavement.

When Brendan and Fox stormed into Cross and Daughters at eleven o'clock, it was packed to the gills. "Summer in the City" was playing at an earsplitting decibel, a tray of cupcakes crowd-surfed toward Brendan, and everyone had a drink in their hands. Momentarily, pride in Piper and Hannah, at what they'd accomplished, eclipsed everything else. But an intense urgency to see his girlfriend swarmed back in quickly.

She wasn't behind the bar.

It was just Hannah, uncapping beers as fast as she could, clearly flustered. She was shoving cash into her pockets and trying to make change, tossing bills across the bar and running to help the next customer.

"Christ. I'll go help her out," Fox said, already pushing his way through the crowd.

Where was Piper?

With a frown, Brendan moved in his friend's wake, nodding absently at the locals who called—or slurred, rather—his name. He went to the dance floor first, knowing it was a likely place to find Piper, although . . . that didn't track. She wouldn't leave her sister in the lurch behind the bar. And anyway, she was supposed to be bartending. Hannah was the DJ.

A hole started to open in his gut, acid gurgling out, but he tried to stay calm.

Maybe she was just in the bathroom.

No. Not there. A lady on the way out confirmed the stalls were empty.

Panic climbed Brendan's spine as he pushed his way to the bar. Fox's expression stopped him dead in his tracks before he could even get there.

"Where is she?" Brendan shouted over the noise.

Hannah's gaze danced over to him, then away just as fast.

She served another customer, and he could see her hands were unsteady, and that terrified him. He was going to explode. He was going to rip this place down with his bare hands if someone didn't produce his girlfriend right the hell now.

"Hannah. Where is your sister?"

The younger Bellinger stilled, took a breath. "She went back to LA. For Kirby's party. And maybe . . . to stay." She shook her head. "She's not coming back."

The world blurred around him, the music warping, slowing down. His chest caved in on itself, taking his heart down in the collapse. No. No, she couldn't be gone. She couldn't have left. But even as denial pounded the insides of his skull, he knew it was true. He couldn't feel her.

She was gone.

"I'm sorry," Hannah said, pulling out her phone and lowering the music with a few thumb strokes. People behind him protested, but shut up and quieted immediately, distracted by the man at the bar keeping himself upright with a stool and dying a slow, torturous death. "Look. There was no one here. *No one.* Until maybe half an hour ago. We thought it was a huge fail. And before that, our stepdad canceled, and you— well, you know what you did." Moisture leapt to Hannah's eyes. She swiped at her tears while Fox hesitantly began rubbing circles on her back. "She'd lost her Piper sparkle. It scared me. I thought if she went home, she'd get it back. But now she'll never know that everyone loves this place."

She'd lost her Piper sparkle.

It was girl language, and yet, he so thoroughly understood what Hannah meant, because Piper did have a singular sparkle. Whether they were arguing or laughing or fucking, it was always there, pulling him into her universe, making everything perfect. That sparkle was positivity and life and promise of better things, and she always, always had it, glowing within the blue of her irises, lighting up the room. The fact that it had gone out, and that he'd had something to do with it, gutted him where he stood.

"I should have gone and found her," Brendan said, more to himself than anyone else. "When she didn't show up at the dock. I should have gone to find her. What the hell did I leave for?"

"She did show up," a woman's voice said behind him. Sanders's wife approached, a half-drunk beer in her hand. "She was there, just late. Blubbering all over the place."

Brendan had to rely on the stool to hold his weight.

"Told her to toughen up," his crew member's wife said, but her tone changed when people around her started to mutter. "In a nice way," she added defensively. "I think."

Jesus. He could barely breathe for thinking of her crying while he sailed away.

He couldn't fucking stand it.

Brendan was still reeling from the news that Piper had come to see him off, that she'd shed tears over missing him, when an older man ambled toward the front of the crowd with a white bandage taped to his head.

Abe? The man who owned the hardware store in town with his sons?

"It was my fault Piper was late to the dock, Captain. She's been walking me to the museum every morning so I could read my paper. Can't get up the stairs alone these days." He fussed with his bandage. "Fell and smacked my noggin off the sidewalk. Piper had to stay with me until Todd came. It took a while because he was dropping my grandbaby off at school."

"She's been walking you to the museum every day?" Brendan asked, voice unnatural on account of the wrench twisting a permanent bolt into his throat. She hadn't said anything about Abe. She'd just picked up another best friend and made him important. It was what she did.

"Yes, sir. She's the sweetest girl you ever want to meet." His eyes flooded with humor. "If my sons weren't married and she hadn't gone and fallen in love with the captain here, I'd be playing matchmaker."

Stop, he almost shouted. Might have, if his vocal cords had been working.

He was going to die.

He was dying.

"Sweet doesn't even cover it," piped up Opal, where she stood near the back of the crowd. "I hadn't left my apartment in an age, since my son passed. Not for more than grocery shopping or a quick walk. Not until Piper fixed me right up, and Hannah showed me how to use iTunes. My granddaughters brought me back to the living." A few murmurings went up at the impassioned speech. "What is this nonsense about Piper going back to LA?"

"Yeah!" A girl Piper's age appeared at Opal's side. "We're supposed to have a makeup tutorial. She gave me a smoky eye last week, and two customers at work asked for my number." She slumped. "I love Piper. She's not really gone, is she?"

"Uh, yeah," Hannah shouted. "She is. Maybe try showing up on time, Westport."

"Sorry about that," Abe said, looking guilty along with everyone around him. "There was an oil rig fire off the coast. A young man from town works there, drilling. I reckon everyone was waiting for news, to make sure one of our own was all right, before heading to the party."

"We really need to get a television," Hannah muttered.

Brendan sat there bereft as more and more proof mounted that Piper had been putting down roots. Quietly, carefully, probably just to see if she could. Probably scared she wouldn't succeed. It had been his job to comfort her—and he'd blown it.

He'd lost the best thing that ever happened to him.

He could still hear her that night when they'd sat on a bench overlooking the harbor, moments after she'd waltzed into the memorial dinner with a tray of tequila shots.

Since we got here, it has never been more obvious that I don't know what I'm doing. I'm really good at going to parties and taking pictures, and there's nothing wrong with that. But what if that's it? What if that's just it?

And with those insecurities in tow, she'd proceeded to touch everyone in this room, in one way or another. Carving her way into everyone's hearts. Making herself indispensable. Did she even know how thoroughly she'd succeeded? Piper had once said Brendan was Westport, but now it was the other way around. This place was her.

Please . . . don't doubt me, Brendan. Not you. Have faith in me. Okay?

There was no way, no way in *hell*, he could let that be the last thing she said to him. Might as well lie down and die right there, because he wouldn't be able to live with it. And no way her last memory of him would be leaving his house, leaving her *crying*, for God sakes.

Brendan steadied himself, distributing his weight in a way that would allow him to move, to walk, without further rupturing the shredded heart in his chest. "It's my fault she's gone.

The responsibility is mine. *She* is mine." He swallowed glass. "And I'm going to get her."

Well aware he could fail, Brendan ignored the loud cheer that went up.

He started to turn from the bar, but Hannah waved a hand to catch his attention. She dug her phone out of her pocket, punched the screen, and slid it toward him across the wood Piper had spent a week sanding to perfection, applying the lacquer with careful concentration.

Brendan looked down at the screen and swallowed. There was Piper. Blowing a kiss beneath the words "The Party Princess's Triumphant Return," followed by an address for a club in Los Angeles. Tomorrow night at nine P.M.

Five-hundred-dollar cover.

People were going to pay five hundred dollars just to be in the same room with his girlfriend, and he couldn't fault them. He'd have given his life savings to be standing in front of her at that moment. Jesus, he missed her so much.

"Technically, she's not supposed to be back in LA yet or I'd tell you to try our house first. She's probably staying with Kirby, but I don't have her contact info." Hannah nodded at the phone. "You'll have to catch her at the club."

"Thanks," he managed, grateful she wasn't punishing him like he deserved. "I'd go anywhere."

"I know." Hannah squeezed his hand on the bar. "Go make it right."

Brendan paced toward the door, pulse ticking in his ears, but Mick stepped into his path before he could walk back out into the cold. "Brendan, I . . ." He bowed his head. "When you track her down, will you apologize for me? I wasn't too kind to her earlier tonight."

A dagger twisted between Brendan's eyes. Christ, how much heartache had his Piper been forced to deal with since he boarded the boat on Saturday? First he'd left, then her stepfather had canceled. No one showed up to her grand opening—or so she thought. And now he was finding out Mick had potentially hurt her feelings?

His hands formed fists at his sides, battling the fierce urge to break something. "I'm afraid to ask what you said, Mick," he whispered, closing his eyes.

"I might have implied that she couldn't replace my daughter," Mick said in a low voice, regret lacing every word.

Brendan exhaled roughly, his misery complete. Ravaging him where he stood. "Mick," he responded with forced calm. "Your daughter will always have a place in my heart. But Piper owns that heart. She came here and robbed me blind of it."

"I see that now."

"Good. Get right with it."

Unable to say another word, unable to do anything but get to her, get to her *by any means necessary*, Brendan strode to his truck and burned rubber out of Westport.

Chapter Thirty-One

Oh, she'd made a huge mistake.

Huge.

Piper sat astride a mechanical unicorn, preparing to be elevated through a trapdoor onto a stage. Kirby shoved a puffy princess wand into her hand, and Piper stared at the object, lamenting the fact that she couldn't magically wish herself out of this situation.

Her name was being chanted by hundreds of people overhead.

Their feet stomped on the floor of the club, shaking the ceiling. Behind the scenes, people kept coming over to her, snapping selfies without permission, and Piper imagined she looked shell-shocked in every single one of them.

This was exactly what she'd always wanted. Fame, recognition, parties thrown in her honor.

And all she wanted now was to go home.

Not to Bel-Air. No, she wanted to be in the recharging station. That was home.

Brendan was home.

The chanting grew louder along with the stomping, and Kirby danced in a circle around Piper, squealing. "Savor the anticipation, bitch! As soon as they start playing your song, the hydraulics are going to bring you up slowly. When you wave the wand, the lighting guy is going to make it look like you're sprinkling fairy dust. It looks so real. People are going to shit."

Okay, fine, that part was pretty cool.

"What song is it?"

"'Girls Just Want to Have Fun' remixed with 'Sexy and I Know It.' Obviously."

"Oh yeah. Obviously."

Kirby fanned her armpits. "Try and time your fairy flicks with the beat, you know?"

Piper swallowed, looking down at her Lhuillier dress, her black garters peeking out beneath the hem on either side of the unicorn. Getting dressed had been a fun distraction, as had primping and getting her hair professionally styled, but . . . now that the time had come to make her "triumphant" return, she felt kind of . . . counterfeit.

Her heart was in smithereens.

She didn't *want* to enter a club on a hydraulic unicorn.

She didn't want to have her picture taken and plastered all over social media. There would never be anything wrong with having a good time. Or dancing and dressing how she chose to dress. But when she'd gone to Westport and not one of these people had called or texted or been interested in the aftermath of the party they'd enjoyed, she'd gotten a glimpse at how phony it all was. How quickly the fanfare went away.

When the time came for her to rise up through the stage,

none of the applause would be for Piper. For the real Piper. It would be a celebration of her building a successful image. And that image didn't mean anything. It didn't count. She thought slipping back into this scene would be easy, that she'd just sink into it and revel, be numb for a little while. But all she could think about was . . . who would have coffee with Opal tomorrow? Who would walk Abe to the museum?

Those visits made her feel a million times better than the momentary bursts of internet stardom. Because it was just her, living in real moments, not fabricating them for the entertainment of others.

Making over the bar with her sister, standing on the deck of a boat with the love of her life's arms around her, running through the harbor mist, making friends who seemed interested in her and not what she could do for them. Those things counted.

This was all for show, and participating in it made Piper feel less true to herself. Like she was selling herself short.

This fame she'd always reached for was finally reaching back, and she wasn't interested.

Piper, Piper, Piper.

The chants were deafening now, but she only wanted to hear one voice saying her name. Why didn't she stay and fight for him? What was he doing now?

"Brendan," she whispered, the yearning for him so intense she almost doubled over. "I'm sorry, I miss you. I'm sorry."

"What?" Kirby shouted over the noise. "Okay, you're going up. Hold on, bitch!"

"No, wait." Piper swiped at her damp eyes. "I want to get off. Let me off."

Kirby looked at her like she was insane. "It's too late. You're already moving."

And she was. So much faster than she'd expected.

This unicorn really had some get-up-and-go.

Piper clung to the synthetic mane and held her breath, looking up to watch the stage doors slide open above her. *Dammit.* *Dammit.* There was no turning back. She could jump, but she'd almost certainly break an ankle in these shoes. She'd break these beautiful Tom Ford heels, too, and that went against her very religion.

Her head was about to clear the stage.

With a deep breath, Piper sat up straighter and smiled, waving at the crowd of people who were going wild. For her. It was an out-of-body experience, being suspended above their heads, and she didn't like it. Didn't want to be there, sitting like a jackass on this unicorn while hundreds of people captured her image on their phones.

I want to go home. I just want to go home.

The unicorn finally settled in on the stage. Great. She was already searching for the closest exit. But when she climbed off, she'd flash the entire club. There was no other way to stay modest than to block her crotch with the unicorn hair and awkwardly slide off, which she did now, people pressing in against the stage. She didn't just feel like a trapped animal. She was one. There was no way out.

Piper turned, searching for an avenue of escape—and there he was.

Brendan? No, it couldn't be. Her sea captain didn't belong in LA. They were two entities that didn't make sense in the same space.

She held up a hand to block the flashing strobe light, and God. *My God.* He really was there, standing a foot taller than everyone in the crowd, bearded and beautiful and steady and salt of the earth. They locked eyes, and he slowly pulled the beanie off his head, holding it to the center of his chest, almost a deferential move—and his expression was a terrible mixture of sadness and wonder. No. She had to get to him. Being this close and not being in his arms was positively torture. He was there. He was there.

"Brendan!" Piper screamed, her voice swallowed up by the noise.

But she saw his lips move. Knew he called her name back.

Unable to be parted from him any longer, she dropped to her butt and scooted off the stage, pushing through the tightly packed crowd, praying she was moving in the right direction, because she couldn't see him anymore. Not with the flashing lights and the phones in her face.

"Brendan!"

Hands grabbed at her, making it impossible for her to move. The arms of strangers slung around her neck, pulling her into selfies, hot breath glanced across her neck, her shoulders. No, no, no. She only wanted one touch. One perfect man's touch.

"Piper!"

She heard his deep, panicked voice and spun around in the kaleidoscope of color, flashes going off, disorienting her. Tears were rolling down her face, but she left them there in favor of trying to push through the crowd. "Brendan!"

Adrian appeared in front of her, momentarily distracting Piper from her maze run, because it was all so absurd. She was trying to get to the most wonderfully real human on earth, and this fake, hurtful man-child was blocking her path. Who did he think he was?

"Hey, Piper. I was hoping I'd run into you!" Adrian shouted over the music. "You look fucking amazing. We should get a drink—"

Brendan loomed behind her ex-boyfriend and, without hesitation, flicked him aside like a pesky ant, sending him flying, and Piper wasted no time in launching herself into the recharging station. A sense of rightness took hold in a split second, bringing her back to herself. Back to earth. Brendan lifted her up, locking his arms around her as tight as they would go, and she melted into the embrace like butter. Her legs wrapped around his hips, she buried her face in his neck and sobbed like a baby. "Brendan. Brendan."

"I've got you. I'm right here." Fiercely, he kissed the side of her face, her hair, her temple. "Stay or go, baby? What do you need?"

"Go, please. Please. Get me out of here."

Piper felt Brendan's surprise register—surprise that she wanted to leave?—followed by a tightening of his muscles. One hand cupped the back of her head protectively, and then he was moving through the crowd, ordering people out of his way, and she was positive she'd never, ever been safer in her entire life. She breathed in the scent of his cologne and clung to his shoulders, secure in her absolute trust of this man. He'd come. After everything, he'd come.

A moment later, they were out on the street, but Brendan didn't stop moving. He carried Piper past the line of gaping onlookers, kept going until the pumping bass faded and relative quiet fell around them. And only then did he stop walking, but he didn't let her go. He walked her into the doorway of a bank and rocked her side to side, his arms like a vise.

"I'm sorry, baby," he grated against her forehead. "I'm so fucking sorry. I shouldn't have left. I should *never* have left or made you cry. Please forgive me."

Piper hiccupped into his neck and nodded; she would forgive him for anything in that moment if he just stayed. But before she could say anything, he continued.

"I *do* have faith in you, Piper. I will never doubt you again. You deserve so much better than what I gave, and it was wrong of me, so wrong, to get angry at you for protecting yourself. You were giving so much already. You give so much to everyone and everything you touch, you incredible fucking girl, and I love you. More than any goddamn ocean, do you hear me? I love you, and I'm falling deeper by the minute, so, baby, please stop crying. You looked so beautiful up there. God, you looked so beautiful and I couldn't *reach* you."

His words made her feel like she was floating. They were pure Brendan in their honesty and depth and gruffness and humility. And they were for her.

How wholly he gave himself, this man.

How wholly she wanted to give herself in return.

"I love you, too," she whispered tremulously, kissing his neck, his mouth, pulling deeply on his firm, welcoming lips. "I love you, too. I love you. I didn't want to be there tonight. I only wanted to be with you, Brendan. I just wanted to hear your voice so badly."

"Then I'll talk until my voice gives out," he rasped, slanting his lips over the top of hers, breathing into her mouth. Accepting her breath in return. "I'll love you until my heart gives out.

I'll be your man for a thousand years. Longer if I'm allowed."
With a miserable sound, he kissed the tears off her cheeks. "I
messed up so bad, Piper. I let my fear of losing you get between
us. It blinded me." He drew back, waited until she looked at
him. Up into all that intensity. "If you need Los Angeles to
be happy, then we'll make it work. I can go up north for crab
season and dock the new boat closer to LA the rest of the year.
If you'll have me back, we'll make it happen. I won't let us fail.
Just let me love you forever."

"If I'll have you back . . ." She exhaled her disbelief, his
words taking a moment to actually sink in. Oh wow. Wow. Her
knees started to tremble around his hips, love surging up inside of her and filling every part of her that had cracked over
the last three days. "You would do that, wouldn't you? You
would change your whole life for me."

"I'd be honored to. Just say the word."

"B-Brendan." Her chest ached almost too much to speak.
"When I was falling in love with you, I was falling in love with
Westport at the same time. That is my home. Our home. And I
don't want to be anywhere else. I knew it as soon as I got here
tonight. Nothing was right. Nothing was right without you."

"Piper," he rasped, their mouths heating, seeking. "Say
you're mine again. Be clear. I need you to be clear. I've been
fucking miserable thinking I lost you forever."

"I'm yours. Of course I'm yours. I'm sorry I ran. I'm sorry I
doubted—"

He hushed her with a hard press of lips, his frame heaving
with relief. "Thank Christ," he said hoarsely. "And no. You did
nothing wrong. Nothing." His thumb brushed against the base
of her spine, his body still rocking her side to side. "Everything

is going to be okay now. We found our way back. I've got you back and I'm not letting you go ever again."

She clung to him. "Promise?"

"I'll make the promise every single day."

A blissful smile bloomed across her face. "I'll try again with Cross and Daughters. I'll be stronger next time at the docks. I can be—"

"Oh God, no. Piper." He ducked his head to make eye contact, his dark brows pulled together. "First of all, you don't have to be tough. Not all the time. I don't know who decided my perfect, kind, sweet, incredible girlfriend needed to fit some goddamn mold, but you don't. You just be Piper, okay? She's who I'm in love with. She's the only woman who was made for me. Cry if you want to cry. Dance if you want to dance. Hell, scream at me, if you need to. No one gets to tell you how to act or feel when I leave. *No one.* And, baby . . ." He puffed a laugh. "When I got to the bar, it was packed. Everyone *loves* it. People just move at a different pace in Westport. They're not all on a strict schedule like me."

"Wait. Really? It was packed?" She gasped. "Oh no. Hannah—"

"Is fine. Fox jumped in to help. And she helped me find you tonight."

"Oh! Oh. I'm so glad." Happiness bubbled up inside of her chest, and she gave a watery laugh. "We better get home, then. I guess I have a bar to run."

Brendan brought their mouths together and kissed her with painstaking affection that quickly started to burn. Her throaty moan met his urgent growl, their tongues winding deep, his hand scraping down to palm her backside. "We could go home tonight," he rumbled, tilting his hips so she could feel the firm rise of his need. "Or we could walk across the street to my hotel room and worry about getting home in the morning."

A sigh shuddered out. "Why aren't we already there?"

"Give me a minute." He jolted into a stride across the quiet avenue that turned into a jog, jostling her all over the place, sending her laughter ringing down the night-draped street, then a euphoric squeal when he threw her over his wide fisherman's shoulder. "So . . ." he said when they were halfway through the hotel lobby, scandalizing everyone in their wake. "Are we just *not* going to talk about the mechanical unicorn?"

"I love you," she gasped through mirthful tears. "So much."

"Ah, Piper." His voice shook with emotion. "I love you, too."

Epilogue

One week later

It was a sad day.

It was a happy day.

Brendan was coming home from a fishing trip, but Hannah was going back to LA.

Piper sat up in bed and pushed off her eye mask, marveling—not for the first time—over how much the room had changed. Before leaving LA, Brendan had driven her to Bel-Air for a quick visit with Maureen and Daniel. Halfway through the stopover, Brendan had disappeared.

She'd found him upstairs in her room, packing her things.

Not just her clothes, although it was nice to have her full wardrobe back. But her knickknacks. Her perfumes, her bedspreads, her shoe display case and fashion scarves. And as soon as they'd gotten home to Westport—okay, fine, after a rough, sweaty quickie on the living room couch—he'd taken the items upstairs and made the room . . . theirs.

Her super-masculine sea captain now slept under a pink

comforter. His aftershave was sandwiched in between nail polish bottles and lipsticks, and he couldn't seem happier about the feminine clutter.

They'd only had a few days of officially living together before his trip, but they'd been the best days of her life. Watching Brendan brush his teeth with nothing but a towel wrapped around his waist, feeling his eyes on her as she bartended, pancakes in bed, shower sex, gardening together in their backyard, shower sex. And best of all, his whispered promise in her ear every morning and night that he would never, ever let her go again.

Piper flopped back against the pillows and sighed dreamily.

He'd be pulling into Grays Harbor in just a few hours, and she couldn't wait to tell him every shenanigan that had happened in Cross and Daughters since he'd been gone. Couldn't wait to smell the salt water on his skin and even continue their conversation about someday . . . *someday* having children.

He hadn't forgotten Piper's attempt to bring up the subject on the night of their argument. They'd tried to discuss it on four separate occasions since getting home, but as soon as the word "pregnant" was uttered, Piper always ended up on her back, Brendan bearing down on her like a freight train.

So. No complaints.

Fanning her face, Piper climbed out of bed and went through her morning routine of jogging and walking Abe to the museum. When she got home an hour later, Hannah was just zipping her packed suitcase, and Piper's stomach performed an uncomfortable somersault.

"I'm going to miss you," Piper whispered, leaning a shoulder against the doorjamb.

Hannah turned and dropped down onto the edge of the bed. "I'll miss you more."

Piper shook her head. "You know . . . you're my best friend."

Her sister seemed caught off guard by that, giving a jerky nod of her head. "You're mine. You've always been mine, too, Pipes."

"If you hadn't come . . ." Piper gestured to their surroundings. "None of this would have happened. I wouldn't have figured it all out on my own."

"Yes, you would have."

Piper blinked rapidly to keep the tears at bay. "You ready to head to the airport?"

Hannah nodded, and—after kissing the Pioneer record player good-bye—she wheeled her suitcase to the front of the house. Piper opened the door to let her sister through, frowning when Hannah pulled up short. "What's that?"

"What's what?"

Piper followed her sister's line of vision and found a brown parcel, in the shape of a square, leaning up against the porch. It definitely hadn't been there when she returned from her run. She stooped down and picked it up, inspecting the delivery label and handing the box to her sister. "It's for you."

Letting go of the handle of her suitcase, Hannah pried open the cardboard, revealing a cellophane-wrapped record. "It's . . . oh." Her throat worked. "It's that Fleetwood Mac album. The one that spoke to me at the expo." She tried to laugh, but it came out choked. "Fox must have tracked it down."

Piper gave a low whistle.

Hannah continued to stare down at the album. "That was so . . . friendly of him."

It was definitely something. But Piper wasn't sure "friendly" was the right word.

Several beats passed, and Piper reached over to tuck some hair behind her sister's ear. "Ready to go?" she asked softly.

"Um . . ." Hannah visibly shook herself. "Yeah. Yeah, of course. Let's go."

A couple of hours later, Piper stood on the dock and watched the *Della Ray* approach, her pulse going faster and faster the closer it came, white wake spreading out around the vessel like rippling wings. The crew's significant others, mothers, and fathers stood around sipping coffee in the cool fall weather, speculating on the trip's haul. They'd been kind to Piper this afternoon, but more important, she was learning to be kind to herself.

Learning to love herself, just as she was.

Frivolous and silly on occasion, determined and stubborn on others. When she was mad, she raged. When she was sad, she cried.

And when she was happy, like she was in that moment, she threw her arms open and ran right toward the main source, letting him sweep her away . . .

Keep an eye out for Hannah's story in . . .

HOOK, LINE, AND SINKER

Coming early 2022!

**Read on for a bonus scene featuring
Hannah and Fox!**

Bonus Scene

$\mathcal{D}$amn.

This pint-sized girl with freckles had just gone toe-to-toe with the captain. Still looked spitting mad, too, underneath the brim of her red baseball cap.

It was a good thing Fox knew enough about women to wipe the amusement from his face. Hannah, the new girl in town, had briefly turned her wrath on him outside the Red Buoy, and he wasn't eager to revisit the moment. Neither was his dick, which had momentarily retreated into itself like a hermit crab at the rare display of displeasure in his company.

Just then, a blustery August wind caught Hannah's hat and knocked it off her head.

They went for it at the same time, his fingers wrapping around the brim before it could hit the ground. Still bent over—and with the most winning grin he could muster—Fox handed it back, his mouth widening further when she only peered at him suspiciously.

Hannah sniffed. "Thanks."

"Anytime."

With a skeptical hum, she pulled the hat back down over her eyes, but he'd already seen the evening sunlight travel over her face. A cute *face*, proclaimed the stubby nose located between two big hazel eyes and a dimple in her right cheek. Her toes peeked out of her flip-flops, showing off a musical note that ran the length of her second-largest toe.

Yup. Cute as hell.

But not so cute that she couldn't turn his manhood into a crustacean.

What are you, his pretty-boy sidekick?

Apparently in addition to being adorable and fearless, she was astute.

The pretty part was obvious. And now, here he was, squiring this spitfire to the record shop so his best friend could get some time alone with the first woman to rouse his interest since the passing of his wife seven years earlier. Thus Fox ticking the sidekick box.

Truthfully, though? He didn't mind not being taken seriously. Let Hannah put him in a neat little category. It saved him from having to try. Trying for anything worthwhile always led to disappointment.

Fox realized his smile had slipped and fixed it back in place, gesturing for Hannah to precede him along the sidewalk. "After you, sweetheart."

She studied him down the end of her stub nose, then breezed past. "You can turn down the wattage, peacock. Nothing I say to Piper about you will affect her decision."

Peacock? Brutal. "Her decision to what?"

"To embark on or decline an affair with the mean one."

The mean one. Savage. "You two seem close. She doesn't value your opinion?"

Hannah stopped short and turned, her expression that of a person jogging back their previous statement. "Oh no, she *does*. She does. But my sister, um . . ." Her fingers plucked at the air for the right words. "She is so desperate to see the good in people, she doesn't always heed a well-placed warning."

"Ah. Do you look for the *bad* in people?"

"Oh, my affliction is way worse than Piper's; I *like* the bad in people."

She showed him that dimple and kept sailing.

It took Fox a moment to regain his stride. Suddenly he was interested in a conversation. More than he'd been in a damn long time. Why? Apart from the fact that she'd gained his respect by refusing to back down from a man twice her size, there was no reason he should be picking up his pace to find out what Hannah was going to say next.

They weren't even going to sleep together.

Doing so could seriously mess things up for Brendan—and Jesus, she wasn't his type, anyway. For one thing, she'd be living in Westport for the foreseeable future. Way too close for comfort. Two, his charm was absolutely wasted on this out-of-towner. The way she speed-walked two yards ahead of him made that crystal clear.

Maybe that's why he wanted to continue talking to her.

He'd gotten the sex-is-a-no-no speech *and* she was immune to him. The pressure was off.

It surprised him how much that pressure was present in his chest when it started to abate, gradually, like the air coming out of a beach ball. "Want to slow down a little, Freckles?" he said, a little testier than he'd intended, because of the weird feeling. "I'm the only one who knows where we're going."

Hannah gave him an eyebrow raise over her shoulder but downgraded from a sprint to a jog. Maybe even seemed a little more curious about him—but what sense did that make? "Really? You think I'm a 'Freckles'?"

"It was that or Captain Killer."

Was that a hint of a smile?

Out of habit, he was about to compliment her on her smile when the phone in his pocket started to vibrate. He made the rookie mistake of taking it out, instead of ignoring it, but quickly put the device back when the name "Carla" blinked on the screen.

Not before Hannah saw it, though. Her gaze danced away quickly, her expression remaining neutral, but she definitely noticed a woman was calling him. There was no reason that should bother him. No reason for the stupid, sinking disappointment in his belly. None at all.

Fox coughed into his fist and they continued to walk, side by side. "What exactly do you mean by 'I like the bad in people'?"

Her dimple deepened while she thought about it. "It's like . . . the bad in someone is also the most honest part, right? When you meet someone new, you dig and dig until you get to the good stuff. Imagine how much time we would save if our biggest flaw was our opening line."

"You're pretty intense for someone nicknamed Freckles."

A laugh snuck out of her, and the weirdness that had been barrel-rolling in his chest stopped abruptly, slowed by satisfaction. Warmth. "Hey, I questioned your judgment. You were firm on Freckles." Her smile melted into a sigh. "And I know, I am a little intense. It's all the music I listen to. Everything is right on the surface in a song. Calamity, heartbreak, tension, hope. It's hard to dip back into normal life after a Courtney Barnett song." She snuck a glance at him. "I tend to overshare almost immediately after meeting someone. It's why I don't have a lot of friends back home. I come on stronger than cold brew."

That made him chuckle. "Hold on, now. I didn't say the intensity was a turnoff."

Her gaze cut to his, mouth in a flat line.

Whoops. Stepped on a land mine. Better backpedal. "'Turnoff' was the wrong expression. This isn't"—Fox seesawed a hand between them—"there's nothing to turn off or on."

She nodded her agreement and they went back to walking.

Shit, this was kind of nice. Having a mildly antagonistic interaction with a girl. *This* girl. There was something invigorating about passing the time with her without expectations attached. Not that a lot of effort went into seducing women. That talent was kind of a built-in mechanism. Trying to seduce Hannah would have been a lot more complicated, and the fact that he didn't have to . . .

The only remaining option was friendship.

Wow. What a turn the day had taken. When he woke up this morning, if someone had told him he'd be chumming around with a girl, he would have called them a damn liar. But here he was. Not even trying to have sex with her. It went against his nature not to check her out *a little*, just for posterity's sake, and she had the kind of twitchy buns that drove him crazy. But he was filing that away under *irrelevant.*

"What kinds of things do you normally overshare about?" he asked her.

She looked up at the sunset-streaked sky but quickly ducked back underneath the brim of her hat when a gull circled above. "My greatest fears, what movies make me cry, my relationship with my mother. Things like that. In Los Angeles, you're supposed to lead with what you do for a living."

"I've been meaning to ask, what do you do for a living?"

An honest-to-God giggle tumbled out of her. "I'm a location scout for an independent movie house."

Yeah, he could see her doing that. Clipboard, earpiece, chewing gum, watching some drama unfold on a movie set. "That sounds like it nurtures your intensity, sure enough. Is that what you want to do permanently?"

"No." She seemed hesitant to say more.

"Come on, oversharer. Don't let me down."

"It's just that I haven't told anyone yet." She dipped her cheek toward her shoulder. Her version of a shrug? "I want to craft movie soundtracks. Not scores. Just, selecting the perfect songs for a scene."

"That sounds pretty fucking cool."

She stuffed her hands in the pockets of her jeans. "Thanks." Was she biting that lip to subdue a smile? Damn. He kind of wanted to see it. "What about you? I gather you're a fisherman like the mean one?"

"That's right." He tapped his inner wrist. "Got salt water running in these veins."

"Does it scare you? When the ocean gets rough?"

"I'd be an idiot if it didn't scare me."

For some reason, that seemed to bring this interesting girl

over to his team. She nodded, examining him a little more closely. "I heard him call you the relief skipper. Do you ever want to captain your own vessel?"

"Hell no."

"Why not?"

"Too much responsibility." He dragged a hand through his hair. "I like things exactly the way they are now. Work a job, don't make any mistakes, come home with cash in my pocket, and end of the bargain fulfilled. Let someone else think about the big picture."

Hannah pursed her lips. "Are you lazy or afraid of messing up?"

Defensiveness stuck in his middle unexpectedly, and using the only weapon he had, Fox dropped his attention to her thighs. "I'm sure as hell not lazy, Freckles."

She gulped, hands balling in her pockets. "So you're . . . afraid, then?"

"Can't help digging, can you?" Laughing, Fox shook his head. "You're not going to find the bad in me that easily. It's sealed up tight."

"Famous last words," she murmured, and they regarded each other for a drawn-out beat. "Is there really a record shop, or are you luring me to a watery grave?"

"Don't be dark, Freckles." He pulled her to a stop outside Disc N Dat before she could walk past it. "This is it."

"Really?" She studied the low white-stucco building. "There's no sign."

"Don't you know that's what makes it cool? I thought you were from LA." Fox opened the door for Hannah before she could respond, grinning as she passed. And yeah, fine, he was a little gratified when her cheeks turned pink. He could be friends with a girl, but it wouldn't hurt for her to at least *recognize* his attractiveness. After all, he worked so hard to make sure it was the main thing people noticed about him.

Hannah set foot inside the record shop and came to a dead halt.

He wasn't a record enthusiast like this girl, but he'd been in Disc N Dat enough times growing up in Westport that he knew there was something magical about it. The fact that he'd been the one to present it to Hannah gave him a surprising sense of pride. Still standing in the doorway, he tried to see the shop through her eyes. The shelves had blue inset lighting, casting the rows of records in a dreamlike glow. Vintage bulbs hung down from the ceiling, amber and gold and silver, paper mobiles turning around them to cast shapes and shadows onto the walls and original flooring. The place smelled like coffee and dust and leather.

Hannah turned to him with wide eyes. She took off her hat, letting loose a tumble of dirty-blond hair, her face awash in jewel-toned lighting, drying up his mouth.

Cute.

Friend.

Fox repeated those words three times each, but he stopped thinking altogether when she took two steps and wrapped her arms around his neck. Hugging him. Snuggling her dips and peaks right up against his muscles and squeezing tight.

"Thank you for bringing me here."

Her breath was warm, her chin propped in that spot where his neck and shoulder met, and Jesus, it felt nice. Too nice. Way too nice. But that didn't stop him from leaning down slightly to compensate for their height difference and pull her closer to his chest.

Hannah shifted slowly, turning her head . . . and their eyes met.

"Fade Into You" played low and entrancing from the speakers. Nothing about this was expected or remotely resembled real life. Not for him. He didn't have moments like this. Not with anyone. But this . . . girl. This off-limits girl.

She was making him need to kiss her. How was she doing it?

Already mentally calling himself a moron, Fox lowered his head—and his phone vibrated in the front pocket of his jeans. This time, he didn't pull it out, but Hannah stepped back, visibly shaking herself free of the moment, because it seemed to hover unspoken between them that a woman was calling. Most likely it was. No sugar-coating it. Fox's hands didn't seem capable of doing anything but dropping heavily to his sides.

"I'm going to browse," Hannah said, hidden beneath her hat once more, already turning for the first aisle. "If you want to take your call."

"Yeah, thanks. I'll just . . . be outside."

But when Fox left the store, he let the call go to voicemail and watched Hannah moon over records through the window instead.

Nisha Ver Halen

ABOUT THE AUTHOR

New York Times bestselling author Tessa Bailey aspires to three things: writing hot and unforgettable character-driven romance, being a good mother, and eventually sneaking onto the judging panel of a reality-show baking competition. She lives on Long Island, New York, with her husband and daughter, writing all day and rewarding herself with a cheese plate and Netflix binge in the evening. If you want sexy, heartfelt, humorous romance with a guaranteed happy ending, you've come to the right place.

MORE BY TESSA BAILEY

Tools of Engagement

Two enemies team up to flip a house, but as the race to renovate heats up, sparks fly as Wes and Bethany are forced into close quarters, trading barbs and banter as they remodel the ugliest house on the block.

Love Her or Lose Her

A young married couple's rocky relationship needs a serious renovation. Never did Rosie believe her stoic, too-manly-to-emote husband would actually agree to relationship rehab, but she discovers Dom has a secret that could demolish everything.

Fix Her Up

Travis was baseball's hottest rookie. Now he's flipping houses and trying to forget his glory days. When Georgie, his best friend's sister, proposes a wild scheme that they pretend to date to help him land a new job, he agrees—but finds there's nothing fake about how much he wants her.

Disturbing His Peace

Danika can't stand Lt. Burns, her roommate's sexy-as-hell but cold, unfeeling older brother. She just wants to graduate the police academy and forget about her scowling superior, until a dangerous mistake lands her under his watch...

Indecent Exposure

Jack Garrett isn't a police officer yet, but there's already an emergency. His new firearms instructor, Katie McCoy, is the same sexy Irish stranger Jack locked lips with last night.

Disorderly Conduct

Tessa Bailey returns with a sexy and hilarious series about three hotshot rookie cops in the NYPD police academy.

Make Me

Construction worker Russell is head-over-work boots for Abby, but he knows a classy, uptown virgin like her could never be truly happy with a rough, blue-collar guy like him.

Need Me

Honey traded in her cowboy boots for stilettos and left her small town for school. She's completely focused on her medical degree—until she meets her newly minted professor, and her concentration is hijacked.

Chase Me

College drop-out Roxy signs up to perform singing telegrams to make some quick cash, but her first customer—a gorgeous, cocky Manhattan trust-funder—has more to his sexy surface and is determined to make Roxy see it.

DISCOVER GREAT AUTHORS, EXCLUSIVE OFFERS, AND MORE AT HC.COM